MW00614981

FALLEN
SNOW

An Erotic Romance

AVEN JAYCE

FALLEN SNOW

Copyright © 2014 Aven Jayce

Cover and Book Design by Aven Jayce

This is a work of fiction. Names, characters, and incidents are the product of the author's imagination and are used fictitiously. Any resemblance to actual persons, living or dead, or events, is entirely coincidental.

ISBN-10: 0991404939
ISBN-13: 978-0991404933

All rights reserved

No part of this book can be reproduced, scanned, or distributed in any printed or electronic form without permission. Purchase only authorized editions. The only exception is by a reviewer, who may quote short excerpts in a review.

Aven Jayce
Connect on Facebook at
www.facebook.com/eroticromanceauthor

For JK

PROLOGUE

*M*y hand digs through a clump of moist tissues and comes across only dirty pennies and lint at the bottom of the purse. I know I placed it in here earlier, wanting to hide it from my brother.

"What's she doing in my purse?" my grandmother seethes, directing her words at my mother.

"Calm down, Ma. She's looking for candy."

"In my purse?"

I step back and hide both of my hands behind my back, waiting for my grandmother to scold me. What a dumbass mistake. There I am, standing in front of my family during our weekly Sunday gathering, caught burrowing relentlessly in the faux-leather handbag, thinking it's my mother's. This is my first realization that all women own purses, not just my mother, and in my family it just so happens that all of the women own cheap, light brown, short-strapped purses. I look up at my grandmother as she quickly approaches me in the kitchen. She grabs my arm and pulls my hand from around my back, giving it a good slap.

"Thief," she exclaims.

"I was looking for my candy," I pout, craving the small bag of gummy worms hidden inside.

"What candy? I don't have any candy in my purse.

You were stealing money from me."

I wait for my mother to step in, saving me from the embarrassment of being thought of as a criminal at the young age of five, but she doesn't even look my way. This is typical of her whenever our relatives are present. Actually, it's an every day occurrence. Conflict avoidance. Ignore the child and maybe he or she will go away.

Family gatherings on Sundays are the worst. My grandmother and aunt arrive around noon, sit in the kitchen with my mother, eat for hours, and disregard the fact that there are two bored children in the house with them. These days are always long and tedious. According to my mother, my brother, Mark, and I need to be on our best behavior, but we aren't exactly sure what that means.

"Sophia, what are you going to do today?" asks my aunt, trying to change the subject.

"I don't know. Play outside?" I offer, looking at my mother for approval. She nods her head yes and I rush out, slamming the side screen door to the kitchen as I go. I'm relieved to be free of my family's madness. On the way out I hear my grandmother ask my mother if I really had candy in her purse. I stop in my tracks, waiting to hear her response, but the only words that come out of her mouth are about whether anyone would like more potato salad.

It's May and a light drizzle is falling from the grey suburban Philadelphia sky. I push my Big Wheel around the yard, pretending that my brother is in the passenger seat laughing. We live on a dirt road, with a dirt driveway, so it's not easy to ride the thing without someone pushing from behind. TV advertisements make the plastic pedal toy look like it moves at an amazingly fast speed, but without pavement or a hill, the Big Wheel often sits motionless in *our front yard. I continue playing, pushing the toy over to our big oak tree next to the driveway. I park the useless red and yellow plastic vehicle under the tree and look up, searching for the branch that's closest to the ground.*

Each year my mother removes the lowest limbs. She's terrified that we'll fall out of the tree, land on our heads, break our necks, or crack our skulls open. Even though it's forbidden, it's the one place I enjoy escaping to when I'm outside. I reach up, but can't quite get my hands close enough to the branch. Where is my brother Mark? I wonder. I could use his help.

I jump up a few more times, finally catching hold of the bottom branch, pull myself up and climb onto the tree. There's no coverage this time of the year, only buds, so I'm completely exposed. The front dining room window of our home has a clear view of the tree, and for that reason alone I know I only have a short amount of time to enjoy the view.

Scanning the neighbors' yard to the east I discover their two black pugs sniffing each other's bottoms. I giggle at the site, then turn my head to the other neighbor's house and notice he's watching me from his living room window.

Our neighbor, Mr. Rudd, is eighty-four years old and senile. He sits in a chair next to his front window all day, every day, often proclaiming that he sees cowboys and Indians fighting in his front yard. I don't know if he's referring to my brother and me, or if it's disorientation from his age.

I decide to put on a show for him. Placing both hands down, I grab hold of the limb that I'm standing on, slowly lowering myself to a sitting position. I let my legs dangle down, both on the same side of the branch, and then fall backward, letting the back of my legs wrap around the limb. I begin scratching my armpits like a monkey, howling and cooing to attract attention to myself. Mr. Rudd turns and says something, probably to his wife, and then points over my way. I can't wait to hear the story that comes out of this one.

"Sophia Elizabeth Jameson, get down from that tree right this minute!" my mother screams, running toward me.

"Oh shit," I bellow, feeling a hard yank on my shoulder. My mother quickly pulls me down and wraps her hand around the locks of my hair, yanking me roughly back inside the house.

"You little piss-ant. Sit there on that chair and don't you dare move a muscle. I'm so tired of you not listening to me, and having to hear your foul mouth each day."

A tear streams down my face as my eyes brim with sadness, humiliation, and pain. A gush of water wells in my eyes as I begin to sob.

"I d-didn't d-do anything," I stutter, trying to catch my breath as my body convulses, snot running out of my nose.

"Shut up. I'm sick of your mouth," she repeats.

My brother walks into the kitchen and sees that I'm in distress. He approaches me and raises his finger, placing it inches from my face.

"Ha-ha, you got in trouble. Ha-ha. Ha-ha," he teases, waving his finger in front of me.

"Go away Mark!" I scream, bawling, and stomping my feet.

"God dammit," my mother shouts, throwing the kitchen towel down and grabbing me by the arm. She pulls me up the stairs, pushes me into my bedroom, and slams the door. I hear her walk down the stairs and demand that

my brother go out and play.

Where did my father go, and why isn't he here to protect me anymore?

I hear my mother's voice calling up the stairs. I open the door, peeking out of the room.

"Sophia," she says in an eerily sweet tone. "I just wanted you to know that I don't love you."

She walks away and I close the door, sitting on the floor with my head up against the wall. I pound against it, bitter about my tiresome, joyless life.

"Love?"

CHAPTER ONE

"She physically hurt you?"

"Yeah, physically and emotionally she hurt me," I reply, as my psychologist takes notes.

I've been coming here for a few months, and the two of us have hardly made a dent in my childhood. I haven't been sleeping, and I can't seem to let go of some of these shameful, demeaning memories. My father pushed me into coming here, and I agreed that it was time to finally talk to someone about all of this baggage. Now I'm starting to realize that it may take years to even begin to unravel my past.

Dr. Rosen's office is painted a beautiful, soothing light blue. A dark mahogany desk rests in front of the far wall of the room, with matching bookcases to either side. A five-foot fiddle-leaf fig plant towers next to the window overlooking the St. Louis skyline. She has three deep brown leather chairs and an odd small settee that seems somewhat out of place. A soft, golden brown, plush rug lies in the middle of the room, matching the pillows tossed onto each chair. I'm sure some consideration has gone into the decor to try to provide a feeling of tranquility for her patients. On top of Dr. Rosen's desk sits the usual; a computer, phone, files, and two frames containing photos of her children. There's also a vase of fresh lilies, filling the room with a lovely scent.

"I might have children some day," I say.

"What made you think of that?"

"I noticed the photos of your children on your desk. They're very beautiful."

"Thank you, Sophia. They're my niece and nephew. Someday I might have kids as well," she replies with a smile.

"If I had a girl I'd name her Violet, and I'd name my son Galaxy."

"Violet and Galaxy?" she asks, raising one eyebrow in curiosity. "How did you come up with such unique names?"

"Oh, I don't know. I guess I want my children to stand out from the common crowd of Jacobs and Emilys, plus I read somewhere children who have unique names have a better chance of being successful later in life. I mean, come on, Sophia is such an everyday name. I never had a chance at becoming anything great right from the start."

A timer goes off and Dr. Rosen looks at her watch. "We need to talk about this in greater detail, especially the story you just told me about your mother expressing that she didn't love you. When are you free next week?"

***

I ride down the elevator, a little disappointed in my session. I need to focus on the issues instead of always trailing off in different directions. *Kids?* What was I thinking? I don't want to have kids. I'd be a horrible mother. Besides, I'm not done satisfying my sexual fantasies. I wouldn't be able to pleasure myself or others with a kid in the house. Talk about lack of privacy. Plus, a kid would eat up all of my time. I'm not ready to give up any of that for anyone, including someone who once lived inside of me and didn't pay rent. God, now I'm starting to sound like my mother. *I need a drink.*

Stepping off the elevator, I hear my name called out by the one familiar high-pitched voice that I love.

"Sophia, I'm so glad I found you. Evan gave me directions to your shrink's office, but I didn't think I'd catch up with you in time."

"Mera, no need to yell," I whisper, pulling her into a tight hug. "The entire lobby doesn't need to know that I just met with my psychologist."

"Shrink," she says pulling away. "You look terrible. What were you talking about this time?"

"The usual. Sex, lack of motivation, and my so-called family from hell."

"Oh my God, have you seen that *My Cat From Hell* show?"

Dryly I tell her yes, and that I'm going to name my son Galaxy.

"What son?" she asks, taking my hand and swinging it as we walk along the sidewalk.

Mera and I were roommates in college. She knows more about me than anyone else, and I can count on her to always be by my side at a moment's notice.

Her hair is long and dark brown in color, always with a full body and shine that reminds me of phony-looking, silky shampoo commercials. It's pulled back into a ponytail most of the time, unless we're out at the clubs. She keeps her bangs long making it hard to see her stunning Irish blue eyes. I notice she's wearing an old, knee length black dress that used to be mine. I shrunk it one day and couldn't squeeze into it again. It flows freely on her.

"What are you staring at?"

"You. You look beautiful in that dress and I'm jealous."

"Well, you'd still be wearing it if you hadn't done laundry that one night after we got home from the bar. You could barely stand and there you went, down to the laundry room to wash your clothes. What possessed you to do such a thing, and at two in the morning no less?"

I'm silent for a moment, not knowing the answer to that myself.

"I guess I needed to be clean."

"Well, duh. Plus, if you weren't like six feet tall and still growing it might still fit you."

"Five feet, nine inches, and growing out, not up."

"You need the weight, Babe. In college you looked anorexic. You were just skin and bones. At least now you look like a curvy vixen. At your height and weighing only... how much do you weigh?"

"One-twenty-five."

"Yeah, you're perfect. Long brown hair, warm brown eyes, small nose and full lips. You're a cross between Alexis Bledel and a young Angelina Jolie. 'Growing out,' as you put it, has turned you into a sexy model instead of a skeleton in the back corner of a science classroom."

I smile at her words, continuing to hold her hand as we head to lunch. We walk along Washington Avenue, finally stopping at The Sportsbook Bar and Grill where they serve the best white bean hummus plate in the entire country. I can tell by Mera's face that she's in the mood for steak, and will have nothing to do with my usual light fare. Her eyes widen when she smells the meat, and I see her moistening her lips with her tongue. She grew up on a farm in Kansas, and I've heard her explain to a handful of boyfriends that she's a big meat and potatoes kind of gal. She could pass as a ten-year-old by her height and weight, and based on her small frame it takes some convincing for people to believe her daily enjoyment of cow and pig.

St. Louis is unseasonably temperate for October. With the sun keeping us warm, we decide to enjoy the weather and have our meal and a beer on the side patio. I take a seat, leaning back in the chair to look up at the brilliant blue fall sky. I notice one small cloud, smirking at its shape.

"What are you grinning at?"

"That cloud looks like a vagina," I respond.

Mera can't help but look up; scanning the sky for the one I'm referring to.

"Do you think we can get through a meal without you mentioning your obsession with sex and cloud shapes?" she asks, still searching for it in the sky.

"Sure, let's talk about the plan for Saturday."

Mera looks down, crosses her legs and places her hands in her lap. "I can't believe you're leaving him. Does he know yet?"

"No, I plan on telling him when I get home today. I may need a second beer in order to do it. He's going to be upset and most likely I'll have to duck from whatever he picks up to throw at me. He has a raging anger like a momma bear protecting her cubs."

"God Soph, he's not that bad. Remember, I met Evan when you did, and I've never seen him throw anything at you, even when you were a total bitch to him."

"You've also never seen him naked or take a dump, but those things also take place in our house, so why is it so hard to believe that he has issues with anger management?"

Mera smiles and her eyes glisten, obviously lost in a memory.

Intrigued by her playful expression, I have to ask. "So what are you daydreaming about this time?"

"I *have* seen him naked, it was quite nice."

"What was nice, his body, or *it?* Wait…when did you see him naked?"

"Last Thanksgiving when you went home to visit your family, we kind of hooked up. *It* was nice. He's got a pretty nice package down there, don't you think?"

I smile, thinking about all of the guys Mera and I have shared over the years. We've usually discussed an attraction and the desire to pursue the other's companion before it actually happens. As far as I know, this is the first time she has kept anything from me.

"I'm surprised you didn't tell me. I had no idea you wanted to sleep with him."

Mera looks at me with her mouth turned down. "I'm sorry, Sophia. I went over to feed your cat because I knew Evan would forget, and he walked out of the shower with just a towel wrapped around his waist. I was going to tell you when you returned, but you were a complete nut case after dealing with your mother. When you told me what happened between you and her, I sort of forgot about Evan. You know you mean the world to me, and I lost myself trying to pick you up and out of that depression. Evan was the last thing on my mind."

"You don't have to apologize. We agreed that if you or I ever come across a *keeper* that he will immediately be off limits. Evan didn't fall into that category, so he was fair game. We both know that my relationship wasn't heading past a sexual friendship with him anyway. Plus, I'm grateful that I had you by my side when I returned from

Philadelphia, and I think you're awesome for feeding Lewis. He enjoys two meals a day, but Evan insists that he only needs one. I'm glad you took care of him; he's a good little cat. Anyway, the thing with Evan is no biggie."

"How is it that we found each other? Do you think the University's housing department knew that we were both nymphomaniacs when they paired us together freshmen year?"

"I don't remember writing nympho on my housing application," I say, smiling at her as she laughs. The waitress places our food on the table and I request a second beer.

"So Mera, if you saw him naked, did you also see him take a dump? He likes to do that right after sex."

"Oh God, please, I'm eating my steak. I take it back, feel free to talk about cloud shapes all you want."

***

Evan carries me into the bedroom, laying me on the bed. "If you're moving out then I'm going to slide inside of you one last time. One for the road, as they say."

I watch him undress in front of me. His skin is tan from painting the exteriors of houses all summer, and his lean body is finely honed like a long distance runner. He unbuttons his jeans, sliding them off to reveal a pair of grey Calvin Klein underwear snug against his body. His erection is obvious, and his face seems somewhat pained by its imprisonment. He places his hands down on the bed, approaching me on all fours as if I'm his prey. His face reaches mine and he lowers his head, taking my mouth into his. His hips sink and his rock hard shaft begins to rub against me, immediately making me wet. I'm wearing a cotton skirt and I can feel every inch of him through the fabric. Slowly he moves against me, up and down and in a circular motion, sometimes hesitating, and then playfully poking himself against my skirt. Clothing stops the penetration, yet his stiff erection feels like he could plow right through the fabric at any moment.

"Are you sure you won't miss this?" he asks in a low voice, nibbling at my ear.

"Perhaps we should stop."

"Do you want me to stop talking?"

"No Evan, it turns me on when you talk. I just don't want you to get the wrong idea. I'll miss certain things like sex with you in the early afternoon, but our relationship is over."

"Do you think you might want to have sex with me after today? I mean, in a few weeks. Do you think you might come back and want to do this again if one of us needs it?"

I hesitate for a moment, trying to think of the best response. It is a possibility. I don't want to be in this relationship, but if I'm out in the world hunting again and nothing hopeful shows up for weeks, then I may need to come back to soothe my cravings until another guy comes along. At least I know he's clean, and he seems to be handling the break-up pretty well. Plus he's asking the question, which means he wouldn't mind being used now and then either.

"Yes, I might come back, for sex," I finally respond.

Evan looks at me with a grin, his dark brown hair framing his face and in need of a trim.

"Well alright then, let's get this show on the road."

"Oh God," I say, rolling my eyes. "It would be a lot easier to stay wet and ready if you didn't say such cheesy-ass things."

Evan reaches down to the bottom of my skirt and wraps his hand over my knee. His fingers slowly run up my leg until he reaches my underwear. Gently, he tugs the cotton panty to the side and places a finger over my opening. There's slight pressure as he slides a finger inside, then a second. I moan and he lets out a sigh.

"You feel wet and ready to me, even with my cheesy-ass comments," he replies, his eyes scanning the length of my body. "When was the last time we did this anyway?"

"Three days ago, you jerk," I say, smacking him on the arm. He laughs and I know he's just kidding. "We both need this. I know that when I end a relationship I tend to run right out and fuck the first person I'm attracted to. It helps me feel better about the break-up, but I also do it because it's usually been some time since I've had sex. People don't fuck much toward the end of things; it's more fighting than sex that usually goes on. I don't know about you, Evan, but this last hurrah will satisfy my needs, at least for a little while."

"Yeah, me too," he says, looking at my face as he brushes my hair off my shoulder.

I grab Evan's arms and roll him so he's laying flat on the bed. I rise to my knees, straddling over his hips. "I need you to understand that I care for you, I'm just not in love with you, and it's obvious from your reaction when I told you I was leaving that you feel the same way about me. We're friends, and it doesn't go any further than that."

Evan looks at me, still grinning. "Sexual friends?"

"Okay sexual friend, enough talking. Let's get this show on the road, as you said."

Smirking, I pull his package through the fly of his underwear, releasing him into the bright daylight streaming through the bedroom window. His body glows in the sun.

"You're not going to undress?" he asks.

"Well, if you insist."

Standing, I pull my shirt over my head and then slide my skirt and underwear down to the floor. I step out of them and lower myself back onto the bed, straddling Evan's thighs.

"Is that better?"

"Yeah, you're not wearing a bra today. Perfect."

I slide forward, taking hold of his solid mass in one hand. Slowly, I lower myself onto him, watching his eyes close and his lips part. I lean down and gently tug at his bottom lip with my teeth.

"Sophia, don't move for a minute. I just want to feel you." Evan's face completely relaxes and I can feel the pulse of his erection. My muscles begin to tighten around him and he moans in response. "You always like to tease me. Keep pulsating like that and I won't last three minutes."

My hands run along his chest, across his nipples, and down his abs. I continue caressing him until I feel his hips lower as he slides slightly out of me. I tighten again, holding him in place. He opens his eyes and smiles, lowering his hips again, this time slamming quickly back inside. He stops and waits for me to make the next move.

"Put your hands on my breasts," I say, leaning down. I clutch his shoulders for balance and begin moving my midsection forward, sliding in and out.

"Soph, go slow."

He gently massages my breast with one hand, wrapping the other around my back. He follows my rhythm, parting his lips once again. I love watching his face when we fuck.

I lower until I feel my clit against his flesh. I begin sliding, putting pressure on the area, nourishing my approaching orgasm.

"That's it. I can feel you, you're so wet."

"Evan, I'm going to come." My head falls back and my chest arches forward. He moves faster, using his hand on my back as a support for his quick movements.

"I'm going to make you come," he says.

My body tightens from my stomach down to my feet. I stop breathing and my chest tenses. A rush of heat travels up my breasts and across my face.

"Oh God," I scream. "Don't stop."

"Do it for me, Sophia. Come."

I fall on top of Evan, panting, feeling a trickle of sweat roll down my chest. He wraps his arms around me and let's me lie on top of him until I'm able to catch my breath.

"Wow, that was fast... and good," I huff.

Evan rolls me onto my side with my back against his chest. We spoon, and I feel his erection against my ass. He slides between my legs and penetrates my opening.

My body shakes. "God, I'm so sensitive right now."

"I can feel your pulse against my dick."

"Are you close?" I ask him.

"After being inside of you for that orgasm? What do you think?"

He begins pushing in and out. His arms wrap around my chest, restricting me from any movement. I feel his breath quickening against my earlobe, and his firm body rocks into me with unforgiving thrusts. "I need this," he groans.

Growing longer and harder he pounds into me from behind, his cock demanding pleasure, sinking deeper inside. My breathing races and I whimper, knowing that my soft cries turn him on. Every sound brings him closer to his release.

"Fuck," Evan says, crushing me with his arms, thrusting himself as far inside as he can reach. "Oh, oh," he cries, burying his face into the back of my neck.

His warm breath runs down my back in deep bursts. I feel his heart beating rapidly and his body vibrating with pleasure. We're both caked in sweat and although I can't see Evan's face, I can sense his smile.

"That was nice," he mumbles against my skin. He slides out and rolls onto his back, panting for air.

We lay in silence next to one another, waiting for the other to speak. I pick up my phone to check the time. It's almost three. I'll have to leave soon, and I start to wonder how long our good-byes will last.

"You can leave if you want," he says. I turn my head to face him, and see a frown. "I saw you looking at your phone. You can go; it's fine to leave."

"Are you okay?" I ask.

"For the most part. I mean, I think I'm sad, but I'll be okay."

"Yeah, me too."

He looks over at me with wide eyes. "You're sad as well?"

"Yes, Evan. I am. I don't want to lose you as a friend."

"You won't."

"Promise?"

"Yeah, I'll always be around if you need me, even after I find someone else."

"Well, I'm not heading out just yet, but soon I'll have to leave for work."

He lets out a chuckle and then covers his face with his forearm.

"Don't laugh at my job. I'll have you know it takes a lot of guts and self-esteem to do what I do. Just because you don't want to show off your wiener to a crowd doesn't mean that you have the right to laugh at me for showing off mine."

"Soph, I'm laughing at the fact that your father owns casinos in Vegas. You're loaded and can have anything you want, and yet you go out each week and do *that.* You don't need the money, so why do it? And by the way, just so you know, you don't have a wiener."

"Well it makes me happy, and happiness in my life is essential right now. Plus I meet interesting people and it gets me out of the house. It would be nice to make my own money at some point and not have to rely on my dad, and who knows, perhaps this will lead to something else."

"I don't see this job as something that will advance your career," he laughs again.

"Then just view it as a confidence builder and let it go," I demand, leaning over to give him a light kiss on the shoulder. "Let's talk about something else."

"Okay, now that we're not together anymore, tell me about the first time you ever had sex."

"What? Why would you want to hear that story?"

"Because you wouldn't tell me before, and it's the first conversation couples have when they hookup and start sleeping together."

"Everyone always asks me that question," I say.

"See, it's very common. People want to hear about one another's past experiences, especially their first time."

"Now? You actually want to hear about this now?"

"Yes. It's something that's always been missing from

our relationship."

"But our relationship is over." I roll over so that I'm facing away from him. I hear him sigh and exhale.

"That's fine, Soph, but we can still talk can't we? It should be easier to tell me about it now, since we're *not* going to be together anymore. Didn't you ever discuss it with your girlfriends at late night slumber parties? Just think of me as one of those friends."

My head quickly turns back toward him. "Slumber parties? Jesus, how old do you think I was when I first had sex, like nine?"

Evan laughs, taking my hand into his. "No, I thought maybe twelve or thirteen. I can picture you being a tall, skinny tomboy, maybe playing baseball or hoops with the boys, and then jerking them off afterward."

"That's sick, Evan. Don't think of me as a little kid jerking boys off. That's so wrong."

"You've always been a mystery to me. I know so much about you, and yet, I know nothing. Talk to me about something other than the present day or your life since we met, and I'll be satisfied."

"If it will make you happy, then fine. But I'm going to tell you about my second time, not my first. The first time was quick, since I think it was his first time too, so there's not much of a story there. In and out and done." Evan starts to say something, but I cut him off. "And, I haven't really kept things from you. I'm not as much of a mystery as you think I am. My past is pretty boring, and that's why I don't bring it up very often."

I settle into the bed so that I'm lying on my back, staring at the ceiling. My second time, now there's a story.

CHAPTER TWO

My phone rings as I'm walking down Pershing Avenue toward Skinker Boulevard. Evan's place is close enough to the university that it seems silly to drive to work on such a lovely evening. The air is still with the smell of decaying leaves, and my mood has lightened since the break up went so well. There's a huge weight off my shoulders. I take my phone out, knowing its Mera seeking details of the afternoon's events.

"Hey love," I exclaim.

"I can tell by your cheery voice that everything went well."

"He didn't throw anything. We had sex one last time, well maybe the last time, and I told him about my second sexual encounter." There's silence on the other end. "Mera, you still there?"

"Yeah, just shocked. I know Evan's always been intrigued by you, but even I'm lost for words right now. Do you want to talk to me about the afternoon fuck, the possible future fucking, or your many past fucks?"

"Yes. All of the above, but I'm heading to work right now," I reply, hearing Mera giggle on the other end. "Why does everyone always laugh at my job?"

"Hey, whatever floats your boat, Sophs."

"I have to get going or I'll be late, but I'll see you

tonight to fill you in on all the details. Thanks again for letting me stay with you while my new place is being painted."

"No problem, I miss having you as a roommate. What do you say we pig out on a pizza from Dewey's and have a girls' night in?"

"You have no idea how wonderful that sounds. See you in a few hours my love." I end our call, placing my phone in my bag as a car horn sounds behind me.

"Looking forward to it." A guy yells out from his car window. Waving, I give him a big smile. He's one of the art students in the class I'll be modeling for tonight.

I miss being a college student, but I've also found my fountain of youth. The secret to staying and feeling young is to work at a college. It postpones the inevitable mundane life that grips so many people after graduation.

The campus is alive with a crowd of students enjoying the evening; throwing frisbees, hanging flyers for events, and playing guitars. A few people are lying on blankets and reading textbooks, while others are hanging out with friends, discussing classes, and smoking cigarettes. There's a blossoming of lives exploding in front of me like fireworks. Students surge through these four years eagerly awaiting the outside world, while I'm scurrying back to the warmth of the womb.

I enter the art building and walk up a flight of stairs to the second floor drawing room. The ceiling rises twenty feet and is engulfed with spotlights illuminating a platform in the center of the room. There are about thirty desks circling around the middle of the space, each one occupied by a young, wide-eyed, eager, soon to be *artiste*.

"Miss Jameson, welcome back. We're ready whenever you are." The professor is a tall lanky man who's about fifty. He walks over to me and shakes my hand as he does at the beginning of every session.

"Isn't Jameson a porn star?" I hear someone in the room whisper, and a few students hoot along at the joke.

I look directly at the student, lifting my shirt over my head, trying to get some kind of a rise out of him in front of his friends. He's definitely an outsider, taking the class for thrills. The typical art student wouldn't show up wearing a green polo shirt and khaki shorts, sporting a buzz cut and white conch shell necklace.

"Um, Miss Jameson, you can undress behind the screen."

I look over at the professor and send an apologetic glance his way. I take my place behind the screen, where there's a coatrack for my clothes, a full-length mirror, and a chair with a white cotton robe draped over it. I slip out of my Prada ballet flats, slide off my skirt and panties, and hang everything on the rack. Glancing at myself in the mirror I tighten my butt cheeks and watch my thighs shrink in closer to my body. I need to start exercising. My hair is slightly mussed from having sex just an hour earlier, and as my eyes travel down my body I make a mental note that I'm in need of a professional waxing. The thought that I'm beginning to look like my mother horrifies me. *Okay Sophia, you shouldn't think about your mother when you're about to expose yourself to thirty people. Keep the panic attack at bay.*

I place one arm into the robe, and then another, tighten the belt, and smile at myself in the mirror. All is well. I walk around the screen back into the open drawing area. The room is cold and my nipples are immediately erect. It's showtime as I feel thirty sets of eyes follow my shape over to the platform. I step up and stand next to the stool, looking out at all of them.

Roger and Diane are in the far row. They're an older couple taking the class through the continuing education program, and my favorite people to talk to during the breaks. They have a son who is an artist and they're hoping to connect with him by taking this course. Two sweet and loving souls who enjoy life and can teach me to do the same.

"Everyone stand please. Let's begin by doing thirty-second gesture drawings, then we'll go on to one minute, and finally end with a few two-minute drawings." The professor looks up at me to proceed. I slip out of the robe and turn to face the outsider. Tonight, this is all for him.

I change positions with each new gesture drawing. The stool is a bonus prop as far as I'm concerned. I use it for support while bending over, and for propping one leg up so that the class can get a detailed view of my crotch, although it's rare for anyone to draw that area. Most of the time it's because the students are shy, or afraid to look *down there*, and other times it's because they don't think they have the drawing skills to do my parts justice. The professor always begins with fifteen minutes of quick gesture drawings as warm-ups. These exercises tend to loosen up his students, as well as me.

"Let's move on to a forty-five minute drawing, your choice of what section of the body you'd like to draw, and then we'll take a break." The professor approaches me and pats the stool. "Please, sit here, facing the north side of the room, and then you can face the other direction for the next drawing. You may cross your legs, or just use the crossbars underneath as a place to rest your feet. Your head can tilt to the side if you'd like, and rest your hands in your lap."

He walks away and I sit on the stool, placing my feet

on the crossbars. I position my hands in my lap and tilt my head slightly to the left. I am fully aware that there are thirty people staring at my naked body at this moment. Every inch is being studied and it's a complete turn-on. Take me in, follow my curves down into every crevice, speculate about my scars, and teach me how to love what you see.

This is what I crave, a quiet moment to think while getting paid to do so. Not that the money matters, I mean it's only fifty dollars to pose for a two-hour session, but it's a bonus. My eyes close and I begin to take deep breaths. The heat from the spotlights warms my body and my nipples relax, expanding back from their shriveled state. The warmth and lack of clothing takes me back to my childhood during the summer months in Philadelphia. I used to run shirtless through the yard with my brother, not realizing that there was a difference between boys and girls. I later learned when I started grammar school that little girls needed to hide their chests from the world. Was it then that I became ashamed of my body?

***

I'm shivering as I run up the stairs to my second floor bedroom, leaving wet footprints behind me with every step. The wood floors are unfinished and I have to be careful not to get a sliver in my bare feet. I grab the beach towel that I have wrapped around my shoulders and begin drying off.

Our above ground pool is still ice cold after being filled for the past three days with the garden hose by my mother. My brother has invited a friend over for a swim and I'm elated since it's not very often that we're allowed to have friends out to the house. First of all, we live in a small community just outside of the city, and our home is rather isolated from the rest of the world. Most people don't want to drive out our way to visit. And second, my mother works forty hours a week and is too tired to entertain, or keep an eye on another child. The same rules will apply to me once I start kindergarten and begin socializing. For now, my only interactions with the outside world are the rare occasions when my brother has a visitor.

I peel off my swimsuit and throw it over the foot of the bed. Water drops bead underneath it on the wood floor. I open a drawer to my dresser searching for a pair of underwear. My window next to the dresser is open, and I can hear my brother and his friend talking below. I walk over and peek through the transparent blue and white gingham curtains. They have towels wrapped around their waists, and are standing in the sunshine on the pool deck, warming their bodies.

I slide my desk chair over to the window, step onto it, hungering for attention. I want to be liked. I need my sibling to laugh at me and think that I'm special. I want to be older, like him, and be able to have friends, like him. I'm so young and often pushed aside from his ten-year-old conversations. Hey, everybody, look at me!

"Oh boooooyyys," I say in a long, drawn out sexy voice, at least as sexy as possible for a high-pitched four-year-old. "Look at meeeeeeee." I swing my hips back and forth in front of the window, showing off my naked body.

My brother looks up at me and smirks, while his friend looks directly over at him, confused by the event. My brother then looks at his friend and begins to walk toward the house. My heart starts to race as I realize I'm going to get in trouble. What did I do? Crap, I don't want to be grounded when we have company.

I jump off the chair and rush to pull my bathing suit back on. It's ice cold and still dripping wet. I panic, racing down the stairs to the ground floor. My brother's voice is coming from the basement; my mother must be down there doing laundry.

"Mom, Sophia just flashed us through her bedroom window."

"I did not!" I yell down to the basement.

"Yes, she did. We were outside by the pool and she showed herself naked from the window."

"No, he's lying, I just got out of the pool," I shout.

"Sophie, don't do that, and put some clothes on," my mother chimes in.

"Is that it? She should get in trouble."

"I didn't do anything!" I yell again. My brother stomps back up the stairs, past me, and out the door. I see my mother walking up the steps carrying a basket full of clothes.

"You shouldn't do that, it's not polite, and you're a girl. Those are boys out there." My mother dumps the clothes onto the kitchen table and begins folding them.

Embarrassed, I run upstairs screaming again that I didn't do anything. I close the bedroom door and yank the suit off, this time leaving it on the floor in a soaking mass. What did I do? It feels wrong and I panicked after I did it, but why do I feel so ashamed by all of this? What's wrong with my body?

"Everyone please put your charcoal down. Take a walk around the room and have a look at your peers' drawings, then let's take a ten-minute break. We'll meet back in here at 5:15 and finish the second half of the class focusing on a full figure drawing." The professor, and the majority of the students take out cigarettes and head for the door. I put on the robe, pulling the middle sash tight.

Roger and Diane approach me and I give them a big smile. "Hello you two, how're you guys doing?"

"Very well, Sophia. We were hoping you would be the model this evening. You have such a beautiful body." Roger nods his head in agreement with his wife as she takes my hand and helps me step off the platform.

"That's nice of you to say. I was just having an upsetting daydream about exposing myself to the world, but you both know I'm here to build my self-esteem, so words like that are always welcome, especially coming from my two favorite artists." Diane laughs and Roger nods again.

"I'll let you know when I sell my first drawing, then you can call me an artist," Diane says, keeping her hand fused with mine as the three of us move to the courtyard for some fresh air.

We take a seat on a bench and I stretch my legs out in front of me. Peering down, Diane asks how difficult it is to sit in the same position for so long, and how much money one can make being a nude model.

"Diane, are you interested in modeling?" I ask.

"Yes, she is," Roger declares in a blissful voice. "And I can't wait to see her on that platform, sprawled out, and visible to all. I love my wife and I want her to see that even younger generations view her the same way that I do. Students will draw her as a goddess, a gorgeous deity, and their depictions of her will be the proof as to how I see her every day."

"Oh Roger, please. College men won't be turned on by viewing a saggy, fifty-five-year-old naked woman. I wanted to try it because I believe that students should draw all bodies, of all ages. It will give them a quality education. Every model we've had has been under thirty, and female. As a matter a fact, Roger, perhaps the two of us should model together. These students could use a male figure in front of them as well."

"I'm game, my love. I'd be happy to show my wrinkled turtle to these boys. It will give them something to look forward to as they age," he says, laughing, as Diane follows. I love how relaxed they are with one another.

"Well, I also wanted to try to model because I've never been naked in front of another person, besides Roger, of course. I think it would be exhilarating."

"It is. It's also relaxing and meditative. I think of it as therapy."

Roger stands and walks over to a group of people from the class. He joins them in their cigarette break as I continue talking to Diane. The student with the conch shell necklace stands in the group with Roger. He glances our way a few times, and once, when our eyes meet, he smiles. I've come to find out, after many requests, that college guys believe women who are nude models will sleep with them. I can tell by his expression what's on his mind. *I've already seen you naked, so why can't we just do it.* Sorry sweetie, I don't put out for everyone. I do have some limits... I think.

***

It's dusk as I walk back to Evan's place to pick up my car. The streetlights flicker as kids ride their bikes along the sidewalk. Evan's 1980s red Saab 900 is sitting in the driveway, the one his father passed down to him eight years ago when Evan received his driver's license. It's been in the family for thirty years. Every part has been replaced at least twice, including the engine. The whole family just can't bear to get rid of it. I'm a firm believer that Evan was conceived in that car, but he insists that his parents would never have sex outside of their own bedroom. In another twenty years, his children will learn how to drive in that beast.

My MINI Cooper is parked in front of Evan's place. The dark grey interior of my Coop matches the color on the body. It still has the new car scent, even after two years of heavy driving and quite a few sexual escapades in the front and back seats. I put close to 600 miles on it the first day, driving from Philly to Cincinnati to show it off to my boyfriend at the time. Mera calls it a girly car, which is fine with me, since I'm a girl.

The car was a graduation gift from my dad, and probably my favorite gift from anyone, ever. I appreciate everything he does for me. He also placed a generous amount of money in my bank account so that I wouldn't have to struggle getting my feet off the ground after college, while also trying to survive in a new city.

My father's a savvy man with two degrees who has made wise business decisions. My mother is not, so when our family went into debt and had to declare bankruptcy because of her spending, my father packed up and left. I was young, and when he contacted us again thirteen years later, he was truly heartbroken by how we had been living. He's still trying to buy our love with outrageous gifts. Sometimes it helps us rise above what we had to withstand during our childhood with our mother, and other times his gifts make me feel guilty. That is, until my brother reminds me that our father enjoys buying us things. *It's his delight so if it makes him happy then we shouldn't feel awkward about it*, he says. I understand that, but what I really need from him is to listen to me. It means the world to me when he wants to hear about my life. Our conversations fill me with love, unlike his gifts of material objects.

Luckily, Evan's Saab isn't blocking me in, so there's no need to go into his place again until I pick up my things on Saturday. I pull away, the bag that I had packed earlier in my backseat, and head toward Mera's apartment.

***

The Auction Space Apartments are the essence of new urban living. The area is young and hip, just perfect for Mera and her outgoing party girl lifestyle. She originally rented the place because it's just a few blocks away from Busch Stadium, completely appealing for all of her boyfriends who were too drunk to drive home after a game. When her jock phase ended she decided to stay in her apartment, based on her position at The Pillsman Center. As an events manager, she's one of a handful of business degree graduates organizing concerts for the city. I've seen some great shows for free, thanks to her. The arena is within walking distance, as is Gateway Arch trail, where the two of us jog three days a week. There's also Lacledes Landing for dinner and a few dance clubs in the area. It's the perfect location for any twenty-four-year-old wanting to be close to the up and coming downtown scene.

Mera's waiting for me as I pull into the lot behind her building. She smiles and points to her tandem spot. I park the MINI and open my door as she runs over to give me a hug before I can even step out of the driver's seat.

"I'm so excited that you're staying with me for a

couple of days. I already picked up the pizza and I've got cold beers in the fridge."

"Thanks, beautiful," I say, stepping out of the car. "After I get settled into my new place we'll have a sleepover, which reminds me; Evan believes that girls talk about their first time at slumber parties."

"What? I guess if you're still having slumber parties when you're like thirteen or older, maybe, but I can't imagine that coming up at such a young age. Kissing, yes, but penetration? No way. Not my friends, at least."

"I know, right? The last time I went to a sleepover I was still playing with dolls. Evan has such strange ideas about women."

"Well, at *our* slumber party this evening, you can tell me all about your first time if you'd like."

I smile and take Mera's hand, as we walk into the building.

***

"I see that you've splurged on some new tchotchkes since the last time I was here," I say, placing my bag down in the entryway as I scan Mera's place with an astute eye. She had a bad spending habit when we were sharing a place in undergraduate school, and I want to make sure she hasn't fallen back into those ways. In the middle of the room is a new violet colored sofa that's very modern and chic.

"The IKEA Store," she says, walking over to the piece of furniture. "IKEA as well," she adds, pointing to a long line of white bookshelves.

"And all the little knick-knacks?"

"The online Anthropologie site," she gleams. "And I

didn't break the bank. I just want to have some things that are a step above a college student's. I was tired of my parents' hand-me-down furniture and all that junk I bought a few years ago."

"Will you let me know if you start spending beyond your budget so that I can step in and save you?"

"Of course, now let's eat. I'm starving."

I slip out of my shoes and enjoy the smooth maple hardwood floors against my bare feet. The apartment is cozy, with two small table lamps lit in the living room. Floor to ceiling windows of the 24-foot high unit toss the lights from the city into the room, swirling them around like a disco ball in a dance club.

"I smell lilies. You know they're my favorite flower."

"On the counter. I thought they'd make you feel at home."

"Yes, and they look wonderful against the black granite. What a nice contrast. I always love coming here. It's such a different world from that old place I've been living in."

"That old place has character. That's why you moved into it in the first place," Mera says, flipping the pizza box open, pulling out a slice. She places it on a paper plate, and slides it across the island to my side. She takes a piece for herself, and then grabs two beers out of the fridge.

"You're a great host. Warm pizza and a cold beer, my life is complete."

"So how are things with the shrink?" Mera asks, taking a swig of her beer.

"She's okay. We talk a lot about my brother, and my mother, but not at all about my dad."

"Why not?"

"We just haven't gotten that far into my life, I guess.

Plus, Dr. Rosen and my father know each other. He hasn't given me any details as to how they met, and I haven't really cared enough to ask. I guess I'll bring it up next time we talk, but for now my relationship with my mother seems to be the biggest issue. My therapist likes to connect my lack of commitment, as well as my '*love em and leave em*' attitude, with my childhood."

"Well duh, your father didn't have to spend a fortune in office visits for you to figure that out." Mera glances over and shakes her head, frowning. "So, you do talk about the current issues you have with men?"

"Yes, all the time. Although I haven't told her about Evan or why I decided to leave him, so I guess I'll have a lot to talk about at our next session."

I look down at the beautiful dark counter and then over to the maple kitchen cabinets. Mera's dishtowels, toaster, tea kettle, and microwave are all light blue, while the walls are pure white. She must have ordered them from an online store. I've never come across that color at any retailer. The rest of the space is elegant and clean, with stainless steel appliances and three low hanging frosted globe lights situated over the center island. I look around the space again, admiring what's hers, and thinking about what I'd like to have in my new place someday.

"What are you thinking about?"

"How quickly our lives have changed in just a couple of years. From the dorm rooms, to the tiny apartments, to all of this." I wave my hand from the kitchen over to the living room. "I hope my new place is just as amazing as yours."

Mera takes another piece of pizza out of the box and sends a thankful smile my way. "I can't wait to see it."

"I can't wait to see it myself. It's being painted right

now, and updated, whatever that means."

"Isn't the building new?"

"No, it's an older building, but it was remodeled a few years ago, so I don't know why they need to renovate it again. It's a bit weird if you ask me."

Mera takes two more beers out of the fridge and places them on the counter. I'm only halfway through my first, not including the two beers I had earlier during lunch.

"Can you play some dinner music?"

"Sure Soph, what would you like to hear?"

"That one playlist we used to listen to all the time back in college."

"Coming right up," Mera says, opening a cabinet and turning on her system. Her surround sound floats music softly throughout the room.

"Today has been one of those perfect days; therapy, lunch outdoors, sex, walk to campus, modeling, beer, pizza, serene music, and an evening with my best friend."

"I couldn't agree more, except for the sex and modeling part." Mera sits back down, her long bangs falling into her eyes as she takes another bite of pizza. "Tell me more about the shrink and then you can tell me about Evan," she demands with a mouthful of food.

"Not Evan first?"

"No, I'm not drunk enough to discuss how you can always get breakup sex to work for you. My relationships end with a fight, not a fuck. It's too odd a concept to process sober. Shrink first."

"Okay, but my family seems far stranger to discuss sober than my sex life." I place a second piece of pizza onto my plate and take another gulp of beer. "At my last session I discussed my hatred for women's purses, my mother's lack of patience, and broken bones."

Mera turns and looks at me, her face confused and hesitant. "I don't believe I've ever heard any stories about broken bones."

"Well, I can only remember bits and pieces."

"Whatever you want to share, I'm always here to listen," Mera gives me a genuine smile and lightly touches my hand.

"Thanks, it's amazing that you can stand to listen to me ramble on about my past for so many years. Most people would have told me to get over it by now."

"Yeah, but I'm not most people, and I know you would do the same for me."

"True." I pause for a moment, putting my beer on the counter. I look across at Mera and admire her gorgeous blue eyes. I've been looking into those eyes for over six years, and I still worship their light color against her dark hair. What a beautiful woman and a heartbreaker. She's been proposed to twice, dated three men all at the same time, been stalked by more than one ex, and has a black book the size of a novel. Her frankness for life and relationships has helped me survive a few wrong turns along my way to adulthood.

"Your eyes match your appliances," I finally say.

"So you've discovered my latest obsession with baby blue." Mera stands up and turns the top of her jeans down, revealing a light blue thong. "I have on a matching bra too," she says with a giant grin.

"How sophisticated," I reply. "That's a definite step up from your last obsession with Pretty Kitty lingerie."

"Come on Sophia, guys loved that shit. They would always get super hard whenever I walked out of the bedroom wearing those sexy things. It was like they were about to make out with a thirteen-year-old, a fantasy come true."

"Yeah, that's because Pretty Kitty *is* for thirteen-year-olds."

"Okay. Fine. But I do look good now, right?"

"Absolutely. You look amazing," I say reassuringly. She does look incredible and I'm surprised she's not dating anyone at the moment.

"Somehow, I broke my leg when I was eighteen months old."

Mera spits out her pizza and glares up at me. "What? You never told me that."

"It was something I discussed with Dr. Rosen. My mother and the way she ignored us when we were little, as well as her lack of protection for her children were all part of that session."

"So what happened? Don't tell me at eighteen months, that you remember that event."

"Well, I know that memories start to form as early as age two, but I swear I can remember a piece of what happened. I have an image in my head of trying to crawl up the steps to the second floor of our home. I tried to stand on one of the steps and looked up to the top. I think it was my brother who peered around the corner. He looked down at me and made a face. I either laughed or was scared, but the interaction with whomever was at the top made me fall backward. That's all I remember."

"And you broke your leg?"

"Yeah. My mother said that she and my father found me lying at the bottom of the steps, crying. I cried for an entire day before they took me to the hospital where they found out I had a broken leg. Child Protective Services questioned both of my parents about the incident, but in the end, I was handed back over to them after a few hours."

"So do you think that's what really happened?"

"I'd like to believe it was that simple and that I wasn't hurt by someone in the house, but who knows. My memory of the event is probably something I made up as a little kid after hearing so many different stories from family members about what they thought happened. My brother has no recollection of it."

"Well, that doesn't surprise me. Do you think any of them would say something if they knew what happened?"

"Probably not," I respond, taking a swig of beer. I open another one, my final bottle of the day, and smile again at Mera. "So, the issue with what happened that day is, where were my parents? Why weren't they watching me? And why did it take them so long to take me to the doctor? It all seems fishy to me. Maybe they were drunk and didn't want to drive forty-five minutes to the hospital. They may have been scared too."

Mera puts down her beer, leans across the table, and places her hand on the side of my face. "Or maybe your parents, at least your mother, is a fucking idiot." She eases back onto her stool and lets out a laugh. "God, you couldn't even catch a break as a baby."

"Alright, I know. I feel like I've always been on my own, even as a toddler."

"That's why you're such a strong person today. You did everything yourself, from cooking, to cleaning, to paying the bills, and maintenance of the house; that is, until your father arrived back on the scene to help out. By that time your personality was formed, and you've been a stubborn goat ever since."

"Well, the good news is that with my required independence, I'll never want to get married to a guy that expects me to be a stay at home mom while he's out bringing home the bacon."

"Actually Soph, that's probably exactly who you should be with, just think about it."

CHAPTER THREE

The morning sun warms the side of my face, gently prodding me to open my eyes. I hear Mera in the living room, picking up her keys on her way out of the apartment. It must be around eight. She's on her way to work and once again I feel like I have no idea what I'm doing with my life. I just left a halfway decent guy because I'm a commitment-a-phobe, and now I have no plans until the big move takes place on Saturday. *Think of this time as a vacation, Sophia.*

"Why do I need a vacation? Shit, I have to get a job, or something," I grumble, pulling the white comforter over my head. Taking in a deep breath, the smell of Tide detergent drifts through Mera's sheets. She's such a neat freak, obsessed with clean scents and tidy rooms. The comforter is too thin to block the sun from my face, and I decide to get out of bed before I roast under the covers. I push the sheets down to my legs and lay flat on my back, allowing time for my body to catch up with my mind.

Looking down, I admire how thin I am when I'm in this position. I wish I could be this skinny on my feet, but when I stand I see fat forming around my hips and ass. I'm five foot, nine inches, and I used to weigh 110 pounds. Then the freshmen fifteen hit, so now I believe I look like a hippo. Gravity and hormones suck.

My black tank has ascended up just below my breasts, displaying my stomach. My finger rubs back and forth over a hole in my belly button where I used to have a piercing. I did it myself when I was fourteen, trying to impress some guy at my middle school. The piercing stayed in for about six years and then I just got bored with it. It's probably the longest I've ever stuck with anything in my life.

Mera's guest bedroom is minimal. The desk, swivel chair, computer, lamp, bed, and side table are all white. It looks elegant, yet sterile against the maple flooring and large window. It's peaceful in an odd, psychiatric ward kind of way. At some point during the night, Mera must have brought the lilies from the kitchen in and placed them on the desk. They're beginning to wilt after only one day of enjoyment, most likely because of the Indian summer heat wave.

Turning onto my side I notice my bag on top of the Kilim rug that used to reside in the apartment we shared back in Philly. Mera's mother gave it to us as an apartment-warming gift. I christened it with drunken vomit the first night we had it in our place. Mera welcomed it to the household on the second evening while doing the nasty on it with her boyfriend. It took us days to get all the stains out. We eventually named him Ken, as we were known to name every object in our place during that time. Now he looks lonely and timeworn, being placed in a colorless room only to fade away in the bright sunlight to a pale semblance of his former self.

There's a low moan coming from the other room and I wonder if Mera really left, or if someone else is in the apartment. I hear it again. A woman's whimper, a pure deprival of pleasure, but it's not Mera's groan.

"Do you want more?" a voice asks.

Where is that coming from? I sit up and take a step onto Ken, peeking out into the empty living room. Mera's definitely not home.

"Keep it up."

It must be the neighbors. I'm surprised I can hear them through the walls. I'll have to tell Mera that she doesn't have as much privacy as she thinks she does.

"Oh. Yes."

I place my ear against the wall, listening to the grunts and moans. Morning sex has never been my thing, but if I'm not the one being smothered with bad breath, it's kind of hot.

My phone sounds just when the wall starts knocking from the bed next door. They're really getting it on now. Pulling my phone out of my bag I see a text from Mera.

GET UP. COFF IN KITCH.

I smile, leaving the love-fest to head over to the kitchen for my morning fix. Opening a cabinet, I'm surprised to see that Mera still has her undergraduate university cup. She also kept all of the lopsided coffee mugs we made in a ceramics class we needed to take to fulfill the college art requirement. I pull one out that was finished with a celadon glaze. It's heavy, and I can barely squeeze my fingers through the handle. It's definitely one of my creations, and I suppose that's why I received a C in the class. I'm better at admiring art, and watching other people create it, than I am at making the stuff myself.

My first sip instantly satisfies my needs, with the caramel spice creamer adding the perfect touch to the lively morning exercise routine that's happening two rooms over. I head back to the bedroom with the "C" mug and the morning newspaper that Mera left on the counter.

A muffled voice comes through the wall, "Oh yes,

yes!"

"You just said that three minutes ago." I yell back at them. There's silence, then laughter as the bedsprings start squeaking, and the bed thumps against the wall once again. I guess they don't mind having an audience. It makes me miss Evan a little, although I suppose it's not Evan that I miss, but rather having a little fun with someone. Mera and I chatted long into the night about him and another failed relationship. I tried to explain my need for freedom, privacy, and not feeling smothered, but she wasn't buying any of it. She knows full well that all I want is to be wholeheartedly adored and loved by someone, and I can't have total freedom or privacy if I'm searching for that as well.

"You love it don't you? You want more. You want my whole body inside of you."

That sounds painful. The junk that people say to one another during sex is unbelievable, and I'm just as guilty as the next person. I sit upright on the bed with my back against the wall and my coffee in both hands. I place the paper next to me and continue listening. Hearing people fuck is nothing new to me, I used to hear Mera on a daily basis, and I've watched my share of porn over the years. It's become a stimulating form of entertainment in my life.

There's plenty of mumbling and grunting over the next five minutes. I wonder how long it will last, and if I should get up and take a shower, or join them by pleasuring myself. The rousing sounds and quickening thumps of the bed are a definite turn-on. With one hand, I place my fingers under my cotton panties and over the top of my spot, moving one finger from side to side. I take another sip of coffee and place it on the end table, lowering my free hand down to my thigh. The sounds continue from the other room. *Give it to me. I want more. Harder. Oh yes.*

Closing my eyes I feel an urge start to build inside my lower abdomen. My breathing becomes deeper, louder, and one finger pressed against my flesh turns into four. The bed in the next room slams into the wall and their cries become louder, their words incomprehensible. I rub faster, sucking in a deep breath, holding it until I can feel my approaching orgasm. There's a final howl from the neighbors and a hard smash against the wall. My body tightens and I hold my fingers over my clit, feeling the pulsations as I come.

My breathing is fast, my leg muscles tight and sore, as my eyes open slowly to the view of the white room. I slide my fingers out from my underwear and pick up my coffee from the side table, taking another sip. What's wrong with me? I just had sex yesterday. Evan must not have satisfied me. Hell, I don't satisfy me. That was another quick one too.

Standing, I leave the paper on the bed, pick up my bag, and head for the bathroom to take a shower. I place my bag on the counter, pulling out my toothbrush. Mera stocks her guest bathroom with plenty of toiletries for guests, including items for her dates, since she never allows them into her master bath. She's the type of woman who is open and flashy with her body, but fiercely guards her privacy. I've never been in there myself, but as far as I'm concerned a bathroom's a bathroom, and I feel no need to wander in there as if she's hiding something from me.

Looking into the mirror I think about my father's eyes. My brother has my mother's blue eyes and blond hair while I have my father's features, reddish brown eyes with deep brown locks. As a child my brother teased that I was the mailman's daughter, until my father returned and my family was reminded of the striking resemblance between the two of us. I'm tall and lanky with a warm skin tone, like his side of the family. He often tells me that I look like his mother and although I've only seen photographs of her, I hope he's right. I want to have the good genes, and my mother and her siblings are all short and plump.

My phone rings as I'm opening the tube of toothpaste. I place the cap on the counter and reach into my bag for the phone. It's Evan.

"Hey Ev, why are you calling me so early?"

"Hi. I just wanted to see how you're doing and if you've changed your mind."

I let out a sigh. "Really? Do we need to go over this again? I mean, haven't we already discussed everything?"

Evan laughs. I hear his lighter flick a few times as he tries to light his cigarette. Finally there's a slight inhale and then a long exhale of air coming from the other end.

"When did you start smoking again?"

"You know I've always smoked."

"Yeah, but only after sex."

"Well that's what I called to talk to you about."

"Evan, I'm not coming over to have sex with you. We're not together anymore, and we just did it yesterday." I look back into the mirror and notice a wrinkle on my forehead. Great, now I have a wrinkle to go along with my expanding hips.

"Soph, I'm not calling to ask you for sex," he pauses, and takes another drag of his cigarette. "I'm calling because I met someone and I want to make sure that it's really over between us. I think I like her."

"You met someone?" My voice suddenly drops to a low and soft tone. "And you had sex with her already? That's why you're smoking?"

"I'm not calling to discuss details, or to hurt you, I'm

just calling for a confirmation. For some reason I feel like I need your permission to continue on with my life."

"We just discussed this yesterday. When people end relationships they tend to run right out and fuck the first person they're attracted to in order to feel better about the breakup. At any rate, no."

There's a further pause as Evan takes another drag of his cigarette. "No, it's not over?"

"I'm sorry, I meant no, you don't need my permission. It's okay to be with someone else, although its kind of fast isn't it?"

"I know. I was invited to a party last night, and since I was alone, well... I had no idea I'd find a match."

"God, you sound like an eharmony commercial. I hope you didn't use the word match in front of her."

"Of course not. So, are we good?"

"Yeah, but I won't be coming over for sex if you're with someone else. It's not fun being the behind the scenes woman who ends up ruining someone's relationship." I place my hand on the counter and lean toward the mirror. I inspect my teeth with a big grin and then back away. "I do need to ask you for two favors though."

"What?"

"First, I'd like you to take care of Lewis until I can pick him up with my things on Saturday. And I want you to feed him twice a day."

"I can do that. That cat loves me, especially when I sing Elvis songs to him."

"Please don't serenade him with Elvis songs. He likes to listen to Johnny Cash."

"Oh, no way! I'm not playing that in my place. I have him for two more days, he's listening to Elvis."

"Fine, just feed him, okay?"

"What's the second favor?"

"Don't invite the new girl over on Saturday. Mera and I will be out on that day to pick everything up."

"I wouldn't do that. Not to you, or to her."

"I know. I just needed to say it."

**

Dr. Rosen has her hair tied back today, which usually means she's in the mood for a critical and intense discussion.

"What does love mean to you?"

Oh crap, I knew it. The age-old "what is love" question. I saw it coming as soon as I told her that I left Evan.

"You know I can't answer that question. Unless I actually feel it, I don't know what it is."

"How do you know you haven't felt it? What do you think it is?"

I place my elbow on the arm of the chair and put my hand up to my chin, resting a finger across my mouth. She's really going to make me come up with an answer this time. "Is it a spark? Perhaps it feels like electricity running through your veins? I suppose it's a desire to be with someone, even when they're at their worst."

"Are you asking me, or telling me?" Dr. Rosen leans back in her chair, placing her pen on her notebook. She looks at the photographs of her niece and nephew, and then over to me. "Love means different things to different people, but at twenty-four, I would suspect that you're not being very honest with your answer." She folds her arms across her waist and gently swivels her chair back and forth.

"I know exactly what love is, based on what I've seen and heard from my friends, and what I've read, but I haven't felt it just yet. I don't think it's as much of a problem as you think it is, Dr. Rosen. I've had crushes, I love Mera, and my father, but I haven't found a sexual partner for whom I have a deep passion. There's nothing wrong with that, as far as I'm concerned."

"So do you want to keep having sexual partners and never develop those associations into something more, say, a healthy relationship?"

"I understand what you're getting at, that there's more to this love thing than sex, but if I'm happy, then what's the problem?"

"Sophia, people your age tend to have experience with at least one long-term relationship. It is a bit unusual for a young woman not to want that."

I put my hand back on the armrest and lean forward. "That's very sexist of you," I say.

Dr. Rosen smiles, and I can tell she's enjoying getting on my nerves. "You know that I've had long-term relationships. I think I proved that I can be involved with someone for some time by living with Evan. We were together for four years."

"No, you've known him for four years. You've been living with him for ten months, and I don't know how involved the two of you were, other than having sex with one another."

"Sex can be very intimate between two people."

"Yes, it can be. Has it been for you? Or is it the same as when you pleasure yourself on your own?"

Dr. Rosen can be such a bitch sometimes. I should have never told her how often I masturbate. "What are you getting at?"

"We're discussing love, intimacy, and relationships. You didn't have any of those with Evan."

"I sort of did."

"How many other men did you have sex with while you were living with Evan?"

I sigh knowing deep down that this is exactly what I need. Someone like Dr. Rosen to wake me up to the fact that it's okay to be emotionally open with another person. I lean back and relax in the chair.

"Like I said, I understand that love isn't purely physical."

Dr. Rosen reaches for her pen and notebook and starts to write something in my file.

"Is it okay if I say a few more things while you're doing that?" I ask.

"Of course, please, keep talking."

"You know I love myself, right?"

"Yes."

"I shouldn't have to defend myself, but I feel like I have to in this case. I love myself. And that's important, isn't it?"

"Ah huh." Dr. Rosen keeps her head down, barely acknowledging my comments.

"I'm a strong woman who overcame an abusive childhood, and I'm not interested in having to compromise, or share my freedom with another person. As a teenager I felt despised by my mother. Sex was the one remedy that actually improved my situation."

"How so?"

"Pure pleasure I suppose. I felt needed, admired by my partners. The other fragments of my life, except for that moment, disappeared. School, my mother, my sibling, our home, missing my father, responsibilities, being poor; all of that was there, but paled next to the gratification of an hour of sex. My self-indulgence over the years has changed from absolute hedonism to an affectionate balance between me and my partner."

"What if you could find that utter sense of pleasure with another person, but it wasn't just on a sexual basis? What if you felt that way just by being with someone?"

"Then I suppose that would be what I call love."

Dr. Rosen smiles. "You know it's out there, and whenever you're ready to let it in that complete connection can exist for you."

"I still think I'm too young to be thinking about this kind of stuff. I'm not ready to get married."

"We're not talking about marriage, we're talking about enjoying life with other people. Your whole life, not just in the bedroom."

"I see. Do you think this has something to do with my mother?"

"Do you?"

"I guess everything does. Feeling abandoned and unloved as a child hasn't allowed me to trust very many people throughout my life."

"Recognizing it is the first step, now we can work to change it."

"If I want to."

"Yes, Sophia. If you want to."

"Dr. Rosen?"

"Yes?"

"I wouldn't be here if I didn't."

"I know," she says, putting her pen down. I'm pleased to see her stern look from the beginning of our session has changed into a more compassionate expression.

"My mother really did try to abandon me when I was

four."

Dr. Rosen stands and walks over to the open window where a breeze has been filling the room with cool autumn air. The weather underwent a dramatic change yesterday evening with rain and cloud cover. The temperature has dropped a good twenty degrees today, and it feels like fall has officially rolled into the city. She closes the window and lowers the blinds. I'm her last patient of the day and I can feel her relief that we only have fifteen minutes left in this session. There's a mini-bar in her office with tea and water, and she offers me a drink for our remaining time together. I take the miniature water, wondering if it will take me two or three mouthfuls to empty the bottle.

"Did she really abandon you? Or did it just feel that way?"

"No, I think she was trying to punish me for something, so she left me at a center and took off without telling anyone who I was, or where I lived."

She sits down and opens her little water bottle, taking a sip before she responds. "What type of center was this?"

"It was a community center. I remember my mother walked me up the steps and patted my bottom, sending me through the door; then she was gone. There were children all around me, so I think it was some sort of preschool. A woman asked me my name, but she couldn't understand my words when I responded. I kept saying Sophie, but all she heard was Opie. I said Sophie Jameson about fifty times with no luck. Another woman with a clipboard went through every name on her list and I shook my head no to each name. I wasn't on the list."

"So, you felt abandoned?"

"I was dumped in that place and my mother wasn't coming back to get me. Yes, I felt abandoned. The women at the center thought that Jameson might be my first name so they started calling me Jamie. As a four-year-old, shorthaired, tomboy with a speech impediment, they never imagined that they might have a little girl in front of them. I watched from the office as the other children played games and made crafts. The women wouldn't let me do anything until they figured out who I was, which wasn't going to happen anytime soon. I sat for hours in that chair, hoping that my mother would come back and get me."

"You don't have any speech issues now."

"Therapy. But only because my grammar school teachers wanted to help me, and not because my mother noticed that anything was wrong."

"So how did it end?"

"A bus came and all of the children and workers got on, including me. I started pointing down the road and every road I pointed to, the bus driver went that way. Thank God I knew where I lived, or else I would have been taken to the police station."

"You may have been better off if the police were involved."

"I know. So I finally made it to my house. When the school bus doors opened I sprinted out and into our home, hiding under the kitchen table. My mother went outside and I crawled out from under the table. When I looked out the front window the bus was parked in front of our house, and the woman from the center was in the yard talking to my mother. My brother was outside as well and I saw the three of them laugh in unison. The secret was out. I was a girl."

"That sounds like a horrifying and life-changing event for a four-year-old."

"Well, I never trusted my mother again. I grew my

hair out, and I started wearing nail polish in order to confirm my gender, mainly to myself. My brother and mother also taunted me. They called me Jamie for months. I used to cry over it, and they wouldn't stop, not even my mother."

"Did you ever ask her about the situation when you were older?"

"Yes, but her only response was laughter."

Dr. Rosen closes her notebook and takes off her glasses, placing both on the desk. "You felt alone."

"I was alone."

"And now you've let your father and Mera into your life?"

"They're the family that I never had."

"Let's keep developing that family. I have an assignment for you before our next session. I'd like you to talk to a stranger, have a conversation with someone, without inviting that person over for sex."

"I have other friends. I'm not isolating myself from the world you know."

"I understand that, but did those friends approach you, or were you the one who took the first step?"

I look up at Dr. Rosen whose eyes are shooting directly into mine. "I understand," my voice soft and defeated, trying to end the conversation.

"Sophia Jameson, you're a beautiful, smart, and exciting young woman who obviously turns heads every place you go. People are drawn to you, and that's a good thing. Now I want you to ponder if you've ever met anyone, or if they're the ones who've met you."

That woman can send a chill right down to my bones.

***

Mera's apartment is welcoming after the discussion with Dr. Rosen. I'm looking forward to a night out with my best friend before the move into my new building. Mera suggested walking a few blocks over to the Landing for dinner before we party. And since I have no plans on heading back to my old place for an outfit, I'll have to see if I can squeeze into one of her dresses for the evening.

I place my bag next to the sofa and notice three candles burning on the living room table. Candles lit in the last apartment we shared used to be a sign not to enter the bedroom. I guess it was similar to people using the sock, or necktie around the door handle. I'm glad I didn't have Lewis back in college. He's the type of cat who would knock these candles off the table with his paw, starting a fire… on purpose.

"How was it today? Are you healed?" Mera asks, walking out of her bedroom with a pure white towel wrapped around her head and a light blue robe concealing her pristine body. She sits on the sofa and I'm happy to join her, propping my feet up next to the flickering lights.

"There's nothing wrong with me, unless you count the anger I have about my childhood, and the fact that I can't commit."

"Commit to what?"

"Exactly. I don't need to be bound to anyone."

Mera unwraps her towel and begins drying the ends of her hair. "Perhaps Dr. Rosen wants you to show some sort of dedication to something besides a relationship. You're the most loyal person I've ever met, so I know you're devoted to me, as well as your father, but maybe she wants you to show some kind of commitment to a career. She could even be talking about an obligation to yourself, and not to others."

"I know she's talking about the whole shebang." Closing my eyes, I start to think about the best way to approach a stranger. What can I say without sounding like the conversation is an assignment from my therapist? *Hi, I'm Sophia. Do you want to go somewhere and fuck?* No, too blunt. Oh, and I have to remember I can't bring them home for sex. *Hello, how are you doing?* God, that's way too boring. "When you walk up to someone whom you've never spoken to before, what do you say to them?"

Mera laughs.

"Don't laugh at me, I'm serious."

"Oh come on. What do you usually say?"

"I don't say anything. I mean, I can't remember the last time I approached someone. People usually walk up to me and start talking, I just listen and respond."

"What about all those guys you brought back to our dorm room and apartment during college?"

"Yeah. I was drunk. I don't remember meeting most of them, I'm pretty sure they were the ones who did most of the talking."

Mera lets out a sigh while wrapping her towel back around her head. She slaps my leg with her hand, and stands, heading back to her bedroom. "Come on, let's find you something sexy to wear and then we'll work on speaking to strangers. I'm assuming that's another shrink request?"

I nod, following Mera to her bedroom closet. "Nice space," I say.

"I almost put my bed in here when I had that night job. It was hard to sleep during the day with so much sunlight creeping through the blinds. Luckily that only lasted for two months."

"Now you're living the high life."

"It does feel that way at times. I have a great place and a cool job, but I still miss having a roommate. It can be lonely here all by myself." Mera pulls out a flirty, black scoop neck dress lined with glitter print around the side and neckline. The sleeves are long, and it has an open shoulder detail on one side.

"That's cute. Black heels I'm assuming?"

"You bet. Here, try this on."

She hands me a plum colored spandex jumpsuit, sleeveless, no less. "No way. I appreciate you letting me wear something, but that? Come on Mera, that's not even funny. Do you have anything else?"

"I wasn't serious. My mother sent me this thing a year ago. It still has the tags on it. It's ugly as fuck and I know she spent a fortune on it, so I can't just throw it away."

"Give it to a thrift store."

"What if she comes over and asks me about it? What do I tell her if she wants me to wear it out?"

I take the jumpsuit, and hold it up to Mera. "Looks hot, baby."

"Shut the hell up." She grabs the hanger out of my hand and places it back on the rod in the closet. "I sent her a photo of me wearing the hideous thing, but that's as far as I'm going to take it."

"You have a photo? No way, I have to see it."

"Never." We both laugh as Mera pulls out another dress.

"Now, that one I like. For a moment I thought you were trying to make me look bad so that all the guys would flock to you." I take the dress and briskly walk over to the bed, laying it out over the footboard. "That's lovely, a beautiful above the knee tank. Did you order it online?"

"Yeah, believe it or not I found page upon page of clubbing dress websites, and this one was only thirty-five dollars."

I pull off my shirt and slide out of my jeans. The dress doesn't have any closures, and I'm nervous about pulling it over my head. "If it rips when I put it on, will you be mad at me?"

"It's not going to rip. Just let me see it on you."

The stretchy material hugs my chest and hips as I tug the dress down over my body. It's a comfortable fit, and looking over into the full-length mirror I can see that it's a slimming cut. The top of the dress, from the breastline up, is solid black. The lower section is a sexy leopard print, with a bright yellow one-inch trim around the bottom.

"I might have to keep this, it will look great with my cowboy boots."

"It actually looks a lot better on you than it does on me. The length is below my knees, but short and hot on your tall frame. I suppose I'm too short to wear dresses that are split with colors and prints just below the breasts. Feel free to keep it. You can think of it as my house-warming gift to you."

I smile back at Mera and blow her a kiss. "Perfect. Let's cake on some slutty make-up, and head on out."

CHAPTER FOUR

L aclede's Landing along the riverfront is the oldest area in St. Louis. The hundred-year-old warehouse and factory buildings have a rich history, having once been the main business district for the city. Red brick facades glow on bright days in the mid-western sun, while the tall paned windows reflect the open skies. It's within walking distance to Mera's apartment, which makes one of the Landing's restaurants, Walker Street Brewery, our chosen spot for dinner. We tend to dine, and then travel further west in a cab to nightclubs.

I'm starting to feel a buzz as we walk out of Walker Street. "I can't believe you ordered meatloaf at the restaurant. How do you eat all of that and still have room for drinks?"

"The meatloaf will help soak up the liquor. You're the one who will suffer, only eating a few crab cakes."

"We'll see. Where to next?"

"Let's head over to Worship and drink our asses off," Mera bellows.

"Keep in mind that we have a lot of boxes to pack and move tomorrow. Let's drink a little, and we can dance our asses off instead."

"We have time to sleep it off in the morning, don't

we? I thought we weren't heading over there until noon, right?"

"Yeah, but we don't want to be dead all day. I don't mind drinking, but we probably shouldn't take it to the point of room spins or passing out."

"We haven't done shit like that since college. Lighten up, Soph. Besides, you need to get drunk in order to approach someone to start a conversation. We're trying to please your shrink."

"I'm not sure I'm ready for that tonight. Let's just have fun and not think about my therapist."

Mera flags down a cab and we head over to Worship. The nightclub is housed in an old church just west of downtown. The pews have been removed and the nave is now used for the dance floor. DJs set up their equipment each night around the altar, and there are two bars, one to each side of the nave. High tables and chairs surround the bar area, and people hang out at the back and side balconies where the pipe organ still stands. The ceilings rise to forty feet, which carries the music up, and bounces it back down to the dancers below. Red and purple lights float around the cavernous structure to the beat of the music, and on most nights a fog machine lets out a cloud that wisps around, and around, sending people into a trance. The space is always loud, with vibrations pounding into your body every other second.

The owner of the club left the religious statues in each niche along the sidewall behind each bar. There are twenty in total, and as the evening progresses the statues' eyes follow me throughout the club, just like in those old haunted house cartoons. Mera can always tell when I'm drunk because I mention the wandering eye statues to her. At that point, it's usually time to head home.

As we suspected, there are only about fifty people in the club. The early hours are the perfect time to have a few drinks and loosen up while there's still access to the bartenders. Once the crowd piles in, we'll have to wait in line for a good twenty minutes in order to get a drink.

I smile at Mera as we pull out our I.D.'s and place them on the bar. "Two redheaded sluts please," I say with a smile.

The bartender is wearing a pinstriped, button-down shirt with the sleeves rolled up above his elbows. He has short copper red hair and is sporting a Snidely Whiplash curled mustache. Tattoos cover his arms and neck, disappearing under his shirt. Smiling back, he picks up our I.D.'s.

"Mera and Sophia, sexy names for sexy women. I'm sure you girls know that redheaded sluts are full of sugar."

We smile back knowing that he's just being friendly, and not trying to pick us up. Male bartenders are overly flattering to women to land good tips, while female bartenders tend to sweet-talk guys for the same reason, and of course it works. "You're right, we'll have two slick panties please," I say.

Mera turns and looks at me, "Starting with some shots, my friend?"

"You bet your little patootie we are."

The bartender laughs as he places the shots on the bar, "Bottoms up ladies."

I take mine and gulp it down, gagging for a second, permitting my eyes to water from the heat in my throat. Mera's glass is already empty when I place mine back on the bar. Somehow, her shots disappear in the blink of an eye, with no expression ever radiating from her face in the process. Glancing at me, she waits for my cue. I nod, waiting to hear what her choice will be for the next round. We've been taking turns at ordering drinks for one another since the day we met.

Mera leans in to the bar and places her hand on the bartender's wrist, pulling him close to her. "My friend will have an STP, and I would like to have a buttery nipple. Please."

The bartender winks and places his free hand on Mera's cheek. "One sweet tight pussy and a buttery nipple coming right up."

"You can be such a slut sometimes."

"What do you mean sometimes? I pride myself on my slutiness," she replies with a grin.

"Okay, but I can't believe you ordered those. I thought we'd do a shot and then drink beer for the rest of the night."

"Is it the alcohol or the names that bother you? Because, you know I wasn't the one who named them."

"The names are clever and amusing for newbies to the bar scene, but can you imagine being forty and ordering a sweet tight pussy?"

"If you're forty, and still hanging out in places like Worship, then you have a lot more problems than sweet tight pussies."

Mera and I laugh as we watch the bartender finish our drinks. Mine is delivered with a cherry on top, and Mera seems pleased with the size of her concoction.

"These should last us a while." I place a twenty on the counter and we carry our drinks over to a table, sitting so we both have a view of the dance floor. There are already a few people rocking their hips, drunk, and acting like fools.

"So Soph, Evan thought that you were jerking guys off at age nine, right?"

"Something like that, why?"

"Well, when did you first see a guy's package? Did it scare you, or did it make you horny?"

"Ha, you sound just like Evan. You know this is not normal girl conversation."

"Sure it is, what else are we going to talk about, shoes and hair? Come on, tell me."

"I'll have you know that I think about shoes and hair all the time... but I suppose penises are more exciting than pumps." I take another sip of my drink and think back to my childhood, a place that I don't like to travel to when alcohol is involved. "A photograph, or in person?" I ask.

"A real, in the flesh penis and balls."

"That would be my brother's."

Mera sends a look of disgust my way and I can't tell if she's about to throw up or hand me money for more therapy sessions.

"That doesn't count. I would think that most people have viewed their sibling's packages, either by accident or on purpose. It was by accident, right?"

"Oh, yeah. You better believe it was, and to answer your question, yes it scared me."

"Thank God. I don't need to hear anymore. I'm sorry I asked."

"Hell no. You brought it up, and now I'm going to tell you exactly what happened so that I can finally share this atrocious experience. You're not getting off that easy," I grin and take another sip of the STP before I begin describing my first experience in the land of third legs.

***

I awake one summer morning to the sound of my

brother and his friend sitting at a dinette table underneath my overhead bed in my aunt and uncle's new camper van. I slowly turn, making sure not to bump my head on the tan fiberglass ceiling inches away from my face. The sleeping loft is tight. Sitting up even slightly is impossible, and to get out of bed you have to roll out sideways, hang onto the safety bars, and lower your body to the ground. This is not an easy task, even for a limber eight-year-old. I decide just to lounge for a while, even though my bladder is about to burst. In my mind it's easier to deal with bladder pressure then to deal with my brother.

The RV is parked in my aunt and uncle's driveway, next to their house. We're having a sleepover, giving my mother a break for an evening.

I have no desire to be lying half naked in a small camper loft bed. My shorts and shirt must be down below where my brother and his friend are sitting. They would never give me my clothes if I asked for them, so I won't even bother opening my mouth. Instead, I lay in bed, having a daydream that my brother takes my clothing and throws it out the door, then laughs because I have to go outside in my underwear if I want to get dressed.

Twenty minutes or so pass and I begin rubbing my feet together to keep my mind off the pressure in my bladder. When my jarring feet stop engaging my brain, I turn onto my stomach and hang my arm down, swinging it back and forth alongside the top bunk. The two below are now aware that I am awake, but don't seem to acknowledge my existence. They are playing cards and waiting for the day to begin just like I am, or at least waiting for someone to tell us what to do.

I hear the door handle turn and my aunt walks up the two metal stairs into the trailer. Now I definitely don't want to get out of bed. There is no way I'm going to show my aunt my underwear.

"Morning. How'd you guys sleep?"

"Good," the three of us mumble.

We're all very quiet and shy when adults are around. My mother's family makes me nervous, so nervous that I walk in a different direction when I see them. Sometimes I even hide in trees or in my bedroom when they come over, so that I don't have to have a conversation with any of them. At the time, I didn't know what it meant to be nervous, I only knew that my stomach was upset, and that when my relatives spoke to me, they made me sad. The sadness stemmed from their laughter at my responses to their questions. Having a conversation with any of them was impossible and resulted in a chuckle if I ventured sharing my own opinion.

My aunt talks to my brother about going fishing. She's wearing white shorts and a tight yellow t-shirt with glasses that are too big for her face. Her glasses remind me of a movie star's extravagant eyewear, and perhaps that's the look she's going for. I'm only focused on my full bladder so most of the conversation escapes me. I hear the word worms, and then a discussion about breakfast. My brother appears from under the loft bed, and he walks over to the side bed next to the door. He sits down, close to my aunt, while his friend walks over and stands next to them. I now have a clear view of everyone from above.

Then I see it. Hideous. There on the bed, where my brother is sitting, squished against the side of his leg, all purple, red, and pink, bulging out, are his balls. They're hanging out of his shorts, and he's clueless. It's a disgusting sight, but what can I do? I suppose I can speak up and say "Hey, your nut sack is hanging out." It's just too nasty to even comment on, yet I can't stop staring. I lift my head and peer down, noticing his shlong is exposed as well. Then I see my aunt sneak a peek and eventually everyone is uncomfortable. My brother sits, oblivious, legs spread wide, baseball hat down over his eyes, his hands on his knees. My aunt finally leaves and before I can speak, his friend blurts out what I've been holding in.

"Your balls and dick are hanging out." The three of us laugh, I more than my brother. He seems a little embarrassed, but only mumbles his usual "shut up" to the two of us. His friend goes on and on about how he was sitting there showing off his balls to my aunt. My brother sits up and walks out of the camper, his friend close behind.

I'm finally alone. I lower myself down from the bunk and put on my clothes. I decide at that moment, while sliding the tiny shorts up my legs, that I am never going to wear short shorts again. Who invented these things anyway, and why? If I sit down and spread my legs, I'm sure my vagina would somehow find it's way out. I sit down on the bottom bed and look. No, it doesn't show, only my underwear is surfacing. Then it hits me, my brother wasn't wearing any underwear, just his shorts. Nasty. Who doesn't wear underwear, especially with shorts that are only an inch down from the crotch? Why not just walk around naked?

I leave the trailer and walk toward the house. It's a sunny day with the smell of pine filling the air. I giggle to myself, thinking that someday I might actually enjoy the sight of bulging balls and a guy's wand. For now, I can't even fantasize about it. The only picture in my head of what one looks like is that of my brother's, and because of that, the package I see in my daydreams will be his. I'm completely disgusted.

***

"Shit, that's nasty." Mera gulps down her drink, repulsed by my story.

"Yeah, I didn't get over that experience until I landed my first boyfriend about five years later. It was even difficult to masturbate for a few years."

We continue our conversation, stopping only to drink two more shots, and have another round of sexy drinks. There are now well over a hundred people in the club, most of who are on the dance floor. We're ready to join them. The music is significantly louder and we have to yell to hear one another.

"Anyone stand out to you, Soph?"

"Nope. Let's just head in."

Mera laughs as I grab her arm and pull her into the middle of the nave. We stay close to one another. Mera enjoys closing her eyes when she dances, rocking around with her arms stretched above her head. I believe a child using a hula-hoop would make those same movements. It's kind of cute in some strange way. I smile as I watch her jerk her hips in a circle and fling her head back. Her hair whisks all around, often flying into other dancer's faces. She looks beautiful once again, and as she opens her eyes, she smiles at me. I love her. I love her more than my parents and my sibling. I love her more than any boyfriend I've ever had. I want this love, and more, with a man.

"I love you too," Mera yells.

"How did you know I was thinking that?"

"I can feel it, and I can see it in your eyes."

"I won't say what I'm thinking because it's too

common of a line in those girly movies."

"You mean the line that if we don't find someone over the next few years, that the two of us should be together?"

"Yeah, that one."

"Total girly movie."

We both laugh as I pull Mera to the edge of the dance floor where there's more room for us to move.

"You know I was just kidding, right?"

"Of course, Soph. Could you imagine either one of us living without that long, throbbing stick."

"Speaking of throbbing things, we should really start to dance, let's get into it a little more, especially since one of our favorite songs is playing. Listen." I point up to the speakers as Macklemore and Ryan Lewis's *Can't Hold Us* blasts out onto the dance floor from above.

"Awesome!" Mera screams, as we raise our arms up and belt out the words to the song along with the rest of the crowd.

"Make sure you get us tickets if they come to The Pillsman Center."

"No problem."

Mera and I dance like we're seeing them live. The music smashes through my body and I find myself getting lost in each powerful beat. My trance lasts until the end of the song, and when I open my eyes I see a face before me other than Mera's.

"I love the way you dance, and you look stunning in those boots and that dress."

I blush and peer around him to see Mera talking and dancing to someone as well.

"I'm Alex, and that's my friend Jay." He points over to the guy with Mera.

"Sophia." I scream into his ear.

He's younger than most of the guys in the club, around nineteen, twenty at the most. He's classier too, dressing in a dark grey button down shirt and a grey skinny tie. His shirt is tucked in to a tight pair of blue jeans, and a white studded belt finishes off his look. The jet-black buckle oxfords on his feet match his hair, which is short, yet long enough to comb forward, as a few bangs fall to the side. He's slick and he knows it.

We dance through more songs, getting close, and then moving aggressively with the faster music. I bounce back and forth between rubbing my body against his, and Mera's.

I notice that the two guys have similar features and I'd be surprised if they weren't brothers. Mera's hookup is also wearing a button down shirt and tie; only his are a deep burgundy color, untucked, with light grey jeans. They have great smiles and seem harmless enough, maybe even a little innocent based on their age.

I'm sweaty and in need of a break. "I need to stop or I'm going to collapse. Do you want to head up to the balcony for a while?"

"Sure, let me tell Jay," he says.

He heads over to his friend and mutters something in his ear. I see them both look my way and they shake hands. I consider that a congratulatory handshake. Mera peeks my way with a large grin and I give her a thumbs up. She nods and knows that a thumbs up from me means the guy will be a good fuck, but I have no further plans. If I had given her the hand fanning my face sign, she'd know the guy could have a future. I point to the balcony and she nods again as the guy, I can't even remember his name, heads back over my way.

Alex. It's Alex. I'll try to remember that.

I take his hand and we wander up to the balcony, positioning ourselves on the side walkway. There's just as big of a crowd upstairs as there is down. People are dancing in the larger balcony area, and the side areas are packed from end to end. Swirls of smoke from the fog machine rise up, settling in the space. The dancers around us are barely visible, yet there's a clear view to the floor below. The smoke stays at eye level here based on the dancers below waving it up, and the ceiling fans above pushing it back down. When you bend slightly over the balcony, you're back in the semi-clear air zone.

We watch Mera dance and I laugh at the freedom she wields with her movements. Her evening fling can't keep up, and he looks like he needs a break as well. I expect them both to be joining us soon.

My arm moves back until I find Alex's side. Pulling him closer, an urge takes over, and I need to feel him. I begin to move and thrust against his jeans to the music. He places a hand on each one of my hips and joins me in grinding to the beat. Most of the couples on the balcony are absorbed with the same movement, enjoying a small break from reality, jobs, bills, and school.

I'm wet and I can feel him growing harder, longer against my ass. The dress I'm wearing is thin, and his jeans definitely don't leave much room for his package. We grind and moan in unison, watching the dancers below echo our movements.

I turn around, facing him, and pull his tucked shirt out from his jeans. He leans in, resting a hand on the side of my neck, while placing soft kisses along the other. I lift my head up and he continues under my chin and then back down to my neckline. I tug on his belt and he steps closer, rubbing against me to the beat of the music.

The smoke continues to swirl around, imitating a veil that envelops us, yielding privacy from the other couples. I look to my left then my right, noticing a few bodies grinding, but no faces. My heart races as I reach below the shirt in front of me, unzipping his pants. Turning back around, I feel him nuzzle close to my ass. He sweeps my hair to one side and continues kissing my neck.

The music feels louder, pounding along with the racing beats of my heart. I'm definitely aroused as I feel Alex's hand slide up my right hip, and under my dress. He slips a finger underneath my thong, and without any hesitation, slides it inside. I groan and raise my head again, leaning back against him. He slides in and out, gently rubbing my intimate spot, as I whimper with enjoyment.

"Do you want more?" Alex says into my ear. "What do you want me to do?"

"I want all of it," I express back to him.

He continues touching me everywhere under my dress, exciting every nerve in my body. Then he slips his finger out, and I feel his hand between my behind and his pants, gently toying to free himself. I yank my thong down around my ankles and kick it off with my feet.

"Is this okay?" he shouts over the music.

"Go for it," I say as I brush my hand down along the side of his face.

There's a muffled crinkling noise from a condom package and then a moment passes before my skirt glides up a few inches. A hard nudge separates my outer lips. He prods again, and then uses his hand to find the right spot, moving smoothly into my wet space.

We let out a breath in unison, continuing to grind to the music. I wonder if anyone else in Worship is enjoying themselves as much as the two of us. I look up, gazing at the lights flickering onto us, watching them trace around the room.

"Jesus, is this really happening?" Alex yells, as he rocks back and forth into me. He's skilled and knows how to move while standing. Some guys have a problem with it, but I can tell he's experienced with the position, and he has the length to keep it inside.

"You're so good," I say, spurring him on to continue. "Keep going, move with me to the beat."

Alex's warm breath travels down from the back of my neck to my breasts. Every heavy puff of air stimulates my nipples, sending a quick rush down to my insides.

"God, this is incredible," Alex exclaims. "I need more," he shouts in my ear.

He pounds against me, and I feel an orgasm approaching.

"I can feel you tightening against me," Alex gasps. "Hurry. You need to come."

His words send me into a spiral. My ears explode and the music deadens. The dancers below blur and move in slow motion. My insides clench and my legs tighten.

"Fuck. I can't wait. I can't stop it." Alex grabs onto the railing in front of me as he pushes clear in as far as he can go. His pulsating flesh against my inner space is the end for me. I exhale, gripping the balcony railing as we're both overcome with pleasure. My body convulses as sweat drips down between my back. Alex let's his head fall onto my shoulder, trying to catch his breath.

"That was great," he sighs.

He gently slides out and tucks himself below his shirt. I turn around lowering my skirt. We both smile. He holds onto my waist, biting my lower lip, as I make sure he's secure in his pants before zipping them up.

"I need to go to the bathroom to take care of things."

"No problem. Thank you, that was some of the best public sex I've ever had."

Alex grins, looking surprised, as he gives me a soft kiss on the cheek. "I was hoping to be your first on the balcony," he whispers.

"You are the first... on the balcony," I smile.

"Find your friend, she's probably worried about you," he says, walking away with a wrinkled shirt, looking disheveled from our undertaking and disappearing quickly into the smoke. I bend down to search for my thong.

A voice stirs from out of nowhere. "You're so slutty."

I follow the legs in front of me up to see Mera standing with her hands on her waist. She's plastered and slurring her words.

"Where did you come from?"

"Jay and I were right next to you guys. Nice show."

"Well, it's not the first time you've seen me fuck someone."

"Soph, he was flucking you. Did you at least talk to him?"

"A little bit, and the fucking was mutual."

"Your shrink is going to be pl-pl-plissed, p-p-pissed about this one."

"Well, I don't have to tell her everything."

"You do if you want to get help."

Mera starts to teeter in her heels so I let her hold onto my shoulder for support. "I'm not in need of sex therapy, I'm in need of family therapy."

"God Sophia, you're a sex addict because you weren't loved as a child. You found comflurt and selurity, se-security in other ways."

"I know, but I don't think there's anything wrong with

71

that. I'm not hurting anyone. And it's comfort, not comflurt."

"You might be hurtling yourself."

"You meant to say hurting, and I need to get you home."

CHAPTER FIVE

I stretch my arms above my head, letting out a deep yawn. The sun entering the window lights my naked body, and I realize I've fallen asleep on the living room sofa. It was a long trek home last night. We decided to walk from the bar back to Mera's, not realizing how far away we really were at the time. Alcohol will do that to you. My body's sore from dancing, among other things. God, what was that guy's name again?

"Mera," I call out, listening for a response. She's going to be hung over after all of that hard liquor, and that means most of the work today will fall to me. I should've hired movers.

Placing my feet onto the warm hardwood floors, I rise from my sleeping spot and search for my clothes. There's nothing of mine in the room. Did I walk around last night naked? Didn't I have a blanket covering me while I slept? I wasn't that drunk when we got home, and now that I'm waking up, I remember I fell asleep in the guest bedroom, not here.

Shit, I hope I'm not sleepwalking again. It's not been since I lived in the dorms at college that I've done that, and it used to get me into a lot of trouble. I'd wake up, half naked in the hallway, or worse, the RA's would find me on one of the couches in the lobby, where I'd fallen asleep for the night. My former therapist at the university thought it was a stress reaction that would come on when I was heading into exams, or had some big paper due. But now, I can't imagine what I'm stressed about. I can only assume that it's because of the move. For the first time in my life I'll be living by myself, and I'm not sure how I feel about that, or if I'm even ready for it. I'll have to take a warm bath each night to clear my mind so that I don't wake up in the lobby of my new building. Shit, that would suck.

The dress that Mera let me borrow is flung over the desk chair in the guest bedroom. The bed's unmade, and my purse is on the floor. I open it to find my thong still shoved inside, and receipts totaling seventy-three dollars. Damn, did we really drink that much? I guess we had another round or two on the way out.

I pull out a clean pair of dark blue boy briefs and a matching tank from my bag before heading into the bathroom to freshen up.

The light was left on from the night before, and the water is still running in the sink. I can imagine myself fumbling in here the night before, trying to wash up, while creating a mess with the water and toothpaste. I turn the faucet off and open the medicine cabinet, searching for Ibuprofen. Mera has a few sample lotions that I take out as well, thinking that they might cover some of the bar stench that wafts off of me. Closing the medicine cabinet, I see my reflection in the mirror and immediately drop the items into the sink.

"Fuck, that mother fucker. Fucking asshole."

I lean in and tilt my head to take a closer look at the hicky on the side of my neck. I'm too fucking old for this shit. Damn, how am I going to hide this from Evan? Fuck it. I pull the items out of the sink and continue freshening up for the morning.

The kitchen and living room are still quiet as I make the coffee. It feels good to have some clothing on while preparing drinks and breakfast. I've always been disgusted by people who cook in the nude. Even if they shave, the possibility of any kind of hair or pubes in my food is downright nasty.

I pull two mugs out of the cabinet, a light blue one for Mera, and a red one for myself. Dry toast and black coffee, with orange slices on the side will be the perfect start for the two of us. The light blue toaster sitting on the counter looks like it's never been used, not a crumb on it, so I make sure to leave a few on top as I'm pulling out the toast. Annoying Mera when she's hung over can be amusing for those who know her personality. She lets out a fake cry of frustration like a three-year-old who has dropped her ice cream cone on the ground. Her face turns red and she jabbers about not having the strength to clean anything ever again. Sometimes she even falls onto the floor with exhaustion from the site of a crumb or a dirty dish, all because of a night of drinking. I can't explain why she does it; except for the fact that she's a baby when it comes to headaches from alcohol, and people making a mess in her space.

With two steady hands, I carry everything on a tray into Mera's bedroom.

"Wake up, sleepy head."

"Hmph."

"What do you mean, hmph? I had just as much to drink as you did, but you don't see me huddled under my blankets like a little wuss." I also know that I have more body weight than Mera does, so I keep my teasing to a minimum.

I place the tray on the nightstand and sit next to her, crossing my legs as I rub her side.

"Hey, let's have a light breakfast and then go for a jog to get our bodies ready for the day."

"Soph, are you fucking crazy? Does it look like I can go jogging this morning?" Mera throws the covers down off of her upper body, turning her head and squinting her eyes. I notice dried vomit on her chin, and mascara smeared down her cheeks. She places her head face down onto the pillow and kicks her feet.

I start to laugh at the atrocious site. "You could be in a horror movie with that face."

"Fuck you," Mera throws her pillow at me, nearly knocking me off the bed.

"Alright, then at least get up and have some coffee and toast. We can talk about exercise later."

"What time is it, and why are you waking me up?"

"It's nine. We're leaving at eleven. I want you wide awake when we get there so that you don't drop and break any of my things, so let's start the morning off right. Come on," I say, smacking her ass. "Get up and eat."

"Pfft," Mera responds, kicking her feet again.

"Don't dismiss me, or I'll have to beat your ass instead of just giving it a light tap."

She finally smiles. "Please do, you got lucky last night, not me. I could use someone touching my ass for a while."

"Don't tempt me, my love," I say, leaning over and reaching for the tray on the nightstand. Mera rises from lying on her stomach and sits up shirtless, letting her breasts hang out as we sip our coffee. She has perfect nipples. Her areola is the ideal quarter size and has a lovely warm brown coloring. Her nipples perk out and her faultless C cup breasts are just what the doctor ordered. Literally.

"Did you notice anything different about me this morning, Mera?"

She looks over and her eyes widen as she sees my neck. "Holy shit, you little whore."

"I didn't know he was doing that. I hate hickies. How am I going to hide this from Evan?"

"Who cares about Evan, I'd be more worried about hiding it from the people in your new apartment building. Talk about a bad first impression. Oh, wait, that's a pretty accurate impression of you."

"You bitch. You think you're so funny all of the time, don't you?" I pause, thinking back to Worship and the night before. "Hey, how old do you think those guys were?"

"Well, they didn't have on wrist bands from the doorman, so they weren't of drinking age. I'd guess about nineteen."

"Yeah, that's what I was thinking. That's a bit too young. I need to start being more careful."

Mera looks at me and rolls her eyes. "She says that now."

"I'm also sleepwalking again."

"No shit?"

"Yeah, I woke up this morning on your sofa, naked."

"You didn't leave any seepage on my beautiful new piece of furniture, did you?"

"Get dressed," I respond, slapping her on the leg as I stand. "I'll be in the shower, trying to rub this hicky off my neck."

"You know that doesn't work," Mera yells, as I walk out of her room toward the guest bath.

"Yes," I say, in a disappointed drawl.

***

There's a heat lamp over the guest shower in Mera's apartment that has made staying at her place like being on vacation. Evan and I lived in an older home, with few updates and no amenities to speak of. The 1950s retro bathroom we shared was pink and black, with the original matching pink tub, sink, and toilet. The fan was broken, and the frosted window was painted shut. The room smelled of mildew during every season, and I'm glad to finally be away from it. Mera, on the other hand, has it all. Sandstone tiles in the shower with small burnt orange, glass tile insets, forming the pattern of a sunburst. The ceiling reaches ten feet, and the walls are a warm grey. I made sure that when I was searching for my new place, to get the same.

I allow the red light to heat my body, standing under the lamp with the water off. The winters back in Philly were long and grey, with snowdrifts that would sometimes reach the height of our car. Now, I'll do anything to keep my flesh warm. Someday I'll move further south, or west where I won't have to worry about extreme cold. For now, St. Louie isn't all that bad, especially compared to the upper east coast.

Turning on the water, I place my head under the stream, washing off the stench of sweat, cigarettes, and liquor. Mera's shower has calming cinnamon oatmeal soap and two of my favorite scented shampoos from her local salon: vanilla spice, and tea tree oil. I usually mix the two when I shampoo my hair, creating my own special scent. Today, I'm keeping it simple, using just the vanilla spice.

I take the massaging showerhead off its post, holding the handle above my head. I rinse my back and then my chest. The spray hardens my nipples as I watch the suds run down my stomach and legs, circling the drain, disappearing into oblivion. Everything from the night before gets washed off. I don't think I'll go back to Worship for a while. It really is time to get a job and find a better way to spend my days, and nights for that matter.

The side of the showerhead lists product specifications and features, including 28,000 pulses per minute. Well, I'm sure that one will make me happy.

Turning the nozzle, I flip through five circles, finally finding the pulsating bursts of water. I place it in front of my face first, letting the water slap against my skin, then move it around to my back for a massage. It loosens my muscles, which should be helpful during the day for lifting boxes during the move.

I sit down on the built-in stone bench and spread my legs, placing one foot up for better access. Lowering the showerhead I lean back and close my eyes. The pulsating water beating against my arousal area produces instant excitement. The feeling of a rapid orgasm overtakes my insides as the heat lamp continues to warm me from the outside. This won't take more than a few seconds. God it feels nice. A sudden rush overcomes my inner body, then into my hips, legs, stomach, finally moving up to my breasts and neck. I let my muscles tighten and shudder, while my breathing stops and my mouth opens. My head falls further back, resting against the shower wall.

I let out a gush of air and moan at the rapid thumping of my deep area. Placing my foot back onto the floor, I sit on the bench discharging deep breaths. My body soaks in a few more moments of the orgasm, and the warming lamp. That will definitely make moving today a little easier.

***

We arrive at Evan's at eleven, a little earlier than I had planned. The move wouldn't take very long if I was smart and had rented a truck to take everything downtown in one trip. Instead, with my MINI, and Mera's little Nissan Juke, we'll have to take at least five trips back and forth unless Evan decides to lend a hand.

I see a note taped to the front door as we walk up the porch steps.

"Is that from Evan?" Mera asks, as she approaches from behind.

"We'll see," I say, ripping it off the door. "Yeah, he had to re-touch paint on a house today, so he won't be around until the afternoon, or so the note says."

"That sucks. Well, at least he won't be in our way, or it won't be too awkward, for me anyway."

"I already forgot that you slept with him, thanks for reminding me."

"No problem. So he's still painting houses?"

"Yeah, I thought he'd find something better to do with his degree after we moved here, but that was wishful thinking." I take out my key and unlock the door, walking cautiously inside as if I'm breaking into someone's house. "It feels weird being here, like I'm a stranger and don't belong inside with him not here."

"Don't worry about it Soph, let's get to work and we can relax tonight in your new abode."

"Sounds good. Let's find Lewis and make sure he

doesn't get out while we're loading the cars."

"Oh my God, I forgot about Lewis. I haven't seen him in months."

Lewis Salami is one lucky little cat. I often tell him that he won the lottery by having me as his mama. He was brought to a shelter when someone came across him starving in an abandoned trailer. A place where his former owners left him to die. His long Persian fur had never been brushed and was so matted that he couldn't walk. I cried the first time I saw him huddled in the back of a cage, shaking, not knowing where he was or what was happening to him. When I lifted him out from that cage he wrapped a paw around my neck and nuzzled under my chin. He let out a big purr and I assured him that no one would ever hurt him again.

Since Mera's allergic to cats I couldn't take him with me to her place, so I left him with Evan knowing that he would care for him.

"Lewis," I call out.

There's a thump on the floor above us as I hear him jump down from his favorite spot in the house, the master bedroom windowsill. A pitter-patter of feet scurries above me and I hear a rumble down the stairs. I see his head peek around the corner and when he sees that it's me, he runs to my ankles and does a quick roll on top of my feet.

"Hi baby boy," I squeal, picking him up and planting a kiss on his cheek. Lewis begins to purr and I hug him for a few minutes.

"That cat is fat, you should name him Chubs."

"Hey, he was left to starve, and as far as I'm concerned, he can eat whenever he wants. Besides, he only weighs twelve pounds, and I've known cats that were close to twenty. If he gets to be fifteen pounds, then I may cut him back a little, but for now, he's happy and healthy."

"Maybe he looks fat to me because he has so much fur. I haven't seen very many Persian cats in person, so it's hard to tell."

Lewis has three-inch thick orange fur and white paws that make him look like he's wearing socks. His eyes are light gold and he has a black nose. Sometimes, when I wake up in the middle of the night, I see his little white paws running by my bedroom door. It's a ghostlike scene when one is half asleep.

I take Lewis back up to the bedroom and close the door. "Sorry baby, I need you to stay in here for a while." He lets out a small cry, and then I hear him hop back onto his windowsill. From there, he'll have a nice view of the day's activities.

"Hey Sophia," Mera calls up to me from the bottom of the stairs. "You have to see this."

Walking back down I round the entryway corner, walk through the living room, and stop in front of four towering piles of boxes. Each pile has a white sheet of paper taped to it, with a word explaining the contents: bedroom, bathroom, kitchen, and living. There's also a small pile of boxes on the dining room table that are all labeled miscellaneous.

"Did you ask Evan to pack all of your things?"

"Hell no, and now I know why he's not here. He's afraid I'll be pissed that he did."

"Are you?"

"I don't know. I suppose not, it does make the day easier for us, but it's freaky that he went through all of my things. I mean, I wonder if he packed my tampons and stuff like that. What if he found my vibrator? Did he know that I had one, and what was he thinking when he found it in my drawer?"

"I'd be pissed."

Pulling my phone out of my bag, I call Evan.

"I doubt he's going to pick up," I say to Mera, as I walk around the dining room examining all of the boxes.

"Leave him a message."

"I will. Look, this box is labeled E-V-A-N. I wonder if he's giving me photos of himself or some of his things. Hey Evan, I'm here, call me." I hang up the phone and place it back inside my bag.

"That's all you're going to say?"

"That's enough. He'll get it."

Mera roams around the boxes and then looks over the rest of the house. "I don't see any of your things out, so this must be everything. Are you taking any furniture, or electronics?"

"Just my desktop, the flat screen from the bedroom, and my stereo. My father's having new furniture delivered for me on Monday, so I'd rather leave everything else for Evan."

"A clean break will be healthy. Starting fresh like I did when I moved into my own place is going to be exciting. I'll help you shop for some things if you'd like."

"I know. It's your favorite thing to do besides drinking and sex."

"I can't argue with that one, you know me well," Mera says, walking over to the kitchen pile, trying to lift a few boxes. She checks the weight of each one, slightly shaking them to see how well Evan has packed my things. "These are pretty light, Soph. I don't hear anything rattling around either. Cheers to Evan."

"Speak of the devil," I say, hearing my phone ring from my bag. My hand starts to shake as I answer, knowing that an argument might occur. "Evan. I see you're still just as anal as when I left four days ago." I shake my head, rolling my eyes at Mera. "No, not that kind of anal, you know what I mean. Anyway, I appreciate all of the time this must've taken you. I guess you don't have much going on lately?"

Mera smiles at me and rolls her eyes back my way.

"Oh, really? You let your new girlfriend help pack up my stuff? You shithead." My voice rises and Mera starts to laugh. "Evan, God dammit. Haven't you ever heard of a little privacy?" I sigh, waiting for his response.

"Let me talk to him." Mera yanks the phone out of my hand and walks into the living room. I'm fuming knowing that a woman other than Mera has been rifling through my most intimate possessions. What if she was the one who found my vibrator?

I follow Mera into the living room, listening to her do a better job than me at scolding my ex-boyfriend.

"And another thing, you know we both have small girly cars, couldn't you help us out a little bit with the SAAB? Where are you anyway?" Mera walks over to the front window with the phone, checking to see if he might be outside. "Really, at work? On a Saturday?"

I claim the phone back from her and lower my voice, slightly, trying not to let him ruin my day. "First, thank you for taking care of Lewis, and second, I do appreciate the packing that *you* did, and I emphasize *you*. It saves us a lot of time, but letting your girlfriend look at and touch my things is just fucking rude."

Mera throws a tough face my way as she holds up a fist, looking like she's ready to punch someone.

"No, I'm not jealous, I just don't appreciate strangers going through my entire life." I start pacing, listening to

Evan bullshit about trying to be helpful, how he was just thinking about me, and on and on about what a saint he is.

Mera swirls a finger in the air cuing me that it's time to wrap things up, and she's right. Evan and I can argue back and forth for hours about certain things, my privacy being one of them. We're good friends who just shouldn't live together.

"Evan," I say in a softer voice. "Please remember that sometimes I feel like my privacy is all that I have. There are things in my past that I don't want anyone to stumble across. If someone were to know everything about me, then what would I have left that's just mine?" Pausing, I listen to Evan laugh. "I wasn't trying to be funny," I say, hanging up the phone.

"Here Soph, let me wipe that fake tear from your face."

"Fuck off," I say with a smile. "I know that was a bit dramatic. I think I'm just nervous about getting a new place after only seeing it online, so I'm taking it out on everyone around me."

"You didn't go there in person?"

"I was in the building, but my unit was being remodeled. I've only seen one that's similar. Perhaps the stress from the unknown is why I'm being mean to Evan."

"No, he was a prick to let his new woman pack your stuff. That's why we both yelled at him."

My phone rings again. Looking over at Mera, I shake my head no, and place it back into my bag. "I'm not answering that right now. We have better things to do." Mera smiles as we head back into the dining room.

We start with the kitchen pile, placing one box at a time into any free nook we can find in our cars. I have to admit, Evan made sure the boxes weren't too heavy for us, and there's no shifting of items inside of them either. It makes me wonder if he just filled them with bubble wrap, and gave all my things to his new woman.

After an hour, the cars are full, and the kitchen pile is down to one box. I tell Lewis we'll be back in two hours, leaving him some food and water in the bedroom. Locking the front door, I walk down the steps and take a seat in MINI. Extending my bottom lip, I blow out a heavy puff of air, making my bangs fly off of my forehead. I look into my rear view mirror at Mera, who's waiting in her Juke. She gives me the thumbs up and I start my car.

In thirty minutes, I'll be walking into my new home.

CHAPTER SIX

M era and I drive west on the Interstate, getting off at her Auction Space Apartment exit, and then head north on Eleventh Street. Traffic is light on Saturdays, allowing for travel with a full load in the car to be less traumatic.

I pull out my phone, and make a quick call to her.

"Hey, turn onto Locust, and then pull into the parking garage on the left. We'll have to carry a small load in from the garage until I check to see what kind of parking is available in my building."

"Which building is yours?"

"You'll see," I say, hanging up the phone while I take a ticket from the parking attendant.

I find the first available space, and Mera pulls her Juke right next to MINI. We each take a box from our cars and head out of the garage, walking east on Locust, and then heading up Eleventh Street.

"I can't believe you got a place in my neighborhood. I'm like two blocks from here," she beams, practically skipping down the sidewalk.

"My dad gave me a list of four properties to choose from, and this was my favorite in terms of location and condition. I hope the inside is as good as the model I was shown. I'm walking into this blind."

"I'm sure your dad checked everything out. He wouldn't let you move into a place that didn't meet his standards."

"I wouldn't call the place I had with Evan high-end living."

"Well, it had character, and it was in a safe neighborhood."

"True," I say, stopping to turn toward Mera. She looks back at me as I tilt my head straight up with a smile, following each floor to the very top of the twelve-story building.

"No fucking way," Mera whines. "You're living here?"

"Supposedly I have a third of the top floor."

"Shit, you lucky-ass bitch, you have a penthouse?"

"Technically, my father has a penthouse, I'm just living in it."

We walk into the North Eleventh Street Building, a national landmark, and one of the most sought after places to live in St. Louis. The historic building was turned into lofts about a decade ago, with businesses on the ground floor including the Baguette Café, a place that Mera and I frequent every week. The original construction of the building took place a few years before the great depression, and it emanates dominance, security, and wealth from that time period. The art deco style is evident with rectangular blocky forms, and smooth-faced large stone pieces that tower over us as we enter the lobby.

"Cripes, look at the ceiling height, and those modern lights, and the floors, and that painting on the wall, and...."

"Mera, stop. Let's try to look like we belong here."

"We *do* belong here Sophia."

We walk into the elevator and I place my key into the

slot, turn it to the right, and then push my floor number. The door closes and I feel a rush as the elevator travels upward. My heart starts to pound like it's going to burst out of my chest. I feel dizzy. My palms are sweaty and my stomach is queasy. Can this elevator move any slower?

"I think I'm having a panic attack," I pant.

Mera laughs.

"No, seriously."

"What could possibly stress you out so much right now that you're having a panic attack?"

The elevator opens and I look at Mera. "Life."

We walk over to my door and I pull out a shiny new key. Mera starts humming an early seventies folk song, *Brand New Key*, by Melanie Safka. I giggle, knowing that she's trying to put me at ease. I turn the key, and open my door.

"Fucking shit, Soph; how much money does your father make each year?"

I'm dumbfounded, unable to speak. I wanted high-end finishes, like Mera, but this is beyond anything I could possibly imagine. From the hallway I see soaring sixteen-foot ceilings, and two floors, with black iron railings on the stairwell and a walkway above. The walls are concrete, painted a warm grey color. Gleaming oak hardwood floors run below, and contemporary light fixtures fill the space above. There's a large glass window above my entry door, covered with an etched texture pattern for privacy. I surrender and step into the foyer, Mera happily by my side.

Placing our boxes down, I open the first door to my left. It's a full bathroom with yellow-grey walls, a white pedestal sink with a round mirror above it, and a grey stone tiled floor and shower.

"This is lovely."

Mera takes my hand, excited to see more, she pulls me into a massive open space that runs a good forty feet. It's definitely an open loft concept with the kitchen, dining, and living area all combined into one room.

"This is gigantic, Soph. You could use it as a dance hall."

"I know. Look at this kitchen." I slide my hand down the speckled brown granite counter of the kitchen island that has enough space for six stools. There's a six-burner gas range, and gorgeous matching high-end refrigerator and dishwasher. All are stainless steel and brand spanking new. The island is the only thing that separates the kitchen from the rest of the room.

Mera walks through the space with me, touching every counter and cherry cabinet. She opens the fridge and gawks at its size. "This is the biggest fridge I've ever seen."

I look in with her, realizing that we both could fit inside the thing. "I think it's about five or six feet wide. This is all just cray."

"Totally cray. Maybe your dad wants you to gain a little weight, you better stock it."

"I could buy half of the frozen section at the supermarket and wouldn't come close to filling this thing."

Mera closes the door and we turn to admire more of the space. The stadium-sized area has six large windows, a double door leading outside, and two half windows toward the ceiling on each side of the room. There's so much light it reminds me of being outdoors. I walk over to the dining area and look out one of the windows at the city view.

"I think I can see your apartment from here."

Mera walks over and opens the double door next to me and we step out onto the balcony. "This runs all the way along this side of your loft. You can put a garden out here. And look, there's my place," she squeals, pointing to the right.

"I thought so. I'll be able to wave to you." We both laugh and I finally relax. This is incredible. I may not want to leave, ever.

Walking back inside we see that the living room extends around to the other side of the kitchen. There's a fireplace on the left wall, and four more windows. Galvanized steel ductwork hangs from the ceiling throughout the room, and lights drop down in groups of three. From the floor to about the ten-foot mark on each wall is concrete with the top remaining six feet containing exposed brick. The room and ceiling are all painted a light grey. It's a warm and inviting space, which I have no idea how I'm going to fill.

"Let's see what's upstairs," Mera says, taking my hand again while practically running up the steps. At the top is a door to the right that she opens with delight. We step into a large storage room, with one window, and a concrete floor.

"You could buy some free standing closets from IKEA and turn this room into an extra bedroom. It's not like you have any need for storage space right now."

"Yeah, well it's not like I have any need for an extra bedroom either."

"True."

"Let's keep looking, we haven't even found the *real* bedrooms yet." Enthusiastically, I skip out of the storage room and follow the second floor walkway to the opposite side of the loft. There's an open space at the end, with a built-in desk and bookshelves. "This will be my office. Look, I can view the entire loft from up here."

"Amazing. Your dad paid a fortune for this place. What do you think, about half a million?"

"At least. But that's not much to him anymore. Plus, he can always sell it and make a profit. I know that some remodeling happened before I moved in, and it looks like that entire kitchen is new. I'll assume he updated the bathrooms as well. It's all an investment for him."

"Well then, why didn't he get us a nice place back when we were college students?"

"Because I asked him not too. I didn't want to stand out, and I wanted us to have a real college experience. You know, eating Raman noodles for dinner, searching under the couch cushions for change to buy gas, and getting free condoms from the health center. It was fun and we have great memories to share because of it."

Mera gasps and latches onto my forearm, "Soph, you have a third floor."

I turn around and see the staircase in the corner of the office. Mera begins to race up the steps, and I pull her back. "Me first chickadee, this must be my bedroom."

I walk up, stopping at the top of the stairs. Mera's right behind, and we both sigh at the sight of the sprawling master bedroom. Floor to ceiling windows line three of the four walls, and a set of double doors open out to a terrace. The oak floors from the first level continue up into this space, with similar concrete walls and exposed brick. The walls have a fresh coat of paint in a cinnamon brown color, and an antique bronze chandelier with frosted golden yellow glass hovers over the room. The galvanized ductwork and sixteen foot ceilings expand into the never-ending space, giving off a surreal effect of continuing out of the building and into the clouds. Mera and I sigh again, taking in the immense beauty that surrounds us.

"I need a king-size bed."

Mera opens the doors to the terrace and a fresh gust of wind flows into the room, dispersing the paint fumes that still hang in the air. The terrace wraps around two sides of the bedroom, providing infinite views of the city. I'm bewildered as to what I'm going to do with all of this space. I don't know if I'm ready for this. I'm not sure I can take on this much responsibility. It's one thing to take care of a MINI Cooper, but a penthouse?

"Are you panicking again?"

"Maybe. Or maybe it's being out here on the top floor of this building. We're pretty high up."

"It's beautiful. I'm moving in with you. Today."

"You might have to. How am I going to fill all of this space? It must be close to three thousand square feet in here." I shake my head and walk back into the bedroom. I'm grateful, but my dad may have overdone it just a bit this time.

"You picked it out, Soph."

"I know, and I love it. I'm excited, but I'm nervous too. Plus, the model I saw was half the size of this one."

A buzzing noise sounds as Mera closes and locks the terrace door.

"Was that the door that just made that noise?"

"Maybe you have an alarm system."

"I don't think so, or it would have gone off when we first walked in."

There's another buzz in the loft down below.

"I think that might be my doorbell."

Mera and I walk the two flights back down to the main floor and I head over to the foyer.

"Don't open it, ask who it is first."

"I know, Mera, I'm not five years old," I say, placing

my hand on the entry door. "Who is it?"

"It's your dad."

I fling the door open and jump into my father's arms, excited to have him here. "Dad, thank you so much. I love my new place. You're amazing."

"You're welcome, Sophia. I'm so happy you like it."

"Hi, Mr. Jameson," Mera exclaims from the kitchen. "Can I live here too?"

My father lets out a deep chuckle as I release him from my hug.

"Mera, I should've known you'd be here," my dad yells back at her. "Here kiddo, I brought you some flowers for your new place, and I have some help for you too, if you want it."

"Lilies, my favorite, and you brought a vase for them as well. How thoughtful."

"You can thank my secretary for reminding me that you probably wouldn't have anything to put them in. She also said to keep them away from your cat, because they might be poisonous if he eats them."

My father's smile disappears as he notices the hicky on my neck. I place my hand over it, trying to hide it after the fact. I try to change the subject, knowing that he'll ask me about it later.

"What are you doing here? Not that I don't want you to be here, I'm just surprised."

"Business."

My father never gives me the details when it comes to his job. He owns a number of casinos in Las Vegas, and has associates in every city. Other than that, I'm clueless as to what it is that he does when he travels.

"Have you seen this place?"

"Not in person. The contactor I hired sent me videos

of the work that he did, but I wanted to check it out today, just in case there are any problems."

"Dad, it's beautiful. I couldn't dream of ever living in a nicer place."

"Oh, you will someday. Think of this as your bachelorette pad. Hopefully you can meet a few promising men with your new home."

"You mean lure them in with money?"

"Well, yes. That's exactly what I mean."

"Everyone is always trying to marry me off."

"I just want you to be happy, Sophia. Now, show me your home."

I walk my father through the space, watching him stop to check every socket, window, floor joint, and all of the nooks and crannies in each room. He looks pleased at the restoration and updates that were made. Mera follows us, pointing out her favorite things in each area.

"Mera, do you like the guest bedroom? I was thinking that you might stay over here quite often so I had it painted in one of your favorite colors."

Mera and I look at my father, taken aback. He walks over to the living area that expands past the kitchen and puts his arm up, pointing to the right.

"In there, on the other side of the kitchen, that's the second bedroom. I guess you didn't head deep enough into the living room to see it."

"Oh Dad, We haven't been here long enough to find all the great spaces this place has."

Mera rushes to the door and walks into *her* room. This time, she squeaks with delight when she sees the light blue color adorning the walls. More oak floors, large windows, and a chandelier that matches the one in the master bedroom complete the room.

"This is perfect for family and friends, Dad. Great color too. Thank you, again." I reach out and give him a big hug and Mera joins in, wrapping her arms around us both.

We break apart and my dad continues through the penthouse, showing us the laundry room off of the dining area, and the beautiful new master bath.

"I had a large shower put in with two shower heads, and the heat lamp that you said you liked. Those are granite counters on the double vanity, and the large-scale tiles are a light grey stone. There's also a Jacuzzi bath next to the new glass block window."

"Wow, Soph. You can fit like four or five people in that shower. It's time for a party."

"No parties," my father chimes in. "You're too old for parties. At this age you need to have what's called a social gathering."

Looking at my father, I grin at his parental rules. "So it's a party, but for older people."

"A social gathering," my father repeats, pointing his finger my way.

The three of us walk back down the stairs and stand by the entrance. My father checks the time on his iPhone and then looks back at Mera and me.

"Now, when I walked in, I said I had help for you. There's a moving company out front that will help you with the rest of your things, and I have some of the furniture arriving in about an hour. I have a business meeting close by, and then I'll come back to meet the furniture crew. You and Mera can follow the movers to pick up the rest of your belongings."

"Our cars are full of boxes, and we're parked in the garage on Locust Street. We'll need to unload first."

My father takes a set of keys out of his pocket and hands them to me. "Here, take my Fisker, it's in the basement in your parking spot."

Mera's eyes widen at the thought of riding in such a luxury car.

"I was wondering if I had underground parking here."

"Two spots. You and Mera can bring your cars around to the back of the building and then head down the ramp on the far right side. You'll have to use your key to open the gate. The underground parking is only for the penthouse residents, so it's secure, and your boxes will be fine down there until we finish with the rest of the move." My father leans in and gives me a kiss on my cheek, then turns and opens the entry door. "Get moving girls," he commands, as he walks out the door.

Mera and I jump up and down like a couple of screaming teenage girls at a sweet sixteen party. I pick up my bag, Mera takes her purse, and we head out the door.

"Where did your father disappear to so fast? I didn't even hear the elevator."

"I don't know. He rushes when he has business to take care of. He may have taken the stairs since he's on some weird exercise kick."

"Yeah, like I couldn't tell. There's not an inch of fat on him, and he's what, like in his late forties or something?"

"He's been tanning too, or maybe that's just the Nevada sun that's bronzing him up like that, but he sure does look healthy."

"I bet he's getting laid a lot too."

"Fuck, Mera. Don't place images of my dad fucking someone in my head."

"Well, he's tall, with dark hair, striking chestnut

brown eyes, thin as a stalk of wheat on the Kansas plains, and rich. You know he probably gets it nightly, maybe even right now."

"Enough, no more sex talk about my father." Locking the door, I hear Mera mumble something as she walks over to the elevator. "What was that?"

"I said I'd do him."

CHAPTER SEVEN

There's a patter of light rain against my windows as a heavy fog obstructs the view of the city. My eyes blur as I try to focus on the bronze chandelier that hangs above my bed. It's pre-dawn and I'm still tired from the whirlwind of activities that took place over the weekend. I couldn't have done it without Mera's help and support, plus it was a godsend that my father showed up to keep everything organized and flowing smoothly. It will take the three of us a few days to recover.

The drowsiness lifts from my eyes and I see beautiful Lewis curled up at the end of my bed.

"Good morning, baby boy. It looks like you feel right at home in our new place."

Lewis opens one eye then rolls onto his back in agreement. He lets out a quiet purr and I decide not to disturb him. He had a long weekend just like the rest of us.

I slide out of bed and wrap the dark red robe hanging on my bedpost around my bare skin. Placing my matching slippers onto my feet, I shuffle into the bathroom to freshen up.

Today I can finish going through the boxes that Evan packed, and then I have to see Dr. Rosen before meeting my father for dinner. It will be good to thank him again before he heads back to Vegas. We didn't have much time to talk over the weekend with the frenzy of the move, so this may be when we can catch up with one another's lives. I'm sure he'll ask me about Dr. Rosen and my sessions. I wish he could stay a little longer, but he did promise to visit again for Thanksgiving, which is only three weeks away.

Heading down the steps, I stop on the second floor catwalk, admiring my massive space. My father and the furniture crew placed all of the new pieces in perfect spots throughout the room. Antique Mexican rugs cover most of the oak floors. An abundance of southwestern tables and chairs fill the room, creating a feeling of being in Santa Fe. He even went so far as buying me bundles of pinion wood for the fireplace. Now I can have the smell of the southwest to go along with the style of my new place.

I continue down to the first floor, making a pot of coffee. Mera was kind enough to unpack and organize the kitchen, as I was busy upstairs putting my bedroom together. My father spent his time rearranging furniture, setting the rugs in appropriate places, and then hanging some paintings on the walls. He's a big art collector, specifically oil paintings, and he enjoys purchasing the works of established artists as well as those who are up and coming. I haven't told him about my nude modeling for the drawing classes at the university, and I think I'll keep that a secret for a while longer.

I take a few moments to light a small fire with the pinion wood. The penthouse is comfortable, but the weather outside is gloomy so a fire will be uplifting with my morning coffee.

Lewis is awake and he hops onto the Saddle Blanket sofa that's in front of the fireplace. His eyes flicker with the reflection of floating embers as he watches the sparks fly upward and disappear into the chimney. Mesmerized, I give him a small rub under his chin then leave him to enjoy the show.

The coffee perks me right up and I feel refreshed and alive. I enjoy rummaging through the final boxes that are left resting on top of the dining room table. Evan packed well, a little too well. He crammed everything that I bought last week at the supermarket, including a box of tissues, and a roll of garbage bags, into any free space he could fill. There's a box with Lewis's toys, and another that has office supplies, including over 300 pens. *A box full of pens; really Evan? What a waste of time.* I'm not sure if some of the boxes are a joke, or if he's just being his usual anal self. Then I see the box that's labeled E-V-A-N. Slicing it open with the box cutter, I find a black velvet cloth. I flip the right side of the velvet to the left, like I'm turning the page of a book, and find one of my favorite possessions inside.

My vibrator is snuggled inside the velvet, looking like its recently had a bath, and then someone tucked him into a sleeping bag for a long nap.

"Oh Evan, you *are* trying to be funny."

My phone rings as I'm reaching into the box.

"Hey Mera, guess what was in that box that had Evan's name on it?"

"Bananas."

"Pretty funny, and surprisingly close. My vibrator."

"And he labeled it Evan? What a weirdo."

"Yeah he was just trying to amuse me, or amuse himself. Can you picture him holding it?"

"Disgusting. I hope you wash it. You don't know where it's been over the past couple of days."

"I will," I say, walking back over to the box, pulling the vibrator out and carrying it with me as I talk on the phone. "I'm glad you called, I wanted to ask you if you'd like to have dinner tonight with me and my dad, around five?"

"That sounds great. I'm assuming you're seeing Dr. Rosen this afternoon, so do you want me to meet you in the lobby of her building?"

"Perfect. I'll have my father pick us up from her building and we can all head out together."

I continue talking on the phone while the dildo swings and slaps against the side of my cheek. Mera is especially cheerful this morning and I wonder if she got laid last night.

"Soph?" Mera says in a happy voice.

"Yeah?"

"How's your place?"

"Oh. My. God. It's fucking picture perfect. Did you get a good night's sleep after all of the work we put in over the weekend?"

"I was exhausted when I got home, but I relaxed with a movie and popcorn, and now I'm getting ready for work. I realized last night just how lucky we are, and how happy I am, so yeah, I'm good."

"I'm glad. See you at five then?"

"I'll be there."

***

Dr. Rosen rocks gently back and forth in her chair as she taps her pen on the top of her desk. I told her about Worship and she's none too pleased at another setback in our sessions.

"On a lighter note, I finally have my own place. It's a very sophisticated loft downtown," I say.

"I don't want to discuss your new place, Sophia. We need to talk about what you did Friday night, and why. Then we need to figure out how you can move past these encounters."

"What if I don't want to? What if I enjoy screwing around?"

"Have you ever thought about why you abuse your body? Why you don't have any respect for yourself? That's what I want to talk to you about."

Dr. Rosen stops pivoting her chair, looks at me, and asks me about my mother's past relationships.

"My mother is a prude. I'd be surprised if she had sex more than twice with my father. You know, once for each kid."

"Why do you think that?"

"Because she never had another relationship after my father. Because we weren't allowed to be naked, or to talk about our private parts, or discuss sex, or our bodies changing as teens. We couldn't even use the word *sex* in the house. My mother was abusive, untrusting, a hermit, and completely asexual."

"So, you want to be the complete opposite of her?"

"Well, of course. Not just because she's my mother, but because I think of myself as an affectionate and outgoing person who likes to have fun. Who would want to have her personality?"

"What I'm trying to say, Sophia, is that you may take some things, including your sexual relationships, to an extreme because of the person who raised you. Your mother wasn't a very good role model. Her rigidity and lack of emotional support may have damaged both of her children. I also believe that you may use sex compulsively to find love. What happened Friday evening is not acceptable sexual behavior in the civilized world. I'm going to ask you to start attending a sex addicts group on Thursday evenings. I think it may help you to meet and listen to other people talk about their behavior. You might begin to see that this style of living has no connection to love."

I look at Dr. Rosen's chest. She's wearing a tight, white, short-sleeved mock turtleneck with a long emerald gemstone necklace dangling down between her round breasts. Her black curly hair is pulled back again, and a few strands drape down around her neck. She places a hand on her necklace, distracting my wandering eyes from her chest. I look up and she sends a warm smile my way, confirming that she's right.

"Okay. I enjoy sex. A lot. And I'd probably do it anytime, with anyone... of legal age of course. What I don't believe is that I need help for it, or that I can't control myself when necessary."

"Well, I gave you an assignment and you didn't show any restraint or control with that. Let me ask you this, have you ever had any negative consequences because of your behavior, such as an unplanned pregnancy leading to an abortion, or how about a sexually transmitted disease?"

"I've been pretty careful."

"Pretty careful? I'll take that as a yes to one of those questions. What about feeling any shame for your one-night stands, and have you cheated on anyone in the past?"

"Well, a lot of people cheat."

"Do you have sex in high-risk locations, like perhaps a bar, and do you leave friends behind to do so?"

"Listen, Mera and I have an agreement when it comes to a night out at a club."

"Have you had more than fifty sexual partners, and do

you enjoy anonymous sex?"

Looking at Dr. Rosen, I can see that she won't let up anytime soon, and her last question throws me off guard. Yes, I do enjoy anonymous sex. It's thrilling.

"Sophia. Have you ever exposed yourself in a window, or a car, and do you masturbate excessively?"

"Those are very personal questions, and things you don't need to know."

We stare at one another, waiting for the other to cave. I listen to her breathe and watch her chest expand out, and in. Out. In. I'm not as smart as she is, and I hate it. Basically, I'm sitting in a room with a woman who thinks I'm a whore.

"Fine," I mumble.

Dr. Rosen picks up her pen and writes something in my file. "I'll let the counselor know that you'll be joining the group this week. You probably won't need to speak your first time there; you can just listen and decide how much of your life and experiences you'd like to share. It will be anonymous."

I slouch down into the brown leather chair, once again overwhelmed by my immense dissatisfaction and frustration about my childhood, my mother, and my relationship with her.

"Sophia, would you like a cup of tea for the rest of our session?"

"Yes, that would be nice. I'm having dinner with my father after this, and I'd like to relax a little after what we've just discussed."

"Why don't we go over to the settee and we'll finish our discussion on some furniture that's a little more comfortable than these office chairs."

I take the cream pillow that I'm resting against and

prop it behind me on the settee. The corner area is peaceful and the peppermint tea calms my nerves.

"I've been having panic attacks, and I started sleep walking again."

Dr. Rosen crosses her legs in the chair across from me as she places her tea on a side table.

"I may need to talk to someone and have you placed on some medication if that continues. When did all of this start?"

"The day of the move. I woke up on Mera's couch but I had fallen asleep in her guest bedroom, and I had two panic attacks while I was walking through my new place."

"When was the last time this happened?"

"College."

"Try to be a little more specific, Sophia."

"There were a few times in the dorms, when Mera and I first lived together, and she was gone for the holidays or staying at her boyfriend's. She never really observed it in person. The panicky feeling seems to go along with the sleepwalking. It happened a lot during final exams too. It definitely comes about during times of stress."

"Can you remember any other times besides college, and over the weekend?"

I think for a few moments, sipping my tea as I try to remember anything that stands out from my childhood. I lean away from the pillow as I recall an event that was similar.

"When I was very young, I woke up a few times in the field next to our home. My brother was always close by, and I can remember him laughing at me. I always thought that he had carried me outside while I was sleeping as some kind of a joke."

"How old were you, and do you remember anything

else from that time?"

"I was probably around four, maybe five," I pause, lowering my voice to a whisper. "I think it was when my father left us. It was also around the time that my mother left me at that center and didn't tell anyone who I was."

"Sophia, is this the first time you've lived by yourself?"

"Yeah," I respond, finally understanding that it's not necessarily stressful situations, but rather fear of abandonment and being alone that causes this to happen. "More problems stemming from my childhood?"

"Yes, but once again you're smart enough to recognize them and move past the issues that may be activating your sleepwalking. I'd like you to start meditating each evening before you go to bed. Try some deep breathing exercises and clear your mind before you get into bed. I'll give you a few pamphlets before you leave today. Also, do the same thing when you feel a panic attack coming on. Take deep breaths." She continues sipping her tea, then flashes a smile my way. "Too much caffeine can put you on edge as well. Do you drink a lot of coffee, or soda?"

"I'm addicted to coffee, but I only drink caffeine free soda."

"Cut back on the coffee for a while. You don't have to stop drinking it all together, just have one cup a day, instead of two or three."

"Six."

She looks at me, her eyes engaging mine. "Cut back on the coffee, Sophia."

I giggle and she smiles again. We both sip our tea and she continues to allocate techniques to deal with my feelings of abandonment, and any future panic attacks.

I check my watch and it's now five minutes to five. Dr. Rosen notices my impatience and wraps up our session.

"Now. I want you to work on that assignment from last week. Talk to someone who you find interesting. Start a conversation without the two of you ending up in the bedroom, or the balcony of a nightclub. Okay?"

"I'll try. I have to model again on Wednesday evening so that may be a good time to approach someone."

"Sophia," she says with a stern look.

"Oh, well I'll put some clothes on before I approach anyone."

"Thank you. Now enjoy your dinner with your father."

"How do you know my dad?"

"We were friends in college."

"Just friends?"

"Yes, just friends," she says, walking me over to the door.

"Did you know my mother back then as well?"

"No, I never met her. Your father and I just had some classes together, and that's it."

"How did you end up in St. Louis?"

"I grew up here, but went to school in Philadelphia, along with my two brothers. They were the ones who were friends with your father, more so than me. They're still very close. You should ask him about them. Now we're crossing some patient and shrink lines here. It's time for you to go."

"You use that term too? Shrink?" I ask, walking out the door.

"Have a nice evening, Sophia," she says, closing the door behind me.

***

The elevator doors open and I see Mera waiting in the lobby. She's wearing a long black sweater dress, with grey tights and a pair of classic two-inch heels. Her hair is down and the ends curve around her breasts. She waves just as I see my father's car pull up outside the building.

"Hi Sophia," she shouts, "Did you have a good talk with your shrink?"

"Hush, Mera. I told you not to say that so loud in the lobby."

Mera points to a sign on the wall that lists the offices in the building. "Look, every floor and every office has a shrink. It's a building full of therapists. It's not like everyone is here for swim lessons."

"Alright. You win. My father just pulled up, let's go."

Mera takes a dark plum lipstick out of her purse and puckers her lips, putting on a fresh coat before we leave the building. I hesitate, deciding against making a comment that she's sprucing up for my dad.

She slides into the back of the silver four-seat Fisker, and I take my usual front seat next to my father. He's dressed in a black suit with a satin-notched lapel and two front flap pockets, also adorned with satin trim. I can see from the passenger seat that his pants are slim legged, but not too slim for his age, and he's wearing a crisp white shirt with a navy blue pin-striped tie. The Fisker smells of Amouage Dia, his favorite cologne, and he's listening to Alabama Shakes. I hate to admit it, but Mera's right, my father probably does get laid a lot.

"You girls look lovely tonight. Thanks for accompanying me to dinner."

"We're women, Dad, and thank you for taking us."

"Mr. Jameson, what kind of suit are you wearing?"

"It's a Lanvin. It was a gift," my father replies to the backseat.

I hear Mera shuffle through her purse; probably pulling out her phone to search Lanvin suits online. A moment later I hear a gasp and I know I'm right. Mera, the girl with a former shopping addiction, still loves to hunt for clothing, wherever and whenever she can.

"Where are you taking us, Dad?"

"We're going to Giorgio's. I'm in need of a good steak, and a good bottle of red wine."

"You're going to share that bottle, right?"

"To share, of course. You like red wine, don't you?"

"We love it," Mera says from the back seat.

"Well, okay then. We may have to get two bottles to satisfy my two girls."

"Women," I interject again.

Pulling up to the valet, I admire the young man's perfect posture in his black suit and bow tie. He calls my father, "Sir," as he opens the doors of the Fisker, lending his hand to Mera and me as we step out of the car.

Giorgio's is just a few blocks from where Mera and I live, but it's not a restaurant at which we dine unless my father is in town. The food and wine are the best this city has to offer, with prices to reflect it. I enjoy fine dining, but the conversation during the meal is what's important, so even fast food would be fine with me. Knowing that my father would disagree, I always let him pick the restaurant when he's here.

The maître d' seats us in a back corner, away from the local businessmen who are regulars at Giorgio's. The room is painted a dark brownish red with mahogany brown chairs surrounding each linen covered table. Low hanging, dimly illuminated fixtures hover throughout the room, casting a warm glow onto every surface. Wine glasses are already set on each table, and as we take our seats, the maître d' turns each glass over, taking the extra one away with her.

I watch and listen to my father speak in fluent Italian as he orders for the three of us. How did this powerful, methodical, and intelligent man spawn such weak children?

"So Sophia, tell me how everything is working out with Devery. Is she helping you?"

"You mean Dr. Rosen? Is that her name? Devery?"

"Yes. Excuse me, I mean Dr. Rosen."

"How do you know her, Dad?"

"She's just an old friend. Her brothers were my roommates during college. Dayne and Doron. Twins."

Our waiter brings a bottle of Chateau Margaux to our table and pours a small amount for my father to taste. My father nods, prompting our wine glasses to be filled.

"She's good, Dad. And yes, she's definitely helping me. I'm beginning to understand more about myself, and the things that I *might* need to change about my life. Most of what we discuss I probably could have figured out on my own, if I was a little more self-reflective."

"Maybe that's what she's doing, helping you to become more self-reflective," my father says, while swirling his wine around in his glass.

"Devery, Dayne, and Doron? How unique," Mera adds. "Creative parents, for sure. I love those names."

"Lawyers, actually. The names have been in the family for generations. I stayed at their home one summer during my junior year of college. Their father gave me an internship in his office, and I made some important connections that proved to be helpful many years later. I don't think any of them have a bad bone in their bodies. If anything, the entire family taught me that loyalty and hard work will take me where I need to go in this world."

"So what happened?" I ask, realizing that it may not be the correct question. "I mean, where did we fit into all of this?"

My father takes a drink of his wine and then places the glass on the table. He folds his hands across his stomach and leans back in his chair. I wait a few moments for his answer, while Mera fumbles with her cloth napkin, trying to look occupied.

"Sophia," my father finally addresses me. "Your mother changed after we got married. When we met during my last year of college, she was a hard worker, loving, and happy. We had a nice home and plenty of savings. Then she changed, and I don't know what sparked it, she just transformed into a completely different person. I took her to a psychiatrist who thought she was bi-polar, but your mother refused to believe him. She also refused to take medication. Our entire savings was gambled away in one month. She stopped talking to me and began isolating herself from the world."

"Why didn't you get her more help? You could have placed her in a clinic or hospital for care."

"She said that there was nothing wrong, and she wouldn't admit that she had any problems. You can't help someone who doesn't want to get help on his or her own. She wasn't suicidal, or threatening to harm anyone, so I couldn't have her institutionalized."

I look at my father, my face calm and sympathetic, "I understand."

"When I left I asked her mother, your grandmother, to take care of you and Mark. She was tough, definitely set in her ways, but a good woman. I knew that she would make sure the two of you were clothed, ate well, and received a good education. I don't know if you remember that far back, but you lived with her for a while. Then my business picked up. I thought everything was going well, and then I lost track of my former life."

"Or you didn't want it back," I say, taking a big slug of wine. "We didn't stay with Grandma for very long. She didn't want us either."

"You're right, Sophia," my father replies peacefully, in a soft voice. "All I can do is apologize. I deserted you, all of you. I thought that if I stayed, the constant arguing would be harmful to my children, so I decided that the two of you would be better off if I left."

"I would've rather had you stay. At least you could have protected us from her. You know she became violent when we got older."

Mera reaches across the table, taking my hand in hers, "You know, I could place a flaming bag of manure on her front porch if you'd like."

I laugh at Mera's playfulness. My father laughs also, and I realize this conversation would be more appropriate in private.

"Dad," I say in a forgiving tone. "Thank you again, for everything. I appreciate your support, not just financially, the therapist as well. She's great."

"I was hoping that you'd like her. Now, tell me more about St. Louis."

"It's wonderful, Mr. Jameson," Mera chimes in. "Sophia and I just love it here. You were right when you said it's a fun city."

"Are you still one of the event managers at The Pillsman Center?"

"Absolutely, it's my favorite job ever. I can't imagine doing anything else. Soph and I have seen some amazing shows, and I can't complain about anyone I work with. It's like one big happy family there."

My father looks at me, smiles, winks, and fills the wine glasses up for a second round.

Our food arrives and a sirloin strip steak with green peppercorn cream is placed in front of me. My mouth waters and Mera performs her usual routine of licking her lips before placing the first moist bite into her mouth.

"Excellent," my father says. "Nothing beats a Giorgio's steak."

I chew and nod in agreement.

Mera holds up her wine glass and we raise ours to hers. "To a wonderful meal with my two favorite people."

"Love you too, Mera," I say, clinking her glass.

We continue to eat and enjoy one another's company. My father tells us about a new casino he's opening next year in Vegas, and Mera and I describe some of the museums we've visited in the city. We disclose a few details about Worship, being sure to leave out the heavy drinking and balcony indulgences. My father looks happy. I'm glad he had the time to visit for a few days.

Mera and I end the dinner sharing a chocolate Tiramisu while continuing to consume wine. We're both feeling the warm rush of red liquid in our veins, which prompts us to giggle incessantly. My father can handle his liquor better than the two of us, and I wonder if we may be embarrassing him.

I take Mera's hand under the table and squeeze it tight, signaling her that we both need to calm down. She gets the gesture, and immediately sits up straight in her chair, shoulders back, engaging my father in a quiet conversation.

"If you'll excuse me," I say to both of them, as I rise to use the restroom.

The dark hallway in the back of Giorgio's leading to the women's restroom is long and winds around a corner. I have to walk past the kitchen and then a small office before I finally find the door.

Finishing my business, I wash my hands in a brown, onyx mosaic tiled sink, before trying out the citrus berry hand lotion on the counter. My reflection in the mirror displays a young woman with flushing red cheeks in a slimming grey suede t-shirt dress. A long red teardrop pendant necklace falls gracefully down my chest, and my hair is pulled back exposing my pale neck. The hicky has finally faded into something that resembles a birthmark. I smile at myself, turn with poise toward the restroom door, and pull it swiftly open to return to my family.

I run directly into someone, rapidly raising my hand onto the person's chest, trying to steady myself.

"I'm sorry," I apologize, looking up to see the valet. He smiles and I blush. Green eyes peer down at me, almost glowing in the dark hallway. His brown hair is combed and slicked back against his head, with not a strand out of place. I smell cigarettes on his breath as he lets out a sigh. His clean-shaven face and freshly laundered suit tell me that he's either new here, or his family owns the place. No college-aged student, working at a restaurant for more than a few months, shows up to work so well-groomed.

He looks down at my hand and waits for me to back away. Standing against him, I feel a light twitch against my hip, and I immediately turn, walking back down the hall.

Mera and my father stand when they see me, and the three of us head out into the rainy November night. The weather is starting to change, feeling more like winter with each passing day.

The valet brings the Fisker around to the canopy and we shuffle happily into the car. I smile at the valet as he swiftly closes my door, and this time he's the one who blushes.

My father pulls away from the restaurant onto Fifth Street, heading toward my place. It's only six blocks and we arrive with little time for conversation. Stopping at my front door, he walks me into the lobby as Mera climbs out of the back and into the front seat. I shoot her a look, making sure that she understands I won't tolerate her hitting on my father. She smiles and blows me a kiss.

"I'll miss you Dad," I say, giving him a big hug.

"You too, kiddo. Call me if you need anything, and keep working on your happiness and your freedom. It's important to me."

"I will, Dad. See you at Thanksgiving, right?"

"I wouldn't miss it."

He heads back out into the rain and I watch them pull away. I send Mera a two-word text before I step into the elevator, hopefully reiterating the look I just shot her.

BE GOOD.

She responds as I'm ascending to my loft.

MOI?

***

Mera's not picking up her phone. I've called her six times in the past two hours. Now, I'm sitting in my MINI on the ground floor of Giorgio's parking garage debating my next move.

It's just past ten. I could've driven over to her place to

see what's up, but instead I decided to give her the benefit of the doubt. She's probably fast asleep after five glasses of wine.

I trust her, but I also know that she's a lot like me and if the moment is right… so I ended up here; lonely, and aroused from my brief interaction outside the restroom.

The valet sent me into a wet mess, and my insides ache for deep penetration. I know that if I wait long enough, he'll be in here to pick up a patron's car.

This is the last time you do this. You're starting group therapy this Wednesday so you need to get your shit together after this.

"Shut up," I calmly whisper, refusing to allow Devery to enter my mind.

The rain continues to fall outside the garage, and my windows fog as warm air flows out of my lungs. I can feel my heart pounding as blood rushes through my veins in anticipation of another possible one-night stand.

A yellow flame flickers a few cars down as someone lights a cigarette. The figure leans against the bumper of the Jaguar I drove past while searching for a parking spot. That has to be him. He probably smokes a cigarette every time he retrieves someone's car. I can't imagine driving cars back and forth throughout the evening to be very exciting. He must chain smoke to erode the monotony of the night.

What's your next move, Sophia?

I pull on the door handle, step out, and walk around to the back of my MINI. The clubman model has double trunk doors that open to each side. I open the left one, leaving a clear view of the valet to my right. He walks toward me as I shuffle around in my trunk, pretending not to notice him.

Looking down at the ground, I see a large pair of polished black lace-up oxfords.

"I'm sorry, but this garage is private property."

I pull my head out from the trunk, and the valet immediately recognizes my face. Grinning, he places one hand on top of my car and leans against the closed door. Taking a slow drag of his cigarette, he looks down into my eyes.

"I'm sorry, I just needed to pull in for a moment to adjust something. I'll be leaving momentarily."

"No rush," he responds, exhaling upward, making sure not to blow any smoke into my car. "Is there anything I can help you with?"

"I was looking for a paper towel, or something to wipe the inside of my windows, my defrost must be broken."

"Wait here. I have to take this Jag over to the restaurant, then I'll bring you back something to use."

"Thank you," I say with a sexy smile, as he walks over to the vehicle.

It's cold outside so I huddle back into the front seat, waiting impatiently with deep breaths of anticipation. My windows fog again, and I notice the trees outside the garage are swaying. A storm is moving in with gusts of wind blowing rain under the overhang onto my front window.

My phone beeps with a text. It's Mera.

R U AWAKE?

I respond jokingly with a big no, and then turn off my phone. She can wait, just like she's kept me waiting for the past two hours.

The passenger door opens and the valet places a small towel on the seat. He closes the door and I follow him in my rear view mirror as he walks around the back of MINI, stopping next to my driver's side door. Opening it, he takes my arm and hauls me out. He closes my door and leans toward me, brushing his lips against my ear.

"I'm not stupid," he whispers. "And I want this too, but not here, not in this small car."

Taking my arm again, he gently tugs me further up the parking garage ramp. We walk around the corner, past more cars and up to the second level. He takes a set of keys out of his pocket and presses the button on the remote. A white Hummer blinks its lights in front of us. My heart beats faster as he opens the back door and I climb inside. He steps up and into the back alongside me, closing the door behind; leaving us hidden from the rest of the world.

I slide my tongue over my lips, swallow hard, and lean toward him, touching his mouth to mine. He places a hand on my side and pulls me closer. His tongue swirls around the inside of my mouth, and we both take heavy breaths, arousing each other with quiet moans. My insides curl with pre-orgasmic twinges, and my vaginal lips swell. The valet puts a hand on my thigh and slides my dress up, revealing a pair of black silk panties.

"You're one sexy woman," he whispers. "I'm solid for you."

"Show me," I whisper back, pulling my dress over my head, baring my breasts to him.

"No bra," he says, swallowing hard and placing a finger on my right nipple, flicking it gently as he leans in for another kiss.

Reaching over I pull his dress shirt out of his pants. He lets out a groan as I grab hold of him through the fabric, feeling his stiff rod.

"We don't have much time," he says. "I have someone covering my cars for me. But I can't be gone for long.

Make me come and I'll do the same for you."

He unbuttons his pants as I pull down his zipper. Placing a hand over the front of his boxers, I reach into the opening and pull out his hard shaft. It's already sticky with pre-cum and throbbing in my hand.

"You're close," I say, grinning with delight.

"Suck on me."

Sliding off the seat, I kneel in front of him. I place my lip on his tip and let saliva run from my mouth onto him. Using my hand to slide it around, I lubricate his shaft with long, slow strokes.

"Jesus, that feels good. Keep going. Put me in your mouth."

I place my mouth on his tip and flick my tongue, circle the top mass then slide it up and down. He moans and lifts his hips, yearning for my entire mouth to encircle him. I grant him his wish sucking in as much as I can, letting him reach in deep to the back of my throat. I slide him in and out, feeling his pulsing veins with my tongue. He grows bigger, choking me at times with his length.

His hand caresses my chest. He alternates from feeling my breasts, to gently pinching my nipples before placing a hand under my forearm, lifting me up to sit on his lap.

"I want you to come too. Ride me and I'll pleasure you," he whispers.

My lower body grinds at his rousing words as I wrap my legs around his hips, taking his shaft into my hand. He pulls out a condom, tears the wrapper, and slides it over himself. Moving my silk panties to the side, I guide him into the tip of my opening, my inner lips tingling with desire. He slides gently inside of me and back out before consuming me with one deep thrust. He grins triumphantly, and fills my body with his.

My head falls back and I push my engorged breasts forward. We both moan as he rocks in and out. Placing my hands on the top of the back seat for stability, I move, shifting along with his movements. His fingers touch my arousal spot, setting me closer to an explosion. He flicks a finger across it like he's strumming a guitar, causing slick juices to engulf his cock. My lubrication sets him on fire as he pushes faster and harder inside of me.

I'm there. My legs, arms, and chest tighten as my throat sets out whimpering screams.

"Damn," he cries in a low voice. His body tensing with mine, while his hips slow into short deep thrusts.

He holds me close against his body, pushing one last blast out through his shaft.

We take heavy breaths, both of us relishing our throbbing and beating parts. It's minutes before he slows and begins to shrink.

Letting out a final deep sigh, I lift up, landing heavily and completely exhausted onto the seat next to him.

"That was totally unexpected," he says, pinching the top of the condom as he unrolls it from his cock. "I wish I hadn't left that towel in your car, I could use it right now."

"Do you want me to get it for you?"

"No," he smiles, tucking himself back into his pants. His calm voice puts me at ease. I watch him tie the condom into a knot, then tuck it into his pants pocket. He rests his head against the back seat, as his hand reaches for his cigarettes. He takes one and places it in his mouth. Eyes open, head back, he looks peaceful. I sit next to him naked, not speaking, enjoying the final waves of post orgasmic pulsations.

There's a soft tap on the passenger door that sends my heart out of my chest.

"Shit," I mumble, reaching frantically for my dress.

The valet laughs, turns toward the door, and shields me from the outsider's view. He opens the door a crack, letting a cold rush of air into the vehicle. I shiver, as the dampness engulfs my naked body.

I hear a low whispering voice from outside.

"Sorry man, I need the keys to that Infiniti."

"Fuck." The valet reaches into his coat pocket, but comes out empty handed. "I left them under the entry desk. Didn't you see them?"

"No, I can't find them," the outside voice murmurs.

The valet sends an apologetic look my way and plants a deep kiss on my lips. "I need to find those keys immediately, how fast can you get dressed?"

I slide the dress over my head, fix my hair, and pull the loose strands back into my hair clip.

"I'm ready."

He opens the door wider and we both slide down and out of the Hummer. He locks it then holds my hand as we walk back to my car, the other valet smiling at the two of us.

"Thank you," he says, pressing his lips against mine. His tongue glides inside my mouth one last time, and I let out a gratifying sigh.

He strolls out of the garage with the other valet, and they disappear into the darkness.

I open my car door and realize I left it unlocked with the keys in the ignition. Fuck. That's one of the dumbest things I've ever done. Sitting down, I pull my seat belt over my chest and turn the car on. MINI starts with the windshield wipers moving and the defrost blasting out on high. I look at the towel on the passenger seat and laugh. Turning my phone back on before pulling out, I see that there's a message from Mera and another text.

CALL ME! It reads.

I listen to the message on the drive home. She needs to talk to me immediately. I turn the phone off, wishing for a good nights sleep. We'll talk in the morning.

CHAPTER EIGHT

"Why the fuck didn't you call me back last night?" Mera whines into the phone.

"What were *you* doing when I called after dinner, and why didn't you pick up for me?" I respond.

Mera pauses, lowering her voice to a normal tone, "I was in the shower and didn't hear the call."

I'm not sure if I believe her. Last night I trusted her, but today I have a different feeling about the way she was eyeing my father. Maybe it was all the wine we drank. Maybe I'm overreacting, or maybe I'm right. I'm not going to start a fight by coming right out and asking her if she ended up screwing around with him.

"I went out, back to the restaurant."

"Why?"

"I needed something."

"God Sophia, now who'd you fuck?" she says in a pissy-ass tone.

"Did you fuck my dad?" I snap back at her, losing control.

"No, I didn't fuck your dad," her voice rising back to a higher tone.

I think about asking if she wants to come over to discuss this, but at the same time, we may just need a day away from one another.

"Mera," I say in a stern voice. "You know you crave sex just as much as I do, so you can't criticize me for having a good time."

"Then you can't be mad if part of my sexual cravings involve having a small crush on your dad. What are you afraid of anyway?"

"If you come onto him and he's dumb enough to reciprocate, and let's say it ends poorly, whose side am I supposed to take? How do we all move past that?"

"Whoa, hold on, you're jumping way too far ahead here, Babe."

"So you're just looking for a quick fuck with him?"

"I didn't say I wanted anything." She pauses for a moment, before continuing on. "Oh, Sophia. I don't know what I want. He's just handsome as fuck."

"And if you're with him, then what if I want to be with you again? I wouldn't want to share someone that my dad's been with, and I should hope that he wouldn't be with one of my former lovers. It's all too weird and awkward."

There's silence on the other end of the phone. I can hear Mera sigh, not knowing how to respond.

"Mera, I know that you and I could never have a real relationship. We'd both cheat on one another, and we can't keep our hands off men, but sometimes I still look at you and I want to touch you."

"I know."

"You being with my dad will take that desire away, and I'm not sure I'm completely ready to let that go."

"We haven't touched one another in years."

"Yes, but we have that past between us and it's not something I'm willing to share with the rest of my family."

"I understand, but I think we need to talk about all of

this in person. There are things I need to discuss with you, but not over the phone."

My phone beeps and I look down to see my father calling.

"Speak of the devil. I need to call you back, Mera. My father's chiming in."

"No, wait. I want to talk to you first."

"You sound like you're in panic mode, what happened last night?"

"Nothing, I just need to talk to you."

"So, you don't want me to talk to my father?"

"No."

"Tell me right now what's wrong," I demand.

Mera pauses, taking in a deep breath. She exhales, obviously being over dramatic about the situation.

"It can't be that bad. Even if you hit on him, it shouldn't be this difficult to tell me, so spit it out."

"I invited him in for a drink. Tea or coffee, and we sat for a while at my kitchen counter, talking mostly about you. He's worried about your promiscuity. I told him that you and I were both still young, and we're just having fun before we settle down. Then your dad asked me if I wanted to make some extra money. A lot of money."

"I'm listening."

"He asked me if I would be on one of his adult websites."

I nearly drop the phone. "What the fuck are you talking about? You must have misunderstood. You did drink almost an entire bottle of wine. I think you heard him wrong."

"He owns, and has an army of workers for online porn sites, Soph."

"No he doesn't," I retort in disbelief, shaking my head

no. "He's a businessman and he owns casinos in Vegas."

"Maybe so, but Vegas is the city of sin. There's a lot more happening there than just gambling."

"Fuck!" I yell. "Fucking hell, that bastard didn't ask you to get involved in that shit."

"I'm sorry. I should skip work and come over," she says, clearly concerned.

"God dammit. What if he's the reason I'm a sex addict? What if it's genetic? He obviously craves it too if that's how he makes his money. Maybe it's not my mother's emotional abuse. Fuck. Now what am I supposed to think?" I yell into the phone.

"Soph, calm down. Do you need me to come over there?"

"No. I want to be alone. I can't believe this. And what did you say to him?"

"I didn't say anything. I was in shock. He could tell that I was disturbed by all of it, so he left in a rush. I think he felt like he made a mistake, and he was probably ashamed."

"Don't make excuses for him," I respond, my voice trembling. My phone beeps and there's a text from my dad. I open it while I'm still speaking to Mera.

CALL ME NOW! It reads.

"Why does everyone send me screaming text messages? Mera, I need to go. We'll talk about this later."

"You going to be okay?"

"Yeah," I reply in a calmer voice. "I just feel sorry for myself right now."

"Call me if you want me to stop by after work, okay?"

"Thanks," I say, letting her know that I'm not mad as I end the call. Before I have a chance to push my father's number, his name shows up on my screen. I play dumb when I answer, waiting for him to divulge any information he'd like to give.

"Hi Dad."

"SOPHIA ELIZABETH JAMESON!" he roars, his fist pounds onto something hard, most likely his desk, as he hollers into the phone. "WHAT DID YOU DO LAST NIGHT?"

Fuck.

"What do you mean, Dad?"

"Don't play games with me. I just spent over an hour on the phone with the owner of Giorgio's, trying to smooth things out and explain your activities in the parking garage last night. Did you know that the owner is one of my business partners? I bet not. And did you know that the man you were with is his nephew? What were you thinking? This is one big fucking mess that I don't have time for," he shouts, in a scolding tone. "Do you think I want to spend the morning in my office, watching a video of my daughter screwing some guy in the back seat of a Hummer?"

"Oh my God. Dad, I'm so sorry," I whisper, my words slow and hushed, reflecting true sadness. I can't think of anything else to say to him. I sit at the dining room table, place my head down, and rest it against my free hand. "I'm so sorry, Dad."

"Sophia, listen to me, and listen very closely. By this time I'm sure you've talked to Mera and you probably know more about me than I'd like you to, so I'm going to tell you something about the video of you I watched. These videos can easily be used on one of my online sites. The owner saw the video and recognized you from my table last night. He called me, first thinking that I was using his property for..." he hesitates, thinking about the correct words to use. "For my business. He caught you on his garage camera, but he assumed that we were producing something without his knowledge. He thought I was cheating him out of a profit by using his property free of charge. Then I had to explain to him that it *wasn't* arranged, and that he couldn't use the video from his cameras to make any money on his own. If he hadn't recognized you from the restaurant and called me, your little escapade in the back of that Hummer would be online right now."

"Dad, I…"

"No, I'm not finished. Didn't you think that someone might walk by and see you? You saw what kinds of cars were parked in that lot; you must know that a place like that has cameras on every corner. God, Sophia, not to mention the fact that something could have happened to you. Something terrible. Did you even know him?"

"I…"

"Don't answer that, I don't even want to hear your response. I'm so pissed right now. Just listen to me. What if he beat you up, or worse? I can't imagine what I would do if I got a phone call from some officer telling me my daughter was dead. Does that scare you?"

I'm speechless. I've never heard my father this disappointed and angry with anyone in my life.

"Are you listening to me? Is all of this sinking in right now?"

"Yes," I say in a soft voice. "I'm sorry."

"Have you been discussing these issues with Devery? Does she know about all of this?"

"Yes. I have to go to a new therapy group for it. We talk about it a lot."

"I thought you were discussing your childhood and

your mother with her."

"We are. We do. But other things come up and we work on those things too."

"My God Sophia, is this my fault? Did I do something wrong?"

My father's a smart man, and I know that once he calms down and thinks everything through, he'll realize this has nothing to do with him. I stay quiet, listening to his anger slowly wane.

"After seeing the first part of that footage, I turned it off, but I need to know if you were careful or not. Please tell me that you protected yourself."

"Yes. He had something."

He exhales the words, "Thank God," then asks me if I've done this before. My silence answers his question as we listen to each other take deep breaths for what seems like a long five minutes. Finally he breaks the silence; changing his tone to a softer, more compassionate voice.

"I think we should discuss my evening with Mera. I made a mistake, Sophia. I'm not proud of what I asked of her."

"I don't know the details, Dad, and I don't want to know. I'm feeling pretty sick right now to be completely honest with you. I need some time to digest everything that we just talked about."

"We need to talk about this so that it doesn't come between us, and I don't want it coming between you and her either. I know she has taken a liking to me, but I want you to know that I respect the relationship that the two of you have. I also wouldn't want to damage what we have. I've been through hell and back trying to repair my relationship with my children, and that's the most important thing to me right now. I've known that for a long time, but it hit me hard last night. I took our relationship for granted, only thinking about money instead of my family. I slipped, and I'm sorry. It happens to me sometimes. Money is a powerful thing."

"Dad, why didn't you tell me that you dealt in adult films?"

"Business is business, whether you're selling sneakers, manufacturing appliances, or creating porn."

"I have to disagree with you on that one. People involved in porn always seem seedy and corrupt to me. It saddens me that you're associated with those low lives."

"This industry is what each owner makes of it. I have a quality product, and I pay well. I never ask anyone to do anything on my sites that they're not comfortable with, and it's mandatory these days that each person is tested and clean. My staff wouldn't be with me if they weren't happy with their jobs. Also, my clientele are sophisticated people, and I've made sure that they get what they want. My business is classy, it's sexy, and it makes people happy."

"So then why do you need Mera's help? It sounds like you have everything you need."

"Like any business, I have to have the best product to beat out the competition. Mera is a beautiful young woman with a perfect body. She could be the next big thing, and if the two of you didn't know one another, she'd be working for me right now. I can offer her more in one month then she makes in an entire year."

"So you expected her to move to Vegas to work for you?"

"No. I have people working for me in many cities, including St. Louis. Videos from those cities pour into my main office, my staff watches, edits, and posts them on one of my many online sites. I have some DVD's still being sold in stores, and most of those full-length movies are made here, but they're not in high demand. I have to keep up with the changing world by finding gorgeous, fresh, new talent, and by making sure everything is created using the latest technology. My online sites are the money makers, especially my live cams."

"Alright, that's enough information about your day job. So tell me. You do own casinos out there, right?"

"Yes. All of that is true."

I suck in a deep breath, exhaling it in a large burst, feeling slightly better about the situation with Mera.

"Do you have any other secrets I should know about?"

My father lets out a chuckle and I can feel a smile radiating from his end. "Sophia, my dear, our entire lives are filled with secrets, but no, you don't need to know about any of them."

"That's not very comforting, Dad."

"How about you? Do you have any other secrets I should know about? I can only imagine after seeing that video that my little girl isn't as innocent as I thought."

"Touché, Dad."

I flop onto the couch next to Lewis after ending the call. I'm exhausted and it's only eight o'clock in the morning.

"Lewis, we either need more coffee, or a nap. What's it going to be little guy?"

***

Oh, fuck me. No, fuck him. I turn and look at Mera who seems oblivious to the fact that he's sitting there on the far side of the room; his head tilted down, preoccupied with a novel. I've never seen him even touch a book before today.

"Oh, Sophia, just ignore him," she sighs.

"Easy for you to say. He's not here to watch over you."

He looks up for a brief moment and nods his head at Mera, then swiftly returns to his reading. I'm trying to hide my anger and frustration at his audacity, showing up here today. Mera takes a seat across the room from him, and I amble over to the check-in area. My shoulders are slouched and I'm aware that being pregnant has made me an emotional wreck.

There's an older woman behind the counter who looks up as I approach her. She's wearing a sweater that has the classic "I made this myself" look to it, and her hair is pulled back into a bun. I wonder if she's a mother, or at this stage in her life, a grandmother. She smiles warmly as I reach the desk.

"May I help you?" she asks.

"Yes, I have an appointment at noon."

"Name?"

"Sophia Jameson," I stutter.

"Date of birth?"

"January 5, 1990."

"And what are we seeing you for today, Sophia?"

Well, some idiot guy knocked me up because he didn't pull out in time, and even though I really want to have a kid, I'm just a dumb-ass college student with no job and no life goals. A kid would bring me down, and put an end to my partying lifestyle that I've grown to enjoy. I'd probably ignore the thing if I had it. I mean, I can't see me winning any awards for raising a child.

"Miss Jameson?"

"I'm here for an abortion," I whisper.

She's still smiling as she hands me some forms to fill out. I walk over to Mera, taking the seat next to her.

"What happened over there? Did you zone out?"

"Yeah, just thinking about my life."

"Well, don't."

"Look, Mera…do you think I'm doing the right thing? I mean, even though I don't want a kid that doesn't mean I should just trash the thing."

"God you sound so nonchalant about the situation. My answer is yes; you're doing the right thing. Nine months being pregnant, and then going through labor doesn't sound like a good way to spend your second year of college. Plus, knowing you, you'd become attached to the baby, keep it, then you'd drop out of school, or worse, ask your dad for a nanny to care for it. I don't even think you want your father to find out about this.

"Never mind," I say, forgetting about my father. I haven't thought about him for the past couple of days while I was trying to figure all of this out. We're in the middle of getting to know each other again and he's only been back in my life for two years. I wonder if he'll call me today, and what I'll say I've been doing this week. I guess if he found out I was at this clinic he'd want to know a lot more than what's been going on just this past week. It's better that he doesn't know the situation that I've gotten myself into. He would definitely be hurt.

"Do you know anything about this Rh status question on the form?" I ask.

She turns and reads the question, then shrugs. I place a question mark in the box and continue filling out the paperwork. Peering up, I notice that he's still reading across from us. From where I'm sitting, the cover looks like some type of horror novel, but I can't make out the title. Fitting for him. He can be quite terrifying at times. I'm doing the right thing. If this child turned out anything like his father I'd be living with yet another abusive person, only this time it would be for life, or at least until the kid was twenty-two and through college.

I finish filling out the pile of forms, handing them back to the woman at the check-in.

"I don't know what the Rh positive or negative information is all about."

She glances over everything, still smiling, and then begins to explain to me that if I'm Rh negative I will need to get a shot, and it will cost me an extra fifty dollars.

"It's a protective injection, my dear. You'll find out about it when the nurse takes your blood."

"If I'm Rh negative will I have to pay the money today?"

"Actually, yes. You have to pay for everything now, including the injection. If we find out that you don't need the shot then we'll send you a refund in about a week."

I say nothing.

"Miss Jameson, will that be cash or check?"

"Cash," I mumble.

***

"Ma'am, you didn't answer me. Is anyone with you who you feel threatened by, or who brought you here against your will?"

The nurse is a heavy-set African American woman with a southern accent. She's pretty, with beautiful full lips that are caked in the darkest red lipstick I've ever seen.

"No," I finally respond. Although I do feel threatened by the fact that he showed up and hasn't said a word to me.

He just sat in the waiting room for a good hour, along with Mera and myself until his phone rang. Then he wandered out as I was finally called to head back for testing. His presence concerns me.

"Ma'am, are you okay?" she asks in a slow, calm voice.

"Yes, I'm fine. Nervous, but fine."

"Oh that's normal, sweetie. I'm just asking because you didn't answer my question. How far along are you?"

"Oh sorry, I'm eleven weeks."

"I'll have to do a sonogram to check the placement."

The room is cold, but the nurse places a warm blanket on top of me, and for a moment I feel consoled, something I haven't experienced in years. Actually, the last time I felt like this was about five years ago when I was dating some older guy. I was just entering high school, and he squatted in the attic of an old Victorian house that Mera's parents rented out. He had an army bag with a few items of clothing, a pair of army boots that he wore daily, a mattress, a blanket, a pillow, and a box of books. He was set up in the northwest end of the attic, next to the stairwell that led to the ground floor, with a door out to the backyard. How he found the space was beyond me. He had a part-time job at a movie rental store, and each night I would come to see him when he got off work. We would have sex in the attic throughout the evening. Bats would fly in and out of the eaves, and when the weather changed, snow would filter in from cracks in the walls. There were nails sticking up from the floor and an abundance of mouse droppings. I didn't care. I would lie next to him under his soft yellow blanket, our arms would be wrapped around one another and I felt his warmth. That was all I needed to be happy. No TV, no music; just darkness. I felt like I do right now. The room is cold and dark, but I have this warm blanket to burrow under, and for the first time I realized that during all those nights in the attic back in Philly, I wasn't there just to fuck. I needed warmth and protection.

I'm quickly thrown back into reality when I hear a faint word come out of the nurse's mouth – twins.

"What?"

"Nothing sweetie, try to take it easy. You'll be out of here soon enough."

Twins will change things. That's a sign that I shouldn't be doing this. Did she really say that? Her voice was so soft. Maybe I should ask her. Would she say it again? Crap. What if she thinks I'm hearing things and she tells the doctor I'm crazy? What if they put me away and no one knows where I am or what happened to me? Why am I so paranoid? What the fuck?

Those damn pills they gave me must be kicking in. I was nervous about taking them because I'm far more sensitive to medications than any other person in this world. Half a pill would've been enough. The nurse explained that the pills would only relax me, and that I shouldn't worry. I took both pills, full dose, and now I'm going to pay. What were they? One was blue and the other white. I feel completely paranoid.

"I feel completely paranoid." How many times have I just repeated that? I feel completely... where am I now? I'm in some dark waiting room. I'm sitting in a chair against the back wall and there are at least fifteen women in this room. They all have their heads down, or they're looking at a television on the other side of the room. It must be around two or three since General Hospital is on the screen. What time zone are we in? God dammit, why

did I take those pills? I can't remember the time zone I'm in. I'm staring down at the floor now. I'm tired, my body feels heavy, but my mind is racing. Twins. I know she said twins. Now I can't speak. My mouth feels like it's full of peanut butter and it's stuck shut. I'll feel better. Just give me five minutes and I'll be able to stand and speak again.

"Sophia Jameson?"

I turn my head and smile. Why the fuck am I smiling? I think they slipped me some acid. Lysergic acid diethylamide...LSD, LSD-25. Damn I'm so fucked up and paranoid. I stand, lose my balance, stumble, catch myself against the wall, stand straight up, and walk over to the nurse. She takes my arm and we walk into a room.

My pants are off and the doctor is in the room. He says I need to relax. He asks me if I'm okay, then he tells me to relax again. I feel my abdomen balloon out, and then he tells me he's going to dilate me, or something like that. It's loud and I have no idea what's happening. The noise sounds like a high-powered vacuum. They had explained everything to me, but then they drugged me and now I'm completely lost. The pain hits hard and I finally understand why the clinic made me take the drugs. It's not to ease the pain or to relax me, it's to paralyze me so that I can't punch the doctor in the face. I can feel everything, but I can't speak or move. He stops and the loud noise stops. He asks me if I'm okay. My eyes are still closed and I say nothing. He walks out, and then the nurse tells me I can get dressed. She walks out, and I'm alone.

***

"What's that?" I mumble, slowly waking. Lewis is still fast asleep next to me, ignoring the noise. Raising my head, I see the phone on the table next to us, jerking around on the smooth surface as it rings.

The screen reads eleven, and I don't recognize the incoming number. It may be Mera using her office phone, or my father doing the same.

"Hello?"

"Sophia," my name spoken with a roar that shoots through my head in a harsh and unloving voice. It's her, the devil in disguise. I turn so that I'm leaning against the back of the couch with my feet on the floor, being careful not to wake the cat.

"What do you want, Mother?" I snarl.

There's a pause before she speaks. I wait, watching Lewis's feet twitch, as he's most likely in a deep sleep.

My mother and I aren't on good terms, and I suppose that's not a recent development. We've never really clicked or could tolerate being in the same room together for very long. Our previous encounter, which was last Thanksgiving, turned ugly with me having to leave the holiday meal to stay in a hotel. My brother drove me, and announced that our mother needs to be able to speak freely to us, and if that means a constant criticism of our lives, so be it. I disagreed. At the time, she told me that she wished that I had turned out prettier, and that I'd always been a stupid, worthless kid, among other things. She has such wonderful parenting skills.

She sighs as I continue to listen for something to come out of her mouth. She also has a knack for making people feel like they've somehow wronged her, as if she's the victim no matter what. Her sigh is a signal that she believes I should be falling all over her right now, so happy that she has called. She's waiting for an apology. Actually, I'm tired of being the adult all the time while she acts like the child.

"Mother?" I say in a stern voice. "What would like to speak to me about?"

"Don't you love me, Sophia?"

"God, Mother. What kind of a question is that?"

"Well, you know, you're supposed to love your Mommy."

Oh my God, the woman has completely lost her shit. Mommy? She's using that trick on me? A sweet endearing term like that one will never apply to her.

"Mother, do you love your children?" I respond in a firm tone.

"I love one of them. I don't know about you though. You have problems, lots of problems. I think you should come home and live with me. You can work as a waitress and maybe you'll meet someone, and then I can have more grandchildren."

"Why? So you can mistreat your grandkids the same way you've mistreated me? Not a chance. I'm quite happy living my life here, with my new family close at hand." I clench my fist and Lewis stirs next to me. He can feel the tension emanating from me.

"You have no family. No one will ever love you."

My mother, with her bipolar tendencies, can flip her demeanor from acting sweet to a raging beast in a split second. This is exactly how she treated me last Thanksgiving.

"Mother, you should really think about what you just said. The reality is, your words apply to yourself and not me."

"You little witch," her voice loud and cracking. "How dare you speak to me in such a tone. If you were here in front of me I'd smack you across the face."

My fist tightens and my knuckles turn white. I stand and pace the living room floor as Lewis watches with one eye slit open.

"At this point in my life, I'd probably smack you right back," I say, not caring about any further retaliation when we already have a permanent wedge between us.

"You know what, Sophia? You heartless good-for-nothing little bitch. Next time, don't even bother picking up the phone if you're going to be this mean to me. You don't care about anyone but yourself."

A response seems pointless. As I'm waiting for her to spew out more trash, I walk over to the kitchen and pour myself a cup of coffee, warming it in the microwave before heading over to the dining room window. The city glows under a fall sun. I know it's cold outside, probably only forty degrees, but the bright cloudless sky makes it seem like summer. I take a sip of my coffee and wonder what I'll be doing next year. I glance over at Mera's apartment building, wondering if she'll still be living so close to me. Lewis jumps onto the windowsill and stretches out his front legs. He sits down and begins to wash his face.

Another sigh coming from my phone takes the peaceful city scene away as I wait for her to speak. I turn my back to the window and sit on the sill next to Lewis, placing my coffee down between the two of us. He stops cleaning his forehead, sniffs the cup, then paces the sill, rubbing against my side with each turn. I pet his head, giving him little scratches behind his ears.

"Sophie?" She says in a calmer voice. "Are you coming home again for Thanksgiving?"

I stop petting Lewis and place my head against the glass, tilting my neck so I can look straight up at the ceiling. It's never-ending with this woman.

***

"Pass the gravy, Mark," my mother says, holding out her hand as my brother places the white ceramic gravy boat in front of her. She pours the thick topping over her mashed potatoes, turkey, biscuits, corn, and stuffing, leaving nothing but a crumb poking out from the brown goo.

"Can you even tell what's under that slop?" I ask.

"It's the way I like it. You used to like it this way too, when you were a sweet little girl."

Mark laughs and I give him the evil eye across the table. He's silent again and his wife ignores the entire conversation. She's busy feeding their son and can't be bothered with my mother.

"You mean, before I knew any better, right? That stuff is full of sodium. You should be careful with your high blood pressure."

"Oh, what do you care if I die? You don't even like me."

"I came out here didn't I?"

"I had to beg you for weeks, Sophia. You never visit on your own. You only show up here out of guilt."

"God dammit, I'm tired of you treating me this way. You've been nasty to me my entire life," I say, raising my voice. "Why do you even want me to visit if all you do is put me down when I'm here? What do you want from me?"

My mother begins to sob. She slides her plate full of gravy over the edge of the table, shattering the plate, and splattering the contents all over the floor. I look down and see food dripping off my brother's pant legs. His son starts to cry and his wife takes the child to the living room to comfort him. It's her way of escaping my mother's *madness. Disappear.*

"You ruined everything!" she screams, tears flowing down her cheeks. "We had the perfect family until you came along. Everyone was happy. We had plenty of money." Her fist hits the table in a loud thud and her other hand rests on her forehead as she looks downward at the table. "And then you happened. You. You destroyed this family."

"I happened?" I scream. "I can't believe you're saying this to your own daughter. What kind of monster are you? I'm done," I say, throwing my napkin on the table and rising to leave the room. My brother places his hand on my arm to stop me, but I pull away.

"Mark, I need you to take me to a hotel."

He sends a pleading glance my way, but then nods his head in agreement.

"Well, whaddya know, Sophia Jameson ruins another Thanksgiving dinner," my mother says.

I give her my dirtiest look, and then the finger, as I walk away.

***

"No. I'm not visiting anymore. I'm having a small dinner here with Dad and Mera."

"Never? You're never going to visit me, ever again?"

"No."

"So, you're going to abandon me just like your father did?" she replies in a condescending tone. "And to think that I spent half my life raising you." I hear her voice waver and crack again. "You little shit. What a waste you've been, a complete waste of my time. All you care about is money and that bastard father of yours has it all.

143

He left me with nothing."

She hangs up before I have a chance to respond. My heart races with anger. I stand and place my phone on the kitchen island, hoping that's the last of my incoming calls for the day. Enough is enough. I mean, first Mera, then my father, and now her. I need to get out of the house for a while.

It's time for a jog and then a quiet lunch by myself. Exercise is a great stress reducer. A jog around the Gateway Arch Trail jolts me back into a better frame of mind and a happier state. It also gives me time to think. I wonder if I'm more like my mother or my father. I think about my mother's words and her belief that no one will ever love me. A smile spreads across my face as I realize how silly my morning conversations were, especially the one with her. I've learned that she manages to lure people into her depression and that she's never happy for anyone. She communicates by arguing, and as the old saying goes, *misery loves company.* I will no longer allow myself to fall into her trap. I'm free.

Each stride I take on my run strengthens my body, and I feel completely alive with a sense of freedom I can't find anywhere else. I have a great life. I love my father and Mera, and I can feel their love for me. My home is beautiful, and my past will no longer rule my future. I need to focus on what my father and Dr. Rosen said about my safety, as well as caring for myself. I guess I should think about loving myself a little more. Do I really need to open my legs to anyone and everyone, with no restrictions? Will power, I need will power.

The trail is alive with other joggers, some of whom are people on their lunch breaks from downtown offices, and a few women with strollers, apparently working off the weight gain from pregnancy. It's chilly and I can see my breath, but the full sun in the cloudless sky keeps me warm. The trees have lost their foliage and the ground has a coating of yellow and brown leaves that swirl in the riverfront breeze. I take the steps up to the arch, reaching the top in record time. Out of breath, I sit at the top and turn to marvel at the water.

Philly this time of the year probably already has snow, so the scene before me does a great deal for my mind. It's nice to be out in November, without having to worry about slipping on ice, or jogging through drifts of snow.

There's a group of children to my right. Most of them are three and four years old. They're with their mothers, who are preparing snacks of carrot sticks, grapes, and apples. Blankets are spread in a circle and the children are giggling and sharing their food with one another. It looks like a nursery school group. Some of the older children are still breastfeeding, which makes me a little uncomfortable. I may feel different about that if I ever have a child, but for now, a little human who can speak, tie his own shoes, and eat without any assistance should also be able to drink from a cup. I understand that whole health and nutrients thing, but damn, when does it end? Will this child still be sucking on mama's breasts in three years when he's eight? What if men were the milk providers? And it came out of their penises and not their breasts? I wouldn't want my five year-old sucking on my husband's penis. It's just all too weird for me. It must be one of those alternative hippie school groups. Put the breasts away, people.

What a hypocrite you are, Sophia, you believe that breastfeeding older children in public is bad, but fucking's okay? Think about that for a minute. Plus, you show your breasts to college students all the time. What's the problem? I guess it's not all that bad. Obviously the group sitting next to me doesn't care what other people think. Breasts are hanging out everywhere and little kids are having a suck fest. I turn away, unable to watch.

I decide to enjoy the view to my left instead and notice a figure sitting part way down the steps. He's facing my direction reading a book. His hair is a lovely deep brown, almost black, and from where I'm sitting, his eyes look just as dark. He has light skin, as if he hasn't been outside much, with a slight olive undertone. I can tell that he's tall, even from this distance. His legs reach out in front of him, and his body looks solid and fit. He's wearing a dark sport coat with a black sweater underneath, and blue jeans. He also has good taste in shoes, wearing a pair of Lucchese grey boots. His hair is layered and a bit messy on top, with the back and sides neatly trimmed. It's strange to see such a sophisticated looking man sitting on the steps of the arch all by himself.

He glances up from his book and smiles at me. I smile, a bit embarrassed that he caught me staring. I look down and pretend to fix and re-tie my sneaker, then look back over to him. He's still looking at me, with an even larger grin.

Standing, he walks up the steps toward me, placing his book in a black messenger bag as he ascends to the top. I see his eyes clearly now, a definite deep brown color with dark eyebrows that match his dark hair. He's handsome as all fuck. As he gets closer I notice his eyes are actually focused over my shoulder on the nursery group. He begins to veer to the left and walks past me toward one of the mothers. He sits down on the blanket with her and her breast-sucking son. He greets her, shaking her hand, as the little boy pulls at his mother's nipple for attention. I look away, feeling foolish for a moment, and simultaneously turned on by his beautiful features.

Without turning back for a final look, I continue my jog back down the steps and home, feeling disappointed.

CHAPTER NINE

Wednesday's here and it's been a week since I left Evan. I spent some time getting to know my new place, hanging more artwork, reading, thinking, and chilling with Lewis. Mera and I spoke a few times on the phone, but I haven't seen her since Sunday. I need to talk to her in person about my father to find out how she really feels about his offer. My mother hasn't called back and my father must have said everything he needed to about the situation, because he's been silent as well.

The floor I live on has been quiet all week and I still haven't met any of my neighbors. I've smiled at a few people at the ground floor gym, but nothing has developed other than a friendly hello. I'm working on my assignment to start a conversation, as Dr. Rosen requested, and the coffee consumption is down to two cups a day. I have to say that I definitely feel less panicky than I did before, and the transition from living with another person to living alone has been nothing but pleasant. I'm actually starting to feel like an adult, and although I still have my father's wealth to back me up, that dependence is something I hope to break away from in the near future.

Like every other Wednesday, I find myself walking into the art building at the university. Students are no longer gathered in groups outdoors due to the change in the weather. The interior lounges are now filled to the brim. Guitars are out, and students are sipping coffees as they listen to music and discuss evening events.

The drawing room is full, and I immediately spot Roger and his wife Diane in the second row from the platform. They must have arrived early to get such good seats. This is probably the only college course offered that students are actually early for, or at least on time, wanting to be as close as possible to the nude model. For some of the freshmen guys, this is their first experience being this close to a female in the buff. I swear sometimes I can see a few of them drool as they follow my curves with their eyes.

I smile at Roger and Diane before I head to the changing area to remove my clothes. There's already a pair of shoes beneath the screen, and I look over to the professor in an inquisitive way. He places a hand on my back as we walk together to the changing screen.

There's an older gentleman unbuttoning his shirt as we enter the little space. The professor flashes a warm smile that immediately puts me at ease.

"Sophia, this is Monroe. Monroe, please meet Sophia, she's our other model for this evening."

I shake Monroe's hand, feeling something sticky on his fingers. He smells like a mix of hard liquor and cigarettes and his body odor makes my eyes water.

"Do you mind getting ready in the same area?" the professor asks.

I look around at the tiny space, but agree that it will be fine. Everyone else is about to see me naked, why not this guy too? The professor walks out to speak to his students, giving them instructions for the class period. I pull my t-shirt over my head, and Monroe looks at my chest then down at his body. He unbuttons his pants and pulls them off, along with his boxers. He has a chub starting, but stands straight, not one bit embarrassed by his half-erection.

"How long have you been doing this?" I ask.

"About two years, and you?"

"About a year now. But I don't know how much longer I'll continue with it. The reality is, I need to get a real job soon."

"So, you don't consider this a real job?"

I look at him, and can tell that he's offended. "I didn't mean that in a negative way. I forgot that some people do this all the time, and not just once a week like me. For myself, it started out as a confidence builder, and then turned into pleasure, and now I'm no longer sure why I do it, besides a way to relax."

"Hmph. That's interesting. I suppose I do it for pleasure as well. I enjoy spending two hours with people's eyes on me. At my age it's hard to get anyone to notice me any other way."

I find that comment sad, and wonder if I'm in need of that much attention as well. I slip off my shoes, pants, and underwear. We both sigh as we look in the mirror, viewing for a brief moment what the students behind the screen will be peering at for hours.

Monroe reaches into his bag and pulls out a large rubber band. He wraps it a few times around his balls and penis, creating a bulge of deformed flesh.

"What are you doing?" I ask in a careful tone, not wanting to offend him again.

"It will keep me down. I want it all wrapped up against myself, and not sticking out at anyone. It's a guy thing."

"Don't you think that alters the objectives of this

class? The students are in here to learn how to draw a nude figure. Drawing that thing…" I point down to the wad of flesh, "it seems to me that anyone who sees a drawing of that will just think the student couldn't draw a penis, and instead, created a jumbled mess."

Monroe unwraps the rubber band and his penis springs free. It's fully erect. The length and width are overwhelming and it points straight out toward me.

"I see. Okay then, wrap it up," I say.

He takes the hard piece in his hand and tucks it down into his balls, wrapping the band around a few times to hold it down. It looked better before I had him unleash it. Now it just seems painfully uncomfortable.

"Do you want me to walk out first, in front of you?"

"No. We'll have robes on, plus they're going to see it eventually. It doesn't really matter to me if it looks funky anyhow, I've done this plenty of times and the reaction is part of the fun."

"Then why not just let the whole thing hang out?"

"Why don't you hide your tampon string?"

Oh shit. I forgot about that. I place one hand down and tuck the string slightly inside, hoping that it doesn't fall back out when I walk over to the platform.

"Just let me do my thing and you worry about yourself. I'd prefer to stay wrapped up than to have my long erection pointing out at some young eighteen-year-old girl."

"Okay, I understand. Are you ready?"

Monroe nods and we walk out in our robes, stepping onto the platform. There are two chairs and a blanket on the floor. I take the blanket, pulling my robe off and lounging on my side. The air in the room is frigid and I have no desire to sit on the cold metal chair.

"I'd like you guys to really focus on the upper torso today; chest, shoulders and head. You can still sketch the entire body and work on proportions, but I'd like details specifically on the top portion of the figure."

I see Monroe's robe fall to my side and I hear moans from a few male students, and a high shriek that I'm assuming is from a woman in the class. One student jokingly asks if the class could focus on the waist area instead of the chest, and there are more moans throughout the room.

"What is that thing?" a voice sounds from the back of the room.

"That's what you looked like when you were born," another student says.

There's a roar of laughter and chuckles. It takes close to five minutes for the comments to subside and the students to settle into drawing mode. I relax on the soft blanket, propping my head up with one hand, looking out at the group. Diane smiles at me, and I watch her eyes move down the front of my chest as her charcoal flows across the paper. Looking around, I notice that most of the students have their eyes on me. Roger is the only person who seems to be peering above, drawing Monroe.

My eyes close as I take deep breaths, relax, and allow my mind to clear. The strong smell from behind wafts over, making my meditation period seem more difficult than usual. I hear Monroe sneeze and there's another shriek followed by laughter. Looking behind I see Monroe's erection flying high. The sneeze forced the rubber band to shoot across the room, causing a few of the younger students to leave in horror. Some freshmen may not be used to college life, and incidents like this can really traumatize them. I don't blame any of them for being freaked out. Seeing an older man's penis reaching out for a handshake wasn't something that I expected to see when I started college either.

"Okay class, calm down. Let's take advantage of what we have here. Sophia, why don't you put your robe back on for a little while and sit with the class. Monroe, please continue to sit on the chair, but place your two feet on the rungs and slightly spread your legs. You can place your hands on your upper legs or hold onto the side of the stool if that's more comfortable. Now, it's time for us to focus on the male form. Go ahead and draw the middle area, focusing on the penis."

"Is it too late to drop this class?" the frat boy who was eyeing me last week chimes in.

"Yes, yes it is. Now, we're going to do a thirty-minute drawing of the penis. I want you to start with your 2H pencil, lightly sketching the shape, then work with your B pencils, defining and shading areas. Let's focus on shape and value."

"Can we draw Sophia's vagina instead?" another student calls out from the back of the room.

"Yes, but not today. Next week. Let's get started, and then we'll go back to the upper torso drawings."

The students moan and rustle in their seats, looking at their phones for the time, and then back at Monroe's erection, their faces wince with each glance. It wouldn't be so bad if his rod weren't purple and red from being confined for so long. Plus the indentation from the rubber band is distracting. I look away, close my eyes, and travel back into my deep breathing exercises.

I spend some time thinking about my sexual habits and the number of men I've been with to date. I've never counted, but on average it's been around two per week for about eight or nine years. I let out a quiet gasp after adding those numbers up in my head. God, that's a lot. And names? I either never asked, or I can't remember the names. Maybe it wasn't that often. Perhaps I only did it with one person a week. That's still… cripes, that's a lot of people. Take another deep breath and think. *How has this really affected you, Sophia?*

The class continues and eventually I find myself back on the platform with Monroe. His erection has disappeared and now his package is a shriveled stump. How do guys live with those things? I wouldn't enjoy having my breasts triple in size and then shrink into my chest on a daily basis. It would drive me crazy. On the other hand, I'm sure guys wouldn't enjoy bleeding each month either, so I guess we all have problems that we have to deal with.

Diane and I have a nice conversation during the break, as Roger talks to Monroe about their first cars. Diane tells me that she's going to start modeling at a small Methodist college in a few weeks. Based on the school's affiliation with the church, she'll wear a bikini, and won't be completely nude. I tell her that's a good place to start, and I give her some pointers on the best positions to keep her arms and legs from falling asleep during the longer poses.

The class ends and I say my goodbyes to Diane and Roger, wishing them an enjoyable weekend. Their son is visiting so they're excited to show him their drawings from the class. After a few minutes, I join Monroe back behind the screen. He already has his pants on and is sliding his sneakers back onto his feet.

"No offense kid, but I hope I never model with you again. All eyes were on you, except when they were forced to be on me. I have to say, it wasn't a pleasant two hours of work."

"No offense taken," I reply, fixing my hair quickly so that I can get home. "It wasn't all that pleasurable for me either."

He laughs and walks out, leaving me alone to get dressed. The smell of alcohol and body odor follows him out the door.

I reach down and pull out my tampon, throwing it into the trashcan next to the changing screen. The gym teachers at my middle school did a bang up job of frightening all of the girls in my class by recounting toxic shock horror stories. Ever since I heard that these things could kill me, I try to change them every four hours.

"Hey."

Surprised by the low voice, I turn to see the crew cut frat boy standing next to me. Even though the weather has drastically changed, he's still wearing the same khaki shorts that he wore the week before. He swapped out his green polo shirt for a navy blue crewneck sweater and a Yankees baseball hat. It's the classy look for any preppy, young college student.

"Hi," I reply, a little stunned by how bold he is. I hold up my shirt, shielding my chest from his eyes, and then slowly lower it remembering that he's been staring at my breasts for a good two hours. "Can I help you with something?" I ask.

"No," he smirks, showing off a perfect smile.

I smile back. "So, then. You just want to watch me get dressed?"

"If you don't mind, yes. You're very beautiful."

I hear a cart roll down the hallway outside the room. It must be one of the janitors. They usually start cleaning the building after evening classes are over. There's a squeak from the wheels, and then a thud as a trash can gets dumped into the cart.

"Anyone in here?" a voice echoes into the open room.

We both stay silent, looking into one another's eyes. He licks his lips with his tongue, and the lights go out. We listen as the door closes and the cart wheels away.

The windows in the room are covered to ensure privacy for the models, and other than a diminutive amount of light from under the door, we're surrounded in total darkness. I can make out a figure before me, but all facial features have disappeared.

He takes one step closer, and stops, probably wondering what lines he may be crossing by approaching a woman in the dark.

"Can I touch you?" he whispers softly.

Dr. Rosen, my father, and Mera all flash into my head, and then just as quickly, they disappear. My insides blaze and my nipples perk from his request. I'm silent as I see the shape move another step closer. His breath smells sweet, like cherry punch, and it's cool as it reaches my face. His cologne reminds me of the overpowering scent of teen clothing stores in the mall, and he definitely bathes in it like all young guys seem to do.

A hand touches my chest, sliding across one breast, and over to the other. Then both hands are on me, cupping, gently squeezing, and circling my nipples. I sigh, drop my shirt to the floor and slip out of my shoes.

He continues to touch my breasts, arousing me from my head down to my feet. My inner lips clench and twitch as small pulses build inside. I can feel my cheeks flush as he takes a final step toward me, urging his body up against mine. His lips are cold, yet soft. He's gentle, laying small kisses over my mouth before pushing his tongue inside and then back out. He pulls on my bottom lip with his teeth, and then licks my lips with his tongue. He continues to kiss me, tracing my lips, chasing my tongue with his. I reach out and slide my hand along his erection that he has purposely pressed against my abdomen. He feels thick and ready for a good fuck. A quiet moan comes out of his mouth as he releases my lips. He steps back, hesitating for a moment.

"I'm sorry."

"Sorry?" I ask, curious as to his uncertainty.

"I don't want you to feel taken advantage of, or trapped in any way."

I almost laugh, but hold it in, not wanting to hurt his feelings or ego. "Have you been accused of that before?"

"No. But I know it's possible when two people are alone that something can go wrong."

"Oh," I say, with a smile on my face that I wish he could see. "I can assure you that I don't feel threatened. In fact, I may be the one who may take advantage of you."

"I just wanted a chance to touch you. I've been looking at your body for so long, and you arouse me more than any woman ever has."

"That's because I'm sprawled out naked in front of you for hours."

"True," he says. "And your body looks like silk. I wanted to touch you to see if you felt like silk as well."

"Well, do I? Do I feel as soft and smooth as silk?"

"Yes, you do. Can I touch you again?"

He seems so young to me, and overly polite. The kind of guy who some women find appealing at first, and then completely boring after a few dates.

"Yes, if I can touch you as well," I respond.

"I don't have anything on me so I can't take things too far. I don't want to lose control and make a mistake."

Bending down, I unzip the front pocket of my bag and pull out a condom. I flick the package so he can hear the crinkling. He steps forward once again and reaches out his hand. I see his outline in the darkness and place the condom in his palm. My eyes are beginning to adjust to the dark and I believe he has a smile on his face.

"My name is Matt," he says. "I know, you're Sophia. Sophia Jameson, but no relation to Jenna Jameson, right?"

This time I do laugh out loud. "No, no relationship at all."

"You're prettier than her anyway. You look real."

"Thanks, I am real." I forgot that younger guys like to talk a lot when they're anxious and turned on. This one's really nervous though, and I wonder just how experienced he is. "Matt, have you ever done this before?"

"Yes. Well... I've had sex, with girlfriends. But no, I've never done anything like *this* before. Is it okay? I mean, is it alright just to do it with someone, without taking her out to dinner? Do you want me to buy you a coffee or something first?"

Oh boy.

"You approached me, so you must want it, and from my end, I don't care either way, so it's up to you I suppose. No, I don't need food or a coffee, but most women will want something. I think it's fine to have sex sometimes, without any expectations, as long as both people agree that that's the way it's going to be."

"Wow. I've heard about things like this before, but I never thought it would happen to me."

"Well then, Matt. Show me what you've got."

I hear a hard swallow in front of me, then his cold, fruit flavored lips touch mine again. His tongue swirls around my mouth and across my lips as his breathing picks up into loud exhales of air. I reach down and feel that he still has his erection, even after minutes of mundane conversation.

"Take off your shorts," I whisper.

He loosens his belt and his shorts slide easily down without having to unbutton or unzip anything. I place my hand inside the slit of his boxers and touch his cock. He shivers and expels a large rush of air from his nose. His tongue moves faster and harder in my mouth as I slide my fingers up his shaft and around the sensitive tip, then back down to his balls, grabbing them in my hand.

I pull my hand out, slide his boxers down, and allow his erection to spring free. He picks me up and carries me over to the platform, laying me down on the soft blanket, while still holding the condom in his hand.

His kisses become deeper as he presses his erection against my mound. I join him in letting out deep moans, my breathing hastens as he wraps his arms tightly around my back. We lay facing one another, his tip pushing at my outer lips. He's teasing me. The young, polite, hesitant boy is teasing me.

He rises above, and I turn to lie on my back. His hand swipes a strand of hair away from my mouth and then the back of his hand brushes gently across my cheek.

"I'm going to fuck you now. Right here, where I see your beautiful body spread out in front of me each week. Then next class, I can sit from my desk, and fantasize that I'm inside of you again."

"So, you're not as sweet and innocent as I thought you were."

"I never said I didn't know how to fuck. I only said that I've never done it with a stranger."

He places a hand on each side of my head, using his

knee to part my legs. He rolls completely over the top of me, and presses his waist down against mine. His erection is throbbing against my stomach, and I hear crinkling as he opens the package. He takes a few seconds and slides the condom on. Using one hand, he swiftly pulls his sweater over his head and then switches arms to pull the other side off. His bare chest hits mine as he lowers his head down to suck on my lips. I feel his tongue pushing inside my mouth then soft kisses run under my chin and down my neck. He sucks softly on my neck making me laugh.

"No hickies, please," I say, remembering what happened last weekend.

"No worries. I'm only going to suck on your tongue, lips, and mouth, but your neck is only for sweet kisses."

His mouth travels over to my ear as he nips at my earlobe. His tongue gently brushes against the inside, and back out, sending a twinge down to my clit. I raise my hips against his, and then lower down. He uses his teeth again to nip at the lobe, tugging gently while breathing heavily with pleasure. His tongue slides in and I feel a small orgasm build as my insides melt. My entire area down there is moist as I press into his erection, wanting to feel his cock inside of me.

Reaching down, I take his shaft in my hand, positioning it over my opening. He takes my cue and pushes inside, reaching in as far as he can before he stops and holds himself in that deep place. Gasping, and needing to feel his thrust I try to move my hips. He presses down and prevents any movement from taking place.

"Jesus, move. You have to move it," I spurt out, embarrassed by my lack of control.

"Wait, I'm not good at lasting very long, so let me take control so I don't come before you do."

Shit. Now he wants to take control, when I'm in a complete state of need. Fuck.

He slowly slides back and I feel every inch of his length pull against my insides. I tighten around him, seeking a greater inner pleasure while arousing him even more. He groans and pushes deep and hard back inside. His body lifts off of mine and he rubs his lower body back and forth against my mound. I arch back, wanting more power and movement than he'll let me have.

He lowers his chest and reaches one hand underneath me. He thrusts in and out, faster and harder this time. His hand tightens around my ass for stability, as his other hand and arm lowers onto the platform next to my head. His mouth latches onto mine. He rocks faster, losing control with every shove.

My mouth lets out high cries, noises that I didn't realize I was capable of making as he continues to pound heavily into me. My body brims with quick pulses, so strong that I almost pass out. He rubs against my arousal with every jolt of his hips. My insides are ready to explode as heat and twinges fill my stomach and inner areas. My legs and chest tighten as my head tilts back.

"I'm going to fuck you so hard and fast until I come all over you."

Matt lets go of my ass and rises from on top of me. Sliding out, he turns me over, grabbing my hips and pulling my waist up into the air. He takes me from behind, driving his ready to burst cock back inside. We breathe heavily in unison as he rams my back end with heavy lunges. His balls slap against my ass with each thrust and his moans become deeper and louder. I let out more high-pitched noises as my muscles tighten once again, my clit swelling, ready to explode.

"I'm going to let it all come out," he cries.

I erupt and fall against the platform, as Matt slides out, and pulls the condom off. He presses my hips down, sliding his shaft between my ass, using his hands on both sides of my body to press my cheeks together against his length. He lets out a loud pant and then moans as I feel the warmth of his cum hit my back. I squirm against the platform, using the hard surface to finish my orgasm. His cum drips down my sides as streams continue to shoot out. I feel each spurt against my flesh as it fires out into the darkness.

"Oh," he tenses, starting to shiver. "That's amazing. God," he gasps, falling next to me, still emitting small spews onto the blanket by my side.

"That *was* amazing," I whimper. Enjoying it every bit as much as he did. I feel the condom next to me and tuck it under the blanket. I don't want him to see or touch the blood from my period.

We lie on the podium and listen to the sounds of campus outside the blocked out windows. My chest heaves in and out as my heart pounds against my breastbone. Matt pants. I touch his body and feel beads of sweat across his chest. He sits part way up and props his head onto his hand for support.

"Sounds like people are heading out to dinner."

"Yeah, and I should be headed home."

"Sophia? Did I do something wrong?"

"No, why?"

"I've never had anyone just say they were going to leave afterwards. Especially so quickly."

"Oh, sorry. I'm not into cuddling."

"Hey, it's fine with me. I just want to make sure it was alright for you."

"You were very good," I say, kissing him on the mouth.

He returns the kiss, reaches his tongue inside one last time, and then leaves a soft kiss on my cheek.

"Thank you, Sophia."

We stand, getting dressed together behind the screen where all of this began. Matt turns on the lights and straightens the blanket as I throw out the condom and find my bag. We switch the lights back off and he asks if he can walk me to my car. I insist it's not necessary, and send him on his way.

I'll consider that encounter to be my last hoorah before group therapy starts tomorrow. Sex Addicts Anonymous, here I come.

CHAPTER TEN

The Tower Grove Park area of the city consists of streets lined with one-story brick homes dating back to 1920's. They sit atop small hills, with steps leading from the sidewalk directly up to the front door. The streets have back alleys with one-car garages and a metal clothesline pole can still be found in the backyard of nearly every home.

The building that is now used as a meeting hall for my sex addicts group was once a corner grocery store. It's a two-story brick structure, with the front door placed directly between two large front display windows. The windows on the second floor, which was most likely used as an apartment at one time, are boarded up, and the interior space of the main floor has been gutted. It's now one open room with concrete floors and a dropped ceiling.

Dark brown folding chairs form a circle in the middle of the room. In the back is a card table with two coffee makers, and a plate of store-bought vanilla wafers.

I walk to the back of the room and pour myself a cup of coffee, adding the powdered creamer that's available next to the cups. I pass on eating the cookies after watching a fly land on each one, staking its claim on the sugary treats.

Two women already sit in the circle and are having a

conversation about a new salon that opened up in the downtown area. They look to be a few years older than me, probably in their late twenties. Both women are heavy set, wearing enough make-up to cover the entire female population of St. Louis. Mascara sticks to their eyelashes in large clumps and foundation is caked on so heavily that it has cracked like soil during a drought. They have on loose, sheer, rayon blouses, with stretch pants and white tennis shoes. One has a black zip hoodie over her shoulders for warmth. Their accessories include shiny gold colored earrings, necklaces, and rings, with pastel color coordinated nail polish and lipstick. The women speak in deep voices, signaling an obvious affection for cigarettes. I find it hard to believe that these people are sex addicts.

They turn and look my way as I take the seat closest to them.

"Hey girl, you're new. We love newbies in this group. It gets kind of boring talking to the same old people week after week." She reaches out her faux gold clad fingers and I shake her hand. "My name's Suzie-Q. You can share your name if you'd like, but last names aren't necessary."

I have a feeling that's not her real name.

"Hello. It's nice to meet you," I say, smiling back. "I think I'd like to stay anonymous until we begin."

"Yeah, most newbies do," she says with a grin; her teeth covered in lipstick smudges. I can't decide if it's appropriate to mention the smudges to her or not, and since the woman sitting next to her hasn't said anything about it, I'll keep my mouth shut.

"This is my daughter, Lil' Sue," Suzie-Q points to her left and the woman next to her reaches her hand out to say hello.

"Daughter? Excuse me for asking, but are you both in

group or is one of you here to support the other?" They look at me and laugh. I can see now that Suzie-Q has wrinkles around her eyes and is definitely older than I thought.

"Honey, you can ask us anything you want, and yes, we're both in group. Lil' Sue takes after me."

Lil' Sue looks at her mother and rolls her eyes. She takes her mother's hand and squeezes it tight. "Yeah Mom. Like mother like daughter," she laughs.

It's interesting and weird how lighthearted these two are about being here, and I wonder if this is really a sex addicts meeting. Perhaps I'm in the wrong building, or I'm here on the wrong night. I'm still offended that Dr. Rosen believes I need this extra help each week outside of my regular therapy sessions. I could be out with Mera right now, having a beer. I'd rather talk to her about my private life than these strangers.

"Hey girl, don't look so worried. Those wrinkles on your forehead won't be very attractive when you're in your forties."

This piece of advice is coming from a woman and her daughter who together weigh close to five hundred pounds.

"You're right, I'm just nervous," I say.

Lil' Sue leans in to the circle, past her mother so that I can see her face. "Hey. No worries. You don't even have to speak tonight if you don't want to. Just chime in if you have any thoughts or can offer help to the rest of us. We're here to support one another, so you have nothing to be nervous about."

"I don't think I need to be here. There's nothing wrong with me."

There's a round of laughter throughout the room as I look up to see that a few more people have gathered in the seats across from us. There are two men and one woman, all of whom look like working professionals in their early thirties, legs crossed, the requisite Starbucks' coffee in their hands.

"Hey group. Many of us were in denial when we first walked through that door. There's no need to laugh at anyone in here," Suzie-Q responds in a scolding tone.

The group nods then quiets down as an older gentlemen walks in carrying a briefcase. He's dressed in faded blue jeans, a brown corduroy button down shirt with a tan sweater vest thrown over the top, and a pair of brown oxford shoes. His hair is neatly trimmed in a classic Caesar cut, with grey creeping in at the temples. He looks like a college professor, intelligent, yet disorganized and taking on more than he can handle.

"Howdy, everyone," he says with a comforting grin.

The group greets him as he joins us in the circle. Two more men walk through the door and are welcomed by the group.

"Okay. Welcome, welcome everyone. Good to see you all here again. For new members, please feel free to join in on any of the conversations and discussions. This is an open group, so you're welcome to come and go as you please. No one is forced to be here, which means you're all here because you want to be. Right?" he exclaims, full of energy and confidence. He waits for the group to respond with "yes'" and "right-on" before continuing the meeting.

"As a new member you will not be forced to speak today unless you want to, but we would like to pair you with a sponsor before you leave. We will need new members to create a list of your compulsive sexual behaviors, and we'll place those behaviors into what we call the inner circle. This is for behaviors that you don't want to practice. The middle circle, as you might hear mentioned today, are behaviors that could lead to a relapse, or lead you into the inner circle. And finally, our outer circle is your safe area. It's for healthy behaviors that don't cause harm to you, or to others. You should discuss and create this list with your regular therapist before our next meeting."

Oh this is dreadful. Inner circles? Sponsors? I wonder if I have to call this person if I find someone tomorrow night at a bar and decide to have a quick fuck.

"Let's begin with an introduction by new members, and then we'll discuss issues and our topic for the day. Now, we have two new members with us this evening. Would the two of you please say your name, first names only, and then you can tell your story if you'd like." The leader of the group takes out a pen and clipboard, ready to take notes.

"I'm Greg," the man directly across from me speaks, in a shaky and quiet voice. "I'm not sure how much I want to disclose this evening, but I can mention that I have been arrested more than once for picking up prostitutes, and unfortunately my wife found out about my most recent arrest. There's a definite strain on our marriage, yet I can't stop paying for sex. I'm getting help, and I hope I don't lose my wife over my addiction." He stops, looks nervously around the room, and waits for acceptance.

"Thank you, Greg. And you're getting help for yourself, not just for your marriage, and soon you'll realize that it wasn't an unfortunate thing to have your wife find out about being arrested. It's a blessing in disguise." The group says hello to Greg and then the leader turns, facing my direction.

"I'm Sophia," I say, everyone greeting me with a

smile and a hello. "I'm here because I like to fuck and my therapist is jealous that I get laid all the time, and she doesn't."

A few members laugh, while others frown and shake their heads. I immediately know who's new, and who's been around this place for a while.

"Whoa, Sophia. I don't think your therapist suggested our group because she's jealous of you. The job of a good therapist is to recognize their patients' needs, finding ways to help them. Don't you agree?"

"Yes. I was only joking, I have nothing else to say right now."

"Okay then. I'm Stephen, and either myself, or my partner Joel will be here each week to work with you. Does anyone have any important issues they would like to discuss, or has anyone dipped into their middle circle... or worse?"

"I had a set back," Suzie-Q immediately chimes in, overly excited like she's deserving of a prize. She uncrosses her legs and moves forward on her chair, sitting on the edge of her seat. Her daughter closes her eyes, and I can see the tension on her face as her mother prepares to speak.

"I found this great new porn site called *smoothies for your ass*."

My mouth drops open in disbelief as Suzie-Q proudly smiles. I put my hand up, motioning for her to hold on a second as I swallow and clear my throat to speak.

"Wait a second," I say. "I'm not sure this group is for me, and I don't mean to be rude, but my sexual life is far removed from surfing the web for ass smoothies."

"Sophia," Stephen halts me from going any farther with my words. "We all have different issues and compulsions in here, but they all *do* relate to sex. You are here to listen and support others with their addictions, just as the rest of the group will do for you."

I sit back and remain silent, realizing I'm being difficult. So what if this woman enjoys watching people eat things that come out of…

Suzie-Q speaks again, interrupting my thought. "Well, I wasn't surfing the web for that specifically, I was actually looking for health smoothies, and then healthy smoothies for your ass just showed up. Of course I clicked on it, I mean, who wouldn't? Then I couldn't take my eyes off the screen. I thought about calling my sponsor, but at that point it was too late. I was on the site watching the videos for almost seven hours. I don't have any restraint when it comes to sites like that, and I don't just mean ass smoothie sites, I'm talking about porn in general. When I'm online and come across anything sexual, I click on it. I haven't been searching for it outright, I have been getting better about that, but if it appears by accident I feel that it's a sign. So I click, and I'm gone. I have to admit, I'm still powerless when it comes to porn."

Stephen shifts in his chair, ready to speak, as I think about those child safe settings you can place on a computer.

"Suzie, we've discussed using safe search when you're online, and you also installed software to filter out sites like that, what happened to that safety net that you set up for yourself?"

See. That was my immediate thought.

"Someone in our house," she hesitates, looking over to her daughter Lil' Sue, "changed my settings, pushing back my progress toward rehabilitation."

"Yeah, so what?" Lil' Sue says. "I can't have that safe

search on all the time *and* that software program. It stops me from enjoying everything that college students enjoy, like YouTube videos of my favorite bands."

"Some of those YouTube videos that you watch are worse than nudie sites, with women's breasts jiggling and bouncing all around," Suzie-Q replies, still smiling. The woman doesn't seem to have any other facial expression except for joy. It must be from watching all those powerful ass smoothie videos. They managed to paint a permanent smile on her face.

"Alright," Stephen says, stopping the two of them from finishing the argument that's underway. "So yes, we have a setback. And that's why we're all here. I'll assume your seven-hour viewing period cost you some sleep?"

"Of course, as well as cutting into my workday by several hours. And, it cost me money because I paid to watch some of the videos."

"Well Suzie, lets try to come up with some new solutions for you, and for you too Lil' Sue, so that the two of you can start to live a healthier lifestyle. Any comments or suggestions from the group will be helpful at this time."

"Yeah," I say, since no one else here seems to be saying anything. "Why don't you just get rid of the computer?"

"I'm a medical transcriptionist and I work from home, so I need it for my job."

Oh dear God, I wonder if she got a certificate to do that back when it used to be advertised on late night TV.

"Well, can you do that without the internet?" a woman across from me asks.

"I still need to process reports and submit work online, plus my daughter needs it for school."

"Well, then you need to show a little more restraint," I

say, instantly realizing that my foot needs to be permanently placed in my mouth. There are a few moans and a headshake as Stephen interjects his view.

"Habits are hard to break, and I know we've already spent some time creating a list as to reasons why you should avoid porn, and you've made a promise to yourself not to do the things that have brought you here. You've tried hobbies, including taking up yoga, and we all know that you can't stay away from the computer because of your job, but there are other ways we can help you with this, Suzie. First, I want you to remember to think positively, even when you have a setback, tell yourself that you can do better. Give it another try, and don't give up. Second, look to your higher power. Seek out the care of God for help. Perhaps this is a good time for all of us to say the Serenity Prayer together."

Oh shit.

I stand and grab my bag from the back of my chair, throw it over my shoulder, and quickly walk out the door without saying any goodbyes, or a thank you. Stepping onto the sidewalk, I feel a light drizzle against my face from a cold November rain. MINI is swallowed by the darkness so I use my keys to flash the lights. Finding my way to the car and then inside, I pull the seat belt over my shoulder, and then lock the door. I'm fine. Breathe in. Breathe out. Deep breaths.

What was that all about? I mean it's not like I don't respect people's beliefs, but God's not going to keep me from fucking whomever I want. And I'm sure God won't help Suzie Q beat her obsession with ass smoothie videos. I guess some people need to feel that they're receiving strength and forgiveness from God above in order to heal.

I'll see Dr. Rosen for the sake of my father and his

guilt, but I'm not attending this group therapy shit. I don't feel damaged, but if I do need to restore my self-worth, then I will seek the help of the good ol' doc, Mera, and my dad. No strangers, and no higher powers to be. And for sure, no ass smoothies.

I feel exhausted as I pull into the underground parking lot of my building. It's still early, but the stress from worrying all day about the group therapy session, and then the session itself, took a lot out of me. Plus, my mind is still strained from last weekend's parking garage mistake. It's funny that I only view it as being a problem because my father found out. I wouldn't feel this bad if it had stayed a secret.

The elevator opens and I'm at my front door. Turning the key, I enter to Lewis's loud meow, as he demands his dinner. We eat together and then I hit the couch, covering myself with a warm, Indian print, wool blanket. Lewis rests on my stomach as I watch the rain slowly drizzle, dripping down the living room windows, hypnotizing me into sleep.

CHAPTER ELEVEN

" *What's that?" I ask, pointing to a giant thing that looks like a hot dog being pushed inside a woman's private area. My brother giggles, making me feel dumb as he turns the page. He flips the magazine on its side and the middle unfolds, revealing a naked woman. She has her legs spread and her fingers are in her naughty space. "Why does she have so much hair down there?" I ask, seeking information about her body. As a three-year-old, I am grossly entertained by the images in front of me.*

"Dad said that these are penises, and those are vaginas, and that people do this when they are grown up."

"Daddy gave you the magazine?" I ask.

"No. He didn't. I saw him looking at it one night. It was hidden inside of his newspaper. I asked him what that was down there, and he said a vagina. He said it's like my penis, only better. Then Mom came in and saw what he was showing me, and she got very upset. She took the magazine away from us."

"And then Mommy gave you the magazine?"

"No, Sophie. I found it in the trash, and you better not tell Mom or Dad that I have it. They'll get mad at me, and I'll tell them that you were looking at it too, then they'll be mad at you."

"I won't tell Mommy or Daddy."

"Good." He folds the big image back up and turns the page. There's a photo of a woman's private area spread open.

"Is that where our stuff comes out when we go potty?"

"Sophie, just let me look. Keep quiet for a while."

My brother studies the photograph. He continues turning the pages, flipping quickly past all of the ones that only have words. He stops on another image of the man putting his thing inside of her thing.

"That would hurt," I say, confused by what's in front of me. "Is he using her as a potty?"

"Sophie, leave me alone, I'm busy." He stands and walks out of the room. I hear his feet stomp up the stairs, and then the door to his bedroom slam shut.

Standing at the bottom of the steps, I call up to him, asking where Mommy is.

"She's out," he yells down from his room.

"Where's Daddy?"

"Work," he yells again with an aggravated tone in his voice.

"I'm thirsty," I whisper, knowing that I'll have to fend for myself.

The kitchen is dirty, with dishes overflowing from the sink onto the countertop. I try to reach a cup but the counter's too high. I turn and look at the kitchen table. The dishes from last night's dinner are still out, including my cup. Walking back over to the sink with it in my hand, I find that the faucet is too high to reach, even on my tiptoes. I take the cup into the bathroom, stand on the toilet, reach over to the sink, and fill my cup. The water is warm and tastes like algae. Yucky.

I put the cup down on the toilet seat and look at myself

in the floor length mirror that Daddy uses for dressing each morning before he goes to work. I smile, and my reflection smiles back. Moving closer I see a booger in my nose so I use my finger to dig it out. I wipe it on my shirt because Mommy told me not to eat them. There's a knot in my long brown hair that I try to untangle, but it hurts when I pull on it. Mommy needs to get that out.

Pulling my pant waist out, I look down at my private area searching for hair, but there is none. I bend over, holding a chunk of my long hair over my spot. It doesn't look like what the lady had in the magazine. Her hair was curly.

Wanting to see my area down below, I search for a small mirror under the sink. Mommy keeps one down there to see the back of her head. I find it.

I place the mirror in front of me while sitting on the floor with my pants off. It looks different from the people in the magazine. It's not as big as what they have. It's the wrong color too, not as red as theirs. I wonder if mine is broken.

I take Mommy's toothbrush from the drawer under the sink and try to push it inside of me. That doesn't feel good. I try the side with the bristles and it tickles, making me giggle. It hurts to try to push it in, so I decide to try to brush the area like I'm brushing my teeth. I place a dab of toothpaste on the brush and rub the area gently back and forth. It tickles and I giggle again.

"WHAT IN GOD'S NAME ARE YOU DOING?" Mommy screams at the top of her lungs. "WHAT THE FUCK IS WRONG WITH YOU?" She pulls me up by my hair and smacks me across the face. I let out a high-pitched cry as tears gush out of my eyes.

"Don't you ever touch yourself down there again, and

with my toothbrush, Sophia? You're a disgusting child. As soon as I can find someone to take you off my hands, you're out of my house and my life. I'm getting rid of you!"

I scream in horror, not being able to breathe. What did I do? Sobbing hysterically, I run and hide behind the couch. I can't catch my breath. I'm suffocating. Tears pour down my cheeks. My mouth is open, but nothing comes out, then I let out a loud cry and I pant and scream again. My eyes lose focus and my head spins. I can't breathe. Panic.

***

"Wake up, you're dreaming. Wake up, Sophia."

I feel a hand on my shoulder, shaking me as a deep voice enters my head. My eyes flutter open as I focus on the rain pelting the windows that lulled me to sleep earlier. It's dark, except for a few lights from the city reflecting into my loft. Lifting my head, I look for Lewis. He must have walked upstairs to bed, his usual sleeping spot each night. The blanket on top of me feels different. It's smoother, like silk, and not as warm. Where am I?

I sit all the way up and place my feet on the floor, letting the blanket slide down exposing my bare chest. It's chilly in here. I never have my heat turned down this low. There must be something wrong with the furnace.

Standing, I see my place has been re-arranged. Wait, this isn't my stuff. Why does it smell like vanilla in here? This is not my house.

"Hello, Sophia."

A deep voice speaks my name from behind and I quickly turn around. "What the fuck?" I yell, placing a hand out in front of me for protection.

"It's okay, don't be alarmed," the voice says in a

softer tone.

"Where am I? Did you kidnap me?"

"No. You're okay," there's a pause and then a sigh before he continues. "I found you outside my penthouse. You were sleeping in the hallway, half naked, so I carried you into my home and placed you on the couch."

"How do you know my name?"

"I've lived in this building for many years. I know when new people move in, especially the people on my floor."

I drop my hand, no longer feeling threatened by this man.

"Put a light on so that I can see you," I say.

"Are you sure you want me to do that? You are topless, after all."

I hold my hands up, using them to shield my breasts from his eyes. It's probably too dark for him to see me anyway, and why do I care in the first place?

"Why is it so cold and dark in here? I feel like we're in a basement."

"I'm sorry, I've been out of town on business, and I like to keep the heat low and the curtains closed when I'm gone. I had one curtain open for you, so that you wouldn't be in total darkness when you awoke."

"Thank you," I say, lowering my arms down to my sides, my nipples hard from the chill in the air.

"Here, let me get you a shirt so that you're more comfortable."

"I really should be going."

"Are you sure? I can make you a cup of warm milk and honey if you'd like."

The invitation sounds tempting. Not the drink, but the conversation. His calm, deep voice is soothing, and I'd like to get to know the people on my floor.

"What time is it?"

"It's two. I guess that's late, or early, depending on your sleep patterns," he says. "I wouldn't mind getting to know the person who lives next door to me a little better, especially if you plan on living here for a few years," he says.

"My thoughts exactly."

"Wonderful," he responds in a gentle tone. " I could use some company. I'll get you that shirt."

The figure moves stealthily through the first floor and over to the stairwell. A dim kitchen light turns on as he reaches the wall and ascends the stairs. He's tall, but I still can't see his face.

This may be the perfect opportunity to work on my assignment for Dr. Rosen. I have to visit with her later this evening, and I haven't made much progress during the past couple of days. More nude modeling, screwing that college guy, skipping out on group therapy, none of these things will go over well with her. This may be one way to redeem myself.

The room is identical to mine except it's reversed, and he has a more sophisticated taste in furniture.

My style is definitely Southwestern Rustic, at least according to my father, with rich hues of turquoise, terra cotta, and brick red on the fixtures. The rugged looking pine furniture is distressed with brightly patterned tile inlays. It's a space were you would expect to see a pair of worn out cowboy boots in the corner and chili peppers on the kitchen counter. It has a feeling of warmth and energy.

The space before me is opulent. I can see now that I was asleep on a dark brown leather couch. There's a matching one across from it, and two, deep red corduroy chairs in-between. The fireplace that the furniture sits next to is ornate, with red, brown, and grey glass tiles framing the interior space. The colors are rich and charming.

Above the fireplace is a life-size black and white photograph of a woman sitting in tall weeds in front of a tree. She's blindfolded, nude, and has her arms wrapped around the front of her body. She looks cold. The woman in the shot is the main focus, with the background soft and blurred. She's shown from the waist up, with tree branches used to frame her head. Her hair is black and cut in a short bob style, while her skin is ghost white. She's young, innocent looking, and gorgeous.

Turning, I see that the wall in the dining area is covered from floor to ceiling with black and white photographs of female nudes, their bodies entwined in bed sheets, leaving very little flesh exposed; a nipple here, and a shoulder there. The photos are staggered closely to one another on the wall, each one captured in an ornate, gold-leaf frame.

The walls throughout the space are a dark grey, and the hardwood floors a deep brown. Each window has a dark velvet curtain flowing across it. Leopard print pillows and rugs are scattered on the furniture and floor, and two large chandeliers hang low from the ceiling. The chandeliers have a Victorian feel, with faux candles mixed between the crystals that hang down like icicles. The end tables and bookcases are industrial with metal legs and wooden shelves. There's an overabundance of white candles placed on every shelf, table, and counter. The candles have to be the source of the vanilla scent in the room. In the space between the living room and dining area is a deep red couch set up in a half circle. It's placed so that it faces the large windows displaying a view of the

Gateway Arch.

Taking a few steps over to the kitchen I admire the splendid craftsmanship of the espresso colored kitchen cabinets, concrete countertops, and dark red tiled backsplash. There are mustard colored placemats on the island, with matching dishtowels, and ceramic pieces topping off the space. Luxuriant beyond belief, this man has expensive taste.

"Here you are, Sophia," he says, reaching the shirt out and placing his head down to give me some privacy.

"Thanks," I say, taking it from his hand, placing my arms hurriedly into the sleeves. The shirt is a soft plaid button up, and it immediately warms my flesh. "You're sneaky. I didn't even hear you come down the steps, or walk into the kitchen." He looks down at the floor, listening to me speak as I button up the front of the shirt.

"That's much better. You can look now."

He slowly lifts his head and I gasp, taking a quick step back.

"Sophia? Are you okay? You look like you've seen a ghost."

"I...I'm fine," I stutter, looking into the beautiful face that I saw the other day in the park. It's the man on the steps, the man who was reading the book. The one who I thought was going to say hello to me, but instead he walked right past me and sat with the breastfeeding mothers.

"Are you sure you're okay?"

"Yes," I say quietly. "You're the man from the park. I saw you the other day sitting on the steps by the Gateway Arch."

He studies my face for a moment, then looks beyond me to the living room area. His eyes flicker from the one dim light that's lit in the kitchen.

"Would you like that warm milk and honey now?"

"I don't know."

"I'm not sure I understand. I thought you were staying for a while."

"Yes. I am," I say, without hesitation. "I don't know about the warm milk and honey though. I've never had that before."

He smiles, showing off perfectly straight white teeth and small dimples on his cheeks. "I think you'll be pleasantly surprised by how calming the drink can be for your mind. It's not just for children you know."

I smile warmly, and agree. He takes the milk out of the refrigerator, pouring a small amount into a pan. He sets the gas range to low, slowly warming the milk, as I sit and admire his kindness. Besides my father, Mera is the only person in the past that has offered to take care of me, and even with a small offering such as this one, it means a lot.

"It needs to warm gradually, and not boil in order for it to be enjoyable. Patience is an important part of this recipe," he says, while stirring the milk. "I believe that fixing it slowly is one of the ways the drink soothes your nerves and puts you to sleep. I'll assume this will be beneficial for you since I found you in the hallway curled up in a little ball."

He's right. I must have been sleepwalking again. The group therapy that was supposed to help me completely stressed me out.

"Is there something that I should be aware of that I can help you with? Did you get locked out of your place somehow? And it's none of my business but if you were drinking, you should probably have a friend with you so that you don't turn up in random places."

His concern for me is overwhelming. His eyes are sincere, and he looks at me in a tender and loving way. I enjoy watching his body flow gracefully throughout the kitchen. His muscles flex as he lifts items and stirs the milk. He's comfortable with himself, even with a stranger in his space. The black t-shirt he wears is tight on his body, and the muscles on his arms and chest are clearly defined against the fabric. I want to touch him, place my hand on his chest and feel him.

"Sophia?"

I look up at his face as I realize he's caught me staring at his chest. "I'm sorry. Yes…uh, I mean no. There's nothing you can do to help. I wasn't drunk, and I didn't get locked out. I was sleepwalking."

"Sleepwalking?" he says in a surprised voice. "I've never met anyone who had that problem," he turns, removing the pan from the burner, and placing it onto a hot pad. Taking two deep red mugs out of the cabinet, he pours the steaming milk into each one. He then takes a glass jar of raw honey out of his pantry, placing one spoonful into each mug, slowly stirring them for a few moments. I take a seat at the kitchen island as he hands me the drink. The mug is warm, but not hot, and even though I haven't taken a sip just yet, it's already comforting.

He sits down to my right at the end of the island, and I turn toward him, enjoying his friendliness and our conversation.

"Go ahead, try it. I want to please you," he says as he takes his first sip. "Lovely. Just like my mom used to make."

I place the mug up to my lips and feel the warm liquid enter my mouth. My taste buds awaken to a slightly sour, yet sweet taste. It slides down my throat, coating my insides along the way while warming my stomach. I take another sip, lulling my muscles to loosen and relax.

I look at his beautifully chiseled face, and smile. There's something mysterious about him, something hiding under that eager to please personality.

"Take it slow, Sophia. Enjoy yourself."

His words echo in my head. I believe he may be referring to more than just the warm milk.

"Can I get you anything else?"

"Yes," I say, looking directly into his eyes. "How about your name?"

He smiles, and pauses for a moment, deliberately forcing me to wait. "Cove," he finally responds. "Cove Everton." He continues sipping from his mug, his eyes looking directly into mine.

"That's a beautiful name, I've never met anyone named Cove."

"It was my father's name, and his father's, making me Cove Ambrose Everton the third."

"Very sophisticated," I say glancing around the room and back to him. "Sophisticated in all ways."

"So, Sophia. What were you doing in the park the other day?"

"I like to jog every couple of days to clear my head. My best friend lives a block away from here, and the two of us used to jog around the arch twice a week. Now that I live just as close to the park as she does, I plan on getting out there more often."

"So you sleepwalk, and you jog to clear your head. If you don't mind me asking, what's stressing you out so much?"

I look at him, wanting to say my mother, but it's more than just her. Now, I think I'm distraught about my sex life, the intervention of Dr. Rosen, and my father's knowledge of recent events. I've always lived the *find em', fuck em' and forget about em'* lifestyle, and now I face an interference.

"You're hesitating. Forget that I asked, I don't want to make you uncomfortable."

I could fuck him right now.

"Well, Cove. How about you? What were you doing in Gateway Park the other day?"

"I was meeting an acquaintance," he replies under his breath while taking another sip of warm milk.

"A friend?"

"No, an acquaintance. Someone I've known for many years."

I set my empty mug down on the counter after taking the final sip of the delightful drink. Yawning, I look at my watch. It's two-thirty in the morning. The concoction has worked and my body is heavy, warm, and ready for sleep; a deep sleep in my soft bed. I wonder if I should ask him to join me.

"Did it help?"

"Yes, I like it, I'll have to make some tomorrow night before I go to bed."

"Try a warm bath or meditation. That might be helpful as well."

"You sound like my therapist," I say, quickly looking down and then back up at him. Fuck. Damn it, Sophia. That slipped out. He sends a concerned glance my way, and I send him a reassuring smile back. "Don't worry, it's by choice that I see her. I'm just talking some things out."

"Good. I'm glad. Some people really benefit from talk therapy. My mother being one of them."

"Your mother?"

"Yes. Haven't you met her yet? She's the other person who shares this floor with us. I'm surprised the two of you haven't crossed paths, she can be a bit boisterous, and nosey at times."

"Why do you live so close to your mother? Isn't that a little weird?"

"No. Not really. She's always been a part of my life, and we're in business together, so living close to one another just makes things easier."

"Yeah, but you practically live on top of one another. I could never live next to my mother."

"Bad relationship?"

"You could say that. We don't talk much."

"Well, if you haven't noticed, Sophia, this is a beautiful building and my mother and I both have exquisite taste. It's also a very private building. We couldn't find what we wanted anywhere else so we agreed to buy these two penthouse units, even though they were next to one another. This building satisfies both our needs, and I *do* get along with my mother."

"I see," I say with a big yawn and heavy eyes.

"I sense that you're in need of sleep, and I fear I may be boring you. Let me walk you to your door." Cove stands, setting his mug on the counter. He takes my arm and helps me off the stool. We walk out his door, his hand on my back the entire way down the hall to my front door.

He stops and drops his hand as I turn to face him. "Thank you. That was nice," I say, beginning to unbutton his shirt. "Would you like to come in?"

"Sophia, what are you doing?"

"I'm giving you back your shirt," I say, tilting my head in an innocent, yet slutty way.

"No, please keep it for now." His hand reaches out

and stops me from exposing my chest. "You can give it back to me another time."

I stop, lean against my door, and my breast falls free from the garment.

He keeps his eyes directly on my face, not even sneaking a peek.

"Good night, Sophia. Sleep well." He leans in, placing a small kiss on my cheek. "Now please, go inside and lock yourself in. I don't want to find you out in the hallway again in the morning."

"Are you sure you don't want to come inside?"

"I have some business to attend to, and you need some sleep. Good night, Sophia." He glares at me, waiting for me to open my door.

"What type of business do you have to do at this time of the night?"

"Another day, another conversation. Now good night."

I look at him as I walk inside, close the door, lock it, and quickly peer out the peephole. He smiles as he turns and disappears, out of sight. "Sweet dreams," I hear him say under his breath as he walks down the hall and back to his place.

I turn and place my back against the door, sliding down the surface, until my ass hits the floor. Lewis comes running, letting out small meows.

"Hello little boy. I met our neighbor. He's just as gorgeous and gentle as you." Lewis rolls onto his back and puts his paws up in the air. I pet his stomach and he purrs. "I love you too, fuzz ball. Come on, let's go upstairs and get some sleep." I pick Lewis up, placing him over one shoulder as we walk the two flights of stairs into the master bedroom. Lewis hops out of my arms and lands on the floor, waiting for me to turn down the bed. After putting numerous pillows on the floor, and placing my sleeping pillows at the headboard, I undress and slide underneath the comforter. Lewis pounces and lands next to me, curling into a little purring ball. My eyes are heavy and fall shut, as the rush of sexual excitement from a minute earlier wanes.

Sleep.

CHAPTER TWELVE

My hand slides down my stomach, coming to rest over my spot. I awoke this morning thinking about Cove, his dark and handsome features penetrating my mind. I'm wet with desire, wanting to feel him slide inside of me.

Straightening my legs, I place two fingers over my clit, gently moving the area back and forth, the motion causing a tingling sensation to shoot inside, down to my most pleasurable place. Deep inside, I feel warm. My body tenses then relaxes, tiny pulsations grow in strength with every passing moment.

Cove is over me, looking down, studying my face with his dark eyes. *Fuck me, Cove.*

I slide a finger from my free hand between my inner lips and into my space, still rubbing my clit with my other hand. My toes point downward toward the foot of the bed, and my legs tighten. I lift my hips as the pulsations increase.

I picture Cove's body, his defined abs and arms hovering over my chest; his powerful smile. *Kiss me.*

My hand moves faster and my chest tightens, as I imagine his cock inside thrusting in and out. I tense and hold my breath, as the throbbing beats begin deep down inside. I stop my hand, feeling each burst of my orgasm.

I relax lying under the covers of my warm bed. Lewis is awake and has wandered downstairs. Looking over at the clock, I'm surprised that it's already ten. I slept straight through the rest of the night, and into the late morning. Milk and honey is my new best friend.

My phone rings as I rise and stretch. Mera's smiling face pops onto the screen. God, I feel like I haven't talked to her in ages.

"Hi Mera."

"Howdy girl," her happy voice chimes in. "Ready for a night of partying?"

"You bet. I have a lot to tell you."

We still haven't discussed my father's offer to Mera about the porn sites, and that will all be good to work out over drinks.

"I heard of a new place, quieter, full of affluent people. It's time to take a break from the college boys."

"That works for me. I'm not in the mood for Worship anyway," I say, remembering the young guy I took to the balcony.

"How about I pick you up at nine?"

"I'll be waiting with bells on."

"Only bells?" she asks.

"Yup, only bells."

"Can I jingle them?"

"Whatever your heart desires," I laugh, descending the stairs to the kitchen to make my morning coffee. "See you tonight."

I end the call and begin my daily routine. Coffee, breakfast, feed Lewis, go for a jog, shower and read. My father sends me a few texts during the day for job openings, all within blocks of my building. Interestingly enough, there's one that I think I might actually enjoy, a film and video editor at his friend's company. I spend some time in the afternoon on my laptop updating my resume to send out to the company, James and Gallo Technologies. Even though it's an entry-level position, it sounds a hell of a lot more interesting than being an administrative assistant in some boring business office. I don't have much experience, so I appreciate my father's thoughtfulness in helping me get my foot in the door somewhere. I text him back, thanking him, and letting him know my resume has been sent off to his friend. I'm actually looking forward to hearing back, hopefully with news of an interview soon.

Mera arrives at my place at eight-thirty and rings my doorbell consecutively until I buzz her into the lobby. I open my door to find her standing in the hallway with a beautiful sleek black dress and three inch, high-heeled shoes in hand.

"Juke or the MINI tonight, Soph?" she asks, walking into my foyer, and through to the kitchen.

"The Cooper," I respond. "Why aren't you dressed?"

"The power is out in my building so I was wondering if I could shower here before we head out."

"Of course, but only if I can watch."

Mera rolls her eyes, freeing a smile from her lips as she looks back. "You just can't wait to see me naked again."

"So, why's your power out?" I ask, trying to think about something other than Mera's breasts.

"I guess some lines leading to our building were accidentally cut by a crew working next door. It's a big mess right now."

"Well, you know you can stay here as long as necessary, remember you have your own bedroom right around that corner," I say, pointing to the far end of the kitchen.

"Thanks, Sophia. I might take you up on that tonight, but for now let's get ready, school girl."

"School girl? That's a horrible nickname."

"I kind of like it," she says, walking up the stairs to my bedroom.

"Alright, just don't call me that in front of anyone. It's embarrassing."

Mera stops on the stairs and swiftly turns around to face me. "Since when do you get embarrassed? Are you feeling okay?"

I laugh and push her up the steps until we reach the third floor.

"God, Sophia. I haven't seen this view at night. It's breathtaking."

"I know. Sometimes I just sit here with my tea and watch all the lights glimmer around the city."

Mera places the back of her hand against my forehead, "Are you feeling okay? You're suddenly embarrassed *and* drinking tea? My coffee nut is drinking tea? What gives?"

"Devery."

"Oh. Say no more."

"Shit, I forgot I had an appointment with her today. She's going to kick my ass next time I meet with her. Damn it."

"I'm sure she has people who cancel on her all the time. Don't worry so much, just enjoy the night."

Mera walks into the bathroom and places her dress on the towel bar, dropping her shoes on the floor below. I follow close behind, take my make-up out of the cabinet, and line it up on the counter.

"I'll be back. I need to find something sexy to wear."

"You should wear that classic black velvet cocktail dress your father bought you last year for Christmas. That looks smashing on you."

"Smashing, huh? I guess that's the winner for tonight," I say, heading toward my closet. I find the dress in the back, hidden behind my heavy winter clothes. I guess it's really that time of the year again.

The dress is one of my favorites, a refined 1950's style with a metal zip closure in the back. It's longer than most of my outfits, reaching down just below my knees with a V-neck front exposing a small amount of cleavage, a tasteful choice for an evening at a new bar.

Mera hums as steam pours out of the shower. The fogged glass doors hide her body, making her outline barely visible.

"What are you humming?" I ask, raising my voice over the fan and running water.

"Nothing," she yells over the shower door. "I'm making it up as I go. Hey, have you heard from Evan at all lately?"

"Nope. I think he's busy with his new woman."

Mera turns off the water and I open the door, handing her a towel.

"That was a quick shower."

"Yeah, I just needed a soap and lather, I'm not washing my hair." She takes the towel and starts to dry off as I walk over to the counter to apply my make-up. I watch her reflection in the mirror, admiring her thin, ivory white body. She pulls a cloth elastic band off her head allowing her dark hair to fall downward, landing softly over her shoulders and breasts.

"An artist would love to have you as a model," I say, turning around to admire her.

"You like?"

Mera places the towel on the counter, and does a poor rendition of a pirouette, spinning in front of me. I watch her hair whirl about as she tries to keep her balance, but as she spins a second time, I notice a dark mark on her right shoulder. I walk toward her and she stops, snatching the towel and wrapping it around her upper body, hiding the mark.

"Mera, what is that?"

Her face suddenly changes from delight to horror. She steps back, wrapping the towel even tighter around her body. "It's nothing."

"Seriously, what is it?" I ask again, putting my hand up to pull the towel off her shoulder.

She takes another step back, into the shower. "It's a surprise. I don't want you to see it just yet."

"Fuck, you got a tattoo didn't you? Show me. I want to see it."

"Not yet, Soph. It really is a surprise, just be patient."

I let my hand fall down to my side, allowing Mera to witness my defeat. She steps onto the bath mat and lifts her dress from the towel bar.

"I'll show it to you soon, but now's not the time. Let's get dressed and head out. We can talk about it later." Mera drops her towel, hiding the tattoo under her hair. She pulls the sleek black dress over her head, covering the black ink for the evening.

"Why are you being so secretive? And I thought you hated tattoos. What gives? Now I'm curious, you have to tell me."

"Soph, just wait," she replies in an uncompromising tone. "Give it another day to heal, and I'll show you tomorrow."

I pout a moment longer, before turning back to the mirror to apply a thin coat of silver rose lipstick and a dusting of blush. I decide to go somewhat "au naturel," letting my reddish brown eyes lure in the men this evening.

"I don't know why you can't show me what it is," I whine one last time. Mera rolls her eyes, turning toward the mirror to apply her foundation, as I walk away to find my heels.

"Don't take too long," I yell back at her. "You're buying the first round."

***

Mera and I arrive at The Dark Scarlett at ten. There's a line of people about a block long waiting to get in as we pull into the garage across the street from the newest wine bar in the city. Parking is a bitch downtown on a Friday evening, and we do our best to find a spot at a distance that won't place too much of a strain on our feet. I should have opted for the two-inch heels instead of going all out and matching Mera with the three inchers.

"Do you think this place is worth the wait on such a cold November night?"

Mera hands me my wool coat from the back seat as she begins to slide into hers.

"I'd say yes, based on the amount of people who are waiting to get in, this must be a great place. It's only been open for a week and everyone at work is talking about it."

"Oh, that reminds me, I applied for a job at some video and film editing company. My father sent me the lead; I guess one of his friends owns the place. I may actually have a job sometime next week."

Mera lets out a chuckle and then snorts, sounding a

little harsh.

"Hey. You find my future job possibility amusing? It's probably better than being a figure model, and I'll make more money."

"No. I think it's great that you're finally getting out into the world. I just had a flash in my head of your father's *behind the scenes* business, and that it's possible you could be editing porn."

"Mera," I say, slapping her on the forearm. I doubt my father would want me to be involved in that. Which, by the way, we need to talk about his offer to you."

She frowns as we cross the street, taking our places at the back of the line. I suddenly sense a slight tension between us as I wait for her response. She stands looking forward, possibly thinking about the discussion the two of them had after our dinner at Giorgio's. She places her hands into her coat pockets and stumbles upon the key for my building and elevator. Mera smiles at my kind gesture.

"Now you can come up on your own, anytime you'd like."

"Thanks, Soph. You know, maybe we should go somewhere else. I forgot how cold it is this time of the year when the sun goes down."

"You're the one who just said it was worth the wait, making me walk over here from the car. We're not moving for a while. Just be patient."

"Fine. I guess our only other choice is Worship anyway, I'll try not to think about the cold."

"Yeah, think about the discussion with my father instead. It's time to talk."

"Drinks first, then talk."

"You're acting so odd and distant tonight. You were fine until I noticed that tattoo. What did you do, get married and not tell me? Is it one of those drunken night tats? Or maybe it's not the tattoo at all, and you really did fuck my dad and you don't want me to find out so you're acting all weird about everything."

The couple standing in front of us glances back, and I send them an apologetic look for my language.

"Soph," Mera whispers. "Chill the fuck out. We can talk in private once we get inside."

"Whoa, that's nice," I say, suddenly realizing that the wine bar has a block long row of heat lamps attached to its building directly above us. "They must have just turned them on."

Mera and I both look up and warm our faces as we take our hands out of our pockets. Yes, this is a nice place.

"Excuse me, Sophia Jameson?"

I look away from the heat lamp and turn to the man standing next to me. He's well over six feet tall, and dressed in a deep grey suit and black tie. His heavy build and slicked back hair reminds me of the standard mob character in any contract killer movie.

"Yes?" I hesitate, sending a confused look over to Mera.

"Miss Jameson, we have a table ready for you and your guest."

"My guest? Um, I'm not sure I'm the Sophia Jameson you're looking for."

He takes a sheet of paper out of his coat pocket, looking down at it, and then at me.

"Yes, you are the Sophia Jameson I'm looking for, please follow me inside."

"Hold on. If this has anything to do with my father, then we'll wait like everyone else in line. I appreciate that he wants to take care of me, but this is a bit too much.

What, does he have a camera on me at all times?"

The gentleman looks confused and then holds his hand up in the direction of the door. "Please, Miss Jameson, I'm not aware of your relationship with your father. I was asked only to lead you and your friend inside and to get the two of you out of the cold."

I glance at Mera and she shrugs, taking a step forward while latching onto my arm, pulling me along with her. We follow the man past the line of people, walking by the doorman, the bouncer, and through the front door of the club.

"Sophia, this is elegant. Look at all of the beautiful lights."

The room is filled with miniscule to gigantic sized low hanging chandeliers set together in groups of five, illuminating black velvet sofas and dark end tables placed around the room. A deep burgundy colored carpet lines the floor with varying shades of light to dark grey paint alternating along the walls. Contemporary electronica lounge music pierces my ears, a category of sound that I have experienced only from living with Mera. This is what she likes to listen to when she's fucking, and from what I've seen and heard in our former apartment, I have to say it is quite sexy.

There's a line of sofas along the back wall, and a more private area to the side, with two bouncers keeping watch over all. It may be for the bar owners, or their wealthy clientele to whom this new place is obviously geared. The man we've been following directs us to one of the seating areas along the back, and we settle into the soft sofa.

"Enjoy your evening ladies. All new guests receive a free bottle of wine."

"Wait," I plead, searching for answers. "Can you tell

me who asked you to bring us inside?"

He looks around the room, undecided about answering the question, before turning back with a smile. "I believe it would be best for you to find that out on your own. I am not at liberty to give out names without permission."

"Well, at least I know it was someone other than my father. Right?" I pause, looking at Mera and then back to the man standing next to me. "Paul Jameson doesn't own this club, does he?"

He grins from ear to ear, obviously enjoying my guessing game. "No Miss Jameson, he doesn't own this club."

Turning, he starts to walk away before Mera calls him back.

"Wait. I have a question too."

He's overly eager to please, and I'm assuming whoever has their eyes on us is also watching him, and he knows it.

"Yes, ma'am. Ask away."

"What artist, or band is playing on your sound system? It's hypnotizing and hot. Makes me want to dance naked."

He smiles, trying not to laugh or look aroused. "Yes, it's very good dance music. I'll get you a copy of the playlist from our DJ."

A woman dressed in a short black cocktail dress, wearing a black wig and dark red lipstick places a bottle of red wine and two glasses on the coffee table in front of us. The bottle has a solid black label with the name *The Dark Scarlett* in red lettering. She pours a small amount into Mera's glass and waits. The man who brought us to this table takes the opportunity to escape, quickly walking away.

"Go ahead Mera, take a swig."

Mera places the rim of the glass against her mouth and takes a sip. She swirls it around, and swallows. Her face shows pure delight and the lounge server pours a little into each glass.

"This is the owner's specialty, girls. I can bring a second bottle out if you'd like." The server sets the bottle back down in front of us and continues on to her other customers in the lounge.

I look at Mera who is staring into space, deep in thought.

"Mera?" I ask, still patiently waiting for her to talk about her secrets. "Can you at least smile for me? What are you so stressed about?"

A sweet smile briefly flashes across her face and then is hidden again by worry and doubt creeping into her eyes.

"Soph, I'm working for your dad. I'm going to do it. I gave my two-week notice at The Pillsman Center. I know you're going to be mad about it but it's great money, and I don't have to do anything that I don't agree to, plus I get to work my own hours." Mera speaks frantically, trying not to cry as I listen and bite my tongue. "Please don't be too hurt that I didn't discuss it with you first, and don't be mad at your dad. I kind of fucked things up and lied to him about the entire situation, telling him that you were okay with it. I don't want to lose you. You're my best friend and I know I went behind your back and everything, but please, please be okay with this and my decision. It's not something I'll do forever, but I think I'll make enough over the next two years to pay off my student loans and buy myself a few nice things. Are you mad? Please don't be mad." She puts her wine down and stops a few tears from rolling down her face, trying to preserve her makeup.

Without looking at her, I stand and move away from the sofa.

"Soph?"

"I'll be back," I say, trying not to show any emotion either way.

The room we're in is large, and I notice a hallway leading to another area of the building. As I walk past happily laughing and very drunk patrons, the floors of the room sway and my face flushes with a wave of heat running though my body. My ears buzz and my palms are sweaty as I try to escape the powerful panic attack that's all encompassing.

A hand takes hold of my elbow, assisting me to the bar.

"Miss Jameson, can I help you?"

It's the man who escorted us in. I shake my head no, waiting for the anxiety to pass.

"Are you sure? Would you like a glass of water?"

"I'm fine. I'm just looking for the ladies room." He takes my elbow again and starts to walk me over to the other side of the room.

"What's over there, down that hallway?" I ask.

"Private rooms."

"Oh." Maybe that's what Mera and I need, a private room to discuss a few things. With music, laughter, and loud conversations whirling in my head, a quiet space would be our best bet to talk this out. "Can my friend and I have a private room?"

He smiles, but shakes his head no, "I'm sorry, they're all booked for this evening." He sends me over to the restroom, then heads back to the bar area to oversee the crowd.

I spend some time in a stall, trying not to think about

Mera being a porn star, or my father viewing her naked body online at anytime of the day. I don't need to fill my head with such images. Mera is an adult and I have to respect her decision, even if it means letting go of a desire to control her and our friendship.

I suck in a deep breath and then let it out as forcefully as I can. The woman in the stall to the right of me laughs, making some smart comment about the lack of fiber in my diet. I take another deep breath, quieter this time, pretending not to hear her remark. My pounding heart finally begins to slow. Focus, Soph; let the situation be. Allow Mera to make her own decisions. Fuck it; she's already made the decision.

I stand and flush, not actually ever using the toilet but knowing if I walked out without flushing, I may look like a pig to everyone in the room.

Mera has finished her first glass of wine and is pouring a second when I return to the sofa. I sit down, gulping my wine to catch up with her. I place the glass on the coffee table and she pours me another.

She longs for words to come out of my mouth. I hold out for as long as I can before she blurts out her frustration.

"Yell, or scream, or do something Soph, but don't just sit there. Don't use silence as a form of punishment on me."

"I want to see your tattoo," I say in a strong voice, being very clear with her that I'm not fucking around. "You need to show it to me now because I think it has something to do with all of this. Lay it all out, all at once, and then we'll talk."

I watch as she brushes her hair off her shoulder with a shaky hand. Gently, and with a slight hesitation, she pulls the fabric from her dress down enough to expose the tattoo.

Property of Jameson Industries

My mouth drops open. "What the fuck is that? He branded you?" I say, nearly throwing up as I realize the seriousness of my father's business. "You got branded, Mera. Please tell me this is a requirement and you didn't do that on your own. On second thought, no, don't tell me. I don't want to know that my father treats his employees like cattle."

Mera tries to speak, but I place my hand up to halt the conversation, closing my eyes while trying to wipe the tattoo image out of my mind. Opening them a few moments later, I find the tat covered and hidden under Mera's long hair. She's quiet, embarrassed, and waiting for my next attack. I sit quietly, trying to understand if this is all about money, or if there's something else to her decision.

"Are you doing this to impress my dad?"

Mera shakes her head no, definitely distraught. A small amount of mascara is smeared under her eyes, and I place my hand up to her face, gently wiping it away with my finger. I cradle the side of her cheek in the palm of my hand and pull her gently toward me, placing my lips against hers. Mera welcomes the kiss, allowing me to have the control that I feel I've lost. I'm gentle, leaving my mouth closed. I warm her lips, letting her feel my support of her decision.

We sit back, as the couple to our left quietly and discreetly holds up their wine glasses in approval.

"When did you decide all of this?" I ask.

"On Tuesday. I called your dad because I had a few questions about the employee contract for his company."

"What contract?"

Mera sighs, knowing that she's digging herself deeper

into a hole. "It was emailed to me the day your dad flew back to Vegas. My tattoo is part of the contract, Soph. It represents my signature, and that I agree to the terms."

"So you've both been lying to me? This has been an ongoing discussion all week and you've kept it a secret? And everything my father has said to me has been complete bullshit? Yeah, now I'm a bit mad, and not about your decision. You guys shouldn't keep things from me," I say in a harsh tone, gulping down another glass and pouring a third.

"You're right, that's why it was so hard to tell you. I've been mendacious, and I hate myself for it. I'm so sorry Sophia."

Mera's apology is sincere, and I believe my father is at fault here more than her. It seems a bit rude and insensitive to approach my best friend and former lover with an offer that could trap her in a seedy lifestyle, something she could easily regret down the road. Plus, he lied to me about it. I watch Mera as she drinks her wine, her eyes saddened by my reaction and disgust. I feel I may be overreacting. I don't want to hurt her feelings any more than I have.

"Mera, if this is what you really want to do, and you think you'll be happy, that's fine and I stand by your decision. Sometimes I say things and realize afterward what a hypocrite I am, and I have no right to criticize you or my father. I have a feeling that you may regret your decision, but who am I to talk?"

"Thanks Soph," she says, giving me a hug. "I'm actually excited about it and I'm glad it's finally out of the bag."

"Do me a favor though." I pleadingly request. "I don't want any details about what you're doing, at least not for a while. All I can picture is my dad seeing you naked all day long. It kind of breaks my heart."

"Soph, it's not like that. Your dad will probably never see me. He has quite a few online sites, and thousands of videos, so unless someone sends him a link that could potentially be an issue for his company, with me in it, you don't have to worry."

I pour a fourth glass of wine, swirling it around before taking a sip. I was feeling tipsy after my second glass, but now I've approached my raging drunk stage. Mera takes her final sip and pours herself another.

"We'll need to take a cab home. There's no way I'll be able to drive."

Mera nods, her cheeks flush from the alcohol. We polish off our first bottle and our server leaves us with a second that I don't believe we could ever finish without passing out.

We're finally able to relax together, once again as friends. It's a rare evening out that we're not prowling for men. The environment inside The Dark Scarlett is part of the reason for that, with customers staying within their circles and not much mingling going on outside of the bar area. Mera smiles a lot as I continue to drink. I recount my experience with the sex addicts group, and my evening of modeling at the university to her. She's not surprised by either one, but rather happy to report that ass smoothies were nowhere to be found in her employee contract. My father mentioned that his clients are sophisticated people, as are his employees, so I will continue to believe that what Mera is getting herself into is not much different than things we've already done in our past. She'll just make a shitload of money doing it.

"I met my neighbor."

"Oh yeah, what's he or she like?"

"He. I think I'm interested in him."

"Sophia? Interested in someone? What do you mean by that?"

"I don't know yet. He's beautiful, and kind, and made me some milk and honey the other evening."

"Wow, milk and honey. Sexy and smooth, right?"

"Yeah, how'd you know?"

"I had a boyfriend who used to make it for me every time he wanted some nooky. He liked how relaxed I got after drinking it. It was easier for him to take advantage of me."

"Ah, I see. Well that definitely wasn't his plan because I showed him my breast and he didn't even flinch. He never looked down at it, or anything."

"Maybe he's gay."

"Oh, I'm so tired of that line. Just because he didn't fuck me doesn't mean he's gay."

"Alright, then perhaps he just jerked off and couldn't get it up again so quickly. What's his name, anyway?"

"Cove Everton."

"Cove Everton? Sounds like he has money."

"For sure. His place is beautiful and elegant. His voice is deep and his body is perfect. I can't imagine him not coming from a wealthy family. And it's Cove Ambrose Everton the third, by the way."

"Whoa. Did you look up the meaning yet?" Mera asks, taking out her phone. I shake my head no as she types in a search for his first name. This is something we've been doing since we were freshmen in college. It's amazing how people's personalities fit the meaning behind their names so perfectly.

"Okay, Cove means *inlet* or *shelter*."

"Yes, that's fitting. What about Everton?"

Mera checks her phone. "Everton means *wild boar*, or *boar settlement*. So you like someone who could possibly be sheltering wild boars."

I laugh, trying to decipher that meaning.

"Well, I didn't see any wild boars in his place, but then again, I was only on the first floor. Oh, and his mother owns the third penthouse."

"Wait, what?" Mera asks, inquisitively. "He lives with his mother?"

"No, she lives next to us, in the other penthouse."

"Yeah, like I said, he lives with his mother. Since when do you like men who are kind and live with mommy?"

"No, it's not like that, Mera. I haven't even seen her in the building yet, so I'm sure he doesn't have issues with privacy. The three of us share a hallway and an elevator, but that's it. It's not like they hang out together or anything."

"How do you know?"

"Good point. I don't. Now stop raining on my parade and let me enjoy the crush I've developed."

"Alright. Is this one sharable?"

"God Mera, I've only met him once. Let's not get into that just yet. Besides, you'll be getting plenty of action soon enough."

She laughs as I pour us each a final glass of wine for the evening. I wink and clink my glass to hers.

"To Cove," she says.

"To your new career," I say. "Hey, are you going to be with women, or just men?"

"Both."

"Really?"

Mera shoots me a warm smile as she places her hand on my leg. "Yes, but don't worry, I'll be thinking about you."

"God you're so corny sometimes."

"No. I'm not horny, I'm drunk."

"I said corny, not horny."

"What does corn have to do with sex?"

I let out a big drunken laugh, spilling some of my wine on my dress as Mera dribbles down her chin and onto her chest. We look like babbling fools.

"Better get home before we pass out," I say, slurring my speech.

"Yeah, I want to be in my own place when the room starts to spin."

"Miss Jameson?"

I look up, seeing the mob character that escorted us in earlier hovering over me. He's a blur, but I recognize his voice.

"Yes, Mr. Big. Biggy. Mr. Biggles." I stutter, giggling at the name I've created for him.

"Miss Jameson," he says with a smile. "You can call me Haverty. I was asked to take you and your guest to the front door. We've arranged for one of the club drivers to take the two of you home."

"What? Who are we? Who are you again?"

"I work for the owners. Please, we've arranged for you to have a safe ride home. And Miss, here is your playlist from our DJ."

Mera stands, taking the sheet of paper, and then falls back onto the sofa. She laughs, tries again and is successful with the help of Haverty. She reaches out to me and I latch onto her hand, allowing her to help me to my feet. I stumble for a moment and then regain my composure, standing straight with my shoulders back. We walk quietly out of the club, arm in arm, following Haverty who leads us to a silver Escalade. A driver opens the back door and we climb in, settling into the warm seats.

"Wait," I say. "I didn't pay for that second bottle."

"Enjoy the rest of your evening, ladies," Haverty says with a wink, as he walks back into the club without taking our money. The driver closes the door, and takes his place in the front seat.

"So this is the company car?" I ask, as we pull away from the curb.

"Yes, this is one of five vehicles for guests of The Dark Scarlett."

"Holy shit, Soph, that's like four hundred grand just in cars. Hey, guy in the front seat. Who owns this club anyway?" Mera asks, leaning forward as she's speaking to him.

He looks back at us in the mirror and grins from ear to ear. "The owners are Leondra and Cove Everton. I assume you've met them since you're allowed to be in one of the Escalades. It's not like they let just anyone get free rides home you know."

Mera turns and looks at me, her eyes wide with delight. She places her head on my shoulder, wrapping an arm around the front of my chest. We ride home in silence, with her holding me tight the entire way home.

CHAPTER THIRTEEN

I arrive home at one in the morning, after making sure Mera's safe in her apartment and her water's been turned back on. The driver walks me to my building and I wish him a good night. Now, as I ride the elevator to the top floor, I wonder if Cove was at the club. How did he know that we were standing out in the cold? He must have security cameras outside the building.

The elevators open and I stumble out, still slightly drunk but no longer wasted like I was at the Scarlett. A soft hand wraps around my wrist as I reach for the wall for support. Turning, I see a woman with dark, very full, shoulder length hair. She smiles, a few wrinkles showing around her eyes and along the corners of her mouth.

"Sophia, sweetie. My name is Leondra. Leondra Everton. I believe you've met my son?" She releases my wrist and her gold bracelets clang against one another as she moves her arm down to her side. She's wearing a silk, golden colored robe that hangs off of her slim body. Her fingernails are painted to match the gold robe, and as my eyes follow her body downward, I'm shocked to see that her entire right leg is covered in tattoos. Classic tattoos, ones you might see on a biker in the 1950's. There's a ship, an anchor, a bird, horseshoe, a heart with an arrow piercing it, and another heart with the word *MOM* written across it.

"Do you like tattoos, honey? I've had these for at least thirty years," she says, placing her leg out for me to get a better look. She lifts her robe to reveal a pair of dice that have landed on snake eyes, and at the highest point on her leg, an ace of spades.

She lets her robe fall over the artwork and steps back, her face suddenly embarrassed. "I'm sorry, sweetie. I didn't mean to be so forward, or to scare you."

"No worries. I'm just a little tipsy right now. You didn't scare me," I reply, my mind still processing the beautiful woman standing before me. She reminds me of an older, modern day version of Snow White, or a fairy tale queen with pale white skin, dressed in gold and wrapped in expensive jewels. I want to tell her she's a knockout, but I'll wait until I'm sober. I may have goggle eyes right now.

"Did you enjoy your evening at the club?"

"Yes, it was incredible. I couldn't believe how calm and elegant everything was, and the wine…oh, the wine. I can't wait to go there again."

"Thank you sweetie, I'm glad you enjoyed yourself. You're welcome there anytime. And you'll never have to wait in line either, we'll make sure of that."

"Mrs. Everton? How did you know my friend and I were outside?"

"Mother, let me help Sophia. Please, go back to bed, it's been a long day for you." Cove's voice echoes down the hall, as he approaches the two of us. She turns and sends a motherly smile his way, then takes my hand in hers, giving it a light squeeze.

"Sophia, darling, it was such a pleasure meeting you. Please come and visit me anytime. I'm just down the hall and around the corner." She waits for Cove to stop in front of us, and then turns her head for a kiss. Cove responds immediately, giving her a gentle peck on the cheek, wishing her a good night. She strolls back to her place, her robe flowing behind her. "Good night sweethearts," she calls back to us, as she rounds the corner of the hallway.

I look up at Cove. He blushes, his dark eyes peering directly into mine.

"Sophia," he says in a gentle and calm voice. "Do you need any help this evening?"

I have no idea how to respond to that question. Yeah Cove, you could help me get naked. I think I might need some help with the orgasm I'd love to have right now.

"I'm sorry Sophia, let me rephrase that. Would you like to go for a swim?"

"A swim? Where? How? Wait, what? It's freezing outside, and its past midnight," I respond, a little shocked. "Do we have a pool in our building?"

"I know of a place, but I'll understand if you say no, especially if you've had too much to drink. I don't want you to pass out in the water."

"No, I'm fine. I mean, I've had a lot to drink, and I'm still kind of drunk, but I'm starting to sober up. Yeah, I'd love to," I say, my insides tingling with delight. Oh my God, I get to see this man wet and half naked. Yes sir, I'll go for a swim.

"Great. Why don't you go inside and get your suit, and I'll wait here for you."

"You're welcome to come inside."

"No, I'm fine. Go ahead, just come out when you're ready."

I enter my place; fling my heels off my feet as quickly as I can and race up the two flights of stairs to my bedroom. Where is my suit? Frantically, I pull open every drawer; clothing flies everywhere as I search for the garment. My heart pounds with excitement as I run to my closet, opening plastic bins, throwing more clothes into the air, still staggering from the alcohol. Where the fuck is it? Finally, my hand touches a nylon fabric, pulling it free from the pile beneath my feet. I grab a towel from the bathroom and head back downstairs.

I stop in my foyer, catch my breath, smooth my hair behind my ears before opening the door.

"I'm ready, I think. Do I need anything besides a suit and towel?" I ask, stepping toward him.

"No, just a suit is enough. I have plenty of towels."

I throw my towel onto the floor of my place, and lock the door, placing my keys and phone into a small purse.

Cove places his hand on the small of my back, directing me down the hallway. "Follow me, Sophia."

"Where are we going?"

"My place."

"You have a pool?" I explode with delight, wanting to skip down the corridor. I'm not sure how long I can contain my ecstasy for this man.

Cove opens his door and I follow him inside, the familiar scent of vanilla still fills the air. The lights are low and a few candles are lit on the first floor. We walk up the stairs in silence, stopping on the middle level of his loft.

He pulls me closer and reaches for the doorknob directly to our left.

"In my place, this is just a small storage room with a concrete floor," I say, suddenly worried that this person who I barely know may have other plans besides a swim.

He opens the door and I immediately feel a rush of warm air. Steam rises from the water of a sparkling deep blue pool that fills most of the room. The space is large, probably twenty feet in length and fifteen feet wide, with floor to ceiling windows along one side. I follow Cove inside. He pushes a button on the wall, turning on the surround sound that plays a tranquil and meditative serenade.

"Our penthouses are slightly different," he says, pleased by my excitement.

"I'll say."

"I use the pool late at night to relax before I go to sleep. I rarely swim in it; it's more of a serene retreat for me, a place to unwind and reflect. After the other evening, I thought it might help you do the same."

He must be referring to my sleepwalking. I nod as he reaches his hand out to mine. I take it eagerly and he walks me over to two tri-fold screens.

"You can change here. I'll use the other one."

There's a wooden bench and a row of hooks along the wall behind the screen. It reminds me of the changing area at the university that's set up for the nude models. That's about all one needs to change out of clothing. I unzip my black dress, sliding it above my chest, out of my arms. The suit I found is my one-piece, I think Mera borrowed my bikini years ago and never returned it. I wonder if he's expecting me to come out in something sexy. It's black, and low cut...

"Cove?"

"Yes, Sophia?" he says over his screen.

"I only have a one-piece."

"A one-piece what?"

"Suit. I don't have a bikini with me. Is that okay?"

Cove laughs. I can see his bare feet below my screen and then his jeans and a pair of black boxers drop to the floor. He steps out of the clothing and picks everything up before he speaks. "Don't worry, it's not like I'll be wearing a skimpy Speedo."

I smile at that thought and wish I could just walk out naked. Wouldn't it be great to jump out from behind the screen and say, "*surprise, look at me, I'm ready for ya.*"

There's a light splash in the pool as I hear him walk down the steps and into the water. Damn it, I missed seeing his body before he got in the water.

He's floating on his back when I walk out from behind the screen. He lifts his head, looking directly into my eyes and not at all at my body. What gives? Mera's right, maybe he's gay. Come on, my suit isn't that ugly.

My foot drops into the water, landing on the first step. It's warm, and without delay I slide the rest of the way in, my muscles loosening while my mind relaxes. This is nice. I look over at Cove who's slowly easing toward me. He smiles and I smile back.

"Nice isn't it?"

"Yes. It's wonderful," I say, moving closer to him. I reach out and he glides away, not allowing me to touch him.

"Float, Sophia. Enjoy yourself. Let go and relax."

I follow his request and turn onto my back, looking up at the ceiling. There's a large glass dome above me that I didn't notice when we walked in. I can see the stars in the night sky as I float around the pool. My hands make small circular motions at my sides, steering through the water from one end to the other. I brush against Cove every so often, aching for skin-to-skin contact with him this evening.

It's a good twenty minutes before I flip back onto my stomach, moseying up to the side of the pool. With my back against the wall, I place my arms over the edge, and lift myself slightly out of the water. My feet rise up as I kick; creating small splashes and waves in the pool.

Cove swims underwater and reappears next to me. His face dripping and hair slicked back.

"Enjoying yourself?"

"I feel like a little kid," I reply, descending back in the water.

"You have a beautiful face, Sophia. I love having you here, watching your eyes light up and your lips when they part ever so slightly."

"Cove," I whisper, moving closer to him, as he once again backs away.

"Sophia, don't." He turns from me, walks up the steps, and out of the pool. A row of chairs line the window side of the room and he pulls a towel from one, wrapping it around his waist. His skin is perfect from behind, with not a blemish in site, and his entire body radiates well-defined muscle tone. His lack of interest confuses the hell out of me, and for once in my life I'm actually angry that a guy won't take advantage of a good fuck. Maybe he has a girlfriend, or he's married.

I follow him out of the water, placing a towel over my shoulders. He stands by the window looking out at a few flickering lights in the distance, as one lonely car drives along Locust Street. His view is nicer than mine, overlooking the Gateway Arch and the Mississippi River.

"Cove?"

"Sophia, stand next to me," he says in a quiet voice.

I walk over and his arm extends, allowing me to curl in next to his body. He lowers his hand onto my shoulder as he continues staring out into the darkness.

"Do you see it?"

I look out the window and see large flakes of beautiful, soft, snow falling onto the city. The first snow of the season. It's one of the prettiest snowfalls I've ever experienced. Something you read about in a book, or see in a movie; the kind of scene that never occurs in real life. Each snowflake spirals down; it's like a feather pillow has been split open and the contents released to the earth. The lights on the building dim behind the quiet flakes, as a white dusting covers the terrace.

Cove gently rubs his fingers in a circular motion around my shoulder. His hands are soft, like the snow falling down in front of us. His body is warm and his muscles are tensed. I don't dare move or make a sound, hoping this moment between the two of us will last.

"I love the snow, especially the first snowfall each year," he whispers. "Some people think it's the end of life, that the cold weather kills and buries living things. I think it's just the opposite. Winter is fresh and clean, bringing change into our lives. During the day it blinds us with its brightness and at night it's hypnotic, sending us into a trance. Snow is pure and that purity is a welcome sight each year."

He continues to look out onto the city. His warmth, generosity, and the proximity of his body completely captivate me. I want so much more from him. I've never really needed anything from anyone, except for sex. I do want him inside of me, but at this moment I'm happy just standing here, listening, waiting, and hoping that I might have a chance with this man.

"Is that your phone?" I turn and look over to the changing screen where the sound emanates from.

Cove walks behind the screen, answering it.

"Cove," he says in a much louder voice than I'm used to hearing. Who could be calling him so late? Perhaps his mother needs something.

He walks out from behind the screen and looks at me, then paces the floor back and forth in a nervous strut.

"I see. Okay, I was planning on it," he responds. "Tomorrow. Yes."

He puts the phone down then walks back to the window.

"Is everything okay?" I ask.

"Yes, it's just business."

"Oh, did something happen at the Scarlett?"

"No, it's other business, but everything is fine," he replies, hesitating between words, then exhaling a big breath of air. "I'm sorry to end this night short Sophia, but I need to get you home." He turns, and I immediately latch onto his arm before he can get away. He looks inquisitively down at my hand and then at my face.

"I'm sorry. I just want to know if we can do this again. I mean, well I didn't mean to invite myself over, but I..."

"Yes," he says before I can finish my frantic sentence. "You're welcome here anytime that I'm not in the middle of a job."

We stare into one another's eyes, and I finally see the craving that he has for me. It's there; his desire, I can see it. He places his hand along the side of my cheek and brushes a few strands of wet hair off the side of my face. We're both finally touching one another, my hand on his arm and his hand on my face. His dark eyes pierce my insides, making my legs tremble and my lips swell.

His phone sounds again, and he swiftly drops his arm away from my face.

"Yes, it's Cove," he says in a forceful voice. "I will. I am. I won't." He hangs up and moves to the changing area, disappearing behind the screen.

"I need to take you home, Sophia. I have some business to attend to."

I change into my dress and we walk out of the poolroom, back to reality. The cold air immediately chills my body, and I wish I were back in the warm water, floating, looking up at the stars. Cove is quiet as we walk down the steps and out his door. Something's on his mind.

"You okay?" I ask, hoping it's not me.

"Just fine. No worries," he says, sending a smile my way as we leisurely stroll down the hallway of the building. "That was nice, I'm sorry I had to cut things short."

"It's fine, Cove," I reply, as we stop in front of my door. "You know I have to ask you if you want to come in."

"And you know I have to say no."

"Because of business?"

"Yes, and only because of business." He bites his top lip and looks behind him, almost as if he believes we're being watched.

"Cove?"

He leans down and whispers in my ear. "Think of me tonight, especially when you're in your warm bed watching the snow fall from the sky."

My phone rings, startling us both. He steps back as I pull the phone out of my purse. It's my dad. What's he doing calling me so late?

"Hi Dad."

Cove's face turns white and he hurriedly walks away.

"Sophia," my father sharply speaks my name, a tone I haven't heard since the parking garage incident. "Stay away from Cove Everton."

"What?"

"Walk into your place, and lock the door."

"Dad, do you have a camera on me? How do you know where I am, and what I'm doing? And how do you know Cove?"

"Sophia, do what I say, and do it now."

"No."

"Sophia, I don't want you to associate with him. Trust me."

"Trust you? To hell I trust you. How the fuck do you know what I'm doing right now? Answer some of my questions and I might trust you."

"God dammit, Sophia. Get in your fucking penthouse and close the door. We'll talk about this in the morning."

I huff loudly, opening my door to a lonely Lewis, and then lock the two of us inside.

"Are you happy?"

"You're inside?"

"You know I'm fucking inside, Dad, you're watching me. You can see what I'm doing right now." I throw my middle finger up in the air and I hear my father laugh. "Oh fuck you, this isn't one bit funny, Dad."

"Sophia, calm down. It's for your safety. I can only see your hallway and foyer. I can't see what goes on anywhere else in your place."

"What do you want, a medal? Am I supposed to be okay now and not hate you because you're only spying on me when I come and go each day? What the fuck, Dad?"

"I'm sorry, but I feel a need to take care of you. I want you to be safe and happy."

"How the fuck do you know Cove?"

"Please stop swearing at me, kiddo."

"No Dad, no kiddos this time. How do you know him?"

"Sophia, let's discuss this in the morning, it's late and I need to go to bed."

"Well good for you, you fucker, you were the one who called me, remember? Just tell me how you know him, and I'll try to let your camera in my foyer and the one in my hallway go for now."

My father pauses, and then says four words I didn't want to hear.

"He's my business partner."

CHAPTER FOURTEEN

"N o, Devery. The shit hit the fan."

"Sophia, please, call me Dr. Rosen and not by my first name."

"Okay, Dr. Rosen," I say scathingly. "What the fuck? I'm so distraught right now and completely paranoid. It's like 1984, and there's a camera on me everywhere I go. I go out with Mera, and we're being watched, and I try to start a relationship, and my father steps in because he's spying on me. Then I find out that my father, Mera, and Cove have all lied to me. What the fuck?"

"Sophia, please," she says in a hushed tone, trying to lower my voice down to hers. "Careful with the harsh language, I have other patients in the waiting area. Now, I understand that you've been hurt by everyone in your life this week, but what you need to do is talk it out with each of them. You need to speak to your father about privacy, and find out from him, as well as Cove, what type of business relationship the two of them have. And ask your father why he's being so protective. There's information that you don't have, and these issues will be difficult to resolve unless you pick up your phone and talk it out with every person involved."

I sigh, pissed off and ready for battle. I've spent the entire weekend hunkered down in my place, not speaking to anyone, and walking purposefully into my foyer just to give my father the finger. Devery's right, giving them the silent treatment isn't going to fix anything or make my problems disappear.

"You still with me, Sophia?"

"Yes. You're right. I need to talk to my father."

"Calling him would be a good place to start. As far as Cove is concerned, I don't believe he lied to you, but he definitely could have mentioned that he knows your father."

"You think?" my sarcastic tone suddenly sounding childish. "I'm sorry. I didn't mean to sound like a toddler in the middle of a tantrum."

"It's okay, Sophia. What you're dealing with, and the way you're handling it is exactly why people come to me for help. Go ahead and show your emotions, but then we need to find the best way to fix the problem, and move past it."

"Again, you're my voice of reason."

Devery smiles, then reaches for her tea. She has a knack for calming me down whenever I fly off the handle. I find comfort in knowing that I have this office, her practice, and her to turn to when I'm in need.

"Would you like to call your father right now, during your session today? It may help to have someone around for support as you discuss this with him."

With wide eyes I immediately shake my head no. I don't think my father would appreciate it if I involved my shrink, his friend, in a conversation about Cove and his porn sites, but then again, maybe Devery already knows about his business.

"Do you know what my father does for a living?" I ask.

"Yes, he owns a few companies. He's a great businessman, full of charisma and highly intelligent. A genius, according to my parents and my brothers."

"Yes, a businessman, but do you know what type of business he's involved in?"

"Sophia, I don't believe his product matters in this particular situation, but to answer your question, yes. He owns a handful of casinos in Las Vegas."

She doesn't know. Or she's not going to say that she's aware of the online sites.

"Yeah, I think I'll speak to him in private."

"Okay, but I suggest you do it soon. He's worried about you."

"And you know this because?" I ask inquisitively.

"He called to make sure you didn't cancel your appointment."

"Once again, I find that to be an issue with privacy."

"I understand, Sophia, but keep in mind that he's paying for your sessions. He'll find out if you were here one way or the other when the bill arrives."

"Alright, maybe we should talk about something else. I'm done thinking about my father for now."

"Why don't you tell me about Cove."

There's no hiding the smile and delight on my face when I hear his name. Yes, let's talk about Cove. Devery listens attentively as I recall the night that I woke up in his penthouse. The story of the milk and honey, and how I proceeded to take off the shirt he let me borrow, only to be rejected in the process. She nods and smiles, as I continue on about the wine bar, meeting his mother, and then the late night swim, all leading to the interruption by my father.

She takes an abundance of notes, her hand trying to

keep up with my excitement of being able to speak about him to someone in such great detail.

"Wow, okay. Is that everything?" she asks.

"Yes. Well no. That's everything about Cove. I had a few other experiences over the past week, but he was the most important."

"Yes, I heard from Stephen that you walked out of the sex addicts meeting."

"First of all, I thought it was going to be anonymous, but everyone used their first name, and second, you didn't mention that it was a religious group."

"You don't have to be religious to attend, it's more about finding support, and showing support to others."

"It wasn't for me, Dr. Rosen."

"Okay then, we'll leave it at that. I can't force you to attend, I only thought it would be beneficial," she says, placing her notebook and pen onto her desk, while she pulls her glasses up to rest on top of her head. "Everything's okay with you and Mera?"

"Yes, we talked. We're fine."

"Well that's exactly what you need to do with your father, and eventually Cove. Now, Cove," she says, looking back through her notes. "You said you met his mother?"

"Yes."

"Does he have any other family members? Did he mention his father?"

"Nope."

"And obviously you didn't talk about his job?"

"No, he wouldn't divulge very much information about that at the time."

"So, you were able to have a conversation with someone, like I asked, without actually having a conversation?"

"What do you mean?"

"Tell me what you know about him, besides what he looks like, how his penthouse is decorated, and how his mother dresses. Tell me what you know, not what you saw."

"Is this a trick question?"

"No."

I think for a moment, trying to remember what we talked about. What did we talk about?

"I know that he was away on business and that's why all of his blinds were closed. He likes vanilla scented candles, oh, and he definitely works out. His body is tight."

"Not what you saw, Sophia. Tell me what you know about him," she requests in a calm voice.

I look past Devery, trying to think back to those two nights. What were those conversations about?

"He said he swims in the evening to relax. It's a form of meditation. I can sense that he has a kind heart. He has a gentle way about him... I can hear it in his voice, and feel it in his body language. He's also a lover of snow."

"I have to say, after spending two hours with this man, you should have more information about him than you do."

"I spent a lot of time just looking at him. I know we talked about some things too, I just can't remember what right now. I might have been overwhelmed by his good looks. I don't know, but yes, we definitely talked."

"Have you thought about why he didn't make any advances toward you?"

"Yeah, over and over again. I can't figure it out. I mean, when a woman flashes her breast at a man, he'll at least look at it. He never took his eyes off my face."

"So do you think he's more than just a challenge to

you? Do you have feelings for this person?"

"I have a crush. I don't know if it goes beyond that or not."

Devery takes another sip of her tea, cradling the cup in two hands. She swivels her chair back and forth for a few moments, mulling over my latest addiction to Cove Everton.

"Would you say you had feelings for Evan?"

"I loved Evan as a friend, and used him for sex, but it never went beyond that. I didn't think much about him when we were apart, nor did I have any need to be with him. He was just convenient at the time. I have a desire to see and be around Cove. There's a clear difference between the two, so yes, I guess I do have feelings for him."

"Is that why you've been holding back as well?"

"What do you mean?" I ask.

"I'm starting to see a change in you. The other men we've talked about during your sessions were people you attacked. You were very forward with all of them, and if you were to act the same way with Cove, then you'd be knocking on his penthouse door right now."

"I don't want to scare him away."

"So then it's serious?"

"Yes, I don't even want to share him with Mera." Devery shoots me a confused look, and I remember that I haven't discussed the agreement that Mera and I have about sharing men. "Sorry Dr. Rosen, that conversation's for another time. Forget I said that."

She writes a quick note in her book and waves me on to proceed.

"I'm confused. What am I supposed to do? I think about Cove all the time. I want to see him and spend time with him. He hasn't made contact with me since he left me standing outside my apartment the other night."

"Again, Sophia. You'll have more answers after you speak to your father. You need to talk to him before you can talk to Cove. You also need to come to terms with the fact that you may be falling in love with someone."

I laugh nervously at her words. "Do I need to do something to prepare for that?" I ask, innocently.

Devery laughs as well, "No, just let it happen, don't be afraid, but be prepared for disappointment if it doesn't work out."

That's probably the worst advice she's ever given me. I want to ask her if she's married or in love with anyone, but I'll save that for another day.

"We're out of time Sophia."

"I need to make longer appointments with you, I didn't even get to talk about my most recent fling."

"Was that before or after Cove?"

"Before."

"Put it in your past and move forward. You have a chance right now, a window to change your attitude about intimacy and how it can be a healthy and meaningful part of a relationship."

I stand and thank Devery for her time. She opens the door to her office, requesting that I come back this Friday, or next Monday for another discussion.

"Sophia," she says, as I'm walking out. "Don't forget to call your father before you speak to Cove."

***

I decide to make the call early Tuesday morning. Cove and Mera have both been silent, and I wonder if my father has talked to them. It's not like Mera to give up so easily, and since she hasn't called since Sunday, I can only assume that he stepped in.

"Dad?"

"Sophia, I'm so glad you're finally calling me. I've been trying to get a hold of you all weekend."

"We need to talk about the other night, and Cove Everton."

"Yes, yes we do."

"First, I apologize for my language. I was shocked and upset, but I think I had a right to be."

"No need to apologize, kiddo. I understand."

"I want to know why you have cameras in the hallway, Dad, and in my foyer. You said it was for my safety. What exactly does that mean?"

"It's for your protection."

"What am I being protected from?"

"My business, which would include my clients, my employees, and the competition, as well as one of my business partners, Cove."

"Go on. I need more of an explanation than that."

"You're right about what you said last week. This is a seedy business. Not mine per se, but in general it can be. I have a few clients who, at times, can be possessive. They try to meet the women or men on my sites, or they think that an online conversation can turn into something more, if only they could see the person and speak to them face to face. There have been a few cases that could be perceived by some as stalking. I've had to call the police on occasion."

"Will Mera be in any kind of danger?"

"No. I'll make sure that she's safe. It's rare for clients to figure out where we film, where we live, and the real names of my employees. It's usually the employee's fault for giving out too much information about him or herself."

"Keep going," I say, still waiting to hear how Cove falls into all of this.

"My employees can get upset with the company as well. I have to let people go from time to time, sometimes it's just because my clients want to see fresh faces online, other times it's because my employees break their contracts."

"How?"

"It's like modeling, Sophia. They gain too much weight, or I can no longer film them based on a poor choice in tattoo, haircut, implant, and so on. It's that simple. There're plenty of beautiful people in this world waiting to take someone's place. Plus, if they make a video for another company, that's an immediate breach of contract. It's moonlighting."

"That seems kind of harsh, Dad. I'm sorry to admit this to you, but I've seen some online porn and there are plenty of overweight men and women, and people with bad tats or blemished bodies."

"I told you I have a quality product for a sophisticated clientele. I give them what they want, and in doing so, they pay a higher price than most. Plus they get guaranteed privacy when viewing my sites."

"So, *your* tattoos are okay? That's not in poor taste?"

My father takes a breath and lets out a heavy sigh. He pauses, and delays an answer. I can tell it's not something he completely believes in.

"The tattoos started many years ago, but we've been having a few discussions about changing that policy. I see it as a company uniform, or a nametag."

"What the fuck," I yell. "That's bullshit. Mera is now branded for life because of you. I have to be reminded of your porno business every time she wears a tank or a strapless dress, you asshole."

"I'm sorry, kiddo, but that's the way it is," he says unapologetically. "This business is paying for your penthouse, and it paid for your car and your degree. You may not like certain aspects of it, but it is what it is."

My stomach sinks and ties itself into a knot at that thought. I'm living in a place that was bought with money by people who needed jerk-off visuals. Fuck.

"So why do you need to protect me? You still haven't explained the cameras in and outside of my place."

"Sophia, hold on a second. I have to make a quick call." My father places me on hold and I'm stuck listening to Michael Bolton. I can't picture my father requesting this music to be used as the background for clients waiting on the other end of the line. How surreal and unfortunate for both my father *and* Michael Bolton.

I hear a phone chime from out in the hallway and I swiftly run over to look out my peephole. It's Cove, he's walking down the hall. As I open my door my phone clicks and my father's back on the line.

"Close the door, Sophia. Let's finish talking."

Cove's gone, already in his place. "Did you call him? Was he coming to talk to me, and you sent him away?"

"Yes."

"Yes? That's all you have to say to me? I want an explanation."

"Let's finish our conversation, Sophia."

I close my door utterly disappointed with my father, and that I missed an opportunity to see and speak to Cove. "Tell me about him, and why I need protection."

"As I was explaining, there are some people, whether they are clients, employees, or the competition, who wish me and my family harm. There are people who want to take my employees for their own business, or who are involved in business deals that have gone awry. The latter have led to threats. I'm referring to the casino business as well. If anyone found out where you lived, you would be in danger. I want to see who walks through that hallway, and who rings your doorbell. For now, most people are unaware that I even have children, and I want to keep it that way," he sighs again, then takes a drink of something, swallowing hard. "The key card for the elevator is your first defense for safety; the cameras are your second. Cove is your third."

"What do you mean by that?"

"Cove is your protection, Sophia. Or at least he was supposed to be. I specifically gave you a list of four buildings to choose from because I have employees, and business partners in all four."

My head spins with this new information and I need to sit down. "Wait, did you have cameras in my place with Evan?"

"Yes."

"Do you have people watching me all the time?"

"Only when I receive a threat, or feel that you're in a vulnerable place."

"Give me some examples."

"I'd rather not, Sophia. The less you know, the better."

"I'm still pissed, Dad, give me some examples or I'm hanging up the phone."

There's another hesitation as my father takes a second gulp of whatever it is he's drinking. I give him time to answer, but there's only silence from his end.

"I'm hanging up now Dad. You can call me when you

want to answer my questions."

"Roger and Diane," he quickly says, not wanting to lose me from the line.

"They work for you?" I respond, completely appalled.

"They keep an eye on you when you're on campus."

"So, they don't really have a son who's in art school?"

"Yes, yes they do. They haven't lied to you, and they really are interested in taking the class."

"Let me guess, Haverty at The Dark Scarlett was another one?"

"Yes, but he works there as well. It was just complete luck that you showed up to that place, and that Cove already had an in-house person to keep an eye on you. Those are the type of places that I worry about the most. Those are the people who know me and who I do business with."

"So you know more about me than you've mentioned in the past. Like, you probably knew about the parking garage before the owner called you. Right?"

"No, it's not that extreme. When I do have someone follow you, I ask the person only to report back if there's a situation. I don't want to hear about your private life and what you do."

"This *is* my private life, Dad; all of it. And so you're saying you don't know what I'm doing, but someone else does? Is that correct? People have seen me having sex?"

"These are people who have worked for my company for many years. They've seen hundreds, if not thousands of people having sex. Whatever you do is meaningless to them. It's all just a job as far as they're concerned. They only care about keeping you safe."

"Well I'm glad you can be so nonchalant about all of this when I'm sitting here feeling completely violated."

"I'm sorry, Sophia. I'm doing this because I love you, and I only have your best interest in mind."

"It's going to take a while for my anger to subside and my brain to process what you've just told me."

"I understand. Unfortunately, we still need to talk about Cove," my father's voice wavers as he says his name. "It's apparent that you like him, but I don't want you to go into his penthouse anymore. There are things you don't know about the Evertons."

"Excuse my language again Dad, but fuck you. You're the one who gave me this building as an option as a place to live. If he's so dangerous, then what am I doing living right next door to him?"

"He can hurt you in ways that you'll never be able to understand. He was supposed to keep an eye on you from a distance... hold on again, Sophia." He places me on hold and I immediately run to my door. Fool me once, Dad, but not a second time.

I swing my door open just in time to see Cove walk into the elevator. His phone rings and he frowns as he views the name.

"Don't answer it, Cove," I say, as my father clicks back onto my line.

"Sophia, don't do this. Trust me, you have no idea what you're getting yourself into. It won't work out, just turn around, get back in your place, and let's finish talking about this."

Cove looks down at his phone again, and then back at me.

"Don't," I say again, ending the call with my father.

The door begins to close and Cove places his foot in its path, he stares at me, conflicted.

I walk up to him, grab the front of his silky, black,

button down shirt, and pull him close to my lips. I can smell the vanilla on his clothing. His breath is warm as he exhales. He places a hand up to my chest, blocking any closer movement.

"Sophia," he says in a soft voice, causing my inner lips to moisten and swell. "I can't. You don't understand."

My phone rings and Cove immediately jerks back, moves his foot and releases the elevator door. He disappears, and I'm left only with my reflection staring back in the stainless steel doors.

***

My phone rings for two hours until my father finally gives up. I spend time with Lewis while cleaning my place and ignoring his calls. The day slowly goes by, and I can't help but walk out my entry door every hour to see if anyone is in the hall. My feet become chilled, standing on the cold, dark, marble floor tiles in the corridor as I wait for the elevator to ding.

Silence.

I walk back inside and wonder what my father said to him. Should I call Mera? I need to talk to someone besides my father.

Her phone goes to voicemail and I tell her to call me when she gets home from work. I make a salad for lunch and then stand on my balcony, gazing at the heavy cloud cover. The sun is what's missing from my life. I wouldn't be so depressed if it would come out and warm my flesh.

My mind wanders back and forth from wishing I had a job, to daydreaming about Cove. I'm anxious, waiting for something to happen.

I spend an hour in the afternoon trimming my pubic

hair, and giving myself a quick wax. I can only go so far before it's time to call in the experts. My skills are limited based on the pain. I finish off the area with a soothing lotion. Lewis sniffs the warm wax and I warn him that if he gets too close, he's next.

Could the day be any more boring? Please, someone call me for an interview.

I'm relieved to hear my phone at five o'clock. It has to be Mera.

"Hey beautiful, I'm so glad you finally called. I think I have cabin fever."

"Sorry, Soph. I've been swamped at work. Two concerts this week, and I'm exhausted from my period. You doing okay?"

"Yeah, well, no. My father and I are fighting about his business, amongst other things. My life is kind of a mess right now."

"I know. He called me to make sure you were okay. I told him I didn't know anything, but that I was sure you were fine."

"Did you know he has a camera in my foyer, and in my hallway leading to the elevator here at the penthouse?"

"What? What for?" Mera sounds just as annoyed as I am about the whole situation.

"He said it's for protection, but I hung up on him before I got all the details. I'm tired of this bullshit."

"You should have just stayed with Evan."

"Mera," my voice surly over such a horrendous comment. "Seriously?"

"I'm sorry, that's not what I meant. I was referring to your old place, and not your old relationship."

"He had a camera there as well."

"Whoa, Soph. What's going on?"

I have an incoming call from my father as I'm talking to Mera, and instantaneously there's a knock at my door.

"Hey, Mera, I've got to go. Someone's knocking, I'll call you back, okay?"

"Yeah, make sure. I want to know what's happening over there."

I set my phone on the kitchen island and head over to the door.

It's Cove.

His arm is raised above his head, supporting his body as he leans against the doorframe. He looks down at me, his dark hair falls forward, his eyes pierce into mine. He smells clean, like he just got out of the shower and dabbed spicy cologne onto his body. He's still wearing the black silk shirt from earlier, with faded blue jeans.

My phone rings again and I ignore it.

Cove uses his free hand to pull a pair of keys out of his pocket.

"Hi, Sophia," he says in a calm voice. "Your car is in the basement parking garage."

My eyes widen as I realize I completely forgot about my car. Mera and I left it across from The Dark Scarlett days ago. I'm surprised it wasn't towed.

"Thank you," my face immersed in appreciation. "But where did you get a key?"

"Your father has the means of getting things when he needs to."

"Of course. My father," I say in a hateful tone. "Did he tell you I was asleep in the hallway? Is that how you found me?"

"Sophia," Cove whispers. "He's only trying to protect you."

"So I've been told, many times."

Cove frowns at my comment, looking past me and up toward the ceiling. My phone rings again, then his. He turns his off and places it in his pocket, and then reaches his hand out to mine.

"Follow me, Sophia. Let's go somewhere a little more private."

I take Cove's hand and we walk down the hall to his place. My heart races and my legs feel like rubber as he closes the door, locking us inside.

He turns and looks at me, a deep hunger in his eyes.

"Have you been thinking about me?" he asks.

I nod, my desire to have him so powerful that I'm incapable of forming any words. He walks past me, reaching for a set of switches on the wall; one dims the lights, the other closes all of the blinds in the room.

In one sudden swoop I'm off my feet and carried abruptly to the dining room table, my ass planted firmly onto its surface. I open my mouth, but Cove places his finger immediately over my lips, silencing me.

"Shh. Not a word," his voice low and restrained.

He slides the mid-length, black cotton dress I'm wearing up to reveal my sheer, burgundy, lace trimmed panties. His eyes close for a moment and he lets out a huff of air, as if he's about to come. I lean back on the table and he slides my underwear down my legs, and then lifts my dress further up past my hips.

My head falls back and my chest rises high the moment his lips brush against my flesh. His moist tongue lunges inside of my inner space, instantly causing my juices to erupt. I'm dripping wet, craving more. He gently snakes around, and then back out, flicking my spot. I moan and Cove hushes me, demanding silence. My legs tense as his finger touches my sensitive skin, replacing his tongue.

Moving his finger gently up and down, back and forth, swirling it over my pounding, female erection. I'm disoriented, unable to focus my eyes.

His warm tongue returns, sliding further into my body as his finger rubs my clit, gradually gaining speed. My hands try to clench the table, in search of stability, but to no avail. I writhe with my approaching orgasm. He tightens his hands around my hips, holds me steady, and continues to pleasure me, advancing into faster and more powerful movements.

The release I've been waiting for is intense, nearly causing me to pass out. Cove's name is on the tip of my tongue as quick pulsations shoot through my body, down my legs, and up through my chest. I gasp in search for air, as my body quivers on the table. He stops, plunges hastily over me, and pushes his tongue into my mouth. I pant heavily, air rushing out my nose. His tongue assaults mine, the breathing between us violent as he lifts me off the table and carries me into a first floor bedroom.

The room is similar to the guest bedroom in my place, only Cove's decorating tastes are far more elegant. A low, dark colored dresser lines one wall, covered from end to end with small white candles. They glimmer in the dark room now that the sun has set, and the blinds are tightly shut. I wonder how long they've been lit, and if all of this was planned. He releases my mouth and lowers me onto a king-size bed covered in a pure white comforter. I sink down into it, like I've been laid in a deep pile of snow.

He takes off his jeans, and then releases himself from his boxers. His erection is solid, glowing in the candlelight.

"Take off your dress, Sophia, I want to feel your skin pressed against mine."

Without hesitation, I slide my dress up over my head,

throwing it down on the floor next to him.

He unbuttons his shirt and walks over to the dresser, pulling open the top drawer. I hear a bottle open, and then a squish of fluid. He walks back to me, his enormous cock hovering between the two of us.

"Turn your body so your head is at the foot of the bed."

I follow his instructions, not questioning how or where he wants me. He straddles my stomach, his shaft resting on my chest between my breasts.

"Make sure you stop me if I start to hurt you. I want you to enjoy yourself."

I nod again, unable to speak as tiny pulsations flow around my inner lips from my still fresh orgasm.

Cove wipes his hand down my cleavage, leaving a line of lubrication on my skin. Pushing my breasts together, he lodges himself between them; sliding himself through the middle space. His crown reaches my chin, and then touches my lips on deep thrusts. He moans with pleasure, closing his eyes, his lips parted in lust. I lift my head and allow him entrance into my mouth with each forward movement.

"That's it, Sophia," his voice yearning for more. "Keep your mouth open for me."

He slides across my chest, squeezing my breasts tightly against his cock until he releases himself. A hand is placed on my head, and his entire length pushed into my mouth.

"I ache for you right now," he groans, fucking my mouth, deeper, faster.

He takes my head in both hands, his shaft moving intensely in and out. My gag reflex takes over as he thrusts further inside.

"Tell me when it's too much," he repeats, looking down at my face. My eyes water, and he diminishes the deep penetration from the back of my throat, moving slowly, with less intensity. My tongue circles around his long mass; flicking his sensitive head as he pushes in, and then sucking hard as he pulls back out.

His shirt hangs off his body, revealing a scar on his right shoulder and a tattoo that says *NOVA* above his left nipple. His abdominal muscles tighten as he prepares for a powerful orgasm.

The penetration of my mouth is fast and deep, prohibiting me from speaking. I'm left only with small gasps of air. My eyes continue to water with each inward attack, his width doubling, as his arousal grows closer to an end. Finally, I grab his hand, unable to take another lunge.

"I'm there," he gasps, propelling a final deep push, nearly drowning me in flesh and cum. His warm juice hits my throat in strong bursts, and he holds himself still until the last drop shoots out.

I turn my head, trying to slide his length out of my mouth. He pulls back as I gulp for air, wheezing with each inhaled breath. He slides down, kisses my mouth, and enjoys the taste of himself.

"Cove," a familiar voice speaks next to the bed. I turn to see Leondra, wearing the same golden colored robe that she had on the other night.

"Cove, Paul needs to speak with you," she says, handing him her phone.

"Oh my God." I jump up and reach for my dress, still panting for air.

"Sophia, please," his mother says in a quiet voice. "Please honey, don't be embarrassed. Just get dressed so I can walk you back to your place."

Cove has a look of hatred on his face as he grabs the phone from her. "You could've waited, Mother. This is completely inappropriate."

"Cove, darling," she replies in a tender voice. "Paul called me. You need to talk to him."

I frantically pull my dress over my head, as he sits on the bed, looking straight ahead, at a loss as to what to do.

"Answer the phone, Cove," his mother says, holding my underwear that I left in the other room. I snatch them from her, nearly falling over as I slide the panties back on.

He places the phone to his ear and sighs; my father clearly hears that he's finally on the line.

"Cove Everton, keep that dick of yours in your pants!" my father screams through the phone. Cove looks down at the bed, as I race out of his penthouse, and back to my place.

Mera's standing in my living room as I walk in and shut the door.

"What gives? You were supposed to call me back, and then when I called you didn't pick up your phone? I was worried about you Soph. And why is your door unlocked? And why are you so flushed? What the hell happened to you?"

"Oh my God, Mera. I don't know. I can't even start to piece together what just happened," I say, tears rolling down my face from the horror of Cove's mother and my father interrupting the two of us. "I was with Cove and all of a sudden his mother was there in the room with us." My body shudders, as I feel reprimanded by Leondra, humiliated by my father, and degraded by Cove. I fall to the floor in absolute sadness, sobbing as Mera attempts to calm me down. She patiently listens, trying to decipher what happened between the blubbering sounds that I spew out.

"Slow down, Soph. I can't understand you."

My phone rings and it can only be one person. Mera lunges for the counter before I have a chance to move.

"Mr. Jameson?" she roars. "Yes, I mean Paul. I don't think this is a good time to speak to your daughter, she's pretty upset."

"Mera, put her on the phone, now."

"No. I don't think so. You've done enough damage for one day. I thought her mother was bad, but now I'm beginning to wonder if it's the whole damn family."

"First of all, don't ever compare me to Sophia's mother. As my employee you should show some respect for your boss. Bite your tongue and keep your words to yourself. Second, you have no idea what's going on, and neither does Sophia, so put her on the line so I can talk to her."

I hear Mera say no again, and she rolls her eyes at me. My father says something else, and she hangs up the phone. She waits, holding it in her hand as an email comes through. She opens it, her face turns white, then she looks my way in a panic.

"I'm sorry Sophia, but your father's right, you need to see this."

Mera hands me the phone and I look down at the site my father just sent. The title of the site is Hidden Live Cam, and it shows Cove and I in the candlelit room. The camera is on him, and now I understand why he asked me to turn toward the foot of the bed. It's a front shot of him ramming his cock inside my mouth.

The scene instantly causes me to vomit down the front of Mera's shirt. It's only a friend such as her who doesn't rally to move away when being thrown up on. My phone rings again and this time it gets tossed across the room. Mera stands to answer it, but I stop her.

"Leave it alone, Mera. I need some time."

"Sorry, Soph. I don't have all the details on what just went down, and this is way too fucked up to stay silent." She picks up the phone and brings it back over, placing it in my hand. "Answer it."

"Dad? Why did you do that? Why did you send me that video?"

"Because you need to know what kind of monster he is, Sophia. He had no right to make that violent video of you, especially without your knowledge. That's not how my business works. I'm flying out tomorrow to speak to him, and I want to meet with you as well. We need to talk about all of this in person."

"What just happened? I don't understand what's going on, Dad? I thought he owned a wine bar, and I thought you hired him as a bodyguard for me. So his business relationship with you is actually the online sites?" Mera listens in on the conversation while rubbing my back as I sob into the phone.

"He used to work for me, but he doesn't anymore, you can count on that," my father slams his fist on something hard, and I hear a crash.

"Answer my question."

"Yes, we're involved in the online business together."

"Just use the word porn, Dad."

"Fine. As you wish. He's also one of my top suppliers of fresh, young…" he pauses, searching for words.

"Meat?"

"No; women, Sophia. Young women. I try not to use words like that when referring to my employees, which is why I'm completely alarmed at what I just saw on my screen. My online sites don't abuse women, and I sure as fuck don't want my daughter to be in any porn. Plus, Cove hasn't been in any videos in years. I don't know what the fuck's going on with him. He just crossed a lot of lines with me, and he's done. I need you out of that building and away from him. I only hired him to keep you from harm if there was a situation. Now he *is* the situation."

"No. I'm not moving. I'm pissed out of my mind at both you and Cove, but I'm not leaving."

"I'll be there tomorrow, Sophia. Be ready."

"Ready for what?"

My father hangs up without hearing my final words.

"Soph, what can I do?" Mera asks. "I feel so helpless right now. Do you want me to go punch that guy in the gonads?"

I let out a brief laugh knowing she's trying her best to heal my mind, body, and heart. "Which one?" I ask her.

"The left one I suppose."

Laughing hysterically now, I stand and head to my bathroom, needing to splash some cool water on my face. "No, I meant which person? My father or Cove?"

"I know what you meant," she yells, sending a giggling snort my way. "Remember his name Soph, you're entering the world of a person who harbors wild boars."

CHAPTER FIFTEEN

Wednesday evening is another session of nude modeling. I'm not much in the mood for it today after suffering through yesterday's events, and I know my father will be at my place when I return home. I'll have to thank Mera again for spending the night at my place. She can really cheer me up when I'm at my worst, and I was close to hitting rock bottom when I saw the online video of Cove and myself. I wonder if my father's talked to Roger and Diane about my knowledge of their job? What a complete joke my life is. What's real at this point is beyond my comprehension.

The class is full as I walk into the room and I know the professor mentioned last time that tonight would be an open class, meaning anyone from the community is allowed to sit in and draw. In the back row are a group of older men. Most of them look like they're reaching the age of retirement, and they might just be here to see a nude young woman without having to be labeled as perverts by their wives.

I slip off my pants and sweater from behind the screen and step back into the classroom. The bright lights block some of the faces, but I can still see the outline of figures, knowing that it's a full house. Close to forty people.

"Okay class," the professor says in a raised voice,

trying to quiet the room. "Sophia will be modeling for us again this evening, and like last week with Monroe, we will focus on her mid-section. Please Sophia, have a seat on the stool." He walks onto the platform, and I sit on the cold metal piece of furniture. He stands directly in front of me, slightly parting my legs with his hand.

"Go ahead and put your hands behind yourself on the stool, and lean back in the same position Monroe was in last class, bringing your feet onto the rungs."

I follow his instructions and lean back, my private area exposed.

"Is this okay for you?" he asks. "Comfortable enough?"

"Fine, thanks," I reply.

My eyes start to adjust and I see Matt in the front row, looking directly at my sensitive area he's about to draw.

"Class, as with Monroe's penis last week, I'm looking for the correct proportions in this drawing, then a change in value from light areas, into the dark folds and shadows. Save the fine details of the pubic hair for last. Let's spend thirty minutes, and then we'll move on to the breasts."

"What pubic hair?" someone calls out, sending the class into instant laughter.

"Okay, or lack thereof," the professor says. "Let's calm down everyone and have a good drawing class. We shouldn't have any incidents like we did last week, so focus and draw. You may begin."

While I'm in this position I can only think about Cove going down on me yesterday, his tongue flicking my sweet spot. I have to be careful not to get turned on while students are exploring my vagina with their eyes. Small twitches and any lubrication that forms will be noticeable, and just as embarrassing as the erection they experienced on Monroe.

"Let's go ahead and play some music to pass the time, does anyone have their iPod with them? If so, feel free to put something on that's appropriate for the masses."

A student stands, connecting his iPod to the system. A heavy metal song blasts out, startling a few people in the room. I question if this is suitable for a figure drawing class; a nice piano concerto would be more relaxing to me, but then again, I'm not the one sitting at a desk trying to draw a vagina.

I scan the rows and don't see Roger and Diane, but then, in the middle of the room directly in front of me, is the one person I'd never expect to see here tonight. My eyes fall to her heavily covered tattooed right leg, moving up to a pair of black capris, a brown suede button down shirt, black scarf, and a plethora of gold jewelry.

Leondra.

She sits three rows back, almost directly in front of me with a clear view of my genital area. Her eyes meet mine and she sends that warm motherly smile my way.

I sit on the metal stool frozen like a statue. Oh. My. God. She can't be my new protection. No way. Maybe it's just a coincidence. Dammit. I want to close my legs and hide. *Don't look down there. Stop looking down there Leondra. Yes, I know your son had his tongue in my vagina. Stop smiling. What's making you so happy? How can you look at my pubic area after your son's face was down there?*

"Students, please remember to draw the vaginal area. I can see that some of you are drawing the hips, and upper legs, but leaving out the part that I'd like you to focus on today. Don't be timid, as an art student, you will be drawing nudes for two semesters, ending the year with a full figure drawing of yourself."

"Naked?" a student asks.

"Yes, you will all be required to draw yourself nude, in front of a mirror."

"In the classroom?" another student asks. "I'm not stripping down naked in front of my friends."

"No, not in the room. It's a two-week assignment that you work on outside of class. This is your time to practice getting used to the male and female form, and how to create observational drawings from what's in front of you. Now, focus everyone, let's get back to our work for today. We are drawing the female body, and yes, that includes the vagina and later on this evening, the breasts."

The entire class lowers their eyes to the area set deep inside my open legs. The women are focused, with wrinkled foreheads and a determination on their faces, while the men's eyes aren't quite as driven. They smile and glare. Some stuck in a daydream, others blushing, taking quick glances down below, but mostly staring at their paper.

Leondra is still absorbed with the inside of my legs, her face beaming with joy as she draws my vagina. I can only imagine what role she has in my father's business - a former porn star? – Cove's manager? - website designer for the St. Louis companies? - or just a concerned mother? Being asked to interrupt Cove and me in the bedroom gives me a better idea of the relationship she has with my dad, and although I haven't asked him about her, I will.

I can't relax, or meditate, or even daydream this evening. My practice of using modeling as a confidence builder, and as a time for contemplation, has been eradicated by Leondra Everton. I count seconds in my head, waiting for each minute to pass as my arms lock and then shake in frustration. It's a difficult pose to hold for thirty minutes, especially when all eyes are focused on one area of flesh.

"A few more minutes everyone, and then we'll take a quick break so that Sophia can stretch," the professor says.

I smile at him, knowing that he can sense my strain, and perhaps even an unspoken embarrassment about this evening's pose. Scanning the room, I finally see Roger in the second to last row, drawing intently as he always does. Diane isn't with him this evening and I wonder if she's okay.

Finally, I'm able to close my legs and straighten my back, bringing my arms forward. I lean down, stretching my arms out toward the floor.

"Class, let's take a walk around the room to view everyone's drawing. Give advice to your classmates for areas in need of improvement, and offer constructive criticism. This will allow our model to have a short break."

The students begin circling the room, chatting with their friends about papers that are due in other classes, and parties that are developing for the weekend. Roger walks up to me and reaches his hand out, wrapping his strong fingers around mine.

"Good evening, Sophia. I'm sorry if you think that my wife and I are only here to watch over you. We are enjoying the class and it's a bonus to be able to learn new skills as we do our other job."

"I understand, Roger. No hard feelings at all. So where's Diane?"

"She has her second evening of modeling at the college she talked to you about. I've never seen her so happy and excited about something besides our son. You've definitely inspired her to try new things."

"I'm glad," I say, while taking a break from the stool. I stand, twisting my upper torso first to the left, and then to the right to prepare for my next pose.

The professor admires his student's drawings, stopping at the best ones to point out areas of excellent shading, blending, and accurate form. "Whoa, what have we here," he says. "Who created this drawing?"

"I did," Leondra says, walking over to him.

"You must have some training in figure drawing."

"Yes, I have a terminal degree in fine art and took many years of drawing back in the day."

"Class, I'd like everyone to walk by this drawing, examine the fine details, the outstanding use of line, and extraordinary photo-realistic results that she obtained through accurate observational skills. She keeps her pencils sharp, and focuses on the most important areas in front of her. This is a beautiful drawing."

I place my robe over my shoulders and walk over to Leondra's drawing, wanting to see this masterpiece for myself. Students are in awe, with true astonishment on their faces as they pass by the drawing. It's beautiful.

She was able to make my body look elegant and sexy, using extreme lights and darks. Her technique and advanced skill creates a drawing that resembles a photograph, and I'm just as bewildered as the rest of the class.

"I hope you like it, Sophia," she says in a soft voice.

"I'm amazed. Thank you." I respond in a stupefied tone. "You are a remarkable artist, although I'm a little embarrassed by the subject matter."

"Oh sweetie, please. I've seen millions of these things. I have one myself you know," she says in her usual warm way. Lowering her voice once more, she continues on in a hushed whisper. "I didn't know you were the model for this class, Sophia. I'm not here spying on you, so please don't think that your father sent me. I came on my own, and only because I miss being around other artists sometimes. If I had known you did this, I would've chosen another night, or another location."

She sounds sincere and I give her an understanding nod. She may be the one person I can trust right now, and after hearing all of this, I'm beginning to like her. Maybe she didn't mean any disrespect yesterday in the bedroom. She could have just been looking out for me, and her son. I look away from the drawing and into her face, giving her my warmest smile back. She looks relieved and places her hand on my arm, rubbing gently in a back and forth motion.

"You're beautiful, my dear," she says. "And don't ever forget it."

***

Leondra left the class after drawing my breasts and didn't stay for the second half of the evening, which was a one-hour full body pose. I was happy to leave wearing my warm clothes, concealing myself from the world. The pleasure I used to feel from nude modeling has waned, and I don't know if that's because Cove's mother was in the room, or because of my new interest in him. I suddenly lack any desire to show my body to anyone else.

I need to talk to him about yesterday to find out if he has any feelings for me, and if he does, then why he would do what he did. I can only assume that his real motivation was simply to make a buck for the company. After displaying so much kindness in the past, and with a gentle voice like his mother's, I'm in total disbelief that he would do such a thing. I'm the type of person who demands answers when dealing with deceitful people, and I need to know what happened between us.

The elevator door to my floor opens and I hesitate, knowing that my father will be waiting for me at my place. I see a small red splattering of what appears to be blood on the wall next to my front door, and when I step into the hall for a closer look I see Leondra frantically pacing outside Cove's door. There's a large gentleman standing outside with her. He holds her back as she tries to squeeze past him, into her son's place.

I hear a thud, and the sound of breaking glass before my mind is able to process the sight before me. I immediately run down to his door, trying to break through the large body blocking the entrance.

"Get out of my way, you fucker," my hands pounding on his chest.

There's a groan from the penthouse, and then a loud smack as a fist comes into contact with the flesh of another person.

Leondra calls out her son's name then pleads with my father to stop.

My knee hurtles into the groin of the man blocking my path, and I swiftly take my chance, pressing through the small space between him and the opening before me.

Cove's on his hands and knees, his head down as blood drips from his mouth and chin. My father kicks him in the stomach and he falls hard against the floor.

"You dumb fuck! How dare you treat my daughter and my business this way," he turns Cove's head and punches him again and again in the face, spewing blood across the room.

I jump on my father's back, kicking and screaming for him to stop. Cove coughs and gasps for air as he puts his arm over his face, shielding himself from the blows. My father stops his violent rampage, and I'm pulled off of his back and restrained by the brute from the hallway.

"Stop Dad, leave him alone!" I scream.

"Let her go, Trey." The guy releases me as I swing my arm, making solid contact across my father's face. He steps back, placing his hand up to his jaw as I rush past him, and down to the floor where Cove is lying; blood pouring out of his nose.

"Cove," I say, sliding his hair off of his face.

My father lifts me up, placing his strong arms around my chest so that I'm unable to move. I kick my legs, trying to wiggle away.

"Put me down, you asshole."

"Take care of your son," he says, passing Leondra on our way out of the penthouse.

My father carries me back to my place, the big guy following close behind. He lowers me to my feet when we get inside, and I slap his face, harder this time, showing my anger.

"I can't believe you just beat the hell out of someone. You're the monster, Dad, not him."

"Oh, so you're okay with some guy using a hidden camera on you while raping your mouth? Is that how you want to live your life, Sophia? I'm not the enemy here, and don't you forget it." His voice is loud, piercing, ruthless. "I spent an entire day trying to remove that video from hundreds of sites and companies that re-posted it online. I've received calls all day from my best clients, demanding to see you and Cove again. What the fuck am I going to do now in order to satisfy these people? Answer me that,

Sophia." He looks over to his body guard, who closes the door, locking us in. "I can't have my daughter highlighted as a star on these sites, and that's exactly what I'm being pressured to do by my wealthiest stockholders. Cove got what he deserved, and he knows it."

"Did you ask him why he did it?"

"Yes, and it's just as I thought. It's also none of your business. My relationship with Cove and Leondra goes way back, and you need to get him out of your head. Now pack a bag, I'm taking you over to Mera's."

"No, I want to talk to Cove to make sure he's alright. I'm not going anywhere. This is my place, and my life."

"No, Sophia, it's not. You're a part of my life, and because of that, you have to do as I say. There is no negotiating, now pack a bag. Either you stay with Mera until I take care of your living situation, or you're flying back to Vegas to live with me. I'll carry you kicking and screaming if I have to, but I'm not leaving you here right now."

"Well, maybe I should just be one of your stars. How do you like that idea? Then this would all be resolved."

"Get your bag," his tone harsh and direct.

I'm trapped. My father is a large man, and powerful as well. Plus, he brought reinforcements along. I have no choice but to do as he says. I stomp like a four-year-old up the stairs into my bedroom, taking a suitcase out of my closet, and throwing my necessities inside. It only takes a few minutes before I'm dragging the bag back down, throwing it at my father's feet.

"Happy?"

"I'm sorry I'm so angry, Sophia, but trust me, I'm doing what's best for us."

"You, not us. I think you're looking out for yourself,

and not listening to anything I have to say. I love my place, and I enjoy my privacy. I'm going to the therapy you set up, and I've applied for jobs. I have feelings for Cove, but would never allow him to treat me the way he did ever again. I think I'm becoming a strong woman and I should be able to make my own decisions. You're basically taking away my freedom."

"You're right. I am. This is an extreme situation, and we'll get through it, but I need you to trust me that it's what's best for our family."

"I don't trust you, Dad. Not now. Not after seeing you beat someone to a bloody pulp. Not after forcing me to leave my home."

He cruelly ignores my words, picking up my bag and walking me to the front door.

"Leondra will watch Lewis for you," is the only response that comes out of his mouth.

***

I place my bag down in Mera's spare bedroom and lay face down on her bed, my head on the pillow, sulking, as my father and Mera talk in the kitchen. She's pissed at my dad and doesn't understand why I need to stay away from Cove.

"Sophia can make her own decisions, and if she has feelings for him, even after what he did to her, so be it." I hear her say.

I place the pillow over my head, blocking out their conversation. If only I had Cove's number. I'd call him right now. My heart tells me he has feelings for me, but my brain is warning me to stay away. I won't know until we're together in the same room again if my feelings are real, or if it's just lust.

I lift my head, feeling Mera's hand on my shoulder.

"Hey, Babe. You doing okay?"

I throw an evil eye her way, burying my head forcefully into the pillow.

"Soph, your dad left, but that giant bear who was with him is parked outside my door making sure you don't leave."

"What?" I say in disgust. Sitting abruptly up on the bed. "I feel like I've been kidnapped."

"Yeah, I have no doubt about that one. Your dad's being a dick. He went back to your place to talk to the Evertons."

"He better not lay another finger on Cove, or I'm going to call the cops on him."

"You'd do that?"

"Yeah, I think so."

"I think your dad isn't able to process what you did with Cove and he's taking it all out on him. Of course, Cove is at fault for the video, but he didn't do anything to you that you didn't want him to, right?"

"That's right. I could've stopped him at any time. He didn't force me to do anything. I actually enjoyed myself until I found out half the world was watching." I pause for a moment, thinking back to the past three hours. "You know it's strange, Mera, I don't mind stripping in front of college students for money, so how is this any different?"

"The only difference is that you didn't know you had an audience," she says.

"My father's concerned about the effect this might have on his company, but if they don't know I'm his daughter then I don't see why he's making such a fuss about all of this. I mean, don't you think he could just post a whole bunch of videos with new young talent to calm his clients? They would forget about me in an instant."

"That's his plan, Soph. He already spoke to me about something for tomorrow. So yeah, that's exactly what's about to happen."

"Oh Mera, I'm sorry."

"Don't apologize. I'm not worried. Come on, let's order some food and have a beer. It'll make you feel better."

"That's exactly what I need right now. I haven't eaten yet today." I send her a smile as she does her best to calm me down. I feel awful that my interaction yesterday has caused her to start business with my father a week early.

Mera and I spend the evening talking about Cove, Leondra, and my father while eating pizza and wings, and drinking a few beers. She calls information, and looks online, trying to come up with a phone number for Cove.

"Is there anything else you want to look up? Should we do some shopping?"

"Actually Mera, yeah. Cove has a tattoo that says NOVA above his left nipple. What's the exact definition of that word?"

"Okay, let's see. N-O-V-A." she types the letters into her laptop. "Well, according to Wikipedia, a nova is a cataclysmic nuclear explosion in a white dwarf star."

"Hmm. Sounds pretty," I respond. "A white dwarf star explosion."

"Yeah, that does sound rather nice. You know, some women have that name, maybe it's a tattoo for a former lover."

"Perhaps. What do other sites say?" I ask, feeling on edge and unable to sleep worrying about Cove.

"There's also a television series called NOVA, and on

another site it's the National Organization for Victim Assistance."

"That's interesting."

"Yeah, I've seen that show once or twice when I was young."

"No, the victim assistance site. Anything else?"

"Not really. Let's type in NOVA tattoos and see what comes up."

There's a knock on the entry door and Mera stands, closing her laptop as she walks over to the kitchen.

"Want another beer while I'm up?"

"No, just see who's at the door."

Mera opens the door to see my father's guard holding a large box.

"Someone left this for you ladies."

"Bring it in, Mera, let's have a look."

She takes the box from his hands and locks her door, carrying the package back to the sofa.

"It has your name on it, Soph. It says it's from Leondra."

"My name? What is it?"

"I haven't got a clue, open it and find out."

I release the tape from the box top, noticing that it's already been cut open and checked by our burly friend outside. He did his best to reseal the box, but it's obvious that nothing's getting into Mera's place without his approval. As I pull the cardboard flaps, a red balloon floats out, with a note tied to the end of its string."

"Cool. That's kind of cute. Is it really from her?"

"No," I say, rolling my eyes. "You know who it's *really* from," I respond, opening the note in a rush. My fingers tremble, as I've been longing for contact from Cove since the interruption in the bedroom.

"What does it say, come on, read it out loud."

"It says, 'I'm sorry. I didn't mean to hurt you'."

Mera takes the note from my hand, turning it over to search for more words. "That's it?"

"It's enough. That's all it needed to say." I smile, looking at the balloon. "Look, There's something tiny on the inside."

"Where?"

I poke the balloon with my finger, but it won't burst. Mera takes one of her sharp nails and pierces the latex. There's a loud pop sending us into laughter as a tiny pill rolls onto the floor coming to rest at Mera's foot. She picks it up, studies it, and then places it in my hand.

"What is it, Soph?"

"I believe it might be my escape."

"What do you mean?"

"I think it might be to drug Trey."

"That guy outside? No way. I'm not drugging anyone. We could go to jail, or worse. What if the pill kills him? Throw it out."

"It's a sleeping pill."

"You don't know that. Get rid of it. Game over."

"Cove wouldn't do this unless he needed to talk to me. What if my father makes him move to another city, and I never see him again?"

"God, would he do that?"

"I wouldn't put it past him, not after what I saw today."

"Yeah, but again Soph, you don't even know Cove. What if he's dangerous like your father keeps saying? Just wait and see what happens tomorrow."

"My father's going to be working pretty quickly over the next day to separate the two of us, and that either means I'm leaving, or Cove is. I think my dad's to a point where he doesn't even want us in the same state."

"What if your dad went to talk to him, to find out if he even likes you? If he doesn't have feelings for you, then this could all be over. Your father will no longer feel threatened."

"I don't know. I guess I have a big head, thinking that I may be in love, and it's mutual."

"Holy fucking shit sticks. Did you say love?" Mera stands and walks to the kitchen, taking another beer out of the fridge for herself. "I need more to drink. Sophia Jameson, in love? I've known you for almost seven years and you've never used that word on any man. When did this come about?"

"Well, obviously over the past week," I say with a smile.

"I don't think you can fall in love that quickly. It must be lust that you're feeling."

"I'm trying to figure it all out, but I think it's more than just a need for his body. Cove's gorgeous, but also interesting, warm, and a delight to be around. I've been thinking about him constantly over the past week, and not just in a sexual way. I wouldn't mind just going out to dinner with him, or having a conversation over coffee."

"Wow, Soph," Mera says, sitting next to me, grinning from ear to ear. "I'm speechless."

"So, don't you think I should take a chance? I need to talk to him before it's too late."

Mera takes a big gulp of beer, then another. And another. I look over at her, waiting for a response. She swirls her beer around in the bottle, then drinks again.

"Mera?"

"I'm thinking," she says.

Standing, she leaves me alone in her living room, shutting herself behind her bedroom door. She may have had enough of me for one night, and my constant chatter about Cove.

Moments later she returns, wearing only a short, silky black robe.

"If we're going to do this, we're going to do it my way. No drugs. I won't give a person something when I don't know what it is."

"What are you going to do?"

"You're going to fix my bed to make it look like you're asleep in my room. Use that mannequin head that I have, and stuff the rest of the bed with pillows. I'll light a candle in there so that it's too dark to make out anything more than an outline."

"Mera, I think we should use the pill."

"I want you to be in the other bedroom. I'll lure our friend, what did you call him again? Trey? into my living room so he can see the fake Sophia sleeping in bed while I entertain him on the sofa. He'll think that he's doing his job, and getting a bonus on the side."

"He'll never go for that. These people who work for my father aren't idiots. He's not going to jeopardize his job for some pussy."

"Excuse me?" Mera's voice is in disagreement with my last comment. She stands in front of me, opening her robe to reveal her beautiful soft white body. She's recently waxed, and again, I'm reminded of Cove's words about the purity of snow. She looks like a new bride, untouched, perfection.

"I take that back."

"You're only two blocks away but you can take my car if you want."

"No, if you can get this to work, I'll be running. It will take me just as long to pull out of your garage, and then find a spot to park outside my building. But, do you really want to do this?"

"Yes. I need to. I haven't in a while and if I'm going to be on camera tomorrow, I want to practice with someone."

"Really? You're really going to do this for me?"

"Yes, Sophia Jameson," she laughs, "I will seduce the guard standing outside my door so that you can escape."

"That sounds so bizarre to me right now. So when are we going to do this?"

"I'm going to start to set it up right now. When I open the door, walk up behind me and say that you're going to sleep. Ask me for a clean bathroom towel."

"Whatever you say." I walk into the kitchen, placing my empty beer bottle on the counter. Mera heads for the entryway; turning to make sure I'm ready. I give her a reassuring nod, and she opens the door.

"Hey stranger," she says to Trey. "Do you need anything before we get settled in here for the night?"

I slowly walk up behind Mera, playing my part. "I'm getting tired, Mera. I think I'll head off to bed."

Mera turns her head allowing the robe to slide off her shoulder, revealing her gorgeous breast. She pulls it immediately back up, turning back to Trey the moment it's covered. His eyes look down, and then quickly back up to her face.

"Excuse me, I'm sorry," she says to him.

I continue with my line, enjoying how incredible she is at all of this. "Do you have a clean bath towel that I can use?"

"Sure, it's in the hall closet, next to the bathroom."

I walk away, hearing Mera ask him again if she can get him anything.

"No, I'm fine. You ladies have a nice night. I'll be right outside if you need anything."

"Are you sure?" she says in her sexiest voice. "A beer or a soda?"

"No ma'am. I'm just fine."

"Well, how about a cold glass of water?"

I can picture Mera leaning against her doorframe, looking like a dog in heat as she speaks.

There's a brief pause, and then he nibbles at the bait. "Okay, a glass of water would be nice."

"Wait here. I'll be right back."

Mera fills a glass, then heads back to the open door, handing him the drink. "You can give the glass back to me in the morning."

"Thank you. I appreciate that."

Mera closes the door and I walk out of her bedroom. I smile, giving her a high-five and a grateful smack on the lips.

"You're the best," I say, hugging her tightly. "I think this just might work."

"All men will jeopardize their jobs for some pussy, Soph. Think about it."

Cove could be referenced in that line, and I nod in complete understanding.

"So what do we do now?"

"We wait," she says. "In about an hour, I'll ask him if he needs anything else before I head off to bed. I guarantee he'll ask to use the bathroom."

"Smart."

"I know, right? When he comes in, you can sneak out from the guest bedroom."

We wait. I pace. Back and forth hoping this will work, and if it does, how will I get to Cove? I wonder where my father's staying tonight and if he's watching Cove's place. Maybe he's at Leondra's, or my loft, or just standing in the hallway of my building keeping an eye on things. If I make it out of Mera's place without being caught, and I can't get to Cove, then maybe I should just vanish for a while. I can take money out of my account early tomorrow morning and stay in a hotel until things blow over. Yeah, that's a good plan.

"Mera, I may not come back."

"What do you mean?"

"Whether or not I find Cove, I think it would be best for me to disappear until my father calms down. He's being irrational and maybe if he has some time to cool off he'll let me go back to my place."

"I don't know, Soph," she says slowly, shaking her head no. "I agree with what you're thinking, but at the same time I don't see how it's possible to hide from your dad. Plus, he'll start watching my every move, waiting for us to be in contact with one another."

"I wouldn't tell you where to find me, and it wouldn't be for long. I'm not saying I'm going to do this. I just want you to know that if I don't come back, I'm okay, so don't worry."

"Well, once you walk out that door you will either get caught at your building or when you come back here. If you don't want to deal with your father when he figures everything out, then go ahead and find a hotel somewhere, but he'll never believe that I don't know where you are," she pauses, placing her hands on my shoulders. "You ready?"

"Yeah, let's do this."

CHAPTER SIXTEEN

T he cold wind cuts into me like a knife as I race the two blocks south down Eleventh Street. Mera was absolutely right. I can't believe I ever doubted her plan. Trey was actually the one who requested to use her bathroom before she turned in for the night. As he came in, I rushed out into the frozen air. I hope she's okay. I won't be able to thank her enough for doing this for me. When Trey walks into the bathroom he'll be able to see the dummy in her bed from a distance, and he might just end up going back out into the hallway after he relieves himself. Mera may decide not to attempt her other plan of keeping him occupied with her body, which would make me feel a hell of a lot better. She's done enough for me tonight.

I have on my black hip-length, wool, double-breasted coat, and a black scarf that's wrapped around my head for warmth. My phone and keys are in my pocket. I arrive at my building and head around back, walking quietly down the ramp and into the underground parking garage. There's an emergency stairwell next to the elevator that will be my best bet to reach the top floor unseen, and unheard. My heart pounds from the swift walk and anticipation of seeing Cove. I stop to catch my breath, calming myself before I reach for the handle of the stairway door.

An arm wraps around my chest and a hand covers my mouth. I'm lifted up from behind, and carried kicking to a dark Mercedes-Benz SUV. The back door flies open and I'm laid on the floor, a body hovering over mine.

"Shh. Sophia, it's me."

Cove's voice puts an end to my struggle for escape. I lay motionless. He lowers his hand from my mouth and rolls off, sits up, but stays positioned on the floor.

"Keep low. Don't stand up. I don't want anyone to see us."

I roll off my stomach and rest on my bottom, staying low in the vehicle. The lights in the garage shine into the window and I can see his battered face.

I reach my hand out toward him and he shudders, turning his head slightly away. There's a cut on his lip, his nose is swollen, his eye black and blue. I'm appalled at the harm my father caused, and his hatred for Cove.

"Sophia, I'm so sorry. I didn't mean to hurt you or to treat you so poorly. I wish I could take back everything that I did yesterday."

"I'm sorry too, Cove."

"What are you sorry for? You didn't do anything wrong. This is all my fault."

"I'm sorry about my father. I'm sorry about what he did to you."

"Don't feel bad for me. I got what I deserved. You're the victim here, Sophia, not me." He pauses and looks around the garage to make sure we're alone, and then slides down on the floor closer to me. "I'm glad you were able to make it back. So the pill worked?"

"No. We didn't use it."

Cove looks stunned and worried that I may have been followed. "How did you get past Trey?"

"Mera. She's a genius sometimes. She decided to seduce him instead of drugging him, with water first, filling his bladder so he'd have to come inside, and then after I made it out, possibly with sex as well."

"Whoa. She'd do that for you?"

"Well, that's what friends are for."

"I wouldn't know." He looks down, and I can tell he has more than just yesterday on his mind.

"Where's my father?" I ask.

"With my mother. He stays with her when he's in town."

"He's never mentioned your mother to me before," I say, thinking about the last time my father had a girlfriend. I actually can't remember him ever mentioning another woman besides my mother.

"He's watching over her, over us I should say. As far as I know, they're not a couple, and if anything ever did happen between the two of them, well, that would be the ultimate deceit."

Cove looks worried again, checking the garage, and then looking back into my eyes. "Your father should be in for the night, as long as Trey doesn't figure anything out and call him. Are you sure everything's okay back at your friend's place?"

"Yeah, if it wasn't, Mera would call me."

He reaches his hand out to mine and squeezes it, just like his mother did the other evening in the hallway. I want to touch his battered face, but I know he'll just back away.

"You must be in so much pain."

"Yes, in my ribs and in my stomach, but my face probably looks a lot worse than it feels. I don't want you to touch it or to try to caress me, but not because it hurts. I'm just not deserving of that form of kindness from you right now."

"Cove, how can you say that?" I ask, seeing the disgust he has for himself about the website. "Tell me, why did you do that? What made you do that to me?"

He gives me another gentle squeeze, places his lips on my fingers and then runs small kisses along the palm of my hand. I melt, not even caring what his response will be.

"I wanted to hurt your father, but instead I ended up hurting you."

"Tell me, what's going on between the two of you?" I ask, taking my hand away so that he focuses on the situation that I'm in, being pitted between the two of them.

"It's your father, and my entire family. How much do you know about his past, Sophia?"

I think for a moment, not remembering much about our time together before he left. "I remember him being happy, and taking care of my brother and me when we were very little. He left when I was young, and I didn't see him again until I was in high school. He just showed up one day filthy rich, showering us with gifts to make up for abandoning the family. He's been feeling guilty about the past, trying to make up for all the lost years."

"Did he ever say what he was doing during the time that he was gone? Has he ever spoken to you about his past?"

"He said he went into business for himself, starting with one casino, then building an empire. I only found out recently about the porn sites. Now I know that most of his money is actually from that business."

"Well, he's made it big because of both businesses, but I think his guilt and the reappearance back into your life seven years ago has something to do with me and my father."

I've never heard Cove, Leondra, or my father mention Mr. Everton. I've wondered if Cove's parents were divorced, or if his father had passed away. I didn't see any family photos on the first two floors of his place, so I assumed they had an estranged relationship.

"I'm not sure I understand."

He looks at me and sighs; trying to speak but instead biting his bottom lip, locking his words inside. I slowly back away, showing him that I'm still weary from what I've heard from both him and my father.

"My father told me not to trust you. He said you're a monster."

Cove shakes his head, obviously repulsed by my words.

"And you believe him?"

"I don't know what to believe. I feel like I don't know anything about either one of you, but I also feel like I want both of you in my life. Tell me why you wanted to hurt my father, and what you mean by his reappearance in my life having something to do with your family."

"I can't tell you everything. If I do, my life and my mother's life will be over. We'll be out on the streets."

"Because of my dad?"

"Yes."

"I won't let that happen."

Cove laughs, throwing his head back in an obvious attempt to show how little I know about the situation. His guilt for hurting my feelings is present once again, and he quickly tries to smooth things over. "I'm sorry, Sophia. I didn't mean to laugh at you. It's just… you can't trust your father."

I'm the one who laughs this time as I feel a moment of déjà vu pass through me.

"Cove, my father keeps warning me to stay away from you, and that you're dangerous. Now I'm starting to hear the same things come out of your mouth about him. What am I supposed to do? Who am I supposed to believe?"

"You've already answered that question for yourself. Think about it. Neither one of us would be hiding out in this car like a couple of teenagers if we weren't sure about the other one. We both want the same thing. I like you Sophia, and I've never had the opportunity to feel this way about anyone. I've never been given the chance."

I smile, even more confused yet happy to hear those words. "Cove, you keep piling more and more on top of me. Tell me what I need to know so that we can figure out what to do next."

"The first thing we need to do is get out of this garage. My mother has set up a hotel room for us. We just need to get there."

"Your mother? She knows what you're doing right now? What if she tells my father?"

"It's alright, my mother's all I have. She'd give her life for me. We'll be safe at the hotel, and then we can talk without having to worry about any interruptions. But right now, I'm not comfortable and I don't want to take the chance of never being able to see you again, so the faster we get out of here, the better off we are."

Cove opens the door as quietly as he can, steps out, and reaches his hand my way. I look at him, not sure how to proceed.

"Sophia," he whispers. "We need to walk, it's only three blocks south of here. I'm sorry it's so cold outside, but it will be safer than taking a car there. Your father knows our cars."

He waits for me to make my decision, his arm

271

stretched out, hoping that I'll reach for him. I look around, glad that I told Mera I might not be back this evening. I'm amazed that Cove and I both had the same idea about disappearing, though I thought I would be by myself. It never crossed my mind that the two of us would leave together.

"Sophia, trust me," his voice hushed, still holding out his hand. I grab onto him and wrap my hand tightly into his as he pulls me out of the SUV. He gives me a warm hug as I reach his body.

"Thank you," he whispers into my ear. "Thank you for giving me a second chance."

We walk hurriedly out of the garage and back out into the city. A light snow starts to fall, disguising our forms as we walk down the street. Cove has his arm around me, steering me quickly along the snow blown sidewalk, keeping me warm.

***

Our room at The Atelier is on the seventh floor. It's exactly halfway up the building, and even though we don't have a presidential suite, I'm still impressed by the high-end finishes. There's a marble floor in the entry foyer that opens into an inviting living room. The space is warm and comforts both of us after being out in the cold. A fire has already been lit, and it glows in front of a large couch that's been placed in the middle of the room. There are windows to each side of the fireplace; each one covered with a heavy red curtain. The walls are painted gold, reminding me of Cove's mother and her opulent styling.

The room comes equipped with a kitchenette, a small table for dining, and a beautiful gold, white, and red Asian rug placed in front of the couch. French doors open into the bedroom with an attached large bath boasting a marble walk-in shower and jetted tub. The king-size bed has two suitcases, both open, and I can see some of my clothes in one. I send Cove a confused look, searching for an answer.

"My mother," he says. "She packed some of your things while I packed a bag for myself. She had everything sent over here. We managed to get it all together before your father came back."

"And what if I didn't show up at our building, or I decided not to come here with you?"

"Then somehow I would've returned your things. Does it matter?"

"No. I'm just not used to having a mother present in my life. Do you feel a lack of privacy sometimes? I mean it kind of seems like you guys are a bit too close. Don't you find that a bit strange?"

Cove throws a stunned look my way, and I immediately know I said something wrong.

"Well, Sophia. Don't you think it's a bit strange that you and your mother *aren't* close?" he inquires.

"No, she's a bitch, and she doesn't like me."

"Well, my mother isn't a bitch, and she loves me," he replies in a direct tone.

"Okay. I'm sorry. I didn't mean anything by it. It's just unusual based on how I grew up. It may take me a while to get used to seeing love come from within a family."

"I understand. Here, follow me. Let's sit by the fire and warm our bodies. I'll make us some tea, and we can talk."

"That sounds more than perfect."

Cove warms two cups in the microwave, while I settle

onto the soft brown velvet couch. I watch as he opens the tea bags, dips each one into the cups, and then wraps the string around them to twist the water out. He places the tea bags in the trash and lifts the two drinks off the counter.

"It's chamomile. That's all that was left in the box."

"That's fine. I'm not picky," I say, taking the cup from him and enjoying a warm sip. "This room is beautiful."

"All the rooms here are nice. My mother makes a reservation here for her sister whenever she visits, and we've used the hotel on occasion for high-end clients. There's only one room per floor with a fireplace, so we were lucky that this one was open. Plus, I would be surprised if your father would look for us so close to our building. He'll assume we got as far away as we could, and my mother was smart not to get one of the top floor rooms. Your dad will be sure to check the executive suites of all of the hotels first, and not the mid-range rooms."

As we sip our tea in silence for a few moments, I study Cove's battered face. Now that we're inside, I can really see the abuse that he suffered at my father's hand. I wonder if my father has ever beaten anyone else up like this, or if he has hired men to do it for him. Cove stares into the fire, his eyes flicker with the moving flames, while his bruises radiate an orange and yellow glow. My hand reaches across the couch and rests on his thigh. I place my cup on the end table and turn, straddling his hips as he leans back and looks into my face. He attempts to smile, but his cracked upper lip seals his emotions inside. I brush a dark lock of hair off of his forehead, placing a gentle kiss in its place. I believe it's one of the only areas showing no sign of injury.

Cove's hands slide below the dark grey sweatshirt that

I'm wearing. They rise up to my chest and then slowly caress my breasts. His eyes are eager, but his movements are slow as I continue with soft kisses on his swollen skin. My lips press against his cheek, his ear, his neck, and to his lips. He let's out a small whimper, either in pain or in pleasure. I stop, knowing his injuries will interfere with any further advancement. He follows my lead, lowering his hands down to my abdomen, and then around to the small of my back.

"Sophia. I've never seen a woman as beautiful as you. Your deep brown hair is soft and radiant, and your body smooth and warm. I love your curves and natural look. Your eyes, a vibrant reddish brown, remind me of the fall leaves. You can't be real, yet at the same time, you're the only experience I've ever had with reality."

"Tell me more, Cove. Tell me what you mean by that, and about my father." I take my leg away from each side of him, and turn to sit back on the couch, waiting to decode his past. Sipping tea once again, I wait to hear his voice.

Cove sighs and exhales before he begins.

"I was threatened by your father many times. Mostly when I was younger, but recently because of you. When you picked our building to live in, your father asked me to shield you from his business. And he meant that in more ways than one. I was to look after you, and guard you without you knowing, but I also knew that the two of us should never meet. I was supposed to protect you from myself. That may sound strange, and what it means is that your father would never take the chance of you finding out certain things about him; certain things that I know. I was surprised that he even allowed you to move in next to us. I guess he trusted me more than I thought he did. Maybe he assumed I was afraid of him. And I am. He terrifies me, but when I saw you looking so helpless, curled up in a little ball in the hallway, it was all over. I never even knew Paul Jameson had children until you moved in, and now I'm torn between your father's control over my family and the woman I've come to adore. I want to protect you from him, and not from myself."

"Cove, what does all this mean? Tell me what my father's hiding and why you feel that you're in danger by being with me."

He places his tea down and leans forward, placing a hand on his forehead and running his fingers through his softly tussled hair. "I can't tell you everything, but I'll tell you what I think you need to know in order for us to move forward. No matter what I say, Sophia, it will be hard for you to hear. You may hate me after I tell you some things, or you may hate your father. It's possible that you'll despise both of us, but I owe you an explanation for the mistake I made yesterday." Cove turns his body and takes my free hand into his. I put my tea down, allowing him to hold the other hand as well. He rubs his thumbs, massaging my palms before he looks up into my eyes.

"There were no cameras in my dining room yesterday. I wanted to pleasure you so that you would know that I have feelings for you. It was real, but when I took you into the bedroom it was to hurt your father. I wanted him to feel the pain that I've felt for so many years. My goal was to hurt him, and my hatred was so strong that I didn't even care what I was doing to you." He continues to circle his thumbs and index fingers over my hands as he speaks. "Sophia, my father went to prison for your father. He's serving twenty years for the mistakes that your dad made. My father took the fall for a man who only cares about himself and money."

"What did your father go to prison for?" I say in a soft voice, beside myself, barely able to get the words out.

"Bad business decisions. Poor choice in product."

"Drugs?"

"No. Worse. But in the end it doesn't matter what it was, it was illegal and my father was set up to cover his partner's tracks. Your father never spoke up to anyone about it, and to this day he lets my father rot in prison. I've spent my adult years without my dad because of Paul. He's a coward and a bully."

"So, is this when he came back into my life?"

"Yes. When my father was arrested your dad made sure that my mother and I were taken care of. I'm assuming he felt guilty about the entire situation, but never talked to either of us about any of it. He's supported us over the years, and when I had enough experience in his company, I started working for him as a partner instead of an employee. I was eighteen when all of this happened, just a year older than you were at that time, and I believe the entire situation, especially having me in his life, forced him to think about his own children."

"My father did this to your family?" I say, my tone direct; my eyebrows slanted in anger. "Why would you even think that I would hate you over this? My week has been spent trying to understand and forgive my father, and now I'm convinced that my heart was right. I can't trust him."

"You should hate me. I used you to harm him. That's not something that's excusable."

"No, it's not. But it is forgivable." I caress his hand as he has done to mine, lifting one of his fingers into my mouth, sucking and teasing him between my lips.

"Sophia," my name spoken from his lips in a low and

longing voice. "I want to touch you. I need to feel you, but I'm afraid. The feelings I've acquired over the past week for you are nothing like any I've ever experienced in the past. I'm worried that I may lose you and I don't know what to do next. We need to think about tomorrow, or if we stay here for more than a day, we need to figure out what we're going to do. I know my mother will be working on a few ideas, but I need to know your thoughts on the situation."

"Do we have to jump back into reality so quickly? Maybe we should enjoy one another's company this evening. We're finally alone, and we can go back to the real world tomorrow."

A hear a text come through and I walk over to my coat, taking my phone out of the front pocket. It's from Mera.

TREY IN HALL, ALL IS WELL.

"Everything okay?"

"Yeah, it's Mera. Our night patrolman is back in the hall and she said everything's okay. I guess we haven't been discovered just yet."

A second text comes through.

OPNED MAC TO NOVA TAT SEARCH – CALL ME

"Still okay?"

"Yeah. She's just wishing me a good night," I say, keeping the last message to myself. Now isn't the time to change the subject.

"I guess your relationship with your friend is like the one with my mother."

"No. It really isn't, at least I hope not. Mera and I used to be lovers."

"Really?" Cove's eyes widen in disbelief. "But, you

do like men too, right? I'm not just imagining that you enjoyed what we did yesterday, am I?"

"No, that part of my life with Mera is over. I've never experimented with any other woman besides her, and now we're just best friends. Actually, she's more than that. She's my family, and the only person I can say that about."

"Since your phone is out, let's do two things," he says, taking his out of his pocket. "First, turn off your location services so no one can track us."

"Good plan," I say, as I change my settings.

"And second, let me set my number into your phone and you can do the same with mine."

Cove hands me his phone and I type my number into his contacts list. When I'm finished, his main screen shows a family photograph. It's him as a teenager, his mother, and a man whom I'm assuming is his father. The three of them stand on the shore of a lake, and Cove is holding a small fish that he must have just caught. His parents are on opposite sides of him, each with one hand on his shoulder, and the entire family smiles. His parents are in swimsuits, and Cove is wearing a pair of cut off jean shorts. His chest is bare and tan; he obviously spent a lot of time outdoors to achieve such dark skin.

"That's my father."

"You look just like him."

"That photo was taken the summer before my father met your father. It was our last vacation together before the business started."

"You look happy."

"I was. We all were happy at one time. My father's a good person and he was just trying to give us the best life possible. When he found out what was going on he tried to step in and change the company, but your father has all of the power and control in this business. My father is guilty of knowing what happened and ignoring the situation. I'm angry at him for that, but I also understand that he really didn't have any way out. When you work for Paul Jameson, you're no longer a human being. You become an item for consumption."

"Cove," my voice wavering in fear as I say his name. "Are you saying that you were his employee before you were eighteen?"

"Yes."

"How old?"

"I'm not ready to go there with you yet, Sophia."

"So it was child pornography that my father was involved in?"

"Yes. Can we leave it at that? It's hard for me to talk about it."

I look down at the photo on his phone once more. Cove said that it was taken right before the business started. He looks like he's around twelve, just skin and bones, his ribs poking out of his chest like you see on most pre-pubescent boys. My stomach ties into a tight knot as I envision Cove forced into my father's corrupt world at such a young age.

"Don't think about it too much. It will haunt you if you do."

"God, Cove. How can I not think about it? I can't believe my father would do something like this to a child."

"Children," Cove says shaking his head in disgust. "It wasn't just one child, there were a few of us."

"I'm sorry. I need a moment to let all of this sink in." I stand, moving away from the couch as Cove looks at me with worried eyes. "Give me a second," I tell him.

I move quickly into the bathroom and lock the door. I

sit on the edge of the tub, bringing my head down into the palms of my hands. A tear forms, and then another. I begin sobbing, for Cove, for the other children; for myself, for mistreating my body and using people for so many years.

Cove knocks on the door and asks if I'm okay.

"Do you mind if I take a bath? I really need to be alone."

"You sound like you're crying."

I try to hold in the tears, but at this point, I'm unable to stop my emotions from pouring out.

"I'll be okay," I say, sputtering out the words.

"Sophia, open the door. I don't want you to be alone when you're hurting so much. Give me a chance to help you."

"Five minutes, and I'll let you in. I promise. Just give me that time alone, please."

There's no sound after that. He's giving me the space that I need.

I slump to the floor in front of the jetted tub; my knees are up with my arms wrapped around them. I turn my head to the side, rest my cheek on my kneecaps, and then stare at the marble wall. I follow the swirls of the lines with my eyes, the movement in the rock is trance-like and meditative. The patterns remind me of typographic maps of unknown lands. I wish I were in another city, just me, Cove, Mera and Lewis. We could all live together in one big house. I wonder if Cove likes cats?

Oh hell, what am I thinking? This isn't a fairy tale. I'll have to face my father at some point, and the reality is neither Cove nor I may be living in St. Louis after he finds us. I sob more, allowing the pain in my stomach and heart to flow out. How can I help Cove move past his years as a teenager in my father's business? Won't he always be reminded of my father when we're together? Won't he see my father in my features? My face? My eyes?

"Cove? Are you there?"

"Yes. I'm still right outside the door."

"What we're doing right now in this hotel, hiding out, is this another way for you to hurt my father like you did yesterday? Are you using me again to get back at him?"

There's a loud crack at the door and I can't tell if he punched it, or struck his head against it. I hear nothing for a moment, and then a voice passes through the door.

"I'm sorry, Sophia. I didn't mean to overreact. I understand your concern and why you might question my motives right now, but I really do like you. I'm not here with you to get back at him. I'm here because I want to spend time with you, get to know you, and unfortunately Paul Jameson is interfering with my life once again."

I had to ask, and I believe him. He's sincere when he talks about me, the tone of his voice changes and he speaks much slower than when he's talking about my father, and the business.

I turn away from the wall, wipe the tears from my face, place my other cheek on my knee, and then watch Cove's shadow move under the bottom crack in the door. He paces, impatiently waiting for me to let him in. I close my eyes and try to think about what I'm doing, what I need to think about and process while I'm sitting in here by myself, but there's nothing. My father is an ass and he broke the law, it's that simple. He destroyed a young boy and an entire family. Half of Cove's life has been spent in the porn industry and the only thing I can do is to show my support to him. I can't change what he's been through, or what I've been through. I can't change anything from the past, I can't stay angry, and I have to stop hiding.

My hands set firm onto the bathroom floor as I push up into a standing position. I blow my nose, fix my hair, wipe the rest of the tears from under my eyes, and take a deep breath. This is life. What I need is outside that door.

I hear a beep come from the other side and Cove's voice enters my space again.

"Sophia. It's been five minutes. Time's up; now let me in. I'm worried about you."

I open the door without hesitation and Cove immediately wraps me in his arms.

"Please don't be sad about this. You can be angry, but don't be sad for me."

We walk back into the living area, and I see that he has taken the comforter off the bed, along with the pillows, making a relaxing place for us to lounge in front of the fireplace. I step out of my shoes, and he does the same, taking his shirt off next. I stare, smile, and pull my sweatshirt over my head.

His eyes stay on my face, as he approaches me in long, fast strides, his lips locking onto mine.

"I can't imagine a more beautiful woman in this world," he says between deep kisses. His large lips embody mine, tugging, nipping, licking, until I feel the area between my legs moisten. He uses his tongue in a swirling motion, gently taking command of my mouth, charging deep inside. He slows the motion, sucking on my top lip, running his tongue along my lips down to my chin; leaving sweet pecks along the side of my neck and then down to my chest. His mouth reaches my breast and he flicks a nipple with his tongue. His hand cups it and pulls it upward, into his mouth. He sucks hard, and then bites my skin, sending shivers down my body.

"Beautiful," he says again, before walking into the

bedroom to pull a pair of red and black flannel pajama bottoms from his suitcase. I watch as he takes off his jeans and socks, folding the clothing, and placing the items on the bedroom chair. His erection is pushing out of his boxers, the size impressive and something I forgot to mention to Mera. "Would you like to put on something more comfortable for the night?" he asks.

I nod yes, and he lifts my black yoga pants out of my pile of clothes.

"My mother didn't feel right about rummaging through your intimates, so it looks like she only packed these for you, I hope they're okay," he says, handing them to me.

I chuckle, thinking about Leondra going through my closet. He looks confused about the humor I find in his mother's apparent modesty.

"So Cove, you know your mother has seen me naked, right?"

"She didn't have much of a choice when your father demanded to speak to me. She had to interrupt us."

"No. I mean she's *really* seen me naked. She was at my figure drawing class, the one I model nude for, she was looking down *there*, studying my most intimate area for over an hour."

Cove laughs, falling down onto the couch and holding his ribs and stomach as he enjoys the image I just placed in his head. He gasps for air, trying to deal with the pain from his injuries as he attempts to control the movement of his chest with each burst of laughter. He tries a giggle and then resorts to a giant smile to ease the pain.

"No, I'm serious, it was embarrassing. I find it bizarre that she didn't want to touch my night clothes and other intimates, but she's okay with looking at my vagina?"

"Stop," he says, laughing some more. "Please, it's too much." Cove's eyes tear and I join him on the couch, smiling at his amusement about the situation.

"Okay, you knocked me off my feet with that one," he admits. "If I didn't know my mother, I might be embarrassed too, but she's been working with nudes since she was a college student thirty years ago. Those photographs hanging on my wall were all shot by her. The nude black and white photograph above my fireplace is also of her. It's her self-portrait from when she was a student."

"At this point, with everything else you've told me, I'm not surprised you have a nude portrait of your mother hanging on your living room wall."

"It's not like that," he says, no longer laughing, but still relaxed. "It's art, and I think she's good at what she does, so I show my support for her, just like she does for me."

"I'm sorry. I didn't mean anything by it."

"I know. She was trying to be polite by not going through your private belongings in your home. It's different from you putting yourself out there in front of her."

"You're right, Cove. You're absolutely right."

"Also, she hasn't seen your most intimate area like I have. You're mistaken if you think that it's here," he says, placing a hand down into my crotch, applying pressure between my legs. "It's actually here," he moves his hand up my stomach and rests it over my heart. "And it's here," his tone passionate as he brushes his fingers along the side of my cheek, looking directly into my eyes. We lean in and kiss. Cove moans this time as my hand reaches down his length. He's rock hard and I'm still worried about hurting him. My hand slides into the slit and I pull him out of his boxers. I lower my head and lick the pre-cum from the tip of his throbbing head. Cove takes my chin in his hand and guides me back up to his lips for another deep kiss. His mouth is moist and warm and we moan in unison at one another's touch.

"Sophia," he whispers. "I'm sorry, but I'm not sure I'm going to be able to do very much this evening with you. I mean, I want to, but I don't know how much I can take. I can't tighten any muscles in my abdomen, and my lips are already sore."

I gently place one finger in front of his mouth, hushing him without touching his lips. I stand, take off my tight jeans then slide into the yoga pants. Cove puts the flannel pajama bottoms on before the two of us settle on the comforter in front of the fire. I lay in front of him, his arm wrapped over me, and we spoon, finally enjoying some down time in silence. Cove teases me, nibbles at my ear every so often and kisses the back of my neck. He runs his fingers through my hair as we stare into the fire watching the flames flicker and the wood crack. His erection stays firm, pushing into my back. It's the last thing I feel and remember as I drift off to sleep.

CHAPTER SEVENTEEN

It's dawn when I open my eyes. There are only a few smoldering embers left in the fireplace as the faint light of day struggles to break through the edges of the closed curtains on the windows. Cove and I slept through the entire night, his arm wrapped around my chest, leaving for only a moment to use the bathroom. I turn to face him, his eyes are open, and we both smile. I nestle my forehead into his chest and he squeezes my body, and then places a sweet kiss on the top of my head.

"How did you sleep?" I ask; my voice muffled in his chest.

"Surprisingly well. I was glad to hear you did too."

"What do you mean?" I question, lifting my head to look at him.

"You have the cutest little snore. You sounded like a kitten with a cold," he laughs.

"I'm sorry. I hope I didn't keep you awake."

"Just the opposite. You pacified me to sleep with each high-pitched snort. It was comforting."

"You look better, but also worse than yesterday."

"I'm not sure if that's a complement or not, Sophia."

I study his face for a moment. "The swelling's down, which is good, but your bruises are darker, more of a reddish-purple color. Especially the one next to your eye."

I lift my hand up and follow the outline of the bruise.

"They'll all go away soon enough, and then you won't have to look at me and be reminded of your father."

"Ha. I was thinking last night that you have to be reminded of him every time you look at me. I am his daughter after all."

"I don't see one small ounce of Paul Jameson in you. I see you, and only you."

He leans in and brushes against my lips, placing little pecks around my mouth. His tongue sweeps inside, encircles mine then sucks on it like it's a sugary treat. I let out a whimper as the entire area between my legs begins to flutter. I push my pelvic bone into his groin, longing to feel his hard erection once again.

Cove thrusts his body over mine, my back on the floor; face up, looking into his eyes. He lowers himself down along my side and places an arm on the opposite side for support. A few of his dark locks of hair fall forward as he leans down for another deep kiss.

I'm unable to move, yearning for this man to slide inside of me. I decide to make a move. Lowering my hand down to his flannel bottoms, I reach below for his stiff cock. He exhales when I latch onto him, lifting his hips so I can stroke him while he bites my lips. His breathing synchs with each movement and he watches my hand pleasure him.

Cove moves his body away, forcing my hand to detach from his shaft. He takes my wrist and lifts my arm above my head, keeping it from his flesh.

"I want more than that," he says.

"Are you feeling better? Can we fuck?"

His eyes have a look of disappointment after I say those words. He releases my wrist and sits up, positioning himself between my legs in a kneeling position. He looks down at the floor between us, almost as if he's looking right through our clothes.

"No. I'm not feeling well enough to do anything like that, and I'm a little confused by what you mean by fuck."

"You know, a fuck?" I say, frustrated by his sudden change.

"Don't be so disappointed, Sophia. You don't understand what this means to me."

"We both like each other, we both ache right now, our pants are dripping, don't you want to put yourself inside of me?"

"Yes, of course I do, but I need more than that from you. I don't know how to explain how I feel. Please, just give me some time. There are no cameras in this room, so..."

"There better fucking not be," I yell, sitting up.

"Sophia, shh. Take it easy. Like I was saying, there are no cameras, we're alone, and I don't need to perform like I've had to my entire life. I can just be with you with no contracts, no instruction, no restrictions on how and when I have an orgasm. Please let me be with you without having to abuse you. Fuck is often an insulting and violent word, and I'm not going to fuck you."

"I think I understand," I respond, lying back on the comforter. "But just so you know, I like to fuck."

Cove leans over me and positions himself back along the length of my body. "God, you can be so nasty sometimes," he says with a smile.

"Get used to it, Babe."

He looks surprised by my choice of words.

"Babe? Do I already have a pet name?"

I laugh as he attaches himself to my lips once again.

My arm is still above my head and I keep it there, allowing him the pure enjoyment of our pre-teen make-out session. It's been years since I've kissed someone so deeply, so passionately, and as we neck I feel my glutes take control of my lower body, tightening and releasing in a rhythmic motion. His tongue swirls, and my clit pulsates. He nibbles along my neck, and my breathing becomes heavy. Our hearts pound against one another's chests as we drive each other into a frenzy of desire.

He moves his mid-section so he's positioned directly over my arousal spot. His cock bulges out against his pajamas as he slowly lowers, finding the area between my outer lips to rest his erection. The pressure sets me over the edge, and I moan in approval.

"You make me feel wanted."

"Sophia," he whispers into my ear as he softly sucks on the lobe. "I've never fallen this hard or this fast for anyone."

"Me either, Cove. I've fallen for you as well."

He kisses my mouth, and slowly moves his hips. He holds the position for a moment, applying weight, causing an eruption of nerves to fire in both of us.

"When I'm with you it's like being blinded by the flurries of a storm. I can't see what's ahead, and I'm engulfed by the swirl of snowflakes melting against my body. I want to find shelter from the fallen snow, but the beauty of it is so captivating that I can't help but delve deeper into the splendor of what's before me."

My heart melts with his words. I take his mouth and tenderly skim my tongue against his. He slides against my mound, rubbing his shaft in just the right spot. I let out a high-pitched whimper as my abdomen and legs tighten.

"Tell me that you like being here with me."

"I'm not going anywhere," I groan, barely able to get the words out. Every muscle in my abdomen tightens as Cove continues to rub against me. His shaft feels incredible, even through two layers of clothing. He lowers his chest against my breasts, his movements becoming faster. My mind is spinning as I fantasize seeing the two of us from above. Cove's hips push into me, the two of us kiss and breath like wild boars, just as his last name implies.

I'm ready. Throwing my head back, I hold my breath. He kisses my neck and I whine with each brush against my pants. I move into him, demanding greater pressure to reach my orgasm. He complies, placing both hands on the floor as he slides faster. His mouth touches mine, and with that final contact I hit my peak. Lightning shoots through me like an intense electrical shock. My lower body is firm against Cove as I release, panting, expanding my hands wide, fingers stretched. I begin to lower my hips down to the floor and air rushes out of my mouth. I lose focus and my mind is blank as my body shudders in the heat of my orgasm.

Cove pushes against me and I cry out in delight. His breathing accelerates as mine slows.

"You're beautiful," he says, rubbing his hard cock on my pounding clit. "I'm cumming for you," he wails, lifting his chest off of me as he straightens his arms. I open my eyes to see that his face is in pure ecstasy. His mouth is open and I feel cum pounding out from his shaft in quick bursts. "Sophia," he whispers, placing his head down as the last pulsation is felt under my pants. He falls next to me, winded, his arms and legs shake.

"Fuck," he gasps.

I laugh, and he joins me. "I thought you didn't like that word?"

"What?" he asks, still winded. "I use that word all the time as an expression of how I feel. It's an emotion. That's different than using it as a verb." He lifts his head and kisses my lips. "I was trying to be intimate for the first time in my life."

"God, Cove. Haven't you ever had a girlfriend?"

There's a knock on our suite door and I immediately stand and run toward the bedroom.

"Sophia," Cove says, as he grabs my arm and pulls me back. "It's okay. Don't worry. It must be 6am, that's just room service. They leave a breakfast cart outside of each room at this time of the morning. We're alright, my mother would call me if she thought we were in danger."

"I'm sorry, it was just a gut reaction to run and hide."

"I understand, but I don't think you'll have to worry about that, plus there really isn't any place to hide in here."

"I know. Like I said, gut reaction."

Cove places his arms around my chest and gives me a comforting hug. I feel a moist and sticky substance on my stomach and as I look down he backs away.

"Oh," he hurriedly walks into the bathroom and proceeds to use a few tissues to wipe some of the cum off of his body. "We should probably take a shower before we eat. Let me pull the cart inside and then we can clean up."

"I'll get it."

"Sophia, no," he says in a raised voice. "I'm sorry, let me get it. We need to be careful when we open the door."

I allow him to take control and I move to the back of the room to use the bathroom. I can hear him unlatch the lock, turn the handle, and pull the metal cart inside. With the door locked again, he places the cart next to the dining room table as I return from the bathroom.

"It looks like we have a pot of coffee, a fruit platter

and some French toast."

"Sounds perfect, let's shower so we can eat. I'm starving."

Cove frowns, realizing he hasn't been the best host.

"We can eat now if you'd like. I didn't realize you were so hungry."

"No, it's fine. Come on," I say, reaching my hand out to him. He smiles, taking my arm as we walk into the bathroom.

The shower has rich brown and black marble walls with a three-sided floor to ceiling glass enclosure. There are two showerheads and a built-in marble seat. I pull off my yoga pants and underwear as Cove turns on both showerheads. He leaves the door open as he pries the flannel pajama bottoms and boxers away from his body. His lower abdomen is moist with his fluid and he wipes more of it off with another tissue.

"Cove, it's fine, just get in the shower and let me wash it off."

I step into one of the massaging streams, lowering my head underneath the warm water. The jets blanket my face, washing away the sweat from our morning workout. I open one eye and see Cove across from me lathering his hair. I take the soap and wash his chest, circling his nipples, his tattoo, and then down low to his semi-erect cock. I rub the bar of soap in my hands, and clean his personal areas, starting gently with his balls, then his shaft, and finally his abdomen. He smiles as he rinses his hair, and then returns the favor. When he finishes lathering me, I rinse and quickly wash my hair as he turns off his showerhead and pulls two towels from the bar just outside the glass door. I turn my water off and he wraps a towel around my body, absorbing the drops of water on my shoulders, back, and chest. Enveloped and restrained within the towel, I'm pulled closer to him with the two ends that are gripped in the palms of his hands. I feel his erection against my stomach, harder than it was a moment ago. He delves into my mouth and sweeps my tongue under his while moaning inside. His hand reaches down my hip and around to my inner leg, rising up and resting on my outer lips. He parts them and slides his finger inside, placing his forehead against mine, looking down at his entry.

"You're so soft and warm. I can't wait to be completely inside of you."

"When?" I whisper.

"When I know I'm ready."

"Ready for what?"

"Making love. Giving myself to you."

I can't keep from laughing and he immediately becomes offended. I'm starting to realize that he's extremely sensitive when it comes to sex.

"Oh wait. Come back," I say, grabbing his arm as he tries to step out of the shower. "I'm sorry, Cove. Your comment really caught me off guard and I laughed out of nervousness. Give yourself to me? Like an offering or what?"

"It's alright. I don't expect you to understand," he says, stepping out to dry off his body. "Let's go ahead and eat while the food's still warm."

I feel bad about spitting dumbass words out of my mouth without thinking yet again. He was forced into child pornography. I should be a little more sensitive to his feelings about this whole *fucking* thing.

I step out and follow him to the bedroom, grabbing a pair of underwear and my black sweater from my suitcase. I put my jeans from the night before back on, and watch as

Cove picks through his clothing. He pulls out a pair of grey jeans and a white button down oxford shirt. The oxford has an expensive look to it, and as I approach him I place my hands on the fabric, feeling its richness. He places it onto his body, covering the scar on his shoulder as well as the NOVA tattoo.

"That scar on your shoulder, I haven't asked you about it but I'm assuming you used to have a *Property of Jameson Industries* brand there, is that correct?"

"Yes," he replies in a hesitant voice. "I tried to remove it on my own with a knife, but then went to a place to have it professionally eradicated. It used to make me sick every time I saw it in the mirror." He rolls up the sleeves on his shirt and buttons the front, leaving the top two open and the length un-tucked from his pants.

"And the NOVA tattoo? Can I ask you about that?"

He's silent as he places a pair of black dress socks onto his feet. I stand and wait, not wanting to push him into an awkward conversation, especially if it's about a former girlfriend. He stands and looks at me, staring into my eyes before he speaks.

"It's also from the company, and just as painful to see each day. I've left it as a reminder of my father, and why he's no longer with us. Whenever I see it I think of him, where he is, and why he's there. I wanted to erase the employee tattoo because I'm no longer involved in those online sites, but the NOVA experience will be with me for as long as my father sits in prison because of Paul. I'll remove it once he's free." His face has a look of sadness, helplessness, and anger. I want to touch him but I keep my distance, knowing that some things can't be fixed.

"You're beautiful, Cove. I'm very lucky to be here with you right now."

"I'm the lucky one, Sophia. Just be patient with me, okay?"

He gives me a kiss and then we head over to the dining room table. I sit and he places the fruit tray in front of me.

"Apples, cranberries, grapes, and figs. What a lovely fall bounty they have at this place."

"I'm glad you approve." He places two slices of French toast on my plate and pours me a cup of coffee.

"Cream?"

"Yes, please."

Cove places the same onto his plate and pours himself a cup before sitting down to join me.

"I'm guessing your father will be checking in with Trey as soon as he realizes I'm not at my place. I'm not sure what's going to happen, Sophia, but it's always best to prepare for the worst."

"And what do you think the worst would be?"

"Being separated from you, of course. But other things could happen as well. I'm worried about my mother."

"If my father lays a hand on your mother he's…."

"Don't say it," he cuts in, halting the hatred that I suddenly feel. "I will take care of Paul if he hurts my mother in any way, you can count on it. I let him do this to my face and body the other day because I deserved it, but if he's not careful I can do some damage to him as well." Cove sips his coffee and eats some figs and grapes before continuing on. "My mother told me not to pick up my phone if she calls. She'll leave a message and we can listen to it before we try to contact her. Your father will make her call my cell to find out where we are, and we both thought of that before I left. That's why we made a plan. I think you should do the same if Mera calls."

"I think that would be best."

"I also wouldn't text anyone from here. I don't want our phones to be hooked up to the hotels Wi-Fi. If we need to send a text, email, or call someone we'll walk a few blocks down from here."

"You've been thinking about this for a while haven't you?"

"Yes, since I packed my bag yesterday," he replies while placing a fork full of French toast into his mouth. He chews quietly and with poise, like he was trained in the number of chews he should employ for each bite before swallowing. "I'm going to do everything possible to keep you safe and in my life."

"Has anyone ever told you how sweet you are?"

He blushes and laughs nervously at my comment, not sure how to respond.

"Cove Everton, I'm becoming very fond of you."

"Well Miss Jameson, I believe you already know how I feel about you," he replies, still blushing and showing off a childish grin. We sip our coffee in unison, asking each other the basic new relationship questions that I often overheard Mera ask her new boyfriends.

"What's your favorite color?"

"Walnut."

"Is that even a color?" I ask.

"In my book it is. What about you?"

"Black."

"See, now that's not even a color."

"Alright then, scarlet red."

"Like our wine bar?"

"Yes, except you spell the word with two t's, like it's a woman's first name."

"True, but it could go either way. I guess that leads me to ask you a question," he says. "When was the last time you and Mera were together?"

"How?"

"Physically intimate."

"So more than just a kiss?"

"Wow, okay. Yes, more than a kiss."

"Three years ago."

"And the last time you kissed her?"

"Exactly one week ago, at the Scarlett."

"Hmm," he says, placing a hand up to his mouth and resting a finger over his lips. "I failed to see that on the monitor."

"Were you there that night?"

"No, I watch the cameras from my home. I was keeping a close eye on the two of you, along with Haverty."

"I see. Okay, my turn. What do you do for my father now that you're not on any of the websites?"

Cove looks at me, troubled by my question. His response is in a much calmer voice than I was expecting. "I shoot, edit, and post. Let's leave it at that for now and get back to the more important questions."

"Ha," I say, placing my cup on the table while taking a few grapes in my hand. "So, how about you tell me what kind of car you drive."

"That's better," he grins. "I have a black Viper and the fleet of Escalades that I own with my mother for the Scarlett. I already know that you have a MINI. What about siblings?"

"Ug, bad subject. I have a brother who is married, and they have a child, but we rarely speak to one another."

"Why's that?"

"We're just two different people. Plus, he's closer to my mother than I am. We don't always get along or agree on very many things about our past, not to mention the present."

"I see," he responds sounding a little disappointed. "I'm an only child."

"Was that lonely growing up?"

"No, we always lived in neighborhoods swarming with children my age, so it wasn't a big deal until we met your dad, and then I became depressed and was forced into seclusion. But enough of that. Tell me what you wanted to be when you grew up, and if you still have those dreams."

"I wasn't set on becoming anything except maybe a housewife with 2.5 kids working a crappy job, and arguing daily with a husband who I didn't love."

"What?" he says placing his coffee down in disbelief. "What's that all about? Didn't you have dreams as a little girl of what you were going to be when you grew up?"

"No, I really didn't. My mother made sure of that. She constantly made comments while I was growing up about how she couldn't wait to have grandchildren, and that I would see how shitty life is as soon as I had a full-time job that I hated, just like her. She also told me I'd soon see how much men suck, and that they're all assholes."

"We are talking about your mother here, right?"

"Yes. My mother never gave me any support or inspired me to achieve anything. She didn't want me to continue my education after high school, and she'd be happy as a clam right now if I was still living with her, poor and pregnant."

"What the hell is that all about?"

"Control. Jealousy. Fear of being alone. Needing to be needed. Dependency. That enough?"

"Fuck. That's nuts. Okay, bad question."

"No, not a bad question. After I left and went to college I wanted to be a nurse, but my father would only pay for my schooling if I was in a business program, so the choice was made for me."

"Of course. Sounds typical of Paul. So being a nude model wasn't one of your childhood dreams?"

"Not that I remember," I reply with a smile, wondering if it bothers him that I put my body on display for college students. "I don't believe I'll be doing that anymore. I haven't been getting anything out of it lately. I don't need it anymore."

"Well, what *do* you need?"

Cove quickly reaches for his phone as a text comes through.

"It's my mother," he says, handing me the phone so that I can view what she wrote.

HE KNOWS SHE'S GONE. STAY PUT.

I look up to see a ghost-like face before me, and I'm sure mine looks the same. I'm immediately queasy and unable to eat any more of my breakfast. Cove places his hand over mine and gives it a tight squeeze.

"It's going to be okay. We need to just wait it out a little longer before we figure out our next move."

"Or before he finds us."

"He's not going to find us," Cove says, deleting and emptying the trash from his phone. He looks into my eyes and reassures me that everything will be okay. "I'll say it again. He's not going to find us."

"Okay. I believe you. You wouldn't have brought me here if you thought we'd be in danger." I pour myself a second cup of coffee and add some to Cove's cup as well, warming up the small amount that he has left.

"Are you religious, Sophia?"

"No. You?"

"No."

"Well, that takes care of that. How about your education? Did you go to college?" I ask him.

"No. I'm not the type of person who would do well in a classroom environment. Could you see me sitting at a desk taking notes?"

"No. You actually seem too sophisticated for school, if that makes any sense."

"I went to an all boys' private school for the gifted when I was a teenager. Beyond that, everything I've been interested in learning I've taught myself through reading and online research."

Cove looks proud of himself for doing so well, despite a few obvious setbacks. I might be more self-reliant like him if I had more time to myself, and didn't go out partying so much with Mera. We have calmed down quite a bit from our college days, and soon I imagine we'll stop our nights out on the town altogether. I'm not sure exactly what age it is that people decide it's better to stay home, but I know it happens at some point. That's why I rarely see fifty-year-olds out in the clubs.

"Cove, do you have any friends?"

He doesn't answer me right away; instead he takes his cup, and sips his coffee. I wait and he smiles. He takes the final bite of his French toast, chews it even slower than before, and ignores my question. He closes his eyes as he swallows, sits back and folds his hands across his stomach.

"Will you think it's strange if I don't?"

"I think you just answered my question."

"You're right. No, I don't have any friends. I have acquaintances, like the woman you saw me meet in the park, but no one I would call a friend. Do you have anyone besides Mera?"

Good call. I hadn't thought of that in a while. I really only have one friend. I used to be friends with Evan, but we no longer speak to one another now that he's in a new relationship.

"No. Only Mera," I respond, leaning back in my chair. "Does that mean you would consider a girlfriend more of an acquaintance than a friend?"

He laughs, obviously feeling awkward again. "I suppose a girlfriend would be a friend, and not just an associate. Are you trying to rummage through my past love life?"

"Well yeah, I wouldn't mind hearing about old girlfriends. You said before that you've had to perform your entire life, and that you were trying to be intimate for the first time. Did your other girlfriends carry out acts with you on camera? Is that what you meant about always having to perform? Haven't you had private moments with people like we're having?"

Cove looks down, his head and eyes tilt toward the floor. He's obviously distraught by my question.

"I'm sorry. I just want to know more about you, and past relationships can be very telling about a person."

"There aren't any," he responds hesitantly, lifting his head and covering his mouth with his coffee cup.

"Wait, what? Haven't you ever had a girlfriend?" I ask, completely shocked that this gorgeous and wealthy man sitting in front of me hasn't had hundreds of girlfriends. "Not one? How is that possible? If I had seen you when we were teenagers I'd be crawling all over you. Just like I want to now. Didn't anyone ever approach you or try to kiss you?"

"You want to crawl all over me?" he says with a smile.

"Don't change the subject."

"I've already explained to you some of the things that happened in my past."

"Okay, but you said that ended about seven years ago. What about since then?"

"It's complicated. You don't understand your father's business. Let's leave it at that."

"No."

"No? What do you mean no?" he places his cup on the table and leans forward again.

"You keep saying let's leave it at that. No. This is important. You don't have to tell me exactly what went on, but why didn't you have a girlfriend?"

"Yes, then I would have to tell you what went on."

"Will you tell me eventually?"

"Eventually."

"Then you can tell me today just as easily as telling me next month or next year."

"Sophia, I just asked you to be patient with me. Please don't make me do this now."

I look at his face and notice his lower lip trembles. How could my father treat a young boy so poorly, and for so many years? And why wouldn't Cove want a relationship as an adult? What has he been waiting for? I guess what he went through was just so terrible that he hasn't been able to heal. If I was forced to make porn as a young teen, I'd be feeling worthless. I wonder if that's how he feels?

"What are you thinking about now?"

"You; your past, what you must have gone through."

A big sigh leaves his mouth as he looks away from me

again. "If I tell you a few things, will you let me decide when the time is right to tell you more?"

"Yes," I say quietly, not sure if I should really keep pushing him to relive the past. "I'm sorry. I'm curious and I want to know everything about you."

"I understand. I feel the same way about you," he says, placing his phone in one hand, and taking my wrist in the other. "Let's go lie down in bed for a while and talk. It's more comfortable, and I want to be next to you, not sitting across from you."

I stand and walk with him over to the fireplace to pick up the comforter. He throws it over the bed and I watch it fall gently into place. He puts his phone on the nightstand and we lie next to one another. Cove kisses my forehead, and brushes a few strands of my hair over my shoulder, away from my face. He gives me a long, soft kiss. His warmth is comforting. His hand moves through my hair and I close my eyes, enjoying his touch.

"You're gorgeous, Sophia. I couldn't believe such a beautiful woman was sleeping in my hallway, her shirt off exposing her soft white skin. I had been watching you for about a week, but only from a distance. I had no idea you were going to cast such a spell on me when I picked you up and looked into your face. You were curled up like you had been abandoned. It was the same position my father found me in after my first NOVA experience. I was crying in my bedroom closet, hiding in the corner in a fetal position. I didn't want him to touch me. He saw the NOVA tattoo on my chest and he knew what had happened. I heard him call your father on the phone. They argued and eventually I cried myself to sleep. When I awoke I pulled a hooded sweatshirt over my sore chest and body. I went downstairs to find both of my parents sitting at the kitchen table eating dinner. I sat down and joined them. Years later I found out that my mother never knew what had been going on, but my father? He knew. He knew and there wasn't anything that he could do. He allowed Paul's employees to kidnap me and abuse me for years."

"Your mother never knew?"

"Not until my father was arrested, no. I never had my shirt off around her after the tat was there, and she probably just thought I was turning into a moody teenager. She knew about NOVA, I mean, she is one of your father's employees after all, but she never knew I was the star. She doesn't work for that part of the company."

"That's fucked up. I figured your mother worked for my dad, but what does she do? And how old were you? And what do you mean people kidnapped you?"

"My mother is a whole other story, let's stay on track here okay?" He kisses my lips again and I feel his body tremble.

"Was that because of me?"

"I wish. But no, it's the conversation. Let me get through this, and then I have a question for you."

"I'm here for you. Tell me what you can, but please stop if it's too difficult."

Cove kisses my lips for a moment before he continues.

"I was twelve when it started. Eighteen when it was finally over."

"Twelve?"

"Yeah, completely unable to comprehend what people were doing to me. I'd prefer not to give you details. We're talking about girlfriends, and that's what I'm getting to."

"Of course."

"So people did things to me and I was disgusted with

my body, I couldn't think about touching or being with a girl. I was abused almost daily, and that left me no time to be with friends, or to be a normal teenager. So no, I never had a girlfriend."

"I can't believe I'm part of this family. I can't believe that my father is this evil."

"It's money, Sophia. People will do anything for money. Your father was also convinced that I was a brat whenever I tried to fight back. He said that any young man would be happy to take my place."

"He said that to you?"

"Yes. I cried a lot during takes, and your father would get upset and say that to me."

"And after? When it was over, you didn't ever pursue any kind of relationship?"

"It took me about a year before I realized I was free from the first experience, but I was still working for your father during that time, and for another two years after that. He owned me from the time I was twelve until I was twenty-one, and even then I was still his property, but no longer on any websites. When I was involved in the adult sites after NOVA, I had a job to do every day, sometimes more than once a day. It was difficult to come home after doing that type of work and then think about starting a relationship with someone."

"What about people you worked with?"

Cove laughs, rubbing the side of his hand along my cheek, then across my shoulder and down my arm. "What I'm doing with you right now, this closeness, this intimate moment, it doesn't exist in Paul's company. You meet someone in the room where you're filming, you barely talk, and then when it's over everyone gets up and leaves. No, there was never an opportunity to have a girlfriend, nor would I want a girlfriend who was involved in the company."

"What about after you stopped? You haven't been involved with the fucking for years."

"Fucking? There you go again."

"Well, you can't tell me you made love to these women, you fucked them."

"No. I never fucked anyone."

"So you had sex with them. I forgot fuck is a violent word."

"Sophia. No. I've never been inside of anyone before. It wasn't in my contract, and it wasn't part of NOVA either."

I sit up, my eyes wide, hovering over him. "Are you serious? You were in porn videos and online sites for almost a decade and you never put it inside of anyone? I don't believe you. How is that possible?"

"It's very possible. You know full well all the crazy shit people do to get off. Think about the other day in my bedroom. There's an example. I've done everything you could possibly imagine, but I've never done the traditional guy in girl."

"Holy shit. Are you really serious? Didn't you ever try to stick it in? I mean you were in a room with someone, naked, getting it on. Didn't you ever just give in and push it inside?"

"Sophia, stop. Why is this so hard to believe? I did what I was told to do, or what was within the limits of my contract, and that was it. There were no substitutions, no improvising. Paul has specific sites for certain clients, and they expect to log on and see a particular thing. Vaginal intercourse was not in my contract. I wasn't involved in those sites."

I calm my voice, not wanting to sound so immature with all of the questions that I have for him. "And after? Why haven't you found a girlfriend after you became a partner in the business?"

"Same reasons. I film and watch body parts pound into one another for a good half hour. Then I have to edit, add music or sound effects, and post. I see the same crap all day long. It can repulse you after a while, kind of like working at a fast-food restaurant and not being able to tolerate eating anything from the place once your shift's over. When I'm not working, I'm not looking for a girlfriend. I have other plans. My mother and I have spent a lot of time opening the wine bar together, and hopefully we can open a second place soon. We'd like to have our own successful business, and then we won't have to work for your father anymore, that is, if he'll let us go."

"What can I do to help?"

"You're not mad at me?"

"Cove, why would I be mad at you?"

"I don't know. You could hate my life. What I've done. Who I am."

"You're a wonderfully kind person who has had some very bad things happen to you. None of this is your fault."

Another text comes through and Cove immediately turns away, picking up his phone from the nightstand. "It's your father," he says in a harsh tone. "See this. This is who he is." He hands me the phone so I can view the text.

YOU DUMBASS PIECE OF SHIT. KEEP YOUR MOUTH SHUT. YOU TALK. HE DIES.

"What? Who?" I ask.

Cove throws the phone across the room and then puts a hand behind his head, sitting up slightly and no longer looking at me.

"It's much easier to kill a man in prison, than to kill a man who's free."

CHAPTER EIGHTEEN

W e sit in silence thinking about the text. Cove has shut down since it came through, and I can tell he feels guilty about exposing the information with regard to his father being in prison, and the business. If I had known any of this, I would have never accepted a dime from my dad. The car, college, gifts, money, and my loft all negated.

"Say something, Sophia."

"Would my father really kill someone? Or do you know if he has in the past?"

"I can't answer that question. I've already made the mistake of getting you way too involved in this world. The less you know, the safer we all are, and that includes my father."

"The more you tell me, the easier it will be for me to help you and your family."

"You're wrong about that, there's nothing you can do. Now ask me something else, and let's leave this subject behind us for a while."

"You said earlier that you had a question for me. What is it?"

"Bad timing," he sighs. "Since you asked me about my girlfriends, I was going to ask you how many boyfriends you've had, and if any of them were significant. I understand if you don't want to talk about relationships anymore. I won't be divulging any further information, so I don't expect you to either."

"And if I don't mind?"

"Be my guest. I still want to know all you're willing to share."

Cove faces me and presses his mouth against mine. I advance my tongue and he captures it with his, gently circling it. His mouth is warm and his kisses moist. He lifts his head, pushing my shoulders against the mattress as he continues to sweep in and out of my mouth.

"I love how my body melts when we kiss," I say, placing my hand under his shirt. "Are your injuries better?"

"The warm shower helped a great deal. But mainly I feel better because of you."

"What can I do to you that's special? Is there something you've always desired sexually, but never experienced?"

"We're doing it. Kissing, touching, being intimate."

"I meant beyond that."

"Isn't this enough?" he asks, taking my lips and tongue back against his. "I could probably cum just from kissing you. Now that's something I've never done before. And what we did earlier, the dry humping, that was a first. How about you?"

"Have an orgasm just from kissing? I don't know. I've never tried it."

Cove embraces my mouth deeper and harder than before. He pushes his erection against my hip and shudders at the contact.

"No dry humping, only kissing," I say.

He takes a breath and places small kisses along my cheek until he reaches my ear.

"Oh fuck," I pant. "That's not fair. You found one of

my sensitive spots."

"Kissing doesn't only pertain to your mouth. I can travel anywhere I want, Sophia. And from what I can tell so far, you have many sensitive areas."

He takes both of my hands and raises my arms above my head while licking my ear. I tighten my inner leg muscles, causing a few small rifts to begin deep inside.

"Remember, no dry humping," he exclaims.

"I'm not, I'm just bucking my lower abdomen. I can bounce, can't I?"

Cove laughs, nibbling my ear lobe, sending a second group of shocks down below. "Oh God, this is going to drive me wild."

"Patience. Just think about my mouth, my tongue, and my lips against your skin. Know that I'm hard for you, I desire you, I want you, but I also need you."

He brushes his tongue along my arm, up past my elbow, stopping at my wrist. He takes my hand, still above my head, and circles his tongue around my palm.

"Fuck," I say again, my clit aching for the touch of a finger or the pressure of his body. "That feels amazing."

He holds my fingers tight against one another while wiggling his tongue between each one. The feeling is intense. It's more pleasurable than I could have ever imagined. Cove takes my ring finger into his mouth. He pushes it into the side of his cheek, then to the back of his throat. My body tightens then relaxes, over and over, until I begin to feel a strong urge build around my clit.

He stops, takes his shirt and pants off, then undresses me down to my underwear. His erection shoots out from his boxers and the head of his shaft rests against my side. I follow the outline of his lips with my tongue, feeling the lushness as they swell.

"You hard for me, Babe?"

"Yeah, I won't last too much longer."

I run my hand down his side, but he stops me before I can reach his shaft. "No. We're kissing, remember?"

"I can't keep my hands off of you."

"Touch me with your mouth and your tongue."

I sit up on the bed and straddle him, placing my lace-hidden clit against his length. "Don't worry," I say. "I'm not going to move an inch. Just keep still underneath me."

"Sophia, if you rock against me, I'm going to cum. I'm that close."

I lean down to his chest and take a nipple in my mouth. He makes a loud groaning sound and grips the comforter with his hands, pulling it up, closer and closer to his side. His chest muscles tighten, showing off his defined abs. I flick his nipple, and then gently bite down on it. Cove wails out in pleasure, trying to stay still.

"Oh fuck, Sophia. That's torture."

I move to his other nipple, flick it with my tongue, nibble, and suck, my lower body still tightly pressed against him. I can feel pulsations along his length as his orgasm builds. My tongue glides down his stomach. His breathing is heavy; head tilted back, tension springs off of every part of his body.

"Sophia, kiss my lips again. Come back to my mouth."

I thrust forward, my movement causing an instant burst of cum to shoot out of him. My mouth attacks his as he battles to stay in control. His whimpering is muffled under our heavy breaths, his lower body locked tight against mine. He tries not to move, not to thrust, and instead grips the comforter tighter, until I hear it rip beneath his hands.

"Sophia," he says with a moan, still cumming onto his stomach.

I lay on top of him, his fluid sticking to my flesh as his orgasm subsides. My mouth rests against his and I feel his lips tremble.

"This time, they're trembling because of you, and not because of our conversation."

"I'm glad," I say, sliding off the top of him and onto my side. He's out of breath but sits up, ready to return the favor.

"Lay back. I have plans for you, Sophia Jameson."

"Little plans, or big plans?" I joke, looking down at his shrinking rod.

He grins, and then slides two fingers deep inside.

"Whoa, that was fast."

He ignores my comment and continues to push his fingers wildly around, brushing my G-spot, and sending quick waves throughout my body. He stops and places both fingers tightly against my upper wall.

"Would you like to have an orgasm, my sweetness?" he asks in a sexy voice.

I nod yes with delight.

"Close your eyes and tighten around my fingers," he whispers. "Now loosen and tighten again." I follow his instructions, tightening with slow contractions. He kisses my nipples and I make quiet whimpering noises.

"Think of me, Sophia. Imagine I'm inside of you, my dick moving. Feel it."

He kisses my mouth, my eyelids, my ears, and holds his fingers fixed inside.

"I can feel your arousal. You're so wet right now. Think of me. I'm on top of you, pushing inside of you, my dick swelling, ready to shoot cum out for you."

"Cove, move for me. Please," I beg.

"Feel the pressure of me sliding in and out. I'm going to come, Sophia. Come with me. Let yourself go with me."

"Oh, Cove. Move," I demand. He stays still. Speaking slowly and quietly into my ear, he moans as if he's going to release with me.

"Do it for me, sweetness. Tighten your muscles, feel my tongue fluttering around your warm clit. Shriek and cry out, yell for more. Feel me fucking you."

I tense and then let out one of the most powerful orgasms I've ever had, calling his name, desperate for more. My legs shiver and spasm, my heart skips and flutters, and my eyes glaze over. Cove flicks his fingers as I climax, sending a shudder of vibrations throughout my inner space. He moves his tongue around my nipple and then bites down as I lose control. I place my hand on his side and dig my fingernails into his skin, feeling the pleasure of a final ripple.

"Jesus, what the fuck was that?" I say, trying to revive my body and mind. "That was one intense orgasm."

He slides his fingers out and another tremor shoots deep inside.

"Hmm. I think you might be able to go again," he smiles, sliding them back in, and then out again. I open my mouth and raise my abdomen, searching for his flesh. "Yes, you're definitely ready."

"What? I just came. No way."

He pushes his fingers in deep, then back out to my flesh, around, and in to my G-spot. In less than thirty seconds I reach my second orgasm, still breathless from the first. I pant and grab his hand, stopping him from continuing on.

"Please stop. No more, I need a break. Let me catch

my breath."

"But you're ready to go again. Let me pleasure you."

"You did," I say winded. "And how do you know I can do this again?"

"I can feel it and see it. Your body is still tense, craving more, one more time Sophia, please?" he says, sliding his fingers inside. I throw my head back and close my eyes, letting out a gasp of delight. "My life has revolved around people making me cum. I need to gratify you. I want you to know how much I desire satisfying *your* needs."

He places a third finger inside, and slowly glides in and out with his thumb against my clit. A quick burst of pre-orgasmic twinges takes place. I moan and tilt my head further back, exposing my neck to his soft kisses. He nibbles while moving his thumb in a circular motion down below, his fingers still in my space.

"Faster, Cove. Don't be so gentle this time."

He bites my neck and groans, his fingers thrusting against my spot. I lift my hips off the bed, squeezing my buttocks tight as my orgasm starts.

"I want to feel you explode against my fingers. You're so warm and wet inside, Sophia. Feel me craving to have you."

Cove places his free hand behind my neck and lifts my head off the pillow, pressing his lips against mine. He pushes his tongue through my tightly closed mouth, separating the opening between my lips and allowing the tense rush of my pre-orgasm to flow out as I reach my peak. "Let it out, Sophia. I want to hear you."

I burst down inside, Cove's fingers stop to feel my throbbing muscles. The pounding beats engulf his flesh and I cry out with each beat. I squirm and grind against him, quivering in defeat.

"Cove," I mumble, still bound in his mouth. I turn my head, bite his chest, and hastily push his fingers away. He swiftly returns them inside and I shake, screaming his name again.

"Cove, please. Stop."

He kisses my forehead and holds himself still against my trembling body. I feel a smile on his lips as his mouth is pressed against mine. He waits for my heart and breathing to slow before pulling his hand away. His head hits the pillow next to me. I open my eyes to see his gorgeous chiseled face, his deep brown eyes and dark hair, his soft full lips; all within inches of mine.

"Cove?" I say in a soft overwhelmed voice.

"Hmm?" he murmurs, grinning from ear to ear.

"No more."

He laughs and I join him, placing my head onto his chest as I snuggle into his warm skin.

"Had enough, my sweetness?"

"Yes. I've had enough for the rest of the week."

"I'll remember that when you try to attack me later tonight."

I lift my head and send a worried look his way.

"What is it, Sophia?"

"Do you think we'll still be together tonight?"

"Yes, I do. He's not going to find us, but we do need to figure out what we're going to do. We can't hide out here forever."

"What time is it?" I ask.

Cove looks at his watch and then shows me the time; it's ten in the morning.

"I'm worried that I haven't heard from Mera. I know my father's over there yelling at her."

"Oh believe me, he's yelling at Trey a lot more than Mera."

"Yeah, well it's still worrisome. I bet she didn't even make it to work today."

"She'll probably never make it to that job again, Paul has other plans for her, remember?"

"Oh God. It's my fault that she's in this mess."

"No, some of it's mine, but Mera became a part of Jameson Industries before you even knew about it, correct?"

"Yeah, how did you know that?"

"I could hear some of your conversation over the crowd last week at the bar. She made this decision, so try not to blame yourself, okay?"

"Perhaps, but I'm still worried. She should have called me by now."

"What's Mera's personality like around your father? Does she stand up to him, or is she submissive when he's around?"

"She has a crush on him."

"Of course she does," he says, rolling his eyes. "Most women do."

"Really?"

"Yes. I've been to expos where women hang all over him, practically getting him off in front of the crowds. It's disgusting."

"Do women hang all over you at these expos?"

"When I was on the sites, yes, but not by choice. It was set up that way for our clients and the press. All of it a facade to sell me as the company's goods."

"Do these expos take place a lot?"

"Usually twice a year. Your father holds them in Vegas in one of his casinos. The perfect spot for this type of business."

I picture a ballroom in one of my dad's casinos packed full of people rummaging through adult magazines, meeting his employees, and women wearing practically nothing; their big fake breasts hanging out for everyone to gawk at, selling videos to men and women who are fans. Maybe even blow up dolls and sex toys available at booths.

"Are there booths at these expos displaying new products?"

"Yes, why?"

"Do people give demonstrations with these products?"

Cove sighs and drops his head. "Yes, unfortunately that does happen sometimes. But usually in side rooms, off the main floor."

"Oh yuck. Really? I was just joking. That really happens? Like, if I saw a big dildo I wanted, there could possibly be someone showing me why that one is better than another one, and how to use it? Like those late night infomercials?"

"Yes. Don't think about it. Tell me more about Mera."

"Okay." I sit up on the bed and notice Cove keeps his eyes on my face, again he doesn't look down at my bare chest. I ignore it for a moment, answering his question. "She has a crush on him, but she also stands up to him. When he hurts me, or he's being an ass, she lets him know it. She'll tell him off without thinking twice about the consequences."

"Not anymore she won't."

"What do you mean by that?"

"She's a possession now. She'll learn fast enough not to open her mouth in front of him."

"Cove, you're scaring me. What do you mean by that?"

"He'll let her know that he's the boss without putting any visible marks on her. He won't want to damage one of his resources for money, but he will set her in her place."

"How? Tell me exactly what the hell you're talking about?"

"Sophia, you saw what your father did to me. He'll beat any man who crosses him, and although I haven't seen him hit a woman I have seen him subdue them in other ways, mainly for his own violent gratification. He'll assert his power over her if she's not careful."

"My father is a complete ass, but he's not going to touch Mera, especially sexually. He wouldn't dare."

"I hope you're right," he says, taking my hand.

"So why don't you like my body?" I finally ask.

Cove sits up wide-eyed and confused. "What are you talking about? I've never seen such a beautiful woman before in my life."

"Then why don't you look at me? I mean, hello? I'm sitting in front of you with my breasts hanging out. You could at least sneak a peek."

He laughs, throwing his head back onto the pillow.

"I'm serious. What gives?"

"There are a couple of reasons I suppose," he says smiling.

"Hey, this is serious, stop smirking," I demand, tapping his leg with my hand. "You're giving me a complex."

"I know it's serious, and I'm sorry. I didn't think you noticed."

"So? Come on, tell me; are they lopsided or something? Not big enough for you?"

"God no. They're perfect; you're perfect, and just so you know I've studied your body in great detail, even that first night when you let your breast hang out in front of me in the hallway. You drove me crazy then. It was difficult to control myself. I wanted to reach out and grab you, but I knew your father would be watching."

"Well, he's not watching us now."

"True, but I still can't control myself. I look down at you, and I don't want you to know what I'm thinking. It's embarrassing. You're just too much, too sweet, and I want to treat you better than staring at you like a piece of meat. Besides, these parts that we all have," he says, rubbing my breasts softly, "they don't mean as much to me as what I see in your face. Your face holds your true beauty."

"What's the other reason?"

"The business, which we've talked about to death, and I won't enjoy bringing up again. So just know that I love your body, you're gorgeous, and I'm in awe of you at all times."

I lean over and give him a kiss, showing my approval of his answer. "I think I can accept that for now, but at some point it would be nice for you to look down, you know, show me that I'm not all eyes and mouth."

He looks at my breasts and purposely opens his eyes as wide as he can, with the obvious intent of making me laugh. "Oh baby, those look so good." He licks his lips and joins me in a good laugh.

"What you just said is the opposite of what I'm used to hearing; all eyes and mouth? Not tits and ass? That was pretty darn cute. Come on, let's get up and I'll order us an early lunch." He sits up, pulls his shirt onto his body, and helps me off the bed.

We dress and I tell him more about Mera. How we met, our time together in college, and our continued friendship afterward. He listens intently, learning more about the one person who I consider to be my family. I tell him very little about Evan and my other relationships, what few there were. I learn more about his mother, and her struggles with losing her husband. She's extremely depressed, blaming herself for not being more aware of what was happening to her son, and not able to stop my father from ruining their lives. She hovers over him now and is noticeably protective of what's happening in his life. Cove mentions her approval of me, even though I'm Paul's daughter. She's just thrilled about the possibility of her son moving forward with his life.

After a light lunch of grilled cheese sandwiches on wheat toast and a small plate of grapes, Cove takes a few Ibuprofens for his pain before we lay back down next to one another. He wraps his arms around me, and I rest my head on his chest.

"I think I should go out tonight once it gets dark. It's one in the afternoon now," he says, looking at his watch. "When the sun sets, maybe around six, I'm going to see what's happening at our building and at Mera's place. It's strange that you haven't heard from her, and that I haven't heard from my mother in a while."

I look up, surprised at his idea. "I'm going with you."

"No. You're staying here; it will be safer that way. Besides, if I run into your father he's going to throw a punch, and this time I'll fight back. I don't want you to have to see that."

Using a strong voice I repeat those four words to him. "I'm going with you." He shakes his head no and I point my finger at him in a scolding motion. "I'm not staying here alone, and you're not going to our building alone either. If I'm starting a relationship with you, then we're a team. No further discussion. We'll go out tonight;

together."

"Yes *darling*, whatever you say," he grins. "Now nap with me for the rest of the afternoon."

I'm elated he's so willing to please, agreeing to my terms quickly and without argument. I smile, snuggling into his side, still puzzled by the enormity of my affection and infatuation; a fixation I've never felt for another person in my life.

We both drift in and out of sleep, waking briefly to run our fingers along one another's flesh, kiss, and smile. This is something I've never done and the similarities that Cove and I have with past relationships is hitting me hard, helping to shape the strong feelings I'm developing for him. Devery would have a field day with the two of us. Two shamefully, sexually active people, one by choice, one not, who are both inexperienced at love and intimacy, find one another and start a relationship as if they're exploring the opposite sex for the first time.

It's around three in the afternoon when I let myself go, falling into a deep sleep, never acknowledging the fact that we still don't have a plan. We'll be walking blindly into the streets in just a few hours, neither Cove nor I wanting to discuss the very real possibility that my father will send us in different directions, far apart from one another, if, or more probably when, he finds us.

CHAPTER NINETEEN

I pick up my phone from the side table next to the bed. It's seven in the evening and I've been sound asleep for four hours.

"Cove?" I say, reaching behind to wake him. The bed is empty and cold. He's been up for a while. I turn and look around the room. "Cove?" I call out again. Silence.

I jump out of bed and check the bathroom then the living room. He's gone.

"That bastard. He left without me."

I frantically dress, falling onto the bed as I try to push my legs hurriedly into my jeans. I hope he's okay. I hope Mera's okay. I can't believe he took off without waking me. I pull my black sweater over my head and wrap my wool coat around my body while thrusting my feet into my shoes. With my keys and phone in my pocket, I head for the door, but stop when I notice a note placed on the floor of the marble foyer. I pick it up, knowing already that it will be an apology from him.

Please don't be angry. My mother needs to speak with me. I'll be back soon. Stay put.

I crumple the paper into a ball and toss it over my shoulder as I head out into the winter night. I'm no longer waiting. It's time to confront my father about his past and talk to him about my future.

A streetlight casts a warm glow on the snow as I leave the side door of the hotel to begin my walk back to our building. I decide to take Tenth Street instead of Eleventh, bypassing my place, and head the four blocks toward Mera's. The air is bitter cold and I can see my breath. The snow crunches beneath my feet making it difficult to be stealthy. There are plenty of people out walking to area restaurants and bars on a Friday evening, making it impossible to try to hide as I walk. Instead, I try to blend in, going about my business like the rest of them. I look up as I approach Mera's building. Her windows are dark, not one light on inside. She's definitely not home and I can only guess that she's out looking for me.

I walk around the back and see her car still sitting in the lot. Wherever she went, she's on foot, most likely to my place. She's probably waiting for me there, with my father, Cove, and Leondra. I hope this isn't a set up for Cove. He's smarter than that. He'd know when the time was right to meet his mother. He must be okay. Maybe I'm the one being set up. I look up at Mera's windows again, trying to see any sort of shadow movement from within her place. Nothing.

The gate to her lot is open and I walk in, taking the back courtyard elevator up to her floor. I expect to see Trey when the door opens, but the hallway is quiet and empty. I place my ear up against her door and listen for people inside. There's nothing, only silence. Where the fuck is she? I look at the bottom of the door for any source of light, but see only darkness. I wish she were here. My heart races in fear of traveling to my building. I press my hands against her door and put my head between them as I lean in, needing her support.

"Mera, where are you?" I whisper, her door escaping

my hands, opening a slight crack in front of me. Surprised, I step back, tightening my fists in case it's my father. It's still quiet and I see no figure in the open space of the doorframe. I place one hand onto the door and push it slowly open, not seeing anyone inside. I walk in, turn on the light switch to my right, and illuminate the entry and the kitchen.

"Mera?" I call out. "You home?" knowing she's not. Everything in the kitchen and living room appears normal, nothing moved, no sign that anyone else besides her has been here. I walk into her bedroom and turn on a light to see that I'm horribly wrong. The mannequin head we set up in the bed is uncovered and thrown to the floor. Mera's closet door is open, and her clothes have been tossed around the room. I see one of her smaller suitcases out, but her two larger ones are missing. Her dresser drawers are open and emptied. Some of her clothing is on the floor and bed, and other items of hers are completely missing. Half of her shoes are gone, her underwear and bras, all gone. Empty hangers line the closet bars or lay tumbled onto the floor. Her bathroom cabinet drawers are opened and emptied, and her countertop is cleared of makeup and personal items. Fuck.

My face burns with heat, my heart pounds out of my chest, and my legs are weak as I fall into a full-blown panic attack. I can't catch my breath and my head spins. She would've left me a note. This isn't by choice. Where is she?

I force my legs to move, rush out of her apartment, down the emergency stairway and back out into the cold. Sprinting down Eleventh Street I lose my scarf that was wrapped around the top of my coat. My feet pound on the sidewalk, as I push past a group of people and fly into the lobby of my building. I hit the elevator button practically prying the doors open with my fingers to get inside. I turn my key and pace, catching my breath as the elevator rises upward. When the doors open, I bound out into my hallway, no longer worried about my father. I only hope that he hasn't done what I think he's done. My door is locked and I open it, rushing through each room as I look for her. She's not here and the place hasn't been touched. I run up my stairs and see that all of my belongings are still in place. I note that the suitcase I had packed for Mera's has been returned and is sitting on my bed. There's a note on top of it that I'm terrified to read. I slowly approach it, knowing the words I'm about to see are going to break my heart. My hands shake as I lift it and see my father's handwriting in front of me.

You and I both win, kiddo. You can have what you want, but I'm taking something that I need, and that's the end to it all.

I place my hand over my mouth and drop the paper, watching it soar down to the floor. I float down with it, in slow motion and disbelief that my father would take away the one person in my life that I love with all of my heart. My best friend, someone so dear to me who has become my family and my support, is gone. I sob and hide his writing under my free hand, trying to make it disappear. He's doing this because of me, and because of Cove? Can someone be this evil?

"Cove," I cry out, realizing that he may be gone as well. "Cove," I yell again, heading down the stairs toward his place. And where's Lewis? Where is my beautiful little fuzz ball?

"Cove," I scream. "Lewis," I belt out running down the hall. I pound on Cove's door, but there's no answer.

"Cove, please tell me you're in there," I whimper, falling to the floor in tears at the foot of his door. I place my hands over my face, unable to bear the fact that the people I care most about are gone, taken from me as a form of punishment. I'm alone.

"Cove," I say again, placing my forehead against his door while closing my eyes. I feel a light push against my leg and open an eye to see Lewis pawing at me. "Oh baby boy, you're here." I pick him up, noticing that he has a lion haircut, and smells like strawberries. "Lewis?" I hold him up and see that he's been to a groomer and is also wearing a black bowtie. "Oh little boy, what happened to you? You look beautiful."

"Sophia," Leondra says in a soft voice, reaching down, gently touching my arm. "I'm so glad you're alright, sweetheart. Please come with me into my place where we can wait for Cove. He'll be relieved to know that you're here and in one piece."

I place Lewis on the floor and watch as he runs down the hallway toward Leondra's apartment. Her tattoo-covered legs are at eye level as I sit on the floor looking straight ahead at all of her inking. I'm overjoyed to hear her words. "Cove's still here? He's okay?" I ask, looking up.

She helps me to my feet and wraps her arms around me, engulfing my body in a warm hug. "He's fine, my dear. I had to talk to him about a few things, but when he returned to the hotel you were gone, so he's been out trying to find you. Why don't you have your phone on you?"

"I do," I say, taking it out of my pocket, noticing that the screen is black. "My battery must be dead."

"We've both been trying to call you," she says, leading me toward her door wearing her usual gold robe and slippers. "Let's get inside so I can let him know you're safe."

She opens her door to an impatient Lewis, who runs inside as if this is his new home.

I follow him and immediately see why. Where my loft is rustic southwest, and Cove's is contemporary and elegant, Leondra has color, and lots of it. Her floors are acid-washed concrete with swirls of auburn gold and terra cotta. Her foyer walls are light blue and red, with bright abstract paintings hung from floor to ceiling. A life size fiberglass horse is used as a coat rack, and Leondra takes my wool coat, adding it to the pile. She picks up her phone to call Cove, smiling and giving me a wink. I'm still upset about Mera, but relieved that my father hasn't hurt the Evertons.

"She's here and she's okay. Yes. Be safe," she says to Cove, hanging up with a sigh of relief. "He's just a block away and he wants to make sure you don't go anywhere."

I smile, feeling anxious to have him here.

"Would you like a cup of tea? I have peppermint, jasmine, and green, all decaf."

"Jasmine sounds wonderful, thank you. Do you mind if I use your restroom?"

"Of course not, my dear. It's to your left. I'll be in the kitchen."

Leondra's front foyer bathroom is in the same spot as mine and I'm immediately comfortable with the familiar layout of her loft. The room is decorated in an art deco black and white tile that covers the floor and continues half way up each wall. The top part of the room is painted a deep turquoise, and where I have a new glass enclosed shower, she has a claw foot tub. It's a graceful space, different from her eclectic entryway.

I relieve myself, and then wash my hands, seeing my reflection for the first time since I got out of the shower this morning. My hair is a mess and I try to smooth it out with my fingers, adding a few light touches of water to help hold it in place. I splash some water on my face and towel off, looking a bit better after tearing up in the hallway a few moments earlier. I wish I looked prettier.

"You're gorgeous," Cove's voice echoes out of nowhere.

Turning, I see him leaning in the doorway, staring at me with a worried look on his face. "I thought your father had taken you away from me," he says, with a sigh of relief.

"I was thinking the same thing about you, and if I wasn't so happy to see you, I'd give you shit for walking in on me while I'm in the bathroom." I hurry over to the door and wrap my arms around him, holding him tight. He places his arms over my shoulders and kisses the side of my head. I hear a phone sound behind us from a distant room, but it stops after the first ring. Leondra must have picked it up. I hope it's not my father.

"I'm sorry about Mera," he says.

"Where do you think she is? What did he do with her?"

"I would say that she's with him in a hotel. He's going to take her with him to Vegas later tonight, or in the morning. She's gold to him right now."

"T-That's what I was afraid of," I say, mangling my words as I begin to cry.

"Shh. Sophia, it's okay. She's going to be alright. Please don't cry." He holds me tighter and kisses my head down to my ear then across my cheek to my mouth. I allow him to press hard against my lips, as he tries to extinguish my tears. "It's alright, we can fix this."

"How?"

"Shh," he whispers again, taking my mouth back into his. He stops and places his forehead against mine, looking into my eyes. "I can fix this. I'll get her back for you."

"Cove, darling," Leondra's voice cuts in, "Sweethearts, please come all the way inside so that we can talk."

He smiles at me and takes both my hands, giving them a good squeeze before turning toward his mother. We follow her into the living room that has a placement of four couches in a square formation with one giant circular coffee table in the middle. Each couch is a different shade of blue, and the table in the middle is a complimentary warm orange-yellow color. The furniture rests on a room-size creamy white, shag rug, which Lewis is rolling around on as if it's made of catnip. He has a six-story cat condo next to the large windows, and as we enter the room he bounds for his pile of new toys, making sure that I see his gifts.

"Wow, you did all this for Lewis in one day?"

"My mother loves animals," Cove says.

"I do. And I hope you don't mind, Sophia. I couldn't sleep last night knowing he was alone in your place, so I brought him over to stay with me. We keep each other company."

"That's fine. I've never seen him so happy, so I guess he's okay with it too."

"Please sit down," she says, showing me to the side dining area. Her table has a natural wood top, with the legs and sides painted a deep red. The wooden chairs are high back, and each one is painted a bright color, orange, yellow, blue, and purple. A painting that's around ten feet in length and height hangs next to me on her one white wall in the space. I admire the thick paint and the subject matter, which is an aerial view of a beach. The water is packed with people, painted using loose brushwork, slightly abstract, but precise enough to distinguish between the men and women. Some of the bodies are nude while others are wearing swimsuits. It's colorful and alive, complimenting the rest of her space. For a woman who enjoys wearing drab clothing, and who has so many tough looking tattoos, her house is quite the opposite. But it does reflect the warmth of her heart and the personality that I have come to know.

"Sophia, I need to speak with Cove in private. Here's your tea," she says setting it on the table. "We'll be back to join you in just a moment."

I take a seat and sip my tea, a white jasmine pearl, soothing to my sad heart that feels frozen in the winter snow. It beats in my chest, but is cold, hardened, and in seclusion from the rest of my body. The warmth I felt a moment ago from seeing Cove is gone as I focus again on Mera. Turning my head, I can see mother and son talking to one another across the room. Cove has one hand on the back of a sofa, and leans against it with his head down, listening to his mother's whispering words. He shakes his head no and she places a hand on his arm, rubbing gently to soothe whatever pain he feels. I stand and begin to walk toward them, needing to know what's going on. Leondra holds up her hand, halting me from taking another step their way. She raises a finger, silently requesting one more minute with him. I keep my distance, respecting her time with her son. He has his back to me. I watch as he lifts his head and runs his fingers through his dark hair and then looks at his mother. I see a resemblance in the two of them that I hadn't noticed earlier. They are both tall, with thick dark hair, and a strong posture. Her eyes have the same warmth and kindness as his, and they both have deep dimples when they smile. She looks up at her son and her brow furrows as she reaches up to wipe his cheek. She's definitely saddened by the bruising on his face, but it's more than that. I think he's crying. What is wrong?

"What's wrong?" I say out loud, stepping forward. "Is it Mera?"

Cove immediately stands upright, turning to see me approach the two of them.

"No, everything's fine. Come on, let's sit down with my mother."

"Actually, I need a few minutes to myself, please excuse me," Leondra says as I'm upon them, seeing the devastation that's now on her face as well.

"Mother, take all the time that you need. We'll be here waiting for you." Cove leans in and kisses her cheek before she disappears into the first floor bedroom. I hear a door close and then he looks at me and tries to smile.

"You don't have to fake anything with me," I say.

"I know," he replies, in a crushed voice. "Please sit back down at the table. I don't think I can stand and talk about this." As we sit, I can see the redness in his watery eyes. He's holding back, not wanting to break down in front of me.

"It's your father, isn't it?" I ask in a soft tone, remembering the text from earlier. "What happened? What did my father do?"

Cove shakes his head no. I reach out my hand and touch his arm. He backs away, something I didn't think he'd ever do again. "Cove, please don't shut me out. Talk to me."

He shakes his head and looks up, exhaling a deep breath of air. "My father's in the prison infirmary. It's not the first time either, so it doesn't mean your father had anything to do with it. Inmates don't have respect for anyone in there for certain things; like any sort of abuse of a child, especially sexual abuse." He takes a moment before continuing on. "He was jumped, beaten, has a broken nose and ribs, a ruptured spleen, and was sodomized, among other things. He's not in the best shape right now," his voice cracks as his eyes pool with water.

"Cove, I'm so sorry."

"It's my fault, Sophia," he says, shouting in a tone of disgust and anger. "I should have let you go."

His words send shivers down my spine. I can't believe that he would say such a thing. "You don't mean that, do you?"

"Yes. Yes I do," he says in a cold voice, glaring directly into my eyes. "Paul was completely right. I should've kept my dick in my pants, and stayed away from you. Now my father is suffering, and Mera is gone. I've hurt you and my mother. I need to leave and apologize in person to your father. It's the only way to fix everything I've done wrong, and to bring Mera back."

"Cove, stop it now," Leondra's voice shoots from across the room. "You didn't do this. You like a beautiful woman and you shouldn't feel guilty about that or believe that any of this is your fault."

"Mother, I did this, and I'm going to fix it."

"You can't beat Paul Jameson," she says moving toward us, her robe flying behind her as she takes the seat across from me. "You know that. You can't even get to him behind his wall of security."

"If he knows I'm coming, he'll come out from behind

his fortressed walls to meet me, especially to see me fall down on my knees in front of him."

Cove's serious, and I'm dumbstruck. I blurt out the only thing that I can think of that makes any sense. "I'm calling the cops."

"No," Leondra and Cove both say in unison, turning their heads to look at me as I push my chair back and stand. Leondra reaches across the table and takes my arm, pulling me back down to my seat.

"I'm sorry sweetie, but I need to protect my husband and my son."

"What if I just tell them about Mera. That my father took my friend."

"We're all connected," Cove says. "Your father will punish anyone you're associated with if you fuck with him."

"But I'm his daughter."

"I would say that as his daughter, your father would feel betrayed if you called the police, and after that he'd no longer consider you to be family. And from what I saw at Mera's apartment, as well as the note he left you at your place, he already feels that way about you."

"Fuck you," I exclaim, aggravated and hurt by the truth. "So that's it? Just like that my father is no longer in my life, and my best friend is gone, and even *you* think we shouldn't be together? I just lost everyone in my life in a day because I fell in love with you? Devery was right. She said prepare for the worst, and I never even thought twice that I would need to do so. Even my cat has abandoned me," I raise my voice, and slide my tea away. "Everyone is gone."

"Devery?" Cove says in a surprised voice.

"You love my son?" Leondra chimes in immediately

after Cove.

"Devery who? Devery Rosen?" he asks.

"Yeah, she's my shrink. Why?"

"Cove, let it go," Leondra says.

Cove stands and walks out his mother's door, slamming it hard behind him. Leondra holds onto my arm, not allowing me to follow.

"Give him some time. He's always like this after something happens to his father. He takes his anger out on everyone around him and says things he doesn't mean. He'll be back."

"How does he know Devery?"

"I'll let the two of you discuss that. It's really none of my business and Cove needs to be the one to speak with you about his life, not me."

I look down at her hand latched around me, and then into her eyes. "You asked me if I loved your son a second ago, and the answer is yes, I think I do, but I'm not sure what that means, or if he loves me in return. What you need to do is let go of my arm," I say, looking down again at the hand that's preventing me from leaving. "Let go of me so that I can talk to him. If I love him, and we have any chance of being together, then he can't just disappear whenever he wants to. We need to talk, and you're keeping me from that."

She releases me and I walk out her door, down the hall, and to Cove's place. I turn the handle, but it's locked. I knock, but hear nothing.

"Cove," I say knocking harder. "Let me in. We need to talk."

There's no answer. I knock one last time. Nothing. I huff down to my door, open it, and bash it shut so that he knows that I'm offended. I stomp into my kitchen and open the fridge, pulling a piece of chocolate cake out of a box with my bare hands, eating it in giant bites. Chocolate calms me down when I'm upset. I hear a knock at my door and ignore it. Yeah, apologize to me from outside that door, you asshole.

I hear Leondra's voice shout from the hall. "Sophia, it's me."

"Come in," I yell with a mouth full of cake.

She walks in and closes my door, waiting for me to join her in my foyer. I walk over with cake in hand, dropping crumbs and frosting as I move. She smiles as I approach, reaching up to wipe cake from my face.

"You can't have your cake and eat it too, honey," she says in her usual calm voice. "Cove knows that. He wants to be with you, I know he does, but there are consequences if he proceeds."

"Mera shouldn't have to be the one who pays for what we did."

"Neither should my husband, but that's how Paul Jameson works, and those are the rules we need to follow."

"I can fix this. I need to talk to him."

"Sophia," her voice low and soft, "I need you and Cove to be in my loft tonight. I can't be alone, and I don't want either one of you to be alone either. You may feel like you have no one, but you have me. I'm here for you. Why don't you get some things together for the evening? I'll make sure Cove is there as well. Then you can charge your phone and call your father, or you can use my phone if you want."

I look down at the blob of dark cake that fills my hand, and then back at the warmth radiating from this woman's face. I start to cry that she cares so much about someone who she hardly knows. I drop the cake to the floor as tears stream down my face, washing away the crumbs on the corners of my mouth. Leondra rubs my arm, and then embraces me with a tight hug.

"Sophia sweetie, everything's going to be okay. Both you and Cove have been through a lot and you're both very emotional right now. That doesn't make for a good start to any relationship. I need the two of you to be strong for one another, for yourselves, and for me." She steps back and looks at me, with a hand on each of my shoulders. "Come over when you're ready, okay?"

"I'm ready now," I say, walking up the stairs to get my clothes that are still packed and sitting on my bed. I wash my hands in my bathroom, and then take the handle of the suitcase, dragging it down the stairs. Leondra has cleaned the cake off my floor, and is waiting for me at the door. I stop at the foyer bathroom and take a tissue, wiping the tears off my cheeks before proceeding down the hallway back to her loft.

"You can stay in one of the guest bedrooms. I have two."

She takes me up the first flight of stairs, stopping at the top in front of the door that is an extra room in my place, and in Cove's loft; a pool. As expected, the room she leads me into is extraordinary and unique, just like her, full of art, passion, vibrant colors and warmth. I put my suitcase down on a black canopy bed that's covered with a lime green and orange striped blanket. A turquoise dresser is in the corner and a dark yellow chair covered with a galloping horse pattern rests next to it. There's a small wooden table next to the chair with a dark red lamp and a picture of Cove as a child. The walls are a golden yellow, and a large green shag rug covers the concrete floor. The room also has a television, a full wall of books, and a row of four photographs in white frames. Each photo is of the same winding road leading into the woods, shot during different seasons of the year.

"I'm going to talk to Cove, do you need anything?"

"No, I'm fine. Thank you," I say, looking away from the photographs.

Lewis runs in and jumps on the bed, sniffs my suitcase and rolls onto his back, playing with the latch for the zipper. He purrs as I rub his chin and the back of his ears. "Good boy," I say, placing a kiss on his head.

"There's a bathroom through that door," she says, pointing to her right. "Feel free to roam around, or to get something to eat or drink. My home is open to you."

I smile as she walks down the steps and out her door.

I'm alone in Leondra's home. A woman I just met eight days ago, who has already seen me with her son's dick in my mouth, who has drawn my vagina, nurtured my cat, comforted me while I cried, and wiped my face clean of chocolate cake. That's more than my mother has done for me in my entire life.

I open my suitcase, taking out my pajama bottoms, bath items, and phone charger, and place them onto the bed. I plug in my phone and wait for a small charge on the battery so that I can see what calls I've missed over the past two hours. My phone beeps over and over as messages and texts pour into my inbox. I check my text messages first, two from Cove, and three from Mera. Cove tells me to stay put and that he'll be back, and the final one asks me where I am. Mera sent me a text when my father was there, telling me that he's an ass. I didn't hear it come through earlier in the day. Her final two confuse me:

XOXOZZZ.

I'LL BE FINE, DDAS.

"Don't worry, I won't do anything stupid, but you better not either," I say out loud. Why would she send me a hugs and kisses text before falling asleep after my father was already there?

I check and see that her final two messages just came through about thirty minutes ago, so I immediately text her back.

CM

"Oh forget it Lewis, I'm just going to call her myself. Enough of this texting back and forth." I dial and her phone goes to voice mail. She must have already turned it off, or my father did. I leave a message telling her to call me as soon as she can, letting her know I'm fine, and that I'm going to get her out of this.

I listen to my voicemail and hear five messages from Cove, and two from Leondra from when they were searching for me earlier. Cove sounds worried that he can't find me, and he demands in each message that I call him and return to the hotel. Then, I hear my father's voice come through my phone. He's much calmer than I wouldexpect him to sound after everything that's happened, but his words still cut through me like a knife.

Sophia, I left you a note on your bed, but you deserve a better explanation from me. I'm calling to let you know that I'm leaving in a few hours and we probably won't see each other again for some time. I thought I could make it work with you, kiddo. That you and I could be father and daughter like old times, but now you know too much about my past. It's better for both of us if we separate, and probably safer for you as well. I'd be lying if I said I wasn't angry. You disrespected me, and went behind my back when I was trying to keep you safe. You have mistreated your body, tossed your friend to the sharks, and deserted me. And for who? Cove Everton? He's not a man. I believe you'll both come crawling back. Maybe this will teach you both a lesson, and if not, well... I still win. Don't expect me to drop my workload and business responsibilities to listen to you. In time, you may hear from me, but not until I make back some of the money I've lost from Cove's mistake. Cutting him out of the business puts a hole in my St. Louis area, and until that's resolved I don't want to think about the two of you. I might be able to forgive you in the future, but Cove? I'm not through with him yet. He'll never be able to keep his big mouth shut. Even though his own words put his father in prison, he'll never learn.

What a coward. The call ends, and my phone beeps with an incoming text from Mera.

TTYS

"Talk to you soon too, my friend," I whisper, and place my phone on the table next to Cove's photo. I guess I won't be calling my father tonight. Fuck, this is messed up. How did Cove's own words put his father in prison?

I look around the room, focusing on the photographs again. The four scenes on the wall should be soothing, but instead they make me feel completely alone. There's a road leading to who knows where, and the lack of any human presence is dismal. I wonder if Leondra shot these, and if the road is in this area. Seasons change, and still there's nothing. The road never changes. The trees bud and grow and then drop their leaves before the snow blankets their bare branches, but the road is always the same. Empty, disappearing around a turn into the trees.

The shelves lining the opposite wall are full of books and little family trinkets. There's a small ceramic piece that could be a bowl, or a vase, lopsided and poorly painted in a bright blue color. It has the look of a grammar school art project, and I can only assume that it was made by Cove as a child. One shelf has a family photo from Christmas morning many years ago, wrapping paper thrown everywhere, and Cove is asleep with a dump truck in his hand. His mouth is open, hair messy, and he's wearing a flannel sleep set. He was a beautiful child. He could have been a model.

I comb through the books, most of which are art related, until I come across a photo album. The first few pages are of Leondra and her husband's wedding, Cove Everton II. An invitation to the event is in the album, as well as a birth announcement for Cove two years later. The album overflows with photos of him as a baby and a toddler. The same album could be found in any middle class American home, timeless shots of a nude baby on a blanket, learning to walk, messy face after eating, crying at the sight of a candlelit birthday cake, and toddler potty training. He smiles in most of the photographs and is absolutely adorable. In one image he's giving Leondra a hug as they face the camera, cheek to cheek, with big grins.

My body aches with his absence. I crave his touch and to hear his soft voice in my ear. I close the album and slide it back onto the shelf, knowing that I'll just fall deeper in love with him with every image I see. I'm getting in too deep with this family, and if he said he made a mistake by being with me, well then I had better start figuring out a way to detach. Rummaging through family albums isn't the way to do it.

I unbutton my jeans, slide them down my legs, and then pull my sweater off over my head, and throw it onto the bed. I'm overwrought, more so than usual, and I need to relax before falling asleep. My grey flannel pajama bottoms feel comfortable against my skin as I stretch my arms over my head, and then reach my hands down to my feet. I hold the pose for as long as I can before standing upright, reaching my arms above my head once again. I continue to stretch, taking deep breaths with my eyes closed.

After a good fifteen-minute meditation session I walk out of the bedroom and stand on the second floor landing, admiring Leondra's keen eye for color and the rich textures throughout her space. From this distance, the beach scene painting with which I was so enamored earlier is drastically altered. The bodies in the painting create the shape of a skull with two eyes, something one would never notice when sitting directly next to the ten foot piece. It's a wonderful illusion, yet again, strikingly depressing like the winding road in the bedroom. I wonder if other objects in her home have the same sense of mystery, and if she planned for people to notice these things on their own, or if she explains the work in detail to her guests.

I take the flight of steps up to the third floor, expecting to see the master bedroom like I have in my loft. A harsh smell of chemicals enters my lungs as I step onto a grey concrete floor, surprised that she doesn't have the wood floors that Cove and I both share. As I lift my head, my eyes travel across the space and fix on a large wooden easel next to the window. The painting in progress is of a nude young man shown in profile. His knees are up, and his arms and hands are wrapped around his lower legs with his forehead resting on his knees. It reminds me of how I was sitting in the bathroom yesterday at the hotel. Like the other work in the house, it has a sense of sorrow, and although this calm and kindhearted woman surrounds herself with bright colors, her depression still creeps in through her work.

There are stacks of paintings that lean against the wall and as I browse through them, I find that they're all of the same man depicted during different ages of his life. In his older years he is sometimes painted with a younger woman by his side, but mostly, he's alone. The scenes are dark, using greys and cool colors. A taboret full of paints and brushes is in the middle of the room. Dried paint splatters and drips are on some of the walls, windows, and the floor around her easel. There are also piles of magazine clippings strewn around the space that I can only guess are used as reference material.

"You probably shouldn't be up here."

I turn to see Cove standing at the top of the stairs.

"I'm sorry, but your mother said I could explore. She's a very ardent and focused artist."

"I'd like you to put on a shirt, Sophia. This is my mother's home and it's disrespectful."

I look down, completely unaware that I'm only wearing my pajama bottoms and no top. Cove keeps his eyes on my face as he makes his request.

"She's seen me naked. I doubt that she'd care if I made myself comfortable in her home."

"I care," he fires at me. "Put a fucking shirt on."

"You're being such an ass."

He approaches me, unbuttoning his shirt, quickly yanking his arms through the sleeves, and then roughly throwing it at me. I catch it and turn around, putting it on to shut him up. He walks around me and rests against a window, smirking at his victory.

"So tell me how you know Devery."

"It doesn't matter, just be careful around her. She knows your father and I'd prefer if you kept information about me to yourself. She doesn't need to know my business."

"Sounds like no one needs to know your business."

"Only you, darling," he says in a cold, dry voice.

"You know, you don't have to do this. You're acting like a teenage prick. Just because you don't have the balls to stand up to my father doesn't mean you..." Cove smacks me across the face with the back of his hand before I can finish. I fall to the floor in a heap, looking up at him in both fear and anger. His face is crushed by his brutal action and he turns away, unable to view the mark that he left.

"Cove!" Leondra yells. "How dare you hit a woman, I didn't raise you this way."

"No, you didn't. Paul Jameson did," he responds with his back to us.

Leondra instantly kneels next to me, places my head against her chest, and holds me tight. "I'm so sorry, Sophia," she says, rocking her body back and forth to comfort me. I break away from her, stand, and run toward the bastard. He turns and holds his hand out, stopping me before I can get close.

"What do you want me to do, fuck you right now, Sophia? Right here in my mother's home? And then what, we live together and everything is fine for the rest of our lives? Do you want to lose Mera forever? Because that's what will happen if I step forward and continue what we started. Oh yeah, and then there's my father. Is getting fucked and screwing around with a woman more important than his life? What do you think? Come on, let's just fuck and get it over with so everyone's life is over."

"Cove, please don't do this to yourself, or to Sophia," Leondra pleads.

I walk up to him, ignoring the fact that his mother is in

the room with us. I slam my knee as hard as I can into his balls, bringing him to the floor in excruciating pain. I lean down next to him and whisper in his ear, "You're treating me the way you want to treat my father. Don't punish me because of him." I walk past Leondra and out of the room. She doesn't move from the floor or say a word, and I don't know if it's because she believes he deserved it or she's horrified by my actions.

I walk down the stairs and back to the guest bedroom, slamming the door behind me. "Fucking asshole."

Opening my suitcase, I take out a white tank, freeing myself of Cove's shirt. I hear two sets of footsteps come down the stairs, one faster than the other. I pull on my tank and there's a knock. Leondra lets herself in without waiting for my response.

"I need you downstairs in the living room. We need to talk, now."

It's the first time I've heard her sound demanding in any way, and I'm right behind her as she descends the stairs. Cove is already sitting on one of the blue couches, slightly bent over in pain.

"Sit on the couch, Sophia," she strains, walking over to the refrigerator, filling a cup with ice before dumping it into a linen hand towel. She comes within reach of her son and drops the bundled towel onto his pants. He grimaces, keeping his legs closed tight as the ice pack sits in his crotch. I take a seat on the sofa next to the one he's sitting on, and she sits across from us.

"I want you both to know that I'm going to the prison to visit my husband."

Cove sits up and waits for an invitation to join her. "When?" he asks.

"Now. He's out of surgery for his spleen, and they're

letting me see him at ten."

"What's going on?" he asks. "That's unusual. We both know that the visitation time for the infirmary ends at nine each night. Is it that serious?"

"Everything is fine. The physician has cleared him, and I'm allowed to check in, but only for thirty minutes."

"I don't believe you. They would never allow us to see him in the past when this occurred."

"Cove, look at me," she says, staring directly into his eyes. "Your father is badly hurt, but he's going to be fine. Yes, this is unusual, but not unheard of. We missed the normal hours because of the surgery. I can see him now, but not for long." She sits on the edge of her sofa, not taking her eyes off him. "I need you to calm down and listen very carefully to me. You're staying here."

"Absolutely not. I need to see him."

"Cove, you're staying here. You need to talk to Sophia before you leave."

"So you're really doing this?" I ask. "You're going to Vegas to speak to my father?"

"Speak? Probably not," he snarls. "He'll either have me on the ground as I beg for forgiveness and my life, or I'll finally have my chance."

"Chance for what? Do you think beating him up will change anything?"

"I didn't say I was…"

"Cove!" Leondra shouts, cutting him off before she turns and stares at me. "And Sophia, both of you stop arguing, now. This ends here. I'm allowing you to go to Vegas to speak to Paul, and that's it. No more fighting. I don't want my son in the hospital, or in jail. I can't lose both you and your father. You're staying here to talk to Sophia, and I'll be back to speak with you about your trip.

You know what you need to do."

He says nothing, leaning his head back to stare at the ceiling. I can see his heart pound against his chest, moving the NOVA tattoo with each beat. He places his hand over it, covering the tat as if he can read my mind. Leondra stands and pulls his hand away. She places her free hand on the side of his face and kisses his forehead.

"I need you to move forward. It's possible for you to have a normal life. Don't fight against it, fight for it. Think about that while I'm gone." She picks up her iPad from the coffee table as Cove looks at her. She holds it up and he nods, and then he leans forward to look at me again. Leondra places the iPad into her purse while she walks to her foyer. She turns back to make a final comment, before leaving her home.

"Cove, for twelve years I've regretted the day we went to the Rosen family reunion and met Paul Jameson. I hated the way I felt when Dayne and Doron Rosen took you aside with Paul and they forced you to undress down to your boxers. I was uncomfortable with their behavior, but when they threw you in the pool I thought they were just playing a prank on a young boy. I had no idea the photos shot that day of you wet, half naked, walking out of that water would lead to other things. I've tried to stay positive over the past seven years, keeping my faith that there was a reason all of this happened to us. Our reason, Cove, is sitting on that couch across from you. Let your past and your anger go. It's time. When I return I want to walk in and feel the warmth return to my home."

She closes the door and we look at one another, waiting for the other to speak.

"I'm going with you."

CHAPTER TWENTY

"I know. I already got your ticket. We're leaving in six hours."

Cove puts the ice pack on top of a magazine that's on the coffee table. He leans back, places an arm on top of the sofa, and looks at me with no expression.

"Why would you get me a ticket to go with you if you feel as though you made a mistake? I thought you were trying to let me go?"

"I was. I am. What I did to you upstairs was the biggest mistake I've ever made in my life. I've been through a lot, but that's no excuse for losing control like I did. You're absolutely right, too. I took my anger for Paul out on you, and I'm a complete ass for doing so. I'm surprised you're not back in your loft right now with the door locked."

"That was my plan, but before I had a chance to leave, your mother came into the room and asked to speak with me downstairs. I felt I owed her that time, but not you."

"I'm sorry, Sophia," he says, leaning forward to look at me. "I'm so sorry I did that to you. You don't have to forgive me, but know that I'll be haunted by my actions for the rest of my life. All I want to do is hold you, and I'm grieving because I no longer have that option. We're going to Vegas, and I'm going to get Mera back, and that's the end. Your father won't let her go unless he has me, and you won't be happy without her, so it's a trade. It's that simple."

"No, it's not. You don't have to be the martyr here. We can figure something out together. I'll talk to him."

"You're only beginning to see who he really is, I'm the one who's been in contact with him almost daily for twelve years. I've seen him put on the sensitive kindhearted act for many women, including you. None of that's real, it's just a game to him. He has me where he wants me, and I walked right into his trap."

"Stop fucking talking shit all the time. What trap?"

"You. I'm convinced now that he completely set me up by having you move in next door to me."

"You're fucking paranoid. If that were the case, why did he give me a choice in buildings, and why would he fight so hard to keep me away from you when we first met?"

"Because he knew if he did, you would become even more interested and curious about me, and vise versa. The more a parent says no, the more a child will rebel and do just the opposite, right? Your father is a brilliant man and he knew we would end up together, and he's also known for making himself look like the innocent one. He plays a good game. I bet those other buildings you looked at were crap compared to this one, right?"

I'm silent, thinking back to the other places I visited. Cove's right, they didn't compare. "So what am I the bait for?" I ask.

"He's been wanting me to do something for him and his business for years, something that will make him a lot of money. He set me up so I no longer have a choice. When we go to Vegas, I'll meet with him and agree to his terms. Then you and Mera can come back here, and life will go on."

"Again, this is ridiculous. I'm just going to talk to him and work this out. Stop acting so calm like this is the end and you've given up. Listen to your mother. Does she know your plan?"

"She doesn't need to know anything. She can stay here, take care of the business we started together, and visit my father. It will be a lot easier on her if I'm gone. She'll no longer have to worry and watch over me once I've given myself completely to Paul."

"And you think I'm the one who's disrespectful to your mother because I wasn't wearing a shirt? Are you listening to yourself? And why did you get me a ticket if you have no plans of fighting for me?"

He sighs and throws his head back, looking up at the ceiling again. "Because I knew that if I didn't get you a ticket that you'd get one on your own and fly out by yourself. At least this way I can keep an eye on you and keep you safe, even if it's only for the brief amount of time that we have left together."

He's not making any sense, so I drop the subject. His confusion about our feelings for one another is causing him to talk in circles, and if I didn't know any better, I'd say he's scared shitless and doesn't believe a word that's coming out of his own mouth.

"I'm going to say one thing to you, and then I'm going upstairs to sleep before we leave."

"I know, I'm an ass," Cove grumbles, trying to read my mind.

"No. I need you to go into battle for yourself, and not for me." His eyes follow my form as I turn and walk up the stairs, into the bedroom, and leave the door open for either

Cove or Leondra to enter at any time. I'm not hiding out, or angry, and they're welcome to talk to me over the next few hours.

I place my suitcase on the floor and set my phone alarm for four hours, giving myself enough time to pack another bag before we leave. As I turn down the bed, Lewis jumps up and begins to bathe next to my pillow. I'm joyful that we have a night to snuggle with one another before I leave. I wonder how many days we're going for, and decide to ask before I lay down for the night.

I walk to the landing and call down to Cove, "How many days do you think we'll be gone?"

He's in the kitchen getting a beer out of the fridge, and doesn't look up when he replies. "No idea. There's an expo there in two days. I figure that will be the best time to meet him, after that, you're probably set to go home unless we have some details to work out. Pack for a week, just to be on the safe side." He sips his beer and throws the bottle cap on the counter. It bounces a few times before it spins and comes to a stop. I decide to turn away as he looks up, not giving him the satisfaction of seeing me. I turn off the bedroom light and crawl into the bed with Lewis, petting him as he lets out a loud purr. I pull off my pajama bottoms from under the covers and toss them on the floor, sleeping only in my underwear and tank. Leondra's home is warmer than mine, and I'm enjoying how comfortable I feel being here.

I awake from a light sleep, hearing voices on the ground floor in the middle of the night. Lewis is spread out next to me, and I gently move the covers, being careful not to disturb him. I step over to the bedroom door to try to figure out what's going on. I can see the clock in the kitchen reads ten, it's still early, and I've only been asleep for about an hour. Cove is sitting at the dining room table with a laptop, and I hear Leondra speaking to him. They must be using FaceTime to talk to one another. A male voice comes through the computer, muffled and slow, and I immediately know that it's Cove's father.

"What happened to you, son? Your face looks worse than mine."

"I'm fine, Dad. I'm worried about you though. Tell me that you're okay. Mom wouldn't let me come with her, and I thought she was going to see you because you were going to die. I can't believe they let her in after hours for any other reason."

"Cove, calm down, I'll be okay. I think Paul may have helped get her in to see me tonight."

"Why would he do that? Don't you think you're sitting in that bed right now because of him?"

"If I am, his concern for our family is making for a great cover, wouldn't you say?"

I quietly slide down to the floor, sitting with my legs crossed, peering out between the metal railings at Cove's face. He places his hand on his forehead and rubs, appearing tired and depressed.

"What's wrong, son? Tell me what happened. Your mother said you met a girl, but she wouldn't tell me anything more. Did one of her old boyfriends beat you up? Does she have a husband or something?"

Cove smiles at the screen, and it's a relief to see that he's still capable of doing so.

"No, dealing with a husband would be easy. How about a Jameson?"

I hear nothing. Cove's father is silent and I wonder if the connection was lost, or if he hung up. I would expect him to scream and throw a fit like my father, but there's only silence. Cove's smile disappears; he rubs his forehead again, waiting to hear his father's voice.

"Son, move your hand so that I can see your face. Don't hide from me."

He puts his hand down and lifts his head, tears welling in his eyes.

"I've never seen you like this, Cove. This is Paul's daughter we're talking about here?"

Cove nods his head, as words get trapped in his throat.

"And Paul did this to you, or was it one of his thugs?"

"Paul."

"Tell me what happened."

Leondra's voice comes through from a distance. "I'll fill your father in on the details, Cove, just say what you need to say. We're running out of time."

"Son, I need to make sure you understand that what happens to me in here has nothing to do with you, it's between Paul and myself."

"I will never believe that."

His father is silent, and I hear Leondra whisper something, but I can't make out her words. Cove is fixated on the screen, and at one point he touches the computer, as if he's trying to touch his father's face.

"Tell me about her. I want to hear about the woman who finally captured my son's heart."

"There are issues, Dad. You know exactly what I'm dealing with right now. I'm stepping back."

"Tell me about her. I want to hear your voice and see your face as you talk about her."

Cove smiles and allows a tear to escape from his eye.

"Tell me. I need to see and hear your emotions, son."

I sit up on the landing, waiting to hear his words.

Finally, Cove speaks.

"She's the most beautiful woman I've ever seen. Pure and innocent, very different from this world that we're wrapped up in, and naive about her father. Her skin is soft, and when she touches me I feel free and alive, something that I've never felt before. I've been in darkness for so long that the light from her is rejuvenating. Her eyes pierce me like a knife, and my body and heart yearn for her when she's not next to me." He stops for a moment and clears his throat, closing his eyes and taking a deep breath. "I need her, Dad. I want to take care of her, keep her from harm, and keep her from Paul. When we're together, I no longer feel cold and abandoned. She comforts me and makes me laugh. I can tell she's brilliant like her father, but in a positive way. She's curious and caring, someone I would want to be with for a lifetime."

A tear rolls down my cheek, matching the one on Cove's. I'm holding on to the railing now with both hands, waiting to hear more.

"So your voice and face show true love. That's all you need in this life, son. You can't take your material items or money with you to the grave, but you can take that love in your heart. That's the only thing I have right now, and it's what keeps me going. Nothing else matters."

"It's more complicated than that, Dad. If it were that easy I'd be lying next to her right now."

"It is that easy."

"The damage on my face and yours proves that it's not."

"What are you going to do, Cove?"

"I'm surrendering myself to Paul, letting him use me to market NOVA again."

"To hell you are," his father says, starting to cough as

he raises his voice. Leondra steps in to control the conversation.

"Cove, you're upsetting your father. Think before you speak, and before you act."

His father recovers from his coughing fit, lowering his voice, showing his determination. "You will do no such thing, and I'll make sure of that. I still have some connections in Vegas and outside this place."

Leondra speaks, her voice steady and direct like her husband's. "You and I will talk about this when I get home, and I will knock some sense into you. If you think we're going to give you up so that Paul can make another big profit...."

My phone beeps with an incoming text and Cove looks up, seeing me listening on the landing. He stands and knocks his chair over in the process.

"Is that her?" his father asks.

I run into the bedroom and pick up the text, embarrassed, not knowing what else to do. It's from Mera.

HE'S WATCHING YOU it reads. What the fuck? I pace for a moment, thinking about how to handle this. That bastard. Sprinting down the stairs with my phone in hand, I show it to Cove, who's back in his chair. He peers down at it and smiles at me, not making a scene in front of his parents.

"Sophia, lean down and let me see you," his father says.

I place my hand on Cove's shoulder and squat down next to him, seeing a broken face on the screen that looks like the man I'm touching. It's hard to tell one's age when a face is swollen and bruised, and at this point, the two of them look almost exactly alike with their injuries.

"Hello Mr. Everton," I say with a smile, not knowing

how to proceed with the conversation, especially since I'm being viewed in my underwear.

"Oh, my God. My son has fallen for a beautiful dove. It's so nice to know that you're there with him. I wish I could meet you in person. I'm assuming you know a little about what's going on."

"Yes, I believe I've been filled in on what I need to know. I'm sorry about my father. I wish I could set things right."

I see Leondra's hand on her husband's shoulder, and she gives him a squeeze. His father's hand goes up to rest over hers, showing us how infinite their love is.

"Excuse me, I'll let you finish your conversation, in private," I say, lifting my head to look around the room. Cove reaches down and takes my hand, and I get the message that I should keep quiet about the text. I kiss the top of his head putting on a show for his father, and then walk up to the bedroom. I sink into the bed pulling the covers over my head, hiding from reality. These are the kindest people I've ever met. My father should be in prison, not Mr. Everton.

I listen as Cove says his goodbyes. The laptop clicks shut and there's a heavy pounding on each step as he races up the stairs. He lifts the covers, and slides in next to me, forcing Lewis to find a new place to sleep.

"Was that text from Mera?" he whispers in my ear.

"Yes. She's sent me a few this evening."

"Let me see them."

I open my hand, passing him the phone. He opens each text, heavily breathing from the run up the stairs.

"Why is she so nonchalant, saying she'll be fine, and sending you x's and o's?" he questions.

"I've been trying to figure that out myself. I'm

starting to wonder if she doesn't mind going with him. Maybe she packed in a rush to leave with him, but wasn't necessarily forced. My father said he took her, but at this point, and after what you've told me, that's probably a lie."

"Shh. Keep you voice down," he says softly in my ear, instantly causing a rush and an arousal in my body. "If she went with him by choice, then she'll regret it once she realizes what she's getting into. You said she has a crush on him, right?"

"Yes."

"And he knows?"

"Yeah. Why?"

"I think Mera's the next Paul Jameson house whore."

I throw the covers back and sit straight up. "What the fuck."

Cove covers my mouth with his hand and hushes me, pulling me down to the bed, throwing the blanket back over the two of us.

"Shh, Shh, Sophia. Quiet. My mother and I have had her place swept for bugs and cameras many times, hoping to find one space for privacy, but he must have planted something yesterday when he was here. I don't know if it's just downstairs, or if he has something up here as well. Just stay as quiet as you can when we discuss him."

I turn and look his way, my lips inches away from his. My feelings steadily grow with each hour we're together. How much more can my heart take before these sensations are so strong that they burst and break me?

"It's obvious by the term house whore what that is, but if that's the case, isn't that the same as being in other areas of his company?"

"No. Paul's brutal, and so are his guards. She's better off in the world of the unknowns where there are at least some rules between employees."

"Shit," I whisper, placing my hand over my eyes. "So, you think I'm naive?"

"About your father? Yes, I do."

"Did you mean everything you said about me to your father?"

"I'd never lie to him."

I take off my shirt and pull off my underwear, lying next to him naked.

"Sleep next to me, in the nude."

"My mother will be home soon, and we still have a lot to talk about."

"Actions can speak louder than words."

"I meant I have to speak with her, not you."

He brushes the back of his hand against my stomach and lets out a deep sigh, actually looking down at my breasts. The room is dark and even though we're under the covers, I know he can still make out the curves that he's touching with his hand. He lets out another deep breath before changing the subject.

"Are there any other messages on your phone? Did Mera or your father call you?"

"Yeah, as a matter of fact, he did."

Cove sits up, holds his hand out, and waits for me to scroll through my voicemail. I hand him the phone and he listens to my father's voice. His fists clench and then slowly release as he listens. He hangs up the phone and tosses it on the side table, lying back down pulling the covers over our heads.

"How did your words place your father in prison?" I ask.

"I went to the police, at least I tried to, which is why I told you not to earlier. I tried to bring his company down, but he set my father up instead, in turn punishing me for thinking that I could beat him. When I say all of this is my fault, and my father's in prion because of me, I really mean it. I was eighteen, and dumb enough to believe I had a friend in NOVA. That person also wanted out, but turned on me and told Paul of my plan. Everything went south after that."

"And your mother? What did she mean earlier about the Rosen reunion? Why was your family there?"

Cove stands and turns on a light, pulling the photo album out that I had looked at earlier. He opens it to the wedding announcement, handing it to me. I sit up, take it from him, and read through the names on the card that I hadn't noticed earlier, Cove Everton II, and Leondra Rosen. Cove places his finger against his lips as a reminder for me to stay quiet.

"Your mother's a Rosen?" I mouth to him.

He shakes his head yes while reaching for the card, placing it back in the book and on the shelf. I can see his erection pushing against his grey jeans before he turns off the light and returns to the bed.

"My mother's cousins are Devery, Dayne, and Doron Rosen. Your father's old roommates and best friends are Dayne and Doron. They were all at the reunion that day, and that's how my parents met your father, and your father found me. He used to call me his young white dwarf star. Some people in the business still do. I was never sure if Devery knew anything about me, or about Paul. I only saw her a few times after that day. Small world, right?"

"Confusing world," I reply. "Cove?"

He looks at me and waits for my question. I place my hand against his erection and I'm surprised that he doesn't back away.

"I'm not going to do this with you right now, Sophia. I've been hard since I saw you looking at yourself in the downstairs bathroom mirror. My balls ache, but partly because you kneed them earlier. I have to get through this night, get us on the plane, and then we can have a full day before the expo to discuss my feelings, and what you heard me say to my father. Until then, I need to stay focused."

He sits up and leaves the room, closing the door behind him as he exits. I listen to his footsteps travel down the stairs and over to the kitchen, where he opens the refrigerator, twisting off another bottle cap. It drops onto the counter and I hear it bounce before it rolls to a stop.

"Drinking won't keep you focused," I yell down to him.

I fidget thinking about his body and that beautiful, yet sadly injured face. I'm unable to fall asleep. I don't want to masturbate with him just a room away. I want him next to me. If he would just rub against me one time I could easily release. I'm that close.

"Fuck," I whisper, getting out of bed and walking down the stairs, approaching him as he leans against a cabinet in the kitchen. He looks at my chest and then down to my lower nakedness. Taking a sip of his beer, he shakes his head, hinting at my poor judgment. I know my father can see me, and I don't care. He shouldn't be spying on the Evertons and if he doesn't like what he sees, he can turn off his fucking camera.

"Sophia, think about what you're doing," he says in a calm voice, taking another sip of his beer.

"At least you looked this time."

"I always see you, in my own way. What do you want me to do? I already told you we're not going to do this, so what do you want?"

361

"I need you, and if you really meant everything you said about me, then you'd come back up stairs with me right now."

He smiles and takes another swig before putting the bottle down on the counter. He folds his arms and stares me up and down again.

"There's a lot more to a relationship than sex," he says.

"Ergh," I respond, stomping my foot. "You piss me off so much, why can't you just touch me?"

He smiles and looks behind me, and I realize we're not alone. I turn to see Leondra standing only a foot away. She's smiling too, and I realize I've made a complete fool of myself.

"Well, I'm glad to see the two of you are beginning to work things out," she says. "Someone famous once said, being naked in front of one another while arguing is a lot better than inflicting pain on each other while clothed."

"Who said that?" Cove asks.

Smiling, Leondra says, "I just made it up."

Cove laughs at his mother as I cover myself, walk back up stairs and pull my tank quickly over my head. I slide on my pajama bottoms and walk out to the second floor landing.

"I'm sorry, Leondra," I yell down, while shooting Cove my middle finger. He laughs again, finding my sexual frustration cute. I turn and close the door, leaving the two of them to talk. Cove's not going to say very much with my father listening, and if I eavesdrop, I'm no better than him. I learned my lesson earlier.

I position the pillow over my head and let out a silent scream, kicking my feet on the bed like a toddler in the middle of a tantrum. It seems cruel to share his feelings about me with his parents, and then to ignore me like everything he said would have no effect on me. Throwing the pillow down to the floor I roll onto my stomach and reach my hand between my underwear and pajama bottoms. I listen for Cove and Leondra's voices to make sure they're still downstairs, not wanting them to walk in on me while I'm having some *me* time.

My fingers find just the right spot, resting between my two outer lips. It's only a few moments before I can feel an orgasm begin. I lift my head slightly off the bed to watch the door for unwanted guests. My lower body pushes into my fingers, and I work them quickly back and forth across the spot. *Fuck, I need you, Cove.*

I put my head down onto the bed and my fingers slow as I reach my climax. I bite down on the sheet, trying not to make any whimpering sounds. My fingers feel the surge shoot across my mound as the orgasm races and pounds, imitating my beating heart. I roll onto my back, rest my fingers down below, and feel both the pulsations and my breathing begin to slow.

That took a whopping thirty seconds. All I needed was for him to touch me and I would have exploded. What is he waiting for? We can do this. We can make this work.

The door creaks open and I pull my hand up from under my pants, turning to see Cove in the doorway.

"You fall asleep yet?"

"Are you kidding me?" I say in a perturbed tone. "What do you think?"

He walks in and pulls his shoes from his feet, unbuttoning his pants and his shirt. He takes everything off except for his boxers and slides into the bed next to me.

"You were masturbating."

"How can you tell?"

"The bed is extremely warm, you're out of breath, and," he takes my hand and sniffs my fingers, "your scent is on your hand."

"So what if I did?"

"Did you think about me?" he asks.

"You asshole, of course I did. What do you think?"

"Sophia, I know you're angry at me. I had no right to take my resentment for your father out on you, and I'm sorry. Do you think we can get past all of that, or are you going to be pissed at me forever?"

"I'm not pissed at you for smacking me," I pause for a moment, not believing the words that just came out of my mouth. "No, wait, yes I am, you can't touch me in such a violent way. Who the fuck do you think you are? You'll never get away with that again."

"Well, you didn't let me get away with it the first time either."

Reaching down to gently apologize to his balls, I come into contact with his stiff erection instead. It's completely out of his boxers and ready for action. He takes my hand, trying to stop me, and I break away from his grip, heading back down to his shaft. He prevents any further encounter by standing up and putting his pants back on. He comes back to bed and lies on his back next to me, eyes glaring at the ceiling.

"I was going to sleep next to you, to comfort you, and to let you know that I'm sorry, but I think that's probably not the best idea right now."

"Listen to me, Cove Everton," I say, lifting my body over his. "I just pleasured myself, with thoughts of you fucking me as my visual, and why? Because I can't get you out of my head and I hate it. I hate the fact that I've fallen for you. I overheard how you feel about me, but you still refuse to get close, or touch me. You're about to burst as well, I see it, and I feel it. And no, I'm not talking about this thing," I say, grabbing his hardness through his jeans. "I'm talking about your voice when you were speaking to your father, I'm talking about the tear that you had running down your face earlier. That was for me. And now you come in here and strip down, but I can't touch you. Fuck you."

He says nothing and just continues to stare at the ceiling. He places his arm over his eyes as if he's blocking out a light shining down into them.

"Sophia," he calmly says. "When and if the time is ever right, I want to be with you forever. You mean more to me than you realize. But you're still not being patient with me, and I've asked you quite a few times already to do so. I don't want this to be about sex, and only sex. I came in here to spend time with you, not to fuck you." He rises from the bed and sits in the horse-patterned chair across from me. The room is dark, but I know he's looking directly into my eyes. "I also don't want to hurt you, and I'm afraid I've already done so, not just physically, but emotionally as well. If I go through with my task for your father when we get to Vegas, then we'll probably never see one another again. I need you to remember me as someone who cared for you, and not just a good fuck."

"So you think you'd be good at fucking?"

He stands and heads for the door. I leap from the bed and pull him back into the room before he has a chance to escape. He turns around and I can see his face glow in the hallway light. He's seriously hurt by my comment.

"Cove," I say softly, while holding onto his forearm with my hand. "I'm sorry. I've never had anyone treat me as well as you do and sometimes my reactions are based more on a lack of self-confidence, or uncertainties with how I'm feeling, than what I'd actually like to say. Maybe I know that this is about to end, so I try to make a joke out of everything to cover the pain that I'm feeling."

He wraps his arms around me and kisses the top of my head as I hold onto him.

"I am sorry, Babe. You can sleep next to me, and we can just talk, or sleep. I promise I won't touch you."

"I need to let you go, Sophia. I'm sorry." He breaks away and leaves the room, closing the door behind him. The light cuts out and I'm left standing alone in the dark, waiting for him to return.

CHAPTER TWENTY-ONE

The alarm on my phone sounds, waking me early enough to pack and get ready for our flight at six. It's three in the morning, and I slept by myself in Leondra's spare bedroom. It took me an hour to fall asleep after he left the room last night. My mind raced with thoughts of him, and what's going to happen to all of us when we get to Vegas. I hope Mera's okay and she's keeping her head above water with my father.

As I walk out of the bedroom, I see Cove asleep on one of the blue sofas. Lewis is snuggled next to him, and they're both sound asleep. Cove has one of his arms stretched above his head and a foot on the floor. He looks prepared to get up quickly if someone were to enter the place. Lewis on the other hand is curled into a little ball, with no plans of stirring, or to protect us from intruders. I reach for my phone and snap a quick picture of the lovely sight before it disappears before my eyes forever.

Cove sits up upon hearing the click of my phone, in search of the noise. He spies me on the top landing and smiles, stretching his arms over his head while he yawns. I can't help but view him as a little boy at times.

"What's so amusing?" he asks.

"You're very cute, even when you first wake up and your hair is all messy, I think you're adorable."

He glides his hand through his hair, tousling it back into place.

"Return the compliment Cove, don't leave her hanging." Leondra's voice calls out to her son from the dining room table where she's drinking coffee and reading the news on her iPad.

"Good morning, Mother. You look beautiful," he smirks.

"Oh not me, say something nice to Sophia."

He laughs and I join him. Leondra smiles and I send her my *I don't care* look.

"No worries. I know I'm hot," I say, walking down the stairs like a model strutting her stuff.

"Why don't the two of you shower, then pack, and I'll make you both some breakfast before you head out for your flight."

She's being very casual about our trip, and I wonder exactly what Cove said to her last night. He was in the bedroom rather fast, and I don't believe they spoke for more than five minutes after she returned from the prison. If my son were heading out to confront and possibly join forces with the devil, I wouldn't be as calm as she is right now. I wonder if she even knows about his plan. Fuck, I just realized I don't even know exactly what he's up to, except for his thoughts on resurrecting NOVA. His parents would never allow him to do that, and I know him well enough to recognize that he wouldn't harm a child. So what exactly would it mean to bring NOVA back?

"What are you thinking about," he says, as he pours himself a cup of coffee.

"NOVA."

He places his cup on the counter and looks at me, his eyes squint as he tries to grasp my intentions. "This isn't the time or the place to talk about NOVA. Not another word about it comes from your mouth, do you understand? And I'm talking to both of you." He looks over at his mother and then to me.

I nod, respecting his past, as well as his mother's presence in the room with such difficult subject matter. She stands and pulls some eggs out of the fridge, as Cove sips his coffee.

"Is it okay if I shower here before I go and pack?" I ask.

"By all means, Sophia, feel free to use the bathroom in the foyer or the one upstairs next to your room," Leondra says, while cracking eggs into a bowl.

My room. I like that. Upstairs I find a clean, long-sleeve black dress that I had packed for Mera's, just in case I was there for a while and we were able to travel out somewhere, like to a bar or to dinner. It's knee-length, and somewhat dressy, but comfortable enough for the plane. I have no bra and I'm out of clean underwear, but I can put those on later in my loft while I pack my bag for the trip.

I decide to use the foyer bathroom, leaving the upstairs one for Cove if he needs it. I'm more comfortable in this space, and it was the last place that he pressed his lips against mine, so I'm happy in here.

The claw foot tub has a long hose with a showerhead attachment that you have to hold by hand. I turn on the water and then walk over to the toilet to relieve myself while I wait for the water to warm. Next to the toilet is a waist basket, only about a foot away from me, and upon sitting down I can see a wad of tissues in the basket that he used to clean up his *stuff*. He must have masturbated very recently. It's good to know he couldn't control himself either.

I stand and flush, smiling as I walk over to the tub. The water's warm and I undress, pulling the curtain around me. As I lather up I hear the bathroom door creak open. I peek out of the curtain to see Cove placing clean towels on the counter.

"Hey," I say to him.

"Sorry to disturb you, I thought you might need these."

"Come over here. I want to ask you something."

He gives me a hesitant look, but then walks over as I peer out from behind the curtain.

"Did you think about me last night?" I whisper with a smile, looking over to the wastebasket and then back at him.

He turns and walks out but I can sense the grin on his face as he leaves and closes the door.

I love the playful interaction the two of us have. It's something I never had with Evan or experienced in any other relationship besides Mera, and I can only imagine Cove feels the same way. The more I think back to living with Evan, the more I realize he was just a roommate with benefits. There was no interaction between us other than sex, and Cove's comment of wanting more than that has me re-evaluating how I've trained my body and mind to find pleasure explicitly through sex. I thought I had feelings for Evan, maybe even loved him as a friend, but now I'm not sure it was anything more than convenience at the time. He was a body in my space that I thought would keep me company, and now I realize I felt more alone with him than at any other time in my life.

With Cove, I have another extreme; he comes complete with a sweet and loving mother, something else that has always been missing from my life. It's weird being in her home, and yet strangely comforting. Maybe I've lost my family; my mother and my father, but perhaps I'm discovering a new one. She wants me here, and I'm sure she's just as lonely as both Cove and myself. We're three insecure people, all with good cause in feeling so, trying to find a way out of our wavering, unstable worlds. It's probably completely unhealthy for all of us to be under the same roof, but the alternative of being alone in our respective lofts is just as distressing. With Cove and I approaching our mid-twenties, we should be out on our own, but our pasts are so uncommon that we don't fit into any sense of a cultured norm. He's still a boy at times, having never experienced his teenage years. Most kids spend time despising their parents, rebelling against them and their beliefs. Cove wanted just the opposite. He needed them to help him, to comfort him, and save him. I believe he's still searching for that from both of them. He's the strongest person I've ever met, having gone through what he did, but also the weakest when it comes to leaving the past behind. And then there's me. I've spent years being cared for by my father, sheltered, spied on, and never developing into a confident adult, while my mother has found me to be worthless and a burden.

We've happily entered Leondra's home, unknowingly seeking a safe haven and her welcoming guidance without acknowledging....

"Sophia," Cove says, knocking on the door. "What's taking you so long?"

"We're fucked," I whisper.

"What?"

"I said we're fucked."

He opens the door and closes it behind him as I finish putting on a small amount of make-up.

"You look incredible, but you need something warmer on your legs. You're going to freeze."

"I have some sweater tights I'll put on once I get to my place."

"So, what did you mean by that?"

"You and I," I say looking over to him. "We…"

"Stop. Everything's going to be fine. You're thinking too much. Stop playing things over in your mind and trust me. I'm taking care of this, and you, Mera, and my mother will all be fine."

"And you?"

"I can take care of myself. I always have."

"That's what I was thinking about. We both have issues. No one ever helped you, and I've been tossed aside. We're both enjoying the comforts of being in this home with a mother figure a little too much, wouldn't you say? We're adults, but in reality we're both still kids. I don't believe you when you say you can take care of yourself."

"You have to trust me. I know what I'm doing."

"Come on, kids. I have breakfast waiting for you," Leondra calls out to us.

I look at Cove and smirk, putting my hand on my side while tilting my hip. "See," I say, lifting my eyebrows.

"Pessimism will get you nowhere," he responds, reaching his hand out to me.

"But it fills me with greater enjoyment when good things do occur instead of just being optimistic all of the time," I smile, taking his hand as we walk together to the dining area. He pulls my chair out for me and I sit in front of my plate, giggling at the sight of two eggs and bacon formed into the shape of a smiley face. "See," I say again, pointing to my plate.

"Yeah, but you're smiling, right?" he says.

"So what does that mean?"

"If it makes you happy, don't fight it," he responds.

"Word to the wise," Leondra says to Cove. "Now both of you eat, so that you can get going. The sooner you talk to Paul, the sooner you'll be back here, and we can begin anew."

Cove looks down at his plate, poking his egg eyes with his fork. He sighs, taking a piece of toast from a plate in the middle of the table and smearing a touch of apple butter onto it. He takes a bite and chews for what seems like minutes before swallowing. He puts his fork down and runs his fingers through his hair, sighing again. He looks around the room and I know he's thinking about my father listening to us.

"Cove, what's wrong?" Leondra asks him in a slow and concerned voice. "Are you nervous about flying? I know you don't do well on planes."

"No. I'm just thinking about our new business. I'm leaving you with a lot of work, and I don't want you to feel overwhelmed."

"Oh, I'll be fine. We have a lot of good workers at the lounge, and Haverty will help me out. Everything will be fine until you get back."

He hasn't told her he might not be returning to St. Louis. I say *might not* because I still have hope that he will, but I know his plan is to stay in Vegas. For how long, I don't know, but longer than Leondra believes.

"Can you handle it if I'm gone for a while? I mean, Paul might have business for me in Vegas, and I may not be back for some time."

"Cove," she says firmly and with no uncertainty. "You will be back next week. I'm sure of it. Come hell or high water if you don't return I'll be the first person on

Paul Jameson's doorstep, with my gun."

He shakes his head, sitting back in his chair. "I just want you to understand that I may have work to do, Paul's not one to forgive, and I'll have to do a few things to regain his trust before I'll be back."

"You're coming back next week, Cove," she says with watery eyes.

Cove reaches across the table, taking his mother's hand. He leans forward, taking a bite of his eggs and then sits back again, turning to me as he swallows.

"Sophia, go pack. I need to have a conversation with my mother. Meet me back here in thirty minutes. Be sure you dress warmly for the plane, but bring light clothes for Vegas. Everyday clothes, and something a bit more elegant."

I look at him, shaking my head no. "I want to be a part of this conversation. I have a right to know what we're doing when we get there, and you can't keep me in the dark forever."

"Sophia," his voice direct and uncompromising. "Go pack, now. This is a private family conversation."

I roll my eyes and stand, grab my suitcase from the bedroom, and walk out to the foyer. I hear Leondra mention my safety in the building. Cove's sure that we're still being watched in the hall, but that I'll be fine.

"Paul has his prize and at this point he's just keeping on eye on us so that we don't go to the cops. She's fine."

I walk down the quiet hallway into my place. I look up in my foyer, expressionless, hoping my father is looking down at me. I don't know if he can only view me from his office or if he has something set up on his laptop, but even if no one's there, I still feel some odd presence. I can't believe he's been watching me for all these years. I stare, motionless for a good five minutes, wanting to make him, or whoever else is out there, uncomfortable.

I wander silently around the loft, running my hands along the fabrics on the furniture and over all of the counters. I don't want to come back to this without Cove living next door to me. I don't think I can live here anymore. I can imagine myself running to the door each time the elevator sounds, yearning to see him appear in the hall.

My phone startles me, and my heart jumps a beat as I reach into my bag to answer it. It's Cove.

"Hello?"

"Are you packing or are you thinking?"

"Fuck, do you have a camera on me too?"

He laughs before saying no. "Of course not, but you've been daydreaming way too much. I know you well enough that I can picture you standing in your place, losing focus at the task at hand."

"Alright, I'm going upstairs right now. Now leave me alone," I say lightheartedly.

Smiling, I hang up my phone and run up the stairs. My suitcase bangs on each step behind me. I stop at the top and see the note from my father still sitting on the floor next to my bed.

"Stay focused," I whisper to myself. I ignore it and head for my closet, dumping the contents of my suitcase onto the floor to start fresh for the trip. I'm running out of clean clothes and need to take care of laundry soon. I can't even fathom finding the time to do that with everything else that's going on. Fuck, what should I pack? Start with the basics and work outward. I place eight pairs of underwear and six bras into the bag, a pair of jeans, a low-cut skirt, five t-shirts, two long-sleeve shirts, pajamas, two above the knee dresses, a sweatshirt, and some socks. I find two of my more formal dresses, one short, and one a bit longer, and I place them into the bag, trying not to wrinkle them too much. I find some shoes to take along, and finally come across my thigh-high sweater tights and garter belt. I slide them on, and wrap a black and white polka-dot scarf around my neck before heading into the bathroom with a smaller bag for toiletries. I make sure to double check that I have my phone, charger, wallet, a small purse, and a book for the flight. I'm ready.

My stomach is queasy as time passes. Every hour is an hour closer to returning here, alone. I'm excited to take this trip, but only because I'll be with him. I wonder how it will be when we have to say goodbye. It's possible that he might disappear, without even saying a word to me. What if I can't let him go?

My phone beeps again, and I see an email come through from Devery. What the fuck does she want on a weekend at four in the morning? I open her message and all it says is *call me*. No fucking way, I'm not calling you. Cove is paranoid about my father, believing that I was bait, and I feel the same way about her. She probably tells my dad every word that comes out of my mouth in our sessions.

I drag my two bags down the stairs and lock my door, hoping I won't be back for a while. The longer I'm gone, the more time I'll have with Cove.

I see him exit his door at the end of the hall. He has two suitcases and a shoulder bag, packing a bit more than me. Leondra meets us by his door. She holds Lewis in her arms, while tears stream down her cheeks. She hands me a brown bag and tries her best to hide her emotions.

"It's a bacon and egg sandwich. Eat it on your way to

the airport, will you sweetie?"

I give her a hug and kiss Lewis on his little nose, thanking her for everything.

Leondra quietly speaks in a sorrowful voice. "Make sure the two of you look out for one another. Keep your phones charged. Stay safe and be back here in one week. Any longer and I'll be there with the troops." She reaches for her son and gives him a big hug. "Be careful. Apologize and make it back here in one piece."

He kisses her cheek, and pulls away, knowing that the goodbyes will never end unless he breaks contact. "Goodbye, Mother. Be safe yourself, and take care of Sophia if I'm not back."

He walks away from her and I join him, looking back to see the devastation on her face. She covers her mouth with her hand; a rush of tears streaming down her face, and then she disappears around the corner to her loft. I hear a door close and weeping from a distance.

"You didn't have to end with that. You could have just told her that you loved her."

He looks at me as we wait for the elevator, his bag over his shoulder, and a suitcase in each of his hands. "It's better to start preparing her now. I'll still be able to talk to her, I just won't be able to see her like she wants me to."

"And like *you* want to as well, right?"

"Yes. And like I want to as well."

The elevator reaches the top and with a quiet ding the doors open, stirring us to step inside.

***

Leondra placed the eggs and bacon between two pieces of wheat toast and the brown paper bag has a drawing of a heart on the outside. I eat the sandwich in the Escalade as we drive to the airport. One of Cove's employees from the Scarlett is driving, which is nice since we're both running on only a few hours of sleep. I yawn and Cove copies my action. He places a hand on my leg and runs it up below my dress.

"Shit. These are thigh-highs, and you're wearing a garter no less. I thought you were putting on sweater tights to keep warm?"

"They are a sweater knit, and very warm. They just stop short."

"You know you have to go through the scanner, right? You'll have those guards drooling for you just as much as I am."

"Well maybe that's my plan. They can search me if they want, and I'd appreciate the skin to skin contact that I'll finally be receiving from someone."

"I'm touching you right now, aren't I?"

I take his hand and slide it further up until he comes into contact with my flesh.

"Fuck, Sophia. No underwear today?" he whispers in my ear. "What are you doing to me?" his breath heavy against my neck. "I would give anything to lay you down in this back seat right now and ram into you."

I start to lower onto the seat, and he pulls me back up, smiling at my playfulness. He places his hand back on my leg, and kisses the side of my head.

"Thanks for dressing that way. You're doing the same thing to me you know."

He gives me a confused look and I take hold of his dark sport coat.

"This outfit. You look incredible and you're driving me mad. Look at you," I say, moving forward on the seat and turning toward him. "You have on these form fitting dark jeans that show off your bulge."

"Well that's only there because of you."

I place my finger over his lips to shut him up. "And, this crisp white dress shirt, with the top two buttons open, and an elegant thin dark colored tie slightly loosened to fall below those two buttons. God you look so relaxed, yet sophisticated. And that black fedora. Classy."

"I like to dress up a bit when I fly."

"Plus that sport coat makes you look important, and wealthy. It's a Cremieux isn't it?"

"Yes, one of my favorite brands."

"Well, thanks for doing that to me. How am I not supposed to think about you in a sexual way when you look and smell that good? What is that cologne you have on today anyway?"

"Clive Christian C," he smiles, and looks out the window, his hand still on my upper leg. "I feel relieved now that we're out of my mother's place and that building. I'll feel even better once we get on the plane."

"Why's that? I thought you didn't like to fly?" I ask.

"I don't. I hate it. But we'll be away from Paul, at least for a while. He's had a bug or camera on me for years and the lack of privacy can be troubling."

"Is that why you were so loving at the hotel, and when we got back to our building you were a complete ass to me?"

The driver looks back at us and Cove doesn't respond. He squeezes my leg and then takes his phone out of his coat pocket, checking the time and for any messages.

"I'll talk to you about some things when we're up in the air. For now, just know that what I said to you earlier hasn't changed. My purpose in all of this is to return your friend to you, keep the prison heavies away from my dad, and unfortunately that means I need to let you go."

I look at the driver who's focused once again on the road, instead of the two of us. "How well do you know him?" I whisper to Cove.

"Don't worry about him, just tell me if you notice anyone following us. I'm still trying to figure out who he has keeping an eye on you. I know most of them, but I haven't seen any recognizable faces just yet."

"My father said he was leaving me alone, no cameras, and no protection."

"And you believe him? See how easy you are to fool?"

"Yeah, I suppose," I say quietly, defeated once again. "I thought he got what he wanted and he was going to leave us alone, at least for a while."

"He's *getting* what he wants. I'm on my way. Let's not have this conversation again."

I finish my sandwich as we pull up to the airport. Our driver opens our doors, and I step out into the chilly air. My dress flies slightly up to show off some skin and Cove immediately places my winter jacket over my shoulders.

"Keep warm, I don't want you to catch a cold."

"You can't catch a cold from being in the cold you know, that's just an old wives' tale."

"Well then, let me keep you covered so that I don't have to view that beautiful body and cum in my pants. Is that better?"

I laugh, smacking him across the upper arm as we walk inside the sliding glass doors. Our driver checks our luggage, and we get our boarding passes from one of the many kiosks lined up along the check-in counters. Cove's quiet as we go through security. We enter the premium lounge for first-class travelers and he orders us each a shot. His is down his throat as soon as the bartender places it on the counter.

"Nervous?"

"I'm fine," he says coldly as he looks around the room. "Recognize anyone?"

"Here, you can have my shot, I'm not going to drink this early in the morning."

"I asked you if you noticed any familiar faces?" he says as he gulps down my drink.

I look around but see no one and nod my head at him.

"Good," he lets out a deep breath. "Perhaps I'm wrong for once. Are you sure you don't want a drink?"

"Cove? Seriously? I'm not even awake yet, and if I have my way I'm going to take a nap on the plane."

He smiles and orders one more, taking it fast, and then sitting down in the lounge area on one of the large couches. I sit next to him and he places his arm around the back of my neck. He's fidgety, tapping his foot on the floor, and crossing his legs back and forth every few minutes. I place my hand on his knee, trying to calm his nerves.

"What's wrong with you?" I ask.

"I said I was fine. I just want to get on the plane."

"Why don't you tell me about your favorite childhood memory to pass the time. It may help you calm down."

"No, tell me about yours. I want to hear more about you."

I think for a moment, trying to find a pleasant story about my past. There aren't many, but I don't want to disappoint him.

"Tell me about the first time you had sex. Was it good?"

I throw him a look, the same one I gave to Evan when

he asked me that question. "What is it with guys wanting to know about the first time a woman had sex? Is it a turn on or something?"

He turns away from me, scanning the room while his foot that's resting over his thigh wiggles uncontrollably. I place my hand on his foot, stopping it from its movement.

"Okay. If it will calm you down, I'll tell you."

"No, you don't have to."

"Cove, stop being a little kid. You asked, so you must want to know."

"I'm curious as to what you liked about it, or what you didn't. Did anything go wrong, or was it just as you expected?"

"It wasn't what I was expecting at all. I thought I was going to have an orgasm and I didn't. I thought that was the whole point, but when he came and it was all over, I was disappointed. He never pleasured me."

"Were you with him again after that?"

"No."

Cove stops tapping his foot and looks directly at me, somewhat saddened by my answer. "Why? Because you didn't have an orgasm?"

"No. Because I haven't been with very many people more than once. I've only had a handful of boyfriends, and most of my sexual interactions have been one night stands. He wasn't someone I was dating, and I had no desire to meet with him a second time."

"I have no idea how all of that works. I mean, I guess I do, it's just like the porn industry, don't you think?"

"Yeah, I've been thinking about that more and more lately. My past is similar to yours, only mine was by choice."

He taps his foot again, thinking for a few moments

before speaking. "Is that all you didn't like about it, or did something else go wrong?"

"No. That was about it. It hurt for only a moment, but not as much as people said it would, and other than my lack of climax, it was fine."

"So, you weren't completely disappointed?" he asks.

"It's hard to explain."

"Try."

"For someone who doesn't want me to remember him just for sex, you sure are asking me the wrong questions right now."

He takes his arm from around my shoulders and sits up. "I'll be right back."

"Where you going?"

"The restroom. Give me a moment. Just don't move, I want you to be sitting in this exact spot when I return."

"Okay. Think of me," I say with a smile.

"I'm not doing what you think I'm doing," he replies over his shoulder as he enters the open restroom doorway. He's gone only for two minutes, and is quickly back by my side. I didn't move an inch and he smiles at my obedience.

"So you weren't really disappointed or even angry at the guy?"

"No, I was confused because I wanted more. I thought I would be satisfied for some time after doing it, but it was just the opposite, I couldn't stop. It's all I thought about because it was the only time I felt close to anyone. Having someone inside of me gave me comfort and security, as if they were in control yet I also had control of them. I craved being close to someone, feeling their flesh against mine, and most importantly I enjoyed the fact that my body was the reason for their pleasure. It's a bit egotistical, but it's how I feel. If I can make someone have an orgasm, and they have that extreme sense of gratification because of me, well that makes me all powerful."

"So that pleasure seeking, or should I say, hedonism, that you want in life, do you feel that way about me? Would you feel disappointment if you couldn't make me come, or if I came before you and you weren't satisfied?"

"Cove, I'm talking about my life many years ago," I pause, looking at the screen to check on our flight. "It's almost time."

"Answer my question, Sophia."

"No, I wouldn't," I say firmly. "For the first time in my life, no. I'm confident that I'm entering new territory here, which is confusing to me. I'm content right now, sitting next to you, having a conversation. It's enough for me. I'm happy with that and sex would just be a bonus. I want to touch you because I'm extremely attracted to you, as I know that you are to me. Our sexual tension is bursting at the seams, but I'm also absolutely and completely fulfilled with what we're doing at this moment. Your presence next to me is enough."

"That's all I needed to hear. Come on," he takes my hand and pulls me out of my seat. "Let's get on our flight. I have a full day with you before I meet with Paul, and I'm going to take full advantage of those twenty-four hours."

He places his hand on the small of my back, guiding me through the check-in, and then down the corridor to the plane. I've never flown first class before and I'm immediately sold on the larger, softer seats with more legroom and privacy. Our seats are in the last row next to the two restrooms, not the best spot, but better than behind the blue curtain. I don't think I'll be able to go back to coach after this flight.

I check my phone but still no word from Mera. I send

her a quick text, telling her that I miss her. Cove sees the worried look on my face, and brushes my hair behind my ear, gaining better access to whisper to me.

"She's going to be fine. You'll see her soon, I promise."

I buckle my seatbelt and he does the same. The engines roar and we start to move down the runway. He tightly grips the armrests and his knuckles turn white.

"You okay?" I ask.

"Fine," he says with an awkward smile. "I could use another drink, but I'm fine."

"You really don't like to fly, do you?"

He looks straight ahead, his foot tapping the floor; his knuckles still white, impatient for the plane to take off. I give him a light squeeze on his forearm before putting my earphones in. I'm not much of a traveler myself, but music helps to control my nerves, and it makes the time go by so much faster.

I scroll through my phone, looking for the perfect song for take off. I decide to play one that Mera likes by Jay-Z featuring Justin Timberlake. It's soothing, with some upbeat sections that will drown out the engines of the plane. I tap my phone and lean back, closing my eyes as we continue to move down the runway. I can think of the mess we're in while I'm listening to this, and once we're in the air, maybe I can read or sleep. The soft music of *Holy Grail* starts and I place my hand over Cove's, letting him know I'm here for him.

It's a rough take off but we're in the air. I open my eyes, and Cove looks like he's holding his breath. He's motionless, staring above at the red seatbelt light. His hands have left the armrests and he's nervously tapping his upper thighs with his fingertips. The red light turns off and he immediately releases his belt, reaching over to mine, freeing me in one quick motion. He grabs my hand and pulls me out of my seat, securing us in the restroom in a matter of seconds.

He pulls my dress slightly up and lifts me onto the sink, placing his hat on the stainless steel shelf next to us. I run my fingers through his hair, wrapping one leg around his waist and placing the other against the wall behind him. He drags his hand softly over my lips and down my neck. I drop my head back, closing my eyes, waiting for his mouth to touch my flesh.

The song still playing in my ear picks up, with voices growing in volume and intensity making me want to tear both of our clothes off. I stay in control, allowing him to decide what he's going to do. I think about Mera, and wonder if and what she's already had to perform.

The hotel room is dark as Paul pounds his dick into Mera. He has her on her stomach and he's holding her hands behind her back. She wiggles, but his grip only gets tighter around her wrists. She's no match for him, or his guard who's hovering over her. She turns her head and sees their shadows move on the wall. He looks twice her size, and she wonders if he's going to hurt her.

"That's right Mera, you little whore. Take all of me," he groans, sending fast lunges into her body, his balls slapping her ass with each thrust.

"Paul," she yells.

He releases her wrists and flips her onto her back. Leaning down, he grabs her chin. "Don't say a word when I'm fucking you."

He stands and rolls her back over. She looks at the wall again and sees a larger figure taking off his belt and unbuttoning his pants. She watches Paul pull out a chair to sit down and watch.

"Try her out, tell me what you think. I think she likes it."

Cove's lips are an inch from mine. His breathing is heavy as he pulls off his tie, and unbuttons his shirt. I pull my dress over my head, and he looks down at my naked body, running his hand down my chest to my garter.

"Fuck, Sophia. You're so gorgeous. I want you. I need you."

He grips the side of the sink with his two hands, leaning down, lightly touching my mouth with his lips. His warm breath flows into my mouth as I wait.

He reaches down with one hand, opening his pants enough to pull out his thick cock. His arm wraps around my back and he finally presses his lips against mine, taking my mouth into his, surging in with his tongue.

"Fuck," I exhale, placing my hand on his chest. "I need you too."

"Oh yeah, you slut. Oh, fuck." Paul's brute pulls out of Mera, coming on her back. He falls onto her, humping her as he continues to shoot out. He huffs and then finally comes to a stop.

"Clean her up, Dayne. I'm not finished with her."

She turns and looks at Paul, remembering the conversation over dinner at Giorgio's. It's hard to forget a name that unique. He's Devery's brother, one of the twins.

He wipes her back with a towel, and grips her arm,

pulling her to a standing position.

"Why don't you shower before we leave so I can have some time alone with her."

Dayne follows Paul's orders, walking out of the bedroom and back to the living area of the hotel suite. Paul motions for Mera to kneel in front of him. She shakes her head no with a smile.

He laughs, leaning back, rubbing a finger across his mouth as he glares darkly into her eyes. "If I ever have to ask you to do something twice...." She drops down to her knees before he finishes, his heartless voice choking the defiance out of her.

"Open your mouth for me."

"Sophia," Cove softly says, placing his forehead against mine, out of breath from our deep kisses. "I don't want to disappoint you." He lifts his head, his warm and loving eyes looking into mine. "Tell me you love me."

I place the palm of my hand against his cheek, and then turn it so the back of my hand lightly brushes against his skin. "I love you."

He reaches down to his shaft with heavy breaths, rubbing his tip between my outer lips to find my entrance. He slowly pushes inside of me, pressing his hand tightly against my back. His head falls to my shoulder as he gasps with pleasure.

"My God, that's softer and warmer than I could have ever imagined."

He slowly slides out and then in, watching his movements down below.

"Jesus, Sophia." He raises his head and devours my mouth, lifting me from the sink and pressing me against the back wall. I place my feet on the sink for stability as he moves my body onto his erection. He's still growing inside of me, consuming my inner space. I've been waiting for this, and it's more than I could have dreamed. I thought he would be the type to plan a cliché romantic dinner with flowers, giving himself to me afterward in a soft king-sized bed. Thank God he knows me well enough to give me a slam against the airplane bathroom wall while we make love for the first time.

"Oh fuck, when can we do this again?" he growls.

"Are you finished? I didn't feel you come."

He smiles, his dimples showing, his eyes glazed over in delight. "No. We just entered the point of no return. You'll know when I come. I just need to hear this isn't over between us."

"We can do this for our entire lives," I whisper into his ear.

His head rests on my shoulder again, as he lets out another deep breath. He watches himself slide deep inside, and I moan with pleasure.

"You like it slow, don't you?" he asks, nipping at my neck.

"Yes, go slow, Babe."

We both watch as he slides in and out, our eyes closing at times, not being able to handle the sight of such intense pleasure. We smile at one another and he kisses me again. I own this moment with him. I don't want this to be over. This time together, this airplane ride, it can never end.

"That's right, Mera. Suck it," Paul says with his hands on each side of her head, pushing her up and down onto his dick. "Make me come. Come on, suck me."

A burst of his seed hits the back of her throat and he leans forward, with his abs tight and hands firm against the back of her head. He slides out, rubbing himself off, and onto her face.

"Keep your mouth open," he commands, circling her lips with his tip. "That's right, taste me. Fuck, that's good." He slows his hand, closing his eyes for the final shots before sitting completely back in the chair, taking deep breaths.

"Stand up. I want to look at your beautiful body," he huffs.

Mera stands, viewing her shadow that's cast over Paul's body. Her outline runs across his face, splitting his cold eyes in half.

"Cove," I say clenching down on my teeth so that no one hears us. "I'm going to come. Oh God, you feel incredible, Babe. Go slow, feel me as I come with you inside of me."

He does his best to stay in control while I place my lips against his. We both groan, his mass sliding slowly against my clit.

"Oh fuck. Cove," I say, a little too loud. I watch his reflection in the mirror as he places his hand over my mouth, his body moving in rhythm with mine. My eyes squint and my fists clench against his back.

"I feel you. I can feel you coming around me, Sophia. Don't stop, I'm going to come with you." He turns and places my ass back on the sink, moving faster to catch up. His shaft is like a rock as he pounds into me. "God, you feel so amazing." He lifts his head and I bring my leg up over his shoulder. "Fuck," he says, and I feel his first rush of fluid escape his body, shooting directly inside of me. He starts to pull out and I push up against him, not allowing him to escape.

"I'm not done, don't stop," I whimper, my body quivering as sweat forms between my breasts. I feel another discharge from him as his semen begins to flow out of my body. My leg shakes and I lower it, wrapping it around his hip. Both of our mouths are open, our eyes in an erotic daze as our pulses sink, firing waves of intense energy throughout our bodies. We feel one another's trembling areas down below, generating pleasurable aftershocks. He shivers, and wraps his arms around me before sliding out. My mouth is deeply kissed, passionately, for a good five minutes.

He looks down at himself again, trying to catch his breath.

"Sophia," he pants. "Did I disappoint you?"

I smile; a tear runs down my cheek as my heart explodes with joy. "Never. You have me Cove, I'm yours."

He looks up and smiles with pure elation on his face. He wipes my tear, placing a sweet kiss on my forehead. His head moves around to my ear, and I feel his soft lips press against my lobe. He holds me, whispering words that have never been surrendered to me in the past.

"I love you."

Paul follows Mera's nude figure from her feet up to her face. He shows no emotion. She looks back at her shadow cast over his figure, trying not to see the man in front of her. Harsh words escape his mouth, slowly echoing throughout the room, words that have never been used on her in the past.

"I own you."

FALLEN SNOW

About The Author:

Aven Jayce is a writer and artist living in the mid-west. She holds a terminal degree from a well-known western university and has been included in group and solo exhibitions, catalogs, magazines, and online interviews for her work. She shares her space and time with her husband and a rescued Persian cat, spending most of her days writing, painting, and being creative.

Aven Jayce's novels include:

The NOVA Trilogy
Fallen Snow (Book One)
Desert Star (Book Two)
Sunset Rush (Book Three)

The Dark Scarlett (available early winter, 2014)

For more information and to connect, please visit:
    https://www.facebook.com/eroticromanceauthor